Facing My Pl

Facing My Phantoms

Sheeba Shah

Rupa & Co

Typeset by
Mindways Design
1410 Chiranjiv Tower,
43 Nehru Place
New Delhi 110 019

Printed in India by
Nutech Photolithographers
B-240, Okhla Industrial Area, Phase-I,
New Delhi 110 020, India

Contents

Acknowledgements

I would like to thank a few people who have stood by me during and after the writing of this book.

Archana Upreti has been like a mentor. Her kind words have inspired me to become a better writer. Her husband, Sanjeev Upreti, who himself is a novelist, is somebody I look up to as a mentor and guide. He goaded me on to produce the best in me.

My dear friend and mentor, Sajag Rana. Words are not enough to thank you.

I would like to thank my dear friends, Rakesh and Ruchee Adukia, for having faith in me and filling me with optimism. A big thank you to Kamana Shah and Geetanjali for standing by me and believing in me.

A special thank you and appreciation for Srinivas Bhashyam, who has designed the cover for this book. You are a blessing. Your support and faith in me amazes me.

I thank my dear husband, and my darling daughters, Eishana and Shaleen, for letting me write.

I thank my publisher, Mr. Kapish Mehra for introducing my work to the world at large.

Thank you everyone.

Sanjeevani

Sunne lai soon ko maala
Bhanne lai Phool ko maal
Yo katha baikuntha jaala.

(A garland of gold for the person who is listening to this
story
A garland of flowers for the person who is narrating this
story
And thus shall this story rise to the heavens...)

Jijumua concluded her stories with this phrase each night, lulling
my fatigued body to sleep and awakening therein my innate
self...my wild self. My grandmother's stories released me, allowed
me to think, ponder, question, understand, long for and even wander
off. More than anything else, her stories kept the truth of my being
alive; submerged yet alive, somewhere inside of me. Now when I
look back, I am convinced that Jijumua's stories actually saved me
from decaying, from disappearing into the oblivion of forced and
falseful thinking. Her stories laid bare the primordial fact of the wild
woman blended with wild nature. It was her fairy tales, myths and
stories of the good woman, the bad woman, the daring woman, the
evil woman, the wicked woman reigning the world of the clouds,

the thunder, the lightning, the rain, the sun, the mud and the skies, the trees and the flowers that nurtured that very innate self in me...the self that is wild, the self that is a wanderer and the self that never stays constant.

Now there rages in me a war between two selves. Am I the wild woman that I am born to be or am I the harnessed woman that I am expected to be? I ask myself this question each day. I am trapped in this dilemma. I suffocate each day, wondering who I really am? Am I Sanjeevani, the one moulded into an accceptable form? Sanjeevani, the gagged one, the unaroused, compressed, harnessed, the socially conscious and socially accepted one? Or am I Sanju, the wild one? Am I Sanju, the one who carries the stories, the dreams, the songs and the memories of the absolute, undeniable and irrevocable bond with the wild?

The thought is scary and chilling. I look around myself, bewildered and completely lost. The cold, steely sense of death is all around me, concrete and hard. It is almost stiff and unyeilding...towering over me like an iron cage, impenetrable and almost suffocating. It is a sense of being trapped, caged in rather. But am I alone in this? I think not. We are in it together. We, my entire family, the remnants of the great Singh clan, established years ago by my dead grandfather. These are people I am supposed to love and care for...feel for. But do I...really?

I know this is not the right time and definitely not the place for me to interrogate my sincerity towards my family. And besides, I have, as Razat has reminded me often, been a selfish person. 'It is amazing, Sanju, that you do not really see people! For you they are nothing but appendages to your selfish needs. You live, madam Sanjeevani, in an intensely lit haze that shifts and shines according to your selfish desires.' Razat's words did not pinch me then for I agree that I am indeed a selfish person and live for myself alone. Did I not think of only myself when I broke my engagement with

Nabin? My parents were shattered after that incident. My father, recently having lost his only son, now walks around haggard and resigned...looking far older than his age. He has no hopes now, and a hopeless man is as good as dead. I know I killed my father...my father who was always hopeful, always aspiring. I took the last breath of hope out of him by being a shameless slut. Yes! That's what I am – a shameless slut. I know people call me that behind my back. It rarely bothers me though. But I am hurt somewhere...knowing and realising that my father too becomes a victim of these stains on my character.

Regardless of what people have to say of me, I am here today to share a moment of grief with my family. I am here to be a part of the death that has sprung unnanounced over my family – my Thulubua is dead. He is my father's only sibling and elder brother. I had received a call from my father this morning. I had felt the slight vibrations of my cellphone on my pillow, where I lay last night, hoping against hope that Razat would call. He could call at any time in the night, which of course he did not, for there are tensions between me and Razat. A relationship that started of on a beautiful and selfless note is now turning dark and grey with unspoken wants and inert dissatisfactions creeping in.

'Dai...is no longer with us, Sanju,' my father had said in a strangely distinct and rather steady voice. It was a shock, for there was nothing ailing my Thulubua lately. Nothing serious apart from his own nagging suscpicions of this and that.

I had immediately rushed along, and now I am here in the midst of this chaotic despair. But I myself, shamelessly, do not feel a thing. I want to. God knows...I want to feel the hurt...the same pain, the same loss that the others around me seem to be overwhelmed with; but it is only Razat who is running inside my mind right now...only Razat and boy, has he been dominant in my mind since I first met him.

The thought of Razat's face, his dark...not black dark, but gentle dark tone of a deep tan and the smooth and soft skin that runs from his face, down his neck and throughout his body...in the same soothing tone that makes me want to smile. 'Krishna...my Krishna,' I have called him often, loving the blending contrast of my marble white skin with the smooth dark chocolate brown of his. He has a playful smile, and I love his smile the way I love his careless laughs. Loving Razat is like an addiction – sweet, inticing, and euphoric, but surely very lethal.

I know I am still very much in love with Razat, although loving him has not done me any good apart from making me an object of contemptable scrutiny by all around me...a shameful disgrace to my family. But still, for two years, I have persisted with my ardour, stubborn and unrelenting. I have rebelled against the rigid trends of my family with my 'shameful act' – the exact words my mother uses when she speaks of my relationship. Not that she speaks of Razat very often, for doing that would seem to give credibility to our relationship and therefore, most of the time she prefers to believe and behave as though the man never existed.

My family is shocked, stunned and after all this time, they still cannot get over my audacity. I think it is not really the shock that makes them behave the way they do, but the fact that I went against what is called 'family honour'. I brought disrepute to the family and this is what pinches them the most. We are a big family...the Singh family. God knows we have been a proud family, although now nothing remains to be proud of. At least that is what I think...

Dada is dead and if you must know, he died three months back. He did not die just like that but was killed, brutally beaten to death by the Maobadi militia. They had come looking for my father that night but he had fled months earlier and had even advised Dada to move in to the town house in Dhangadi, but Dada refused to leave.

'This is my home, these are my fields and my farms, this is where I belong,' he had said, nearly mumbling to himself. Dada rarely spoke to my father. Unless imperatively neccessary, they did not communicate. Often times, it was me or my mother who acted as mediators between them. That day my father had sneaked into Ganeshpur, riding pillion on a neighbour's motorcycle. He had come to Ganeshpur to retrieve some neccessary land papers that were locked in my mother's grey aluminium cupboard in their bedroom.

He had walked around the house and the kitchen garden, and then went up to the Dhansaar where our grains were stored. I had walked beside him while he assessed columns after columns of gigantic mud-baked granaries. He had squatted in front of one of them, peeled out the bundle of straw stuffed in the mouth of a little round opening from where rice had spilled out. He grabbed a handfull of rice grains and assessed them with his experienced fingers. Although he said nothing, I noticed a glint of pride in his old sunken eyes.

'Sell it off immidiately,' he had told Dada as we walked around the stables. 'Keep a year's stock for yourself and sell the rest. Do that immediately and by next week, I want you all to vacate this house and come and live with your mother and myself in Dhangadi.'

'There is no danger for me,' Dada had said, walking alongside my father. 'I have met with and spoken to the area commander here. They had sent a notification last week asking for 1000 quintals of dhan. I have arranged for a few more bullockcarts next week so that I can hand over their demand.'

'You are going to give in to their demands so easily? This is outright betrayeal to the king and the country. We feed them, we support them.' My father had started shaking his head in agitation.

'Are we left with any other choice?' my brother had mumbled again. 'The king and the country are far-fetched for me. I live here,

I work here and unless the king is not going to support me here, I will do whatever is neccessary to get my living.' Dada had stated his firm decision, looking down at his soiled farming boots.

'You mean to say, you will blatantly join hands with them, call them over to my house and have them eat my grains and sleep on my cots?' It was clear that my father was angry and felt cheated. 'Have you heard their slogans lately? *Samanti ko nash, ragat ko pukaar...dhesh lai uddhar.* Does it not insult you in any way? Walking down the village, not one tharu comes to greet me these days. They all stand in their courtyards, shameless and indignant. A whack on their ignorant heads, that's what they need.'

Dada had laughed at this retort by my father. Dada was never a man of many words but he understood well that for our father, it was difficult, and nearly impossible to accept this drastic change that had come over our villagers and how recently, each one wanted to be treated as an equal. Dada had come to terms with it in the course of the past year when villagers ignored calls of some manual errand in our farms and house. This would never have happened in Bua's time. Then the entire village would have accumilated at an hour's notice. The villagers of Ganeshpur would have left behind their own pending work to first finish my father's errands.

Bua had left shortly after lunch. 'Not too safe to travel in the evening,' he had said, masking his face with the helmet.

That evening, as we sat by the fire out in the lawn, I had voiced my own pent-up fears. 'They say that Hikmat Malla's farm was raided a few days ago. The women were all shoved into one room while all the male members were assembled in the courtyard, keeping them at gunpoint there. The entire house was plundered and looted. They even took the mattresses.'

He was staring silently into the fire. Dada's eyes did most of the talking with me for he said so little. It was the gestures of his body, expressions on his face, the glint in his eyes through which

I had learned to read his thoughts. Now they stared into the fire with a sheer sense of helplessness but somewhere in them I could see a glimmer of hope, more of a resilience, rather.

'So, you want to go down to Seeta Kund tomorrow? We can actually take Shanti and the baby. Will be a nice outing for them,' he had said, ignoring my apprehensions. His face had suddenly brightened at the thought of next day's outing. It brought a glint in his eyes.

'Remember Da, how each Maghi Sangranti we all went to Seeta Kund and how you scared me on the way, saying Jamjutwa would get me. I remember crying in real fear! How stupid I was . . . scared of ghosts!'

'They are for real, Sanju,' my brother had said, staring into the fire, 'not in the mango grove, not in the jungles, not Madhakunti, but here, within ourselves. Don't we carry the ghosts of us, our weaknesses, our sorrows, our dead aspirations, our dead predeccesors? I carry my ghosts with me, Sanju, and I know you do too.'

We rarely talked . . . Dada and myself . . . never this intimate, and instantly I froze. It was as if his words had awakened my own ghosts, the jeering phantoms from within me. 'Da,' I had wanted to say, 'do you know that I am a slut? That I hate my body and my soul feels trapped in it and I suffocate each moment that I breathe? Da, help me fight my ghosts.' Instead I had heard myself say, 'Seriously Da, your daughter needs a name. She is nearly three years old now. We cannot go on calling her "Baby" for the rest of her life for God's sake!'

'Ha ha! She is a special girl and special girls need time . . . lots of it to be named,' he had replied, still laughing.

Now Thulubua is dead and we are living hand to mouth in a shabby little apartment in Kathmandu. Forced out of our homes and our lives, what is there to be proud of? Old glories now remain hazy memories, buried within our minds.

If we have changed, so has the country. So much has been the change that my own childhood memories seem unreal. People have changed, landscapes altered...and the place I called home is now a ruin, with broken walls and cattle grazing inside the rooms that once were. All this happened in the name of development and progress, of which little has been achieved. More focus has been given to demolishing the age-old social structure and instilling the mind of the common man with issues of human rights.

'Everyone is equal...'

'There is no master and no servant', and blah, blah, blah.

......'

These, after all, are only slogans. They are never given any meaning by the reformers apart from destroying the affluent, killing their honour and even cremating their age-old traditions. *Bandhs, chakka jams, masaljulus* and *dharnas*, words used by political parties, identity movements, economic associations, teachers' associations, public transport owners, who are capable now of bringing the entire city to a halt causing more distress and inconvenience to many. Even the locals now are used to bringing the entire movement of traffic to a halt, should there be an accident in their area. People will not only throng to the accident site but block the entire road in protest. Protesting against what, and punishing whom? Yet, closures of streets, roads, offices, schools, hospitals and even the entire city has become an everyday affair now. It is amusing to see how the Nepalese mind so easily adapts to these inane obstructions in daily lives. 'Oh, there's a bandh coming up tomorrow, let's all get together and play cards,' is how the general Nepali mind has started to think. Or maybe it is that the public is left with no other choice.

Perhaps it is the mentality that has altered over the years. Values have changed along with prerogatives and so the Nepalese people now want answers for their actions, reasons for their submissions. For my family and families like mine, it is hard to digest that today a common Nepali does not repect the ancient social hierarchy. The common man will not stoop, will not humble himself, even in want and despair, for he has developed wings and is soaring high into the wide horizon of Bikas. Where once they sang praises and only praises for the ruling monarchy. And when that started happening, the roots of families such as mine, that were placed higher up in the social heirarchy, began shaking. They did not see this social change coming. Even if they did, they disregarded it....

Talking of choices, a lot of them have been presented to the common Nepali. Choose between autocratic monarchy or constitutional democracy.

Choose between the Congess or the UML.

Choose between the elected parliament or the People's Liberation Army.

Choose between conflict and peace.

Ironically enough, though choices are many, the people are left with hardly any ability to make that choice. For choices are so many and do they not keep changing more often than do seasons? Not only have they created a common confusion, but even more of mistrust, insecurity, instability and civil strife. Our new democracy is left in a complete state of hysteria.

It was the hope, I think, that led to all these choices in the first place. A hope that changed it all. As the hope persisited in the common mind the social strata began crumbling and down fell the likes of us...in shame...in total shame. Since the wealth and grandeur was already long lost, the likes of our family suffered more. It was an unforseen nosedive for our familial dominance, ancestral esteem, honour and repute. It is this very hope of a bettter nation, a better society and a better life that has made Nepal remain in a bewildered state from one course to another in the near three decades of my lifetime. *Panchayati, razat razatantra, loktantra* – only the slogans have changed. The people chanting them remain where and as they were. Changing leaders and political opinions with each passing season, again...only in hope.

I remember, after Dada's death, my father pinning all his hope on the king. 'This is temporary,' he said, with strong conviction and endearing hope. 'I had a word with Maharajdhiraj. He says the time is not right but when it will be, he will resume authority and then that shall be the end of this People's war nonsense and then we can all go back to our homes.'

'Yes!' Thulubua had added his conviction, his allegiance to King Birendra. 'He has dispatched his envoys to all the districts. He is studying the political landscape sharply, reading people's minds. Once he is ready, he will send the Royal Nepalese Army against the rebels.'

I was sitting out in the sun with them, on the terrace, peeling oranges and laying them on the plate for the two old men. Deeply engrossed in their political discussion, their hope, belief, and allegiance to the king made me laugh. 'The king is not going to do anything, for a loooooong time,' I had intervened, making the two of them look at me in surprise. They had begun to give a little credit to my political opinions since I had joined the *Kashtamandap Weekly* as a sub-editor. Somehow, my working there, gave them the impression that I got news of the dealings of the monarchy underhand. 'He is enjoying all this chaos and wishes for some more...more pains inflicted on the general public, more homes uprooted, more families displaced and more sons abducted and killed,' I had said carelessly, shoving a piece of orange into my mouth.

'Ke...Ke, *bhancha*. why...why would His Majesty wish harm to his subjects?' Thulubua had stammered. He always did so when excited.

'The king wants his powers back, his authority back. And the insult of the 1990 democratic movement, that forced him to give up all his autocratic powers, has not been forgotten by the monarchy. The king now waits. He wants the public to suffer all they can and then beg him, surround his palace with banners, just the way they had done in 1990 asking for a democracy, but this time pleading him to resume authority. Why else do you think the Royal Nepalese Army refrained from helping the armed police force in Dune Bazaar of Dolpa. The army could have reached the conflict zone in half an hour if they wanted. But no, they stayed put in their barracks, safe and sound and let the armed police force get beaten like stray dogs.'

Thulubua had started twirling the tips of his moustache and wetting them with his tongue, something that he always did, a mechanical and rather purfunctory action, when in deep speculation. My father began to nod his head up and down, his gesture of intent speculation. Sometimes, I think he does not even know how fast his head is bobbing up and down. There was a tremour in his hands as he picked up pieces after pieces of the oranges and began stuffing them into his mouth. My father never chewed his food, he was always in a hurry to swallow it for some reason I have never understood.

I was begining to enjoy myself. I knew this would barely help in removing their inherent allegiance to the monarchy but I knew I was shocking them and gloated upon that prospect. So I continued.

'The greater the chaos in the country, the more reasons for the monarchy to assume power. The longer he keeps this blind eye to the sufferings of the people, the faster he will regain his authority. Why else do you think King Birendra will not permit Girija to deploy the Royal Nepalese Army against the armed rebels? Everyone is playing politics to achieve power and authority at the cost of us...people like us suffer.'

There was silence after my outburst. I knew they understood what I said but I also knew that the two would never ever accept it, for their own belief in the monarchy was so firm and well-grounded since generations. For them monarchy was imperative for their own survival. Each complimenting the other. We, the Thakuris and the Ranas and the Chetris were the base of this big foundation and the king was the pivotal point. The likes of my family live with this belief that the king should and would support them for they were the holding base of his social status. What they do not realise is that the king is into other games. He does not care for this base. He has devised other means to keep himself at the pivotal point.

'You are a lost soul,' I can hear Razat's voice, my illegal lover of two years, whispering into my ear, nibbling the tips of my lobes. His way of telling me seemed like he wanted more of me. 'Sanju...you are a lost soul.' His words now make a real impact. I am indeed lost...caged in, yet terribly lost. I do not know where I belong with these weeping people that I see around me. Do I belong with Razat...or somewhere else?

'I am lost...I am lost,' I can hear my mind chant within the gloomy silence in me as I continue staring at the chaos in front of me. I rest my head on the wall against which I am standing and close my eyes to relieve myself of the blatant image of pain and suffering in front of my eyes. I let myself go, slowly sink, submerge my conscious being into a darkness...a peaceful darkness, where there is no mourning, and no voices of myself jeering at me.

I can feel the tranquility seep into my skin and bones. I feel the emptiness in my soul making me one with its obscurity.

'Mero chora...mero chora....' Jijumua's distressing lament forces me back. I am living again...hurting, cursing all over again.

All around me are moans of anguish and loss. My grandmother is crumpled upon the floor; worn and shrivelled with the beatings of age. She lets out her own grief with loud wails. Her beloved son is dead. It is not the first time Jijumua has seen death. She is a little over eighty now and her slowly diminishing mortality has certainly seen many pass away before her gradually fading senses.

I cannot breathe. The room around me reeks of sympathies of relatives and friends who have come to comfort and console. Some sprinkle water on the unconscious bereft, some caress with compassion the sagging head of my grandmother that is forced about with a frustrated grief while the rest stand...silent spectators, shaken by the certainty of death. Amidst this crowd, I stand alone, the pariah, feeling sceptic eyes and glances of chastisement on me. For in this crowd, I do indeed stand alone. My cousins have come in respectably, with their husbands and wives and children; whereas I come in with a tag trailing behind...of being a dishonourable woman.

I am going to be thirty in a few years and I am still umarried and shamelessly seeing a married man. I am well aware that the chastisements that I receive from my family and others are not for my being a second woman and a mistress to a man, but more for loving a man out of my caste. For loving a Marwari. Razat is a Marwari...rich, but a Marwari. A good man, but a Marwari. A stable man, but a Marwari. At home he speaks a different language and although he is a Hindu like myself, his traditions are different, his customs are different. And the most horrendous part is that he is not a Thakuri – the ruling class. He is not a Shah, Singh, or a Chand. Even Basnyat would have been acceptable. But sadly, he proudly holds the surname of Aggarwal. And when that is spoken aloud, if ever, by my family, it is spoken as though the mere mention of him had suddenly soured their minds.

I had never wanted to marry Razat, nor him me. Even today, I cannot imagine him fitting in with my family. Besides, Razat had defined our relationship from the start and in a way I think he even dictated it. I was given a little space outside his marriage and I never complained. I accepted the little that I could get of Razat.

Razat loves his wife...I know that. He speaks very rarely of her but when he does, not only is love explicit in his words but more of respect and commitment of a lifetime.

'Then what is he doing with me?' I have asked myself often and am left with no answers. Leave alone that, I do not know what I, myself am doing with him.

'Is this right? Are we doing the right thing? Where does this lead to and where does this end?' I had asked him once, shamelessly burrying my face into the immensity of his chest.

Embracing my little frame within his large bulky arms, he said, 'We share a perfect union, Sanju...you and me. There is unconditional love between the two of us and that makes our relationship very different and very special. I make you happy and you make me happy and that is all that matters...does it not?'

I never told him then that since we started seeing each other, I have had no peace. I have longed for him when not with him and when with him, constantly feared that time was passing too fast and that soon he would be gone, back again to his wife and family. So I have continued for the past two years, bearing the spiteful glances, the silent murmers of rebuke from my social circle, keeping myself busy in my own little world...where I write and write and only write.

At the outset, my life is perfect. I am the sub-editor for the *Kasthamandap Weekly*. I make 15000 rupees a month, besides the little extra I get from my freelancing for other papers. I spend my free time volunteering with the oldest politcal party of Nepal. I have a rich lover who visits me now and then in shady places besides my own, which I have rented with another girl who teaches little children at the British School. We have seperate rooms besides a common lounging area and a little kitchenette. And when I am alone in my room and have tired myself from either waiting for Razat or his calls, drained my evil thoughts of him with his wife and children, I sit and write the novel I am secretly writing, about my grandmother. Having said all that, I guess I am not really happy with my perfect life. I guess there is a part in me which is wanting more...but more of what is a question that has been difficult to answer.

My eyes are dry, but I can feel my heart resound to the heavy tolls of grief. There is an urgency in me...surfacing from the pit of my stomach, making me want to cower into the darkness that I perceive all around me. I rest my head on the wall behind myself – my refuge, my hiding place for today and yet again, I desperately hope to dissappear.

I think of Dada, my only sibling. He died three months ago and it seems that his reflections in my mind are slowly fading away. I can no longer see him now. As much as I, in my desperation, try to hold on to his memories, he slips away. He is no more there, and although I cry for him each time I think of him, he is fast becoming a dream...hazy and unreal. When Dada died, we all wondered where he'd gone. It was like an amputation of a body part. The remaining bearing the pain for the part that was cut off and thrown away. I stood stunned and bore my own part of the pain. I tried to console myself with the thought of Dada playing cricket in heaven. Dada loved playing cricket and when he was not playing he was either listening to some commentary of it with his little 'onety onties' radio stuck to his ear or discussing it with his friends. He loved cricket. It was one of his few passions. Speaking of passions, hobbies, likes and dislikes, Dada barely had any and even if he did, he had it all shut in himself. He was a mysterious man. On rare moments, he opened his heart out to the rest of the world; and in moments like that, we all seemed to rush in...my mother, myself, his two wives and his friends. We all swarmed in, curious and cautious at the same time...searching, fiddling and scooping all that we could get. That was him, my brother...now dead. His face is slowly fading away from my memory. I have to really think hard, close my eyes and really, really concentrate on his image that once was. But the pain, the anger and the resentment that he let me down...he left me all alone to bear ALL THIS. I shall never forgive him for that.

Behind the faded curtains, I can see light. Pale and faded in excellence... nearly blending in with the gloom that is striking all around. 'I need air,' I can hear myself aloud amidst the din of the wailings around me and I walk out to where the body is lying. The air outside seems as still as it is inside the house. The skies above seem to share the same mourning sentiment of my family. Clouds are getting thicker. They look like grey masses of gloom fixed tenaciously over our heads. The gloomy sky strike forth as an eerie omen, foretelling our retributions to come... for the savageries committed by my family. 'In innocence....in ignorance...' I want to scream in defence. 'What my family did...how my family lived was a way of life, a tradition passed on for generations. They did not know of any other way but theirs,'...or so I want to think.

The body is on the floor upon a stretcher – a bulky mass of already decaying flesh. It is nearly covered with flowers. I can see the top of his forehead smeared with red and yellow vermillion. I think I want to touch it....feel his skin for the last time. His face is calm and serene....not an ounce of regret, remorse or anger that this dead man was filled with in his last days. My Thulubua died this morning. He was out on his morning walk when his long weary heart had refused to function any more. It must have been an adamant refusal from his exhausted heart for taking any further, the loads and liabilities of his mysterious ways. He had died in the arms of a stranger, the long weary reminiscences of his life flashing in an instant upon an alien face.

Never before have I seen that peaceful look on Thulubua's face. His mind like mine was always shuffling from one thought to another, as his fingers twirled the tips of his moustache...careless and instinctive. There were times when his tongue slipped out and he licked the tips of the twirled moustache...but that is all I shall remember him by. That and the glint in his eyes that spoke of the glories lost.

There is a chaotic movement all around the dead body as the men prepare for the cremation and in the midst of this flurry, I can see my father. He moves around like a ghost for there is not an ounce of emotion upon his face. His senses have gone numb. There is much to do for him now. He shall grieve later. But I can hear the thuds in his chest for the ones in mine come from him. And with this thought comes the realisation that this biting pain in me is more for the silent poundings in my father's heart than for his dead brother lying upon the floor.

I watch my father. His greying scalp, that he does not bother to colour, is not shaking as it normally does in moments of extreme excitement. Neither did it wobble when his only son died. I could almost feel the overpowering resilience in him when he had taken hold of my hands and his grim but firm voice had told me to be strong, moments before he went into the morgue to see the lifeless body of his thirty-four year old son. For my father, I had forced back the tears and the helpless cries that were bursting like painful sores from inside me then, and have continued since, with the trend of suffocating my feelings...never letting myself surface from this barricade of resoluteness that I have created around myself.

I think in a way, Dada's death changed us all. It came in unexpected but left an irrevocable impact upon each one of us. My mother is somewhere around here, helping perhaps in getting things ready for the cremation, and the mourning to be formally conducted by the three widows of my dead uncle. Perhaps she is the only one not really mourning. She probably does not even sympathise. Not that she is cruel and has no feelings at all, but because she is yet to get over the immensity of her own grief. The loss of her own beloved son is still fresh and stinging since he was beaten to death by Maoist hooligans who call themselves reformers of the society and country. To this day she walks around, silent in her own contemplations, conducting her daily chores religiously. But what the others cannot see, I do...clearly. There is a bitter resentment in her now....for the world at large. She quietly assesses each face around her with a vindictive spite.

My grandmother, wept too. She sympathised with my father's grief as it added to her own. She was seeing too many people leave her and go. She is slowly withdrawing into a selfless coccoon.

Then there were my cousins, children of my dead uncle, both a few years elder to Dada. I think Hemlata Dijju has taken it quite well. Now that she has moved on, married a rich, stable man from the caste and has children of her own, problems of her own, she weighs and balances her reponsibilites, obligations, and even her feelings. She wakes up on time, gets the children ready, pampers the husband, does her puja, sits with her in-laws nodding her head in silent agreement, and fucks her husband. I think her life has become a mechanical clock that moves along with each tick; robotic, I should say, but she never complains. I see her walking around helping to get the cremation organised in a responsible manner. I can see her behind the staircase, wiping the corners of her eyes with a portion of her chiffon sari. Her children instantly corner her. All three of them are toddlers, and she immediately gets caught up with her maternal responsibilities. And then there is Hemant Da. He is inside the room, sprawled near Jijumua's feet. He is Thulubua's only son. The pride of my Jijumua. Her eldest son's only son and the first male child of our generation.

Hemant Da is weeping. Actually, he is wailing. His head thrown back from time to time, he releases these moans that seem to pierce into my own body with a sting. The two of us share a history...a past with dark shades drawn around it. Within their enclosures stands firm...the secret, our secret. He knows and I know and though I should hate him for it, I don't feel a thing. There are no indictments and no charges from my side and after all these years, we still pretend to be brother and sister.

Standing by the doorway, I watch Hemant slumped grief. Crouching into a miserable bundle, he mourns for his father. Perhaps there is resentment in his wrenching sobs, and I wonder whether he has already forgiven his father.

I see him sprawled on the floor, his long legs spread out. Unconsciously, my eyes slip to the area between his legs. It was him who had first made me conscious of that bulge he carries between his legs. But that was much later. My memory plunges back in time. I may have been a toddler then. Images of him flash in front of my eyes. There he is, Hemant Da, standing in the verandah, my stuffed doll in his hands. 'Aiijaa...aiiija. You want your *putali* back? Give a kissy to Hemant Da.'

I walk to him, with my hands outstretched. He embraces me. But he is tall and my head reached his waistline. What goes unnoticed by everyone else is that my face remains buried in his crotch for the longest time as he croons softly, 'Mero bahini...my darling little Nepti.'

Yes, that's what Hemant Da called me and still does in family functions. Just the way he had said that morning when I had returned from my tuitions. 'Nepti, come here.' His door was open and he was still lying in bed, his body covered with a quilt.

Although I have buried those moments somewhere in my mind, I feel them popping up from time to time. Every time he says 'Nepti' in his loud authoritative voice, those images spring back. My mind tells me to flee but my feet mechanically move towards the open door. 'Your Bhauju has gone to make some tea to the kitchen. Sit down,' he said. Or was it 'Returning from tuition, are you? How much trouble do you give to your poor sir, you naughty girl!'? Or perhaps he even said, 'Why do you run away from me? I am not going to eat you.'

Whatever he said that morning is a jumble in my mind, but what he did, how his hands moved and grasped mine and slid it under the quilt is clear. Crystal clear. As much as I would want to wipe it out, rub, rub and rub till it is there no more; it hangs on stubbornly and remains a dirty stain.

I had first gone to the kitchen and picked up the soap from the sink, ignoring his wife's 'Good morning Maharani'. I went straight to the bathroom and washed my hands for hours, scrubbing my hands till I saw skin peeling off and blood oozing out and slowly blending in with the water flowing from the tap.

I have stopped acccusing Hemant Da for anything for I want to believe that it never happened. Just like that afternoon when I returned home to find everyone gone out and only us children at home. Dada was flying kites on the terrace. He had seen me walking into the house and even called out to me. 'Come up quickly' he had shouted, 'I have just cut Beeraj's kite and am after Binod's.'

I had leaped up the staircase and was about to cross the landing to take the stairs to the terrace on the other side of the corridor and found him standing outside his sister's bedroom door. I knew she was inside for the blaring lyrics of 'disco deewane...aaha' were rocking the walls of the entire house.

I should have run down and left the house or maybe just gone down and kept talking to Dada from there but I panicked. I tried to creep by him hoping that he will allow me to pass. But he smiled and the look in his eyes confirmed my latent suspicion that he would not. I rushed to Hemlata Dijju's door and remember banging it with all my might but then her music was so loud.

I remember the feeling very well. I wanted to dissappear into the door, merge into the hardwood in front of me. But that did not happen. Instead I felt him behind me, pushing his weight on to my back side. I felt a snaky, slimy thing stirring on my buttocks. Then he began to slide it. His hands grasped my hips, and he began thrusting. 'Hemant Da, no. No, Hemant Da!.' I remember a strangled plea amidst my banging on the door and Hemlata Dijju's blaring music.

When she opened the door. He was gone and I was still slamming my clenched fists onto the door. I had walked in straight-faced. I went straight to the stereo and switched it off. Then I had gone to the toilet and felt wretched. It was as though my entrails were on fire. I never cried. I never told anyone but I kept telling myself that it did not happen...it could not happen. Although I will not accept it I still seem to be carrying it along day by day, moment after moment. I can feel the weight of it on my hands, rubbing against my back side. This heavy burden I shall always carry.

I walk out to the little car porch that we have always used for our gatherings as we do not own a car. Placing plastic chairs for visitors that begin to arrive from early in the morning, this place has become more of an entertainment area for my father. Here he sips his morning tea, debating loudly the country's fate if left to the Maobadis. 'We must not keep quiet' he would say, as others around him would nod in approval. 'We have to fight. The king must understand we are there for him. He has only to give us a nod and we will create our own private militia.'

Thulubua too, used to sit here with Bua, twisting and licking the tips of his moustache and nodding and sometimes even adding his own opinion. 'We must push Marichman forward again. We have stayed in the background for too long. Congress is nothing but a pawn for India. The junta understands that. His Majesty should just take over the present Girija government and instate Marichman as the new prime minister.'

Thulubua never rose from his past glories, and his days of political authority. Though vast changes have come in the country and the political scenario, for Thulubua, his flattering allegiance to the king remains his only politics.

He lies still on this same porch and I watch my father sit beside his only sibling's corpse, waving the flies away from his dead face. I feel a stab for my father's loss.

Losing a sibling is the cruelest loss ever. I know for I have too lost my only sibling. Although there was a gap of eight years between my elder brother and myself, and we did not whisper intimate details into each other's ears before we slept; nor did we share the same games. Yet he was there for me and I for him . . . separate halves of one big piece, and after his death, there is this strange consciousness that continually jeers at my distortion.

Although I have never said it aloud, I think I have always blamed my father for the death of my brother. My grudges have been strong against the entire family and their ways too, which led to that dreadful night when they had arrived with guns and lathis in hand. . . . kicking, shouting and abusing. They had led my brother to the courtyard where all the male descendants of my late grandfather had been already assembled. Here they were kicked, butted, spat at, laughed at until one after the other, the great Singh family boys had begun to crumble and fall. The Maoists were only enlightening the ignorant villagers. This use of violence upon my brother was their way of bringing social transformation. 'There is no master and there is no servant . . . we are all equal' is what they meant to say with their violent actions that night.

And that was the night that made my family a refugee in its own country. Seeking an asylum from these political bandits, they had all flocked into Kathmandu, seeking protection and even solace for their shattered egos, leaving behind all their material wealth to be devoured by the mutinous villagers who had just woken up to the dawn of parity.

How I had wanted to wake him up . . . but he remained there still, stiff and stubborn. He was gone, taken in by the inexplicable chasm of infinity that we all call death.

'Prashant,' someone calls my father, and he is whisked away to coordinate the ceremonials of the cremation. A small regiment from the police have arrived to honour my dead uncle. 'Was he really worthy of this token of esteem?' I question his credibility, standing by his corpse and wishing in earnest to mourn for him. 'Who else in this family can boast of accomplishments to equal his?' A defensive thought retaliates back. 'He was minister of state not once but three times in his life time. But what was accomplished? Any gains to be proud of? There I stop. For there is not a shred of noble and worthy accomplishments reflecting upon his three terms as minister. Only that the country changed the course of history from an autocratic monarchy system of governance, of which he was inherently a part of, to a democratic one with a constitutional monarch while he served as the Home Minister for the last and final time. But that was ten years back. Since then, he has merely reflected upon the glories of his esteemed positions that were but once upon a time.

Of course, he did not stop meddling with politics in his own ancient ways, trying to revive the influence of the king amongst the masses. But he failed terribly. As political opinions had changed, even the political principles garnered by the new lot in politics had left him far behind. And no matter how hard he tried, he never managed to regain his popularity as a leader gain.

I look at him now, cold and dead on the floor and cannot help mixed emotions brewing in me. I see him as a terrified infant...standing in the courtyard....a huge, frightening object roaring into the stillness that he has created all around. With this intimidating image of him stands in congruence the fond memories, the ones I shall probably choose to remember him by. When I led him by his hand out to the same courtyard, forcing him to watch me dance, he obliged me each time by clapping and laughing, pretending to be in tune with my childish amusement before he picked me up and placed me upon his lap where I would remain for the longest time.... playing with his moustache, rubbing my little hands over the softness of his chubby face and sometimes even biting the rubbery skin of his cheeks. My father and my uncle then seemed to me these large, giant figures, protective barricades rather, within the embraces of whom I was innocently content and secure.

I look at them now, one dead upon the floor and the other lost and haggard. The thought sends shivers down me....cold and icy and I look away desperately in search of another refuge.

I have thought of death on many occassions. To me death has never been a scary prospect. It seems to lure me from its infinite calm, enticing me with promises of eternal peace and sanctuary. Sanctuary from what? This life and its complexities and perhaps even the shame of living in contempt. Imagine, hating it and having to live it all, day after day, suffocating with the pressures of its burdens...waiting for each day to pass and bring me closer to the final day of my annihilation. It is pathetic to continue living each day hoping that it is the last or do I have in me submerged hopes of a better life? Is there any better life?

The women are walking out now, and with them they bring along wails and loud cries for it is time now for the body to be taken to the ghats of Bagmati. I see my grandmother. She is barely walking. Others have nearly lifted her in an attempt to bring her closer to the dead body of her son so that she can give her last farewells. She seems dead herself. Her body is limp and lifeless and her eyes are open but vacant. Her white feathery hair is scattered all over her face and her sari is nearly torn apart because of physical exertions. Beside her are my two aunts, the two wives of my dead uncle. They seem in a trance themselves.

'My son...my dear son, the pride of my family...leader of a nation to die this way, unplaced and indigent. Oh! what more have you in store for me, dear lord? she stares in amazement at her bare hands, searching as though for an answer in the hardened furrows of her aged palms. I have never seen Jijumua break down like this before...so vulnerable and helpless. She has, since I can remember, been an epitome of authority, strength and perseverance. For the first time since I heard the news of this death, I let tears fall down my face. Tears of symapthy for my grandmother and for bewilderment at myself for knowing who I was weeping for.

The chaos is slowly lessening. The body I, secured and wrapped in a white cloth, is carried away on a stretcher. I can see my father leading this little band of mourners to the ghats. I stay back with the women in the house. We shall wait for the call to come after his cremation rites are concluded. Then we will all bathe in order to cleanse our mortal selves of the death that has just befallen us, after which the Singh family shall commence the thirteen-day rigid mourning rituals for Thulubua.

There is silence in the room now. No more wailings; only sighs can be heard now and then coming from different corners of the room. I sit at my grandmother's feet, massaging them. She lies prostrate with her eyes staring vacantly at the white ceiling above her, Her face an apparition of an ephemeral ghost.

'Jijumua, you have to be strong,' I can hear my voice. 'Talking always helps,' I continue in the same flat tone. 'It is always good to relieve yourself. Speak of him as you think of him. It will ease the pain.'

'I feel no pain, ba,' she finally speaks. 'It is the past that refuses to let me be. It drags me along each day as I see all others around me disappear. One after another I have seen people pass by me, leaving me alone with memories of them to endure. I feel no pain, ba. I merely suffocate in the endless sagas of the eras gone by.'

Sanat

Sanat crouchs in fear and anxiety. Strange faces peep and peer, and even poke her tear-stained face; some with curiosity, some with animosity and some merely to feel the gleaming, impeccable skin that stretches down from Sanat's face down to the rest of her lanky body. They had brought her to Kanda all the way from Achaam last night. A grand wedding procession playing drums and sarangis, singing and dancing had led her palanquin after a tedious journey of days, into the durbar of the Raja of Kanda.

'Buajiu...Buajiu,' she had clung on desperately to her father's bosom. 'Buajiu, Buajiu...' she had cried hoarse with panic and alarm, 'do not leave me behind...I am your flesh and blood...how will you live without me?'

'My daughter...my angel...my beautiful Sanat, you were a jewel given to us. Precious as you were I am now returning you to your rightful owner.' Her father had choked in his own grief, his body trembling with his own helpless plight.

'Buajiu...Buajiu...I beg you, do not leave me behind. I promise to work for you, clean for you, cook for you, and slave for you. Buajiu, take me back home.'

'Bless you my child...bless you...but you were born with a privileged fate. You will never have to cook and clean. In this place, you will reign as a queen...' His words were choked, his heart was heavy and tears flowed in the pain of leaving his little daughter behind. He had pushed Sanat away, yet she had clung on in desperation, dragged on, holding on to his fleeing feet. People had rushed in, women mostly, weeping and helping to separate the father and daughter.

Her hands outstretched, fingers curled in desperation, Sanat wailed her last desperate appeals to her departing father. 'Buajiu...Buajiu, who will bring your hot glass of milk every morning? Who will oil your hair at night by the fire? Buajiu, who will sit on your lap and playfully pull your moustaches? Buajiu, you too will suffer, I know...you have cut a piece of yourself and are leaving it behind. You will open your eyes to this ache each morning and will end the day with the same pain...I beg you Buajiu, do not leave me behind.'

Her father had not turned around but walked away with the stinging pain of his own amputation.

Later, while she was inside the room with the women, overwhelmed in her own gloom of abandonment, Sanat's anxious eyes – moist and panicky – had scanned her surroundings. Bright colours, rich and ornate, fill the room with articles of luxury that she never knew to existed. Her panicked gaze falls from one face to another. Women of all ages, were busy with instructions and merry chatter. Beyond these by the doorway had stood a large bulky figure, loud and dominant, severe and critical...staring at her. Their eyes had met. Sanat's confused curiosity met a glare of sheer hostility. Lost in her own quagmire of bewilderment, Sanat then had failed to comprehend this establishment of a conflict that would eventually help her understand her own position in her marriage.

Tara, that was her name. The women had called her and she swayed over everyone else, a commanding and an imposing figure.

'Change the Rani Saheb's attire before she is taken down for her meal...remember to have her washed before that...go down to the Jiunarghar and see whether her meal is ready.' Instructions floated out of her, easy, plain, dull and prosaic. The others simply complied, never seeming to refute her commands.

It is Tara's loud and commanding voice that has woken her up this morning, forcing Sanat out of a beautiful dream. 'Wake up you log!' Tara kicks Sanat's maid who was sleeping on a pile of hay in one corner of the room. 'Get the Rani Saheb ready for the Dhara puja.'

Phoolmaya makes a bundle of clothes given to her by Tara to be worn by Sanat after her Dhara puja. She walks behind Sanat who has been yet again placed on a palanquin. A shrill note of the sarangi cuts through the near silent morning. Then the Damais begin beating their drums, leading the palanquin all around the entire expanse of the massive, imposing structure of stone that is the home of her husband. Prayers are chanted along by the family priests as the retinue moves along and finally deposits Sanat to the source of water to the house. Here, a short prayer ceremony takes place after which the men go, leaving the women behind to help the bride take her first dip into the waters of her husband's home.

Sanat is a little hesitant. She embraces her lanky frame with her arms and looks up at the skies. The still darkness, lit up with a shimmer of stars that were beginning to fade, was being taken over by the pale hue of the slowly rising sun. A cock crows in the neighbourhood and distant sounds of the *dhikki chiau* going *dhuk...dhuk...dhuk* sends a sweet sensation of nostalgia in Sanat. Her mother too would be up at the crack of dawn. Fighting the clutches of sleep, she would now be holding on to the fastener that fell from the verandah's ceiling. Her feet would be pounding the end of the wooden log, the other end of which would fall into the little pit filled with rice, beating it flat. Then she would go into the house and wake her brothers sleeping by the hearth and send them with pots to bring water for the day from the water source. Her mother would then light a fresh fire and start heating the milk. Her father would sit up on his bed at the end of the room and wait for her to bring the glass of milk to him. Here Sanat stops, for the fact creeps in, biting into her chest...that she is not there anymore...she will not take the milk to her father but he will drink his milk this morning regardless. Her brothers would bring water and her mother would begin cleaning and cooking, and the lives of her loved ones, left behind, would move on...slowly attuning themselves to the vacant gap that she has left behind.

'Do it, Rani Saheb...the more you dilly-dally, the colder you will be. Just plunge in,' voices persuade.

Sanat squats by the water, dipping her hands into the softly gurgling flow of the stream. A transient layer of steam rises from it and disappears into the chill of the morning. It is also the shame of having to undress in front of strangers. Shy and fearful she pleads with her black round eyes to her maid, who is instantly by her side. Sanat's long and thick plaited hair is undone and her blouse unbuttoned. The petticoat tied at her waist, is pulled up and refastened just above her tender and newly blossoming breasts. It is now that the gaping women move in...smiling, giggling and laughing.

'All bones, Rani Saheb...*chya chya*...won't do. Men like flesh!'

Sanat can feel hands all over her, exploring and assessing. 'Big buttocks men like,' a woman with fat rounded hips turns her bulging back towards Sanat and adds emphasis to her statement by giving a slap to her own behind. 'Big buttocks like these they like, big hips full of flesh, something that they can hold on to, pinch, bite and even suck. Bones won't do, Rani Saheb...bones won't do.'

'Nani Saheb...' someone calls out to Tara who is standing, separated from the crowd, quiet but vigilantly observing. 'You would know best what Raja Saheb likes. Does he prefer bones to meaty flesh?' there is more laughter.

'Get in Maiya Sab,' Phoolmaya is urging Sanat to step into the freezing water. There is a strong resistance from Sanat. 'Help her...' Women are now screeching in near delight. 'Push her in...', 'splash some water on to her first.'

Phoolmaya, determined by now, and to prevent her ward from becoming a laughing stock to these jabbering women, picks up a jug. Filling it with the cold water from the gurgling stream, she pours it over the head of the shivering girl.

'*Ooiee...*' Sanat can hear her own chattering teeth and then with a forceful determination, she shuts her eyes, takes in a deep breath and plunges herself into the biting cold of the menacing flow in front of her.

Sanjeevani

Sanju Two

That I should marry and marry into a suitable family was perhaps the first thought that came into my mother's mind, the moment she laid eyes on me. She probably even began imagining my trousseau and short-listing the suitable and fitting families that I could some day wed into. Being born a female, I would not say I was a disappointment to my parents, as they already had Dada by then and were quite content with their male heir. I could surely be accommodated into their lives until I was ready to be given away; subsequently creating this grand and perhaps an envious matrimonial alliance that would one day be the talk of all the other relatives who too had daughters.

So I was brought up to be given away eventually. I was kept as a precious valuable, handled with the gentlest of care and treated with utmost concern. Not that I would have accepted it any other way...for I have been one hell of an imposing character since my early days. I made it clear from my first demanding wail that I got immediate and complete attention right away.

Pathetic as it may seem, the fact remains that I was educated and groomed only to get a suitable husband who would in return boost my parent's own social status, I think that is why my parents never showed any keen interest in my academic skills. My mother had this silly notion stuck in her brain somewhere that good girls from good families must go to good convents. So I was shut away with the nuns for nine months in a year and the three months that I was home, I ravaged the fields and jungles around my home as though looking for something lost... my soul perhaps.

Very early, in my growing-up years, I began to sense the differences between the way they treated me and my brothers. 'He is a boy and you are a girl, that's why,' was the only answer for all my 'whys'.

'Why can I not go out to the market? Dada is going.'

'Because he is a boy and you are a girl.'

'Why can I not stay up on the terrace? Dada is flying kites there.'

'Because he is a boy and you are a girl.'

'Why can I not go over to spend my holidays at my friend's place? You always let Dada go to Bimal Da's place.'

'Because he is a boy and you are a girl.'

I started rebelling for being a girl and most of my teenage years were spent in forcing myself to believe as I would want others to think I was a boy. I liked my hair short, wore only pants, and completely stayed away from female fancies. While Hemlata Dijju painted her nails and brought matching bangles for her new salwar kameez, I forced myself to say I was not interested.

I remember sauntering into the courtyard, where all the females of my family spent their idle afternoons; chest held back, arms swinging in the air and wanting each woman there to feel my manly presence.

'Teach her to sit, Kanchi Buhari. No girl from a proper family sits with her legs stretched apart the way Sanjeevani does, as though she were a man and has nothing to hide.' My grandmother would nearly have a panic attack each time she saw me.

'Why do men have nothing to hide, Jijumua? They might as well walk around naked then,' I would retort, bending over my torso and placing my elbows on my knees.

'Learn some decency, Sanju. You are big girl now. You cannot go around the house walking and talking like a man. Look at the way you dress...disgusting! Those pants clearly outline your crotch. In our days only *those* type of women dressed like this and that too in secret.' Jijumua would tell her daughters-in-law, her hand nearly covering her mouth, a gesture of being discreet.

'What kind of women, Jijumua? Ohhh! Lesbians? You had them in your time too?' I'd run to Jijumua's side in my excitement. 'Jijumua, please, please tell me who was a lesbian in your time? What did they do? Wow! Imagine, man! Lesbians in the onety onties!'

'Shameless girl!' and a whack I would get from Jijumua as she would turn her back to me, pretending to be disgusted with my brazenness. But I knew that Jijumua, despite her rigid stance of being a prude, is hardly shocked with my ways. More than that, I think she is envious. She envies my spirit and my boldness. Sometimes, I feel all the women around me who hold me in contempt for being a social tramp, envy that I am at liberty to live my life at my will and that my life is not dictated by any mama, papa, sasu, sasura or even any didi, bahini, dais and bhais.

Did they consciously neglect my talents, my dreams and my ambitions? I would think so. I still remember very clearly, the day I got my graduation results. I felt elated at the thought of starting a fresh, mature adult's life, getting a job, and getting a place of my own. My effervescent spirit and plans were waved away as futile and a load of nonsense by my mother, who for her part, was content with the fact that I could speak in English and had not a flaw on my face – essential criteria to trap a rich and worthy husband. So, I was sent to Kathmandu to associate with my rich aunts so that I could trap someone of an enviable status for a husband. This did not mean that she hadn't started her own devious strategies. Much before I entered the Kathmandu society, photographs of me, sitting in pink, yellow and green, printed chiffons, one hand on top of the other, head poised at an elegant angle and a gentle woman's smile on my dolled-up face, attached with my birth charts that had obvious hints of my lucky stars brightening up the fate of my would-be husband, were flying all around Kathmandu as would pamphlets of fresh news.

I am not clear how it all fell through, but I remember the day I was raving, ranting, screaming and pleading all at the same time...trying to make sense to my mother and explaining to her the advantages of establishing a career for myself first. However, I guess she was stuck with this notion that the quicker the better to get a daughter suitably settled. To wait another two to three years for me to establish myself would be too late for her. All my suitors would probably have got themselves pretty little young things by them. If I waited that long, she thought that I would end up an old maid.

It was not that only I was subjected to my mother's senseless dictations; my brother, too, was a victim to her tyrannous ways. But there was a difference there, too. For me, the girl child, they were loud and direct commands whereas for Dada, her son and heir, her wishes were relayed in subtle ways. She would soften her stance, her words would sound more like pleas, making them seem more like a cry for help.

He gave in each time; she sat by him, feeding him with her hands, fussing over him, stroking his hair, and dusting his collar. Many a time, she even kissed him on the head when he sat brooding in front of his computer...it was very eerie to me. She seemed like a scary ghost creeping in unannounced over him and cajoling him into agreeing to her demands. He would smile. I think it was a knowing smile. The gentleman that he was, he never made it apparent to our mother that he knew; he knew that the fussing and pampering were her ways to get him to do what she wanted. Dada gave in easily, too easily always without a fight. Sometimes, he even sacrificed his own wants and desires... unlike me. I always put my own self before all else and for that I had no choice but to make rebellion my religion.

Sometimes I rebelled for the silent submissions of my brother, too. Like for instance, when they decided to get him married. 'Always get your daughter married into a family richer in wealth, name and fame than your own and always bring a daughter-in-law who is lower in terms of your own wealth, name and fame' was my mother's favourite line as soon as (according to her) the two of us became eligible for marriage. I could not believe that she had got his marriage fixed with a girl seven years younger to him, barely educated and who had never walked outside the periphery of her own little village.

Although I was the last to be informed, the engagement having been conducted when I was away from home and busy with my high school examinations, I know she knew that I would as always oppose her decree, and perhaps even influence my brother into refuting her command.

'How could you, mamma?' I had choked in utter shock even though I was aware of my mother's devious ways. Even though my brother dreamt of pursuing a medical career, she had coaxed and cajoled him into taking care of the farm.

'All this belongs to you, Sanjay. We have only taken care of it so that we can hand it over to you some day. You think your Bua did not have dreams and ambitions of his own? We both did, but we gave it all up for the family. Your father left his job in Kathmandu at the land revenue department so that he could take care of the family assets... and now the responsibility is handed down to his son, you.' Kaput went his dreams of Poona and the medical institute.

Instead, I saw him quietly push away his own dreams and make our parents' expectations rule his life.

'How do you expect the two of them to get along? She is not even out of school and he has a bachelor's degree. He's been places, he's seen the world...what the hell are the two going to talk and discuss for the rest of their days?' I asked in sheer bewilderment.

'They don't need to,' her eyes had smoked with anger at my seditious image in the mirror in front of which she sat every morning, plucking and tweezing her eyebrows, powdering and beautifying her face. I had grown up watching her do this religiously right after her morning puja. She would enter the room after taking a bath, half naked, with wet hair and only a petticoat wrapped over her chest. After finishing her prayers, she would sit on her dressing table and prepare herself for the day; make herself look appropriate in her own eyes. I remember as a child, I would wait for her to come out from her bath, and join her in the puja room. My hands folded, I would sit by her as she lit the diyo and the room would fill with the essence of sandalwood. Her voice would echo in the silence of the morning. I would wait for the prasad, a little piece of gur that she placed in my hands religiously after she was done with her gods. For a split second after that, her hands, loving and compassionate, I would like to believe, fell on my little head and then she would go back to her commanding voice, giving orders for the day to the domestic staff. I would not say I do not love my mother...but I hate her when she imposes herself on me and more when she did it to Dada.

'How can you say that, Mamma? As husband and wife, they need to relate to one another, understand each other...there has to be compatibility, you know?'

'What compatibility do you talk of, Sanju? That's all crap that they teach you in modern schools. Is there any similarity between your father and myself? Yet we have stuck it out all these years...have we not?' She had almost growled back.

'But, Mamma...' I had insisted, 'that was in your days...these are different times, we are different people...we have different expectations and we think differently.' I had adamantly persisted, banging my hands on her dresser.

'That you think. Only you think differently, Sanjeevani...Sanjay does not. He is a good boy. He listens, he understands his parents and his obligations to his family first before wanting to understand other people.'

'Mamma...' but she was gone before I could have said that his to-be wife was not any 'other people' ...she would be his life partner and that it was imperative that he understood her and she him for them to live together.

That was the end of our discussion over Dada's wedding. I never asked him how he felt about the entire affair, and he never confided, either in me or to anyone else. But I saw him, felt him swallow his frustrations, keep them there until they kept piling one upon another. Eventually, the burden became too much for him to bear. It was then that he took to drinking. No matter who says what, I know my brother and although he is dead and gone now, I always will continue to love him. The gap he has left behind will always remain, forcing itself in, inch by inch until I fear it will consume me entirely.

I think that is exactly what is happening to me now...this gap that Dada left behind is growing into me...I can see myself slowly blend into its emptiness, becoming a non-entity, with no feelings, no dreams and no passions.

I ask myself whether I really am without any dreams and passions and if so, then what is it that I feel for Razat?

My sweet Razat, my darling Razat, my loverboy Razat...my sex mate Razat...my punching bag Razat, my friend Razat, my companion Razat...my world is shrunk into this one word and that is Razat.

I met Razat accidentally, or was it a grand design of fate? Whatever it may be, I saw him walk into the Salsa Bar where I was with my group of friends waiting for the grand finale of the 1993 World Cup. He was all dressed up, looking sophisticated in his purple shirt and grey Armani suit. I remember it well, for that night changed my life, steered the course of my fate and landed me where I am right now.

We were all there, eager and expectant, and cheering on for Ronaldo. I had a strong gut feeling that he would work wonders that night. We were drinking, too. Wine, beer and vodka were flowing like the surging rivers of Nepal. He walked in minutes before the game began. People had started seating themselves in front of the huge screen placed by Rakshya, the owner, on the wall behind the dance floor. My friends and I were moving from the bar to get the best seats and that is when I saw him. He was with friends too, surrounded by a group of men, who I had noticed a little later were seeming to give him some kind of special attention. Our eyes had met across the room and he had smiled. Obviously not at me but at the person who stood in between the two of us talking to him. But I chose to think that that angelic smile had been intended solely and much intentionally for me alone.

Instantly, Sanju came alive. She pushed Sanjeevani back. Did Sanjeevani fight? No, she quietly gave in, perhaps even willingly, for Sanjeevani was tired by now. She was wary of taking the lead for so long, her goodness had drained her out... she needed to rest for sometime. Sanju, the forceful one, the spirited one and the one who truly loves the self, came to the forefront.

Sometimes, alcohol does act as a magical catalyst in creating a destiny. Either way, good or bad, people have found their lives changed, altered forever, after having consumed this miraculous potion. The few vodkas that had gone scorching down my throat, had, I have to admit, ceased all senses of rational understanding and to an extent, begun to manoeuvre my bodily functions that night. I was flying in spirits and the intoxicant was speeding my rhetoric competence. My feet seemed to have wings planted on them and I flittered from one corner of the room to another...effortlessly and deliberately trying to show myself to him, catch his attention and make him feel the same ardour, that was both weird and wonderful.

He did not acknowledge my giddy presence until the end of the game. Even if he did notice me, I would have barely known for I was myself, too engrossed in my attempts at seduction. I was swaying my head so that strands of hair flittered in the air to give me an angelic look. I lifted the strands of hair from my face and tucked them behind my ears so that he could get a glimpse of my side profile. I pouted my lips when I spoke so that he could see the fullness of my mouth. I squinted my eyes to give myself an enchantress look; laughed loudly and cheered loudly so that my voice could travel to him. In short, every bewitching endeavour was made to catch his fancy. We watched the match together, he with his own group and I with mine...standing up to cheer, clapping in elation each time the team had the ball and slumping down with despair each time it was taken away. I made certain that the object of my interest did not disappear. Our eyes kept clashing from time to time throughout the course of the game.

His reactions to the game, unlike mine, remained more reserved. He did clap and cheer and get up from his seat from time to time but all this was done in a very composed manner...not jumping out of the chair and grabbing my nearest friends in a frenzy as I did, impulsive and energised with the beatings of my heart that seemed to get louder by the minute. They even seemed to drown the din of cheering and booing.

There were reasons one too many for celebrations by the end of the game. Brazil had won over Germany by two goals. Ronaldo had struck twice in the last twelve minutes, giving the South Americans yet another world crown...and I was richer in drinks for the bets that I had made with this one and that. I could feel his eyes on me. At least I remained under the impression that it would be nearly impossible for him to take his eyes away from me...the captivating enchantress that I was. So I went around grabbing my winnings that made me drown tequilla shots one after another, small in size but much larger, in capacity to devour all sense of right and wrong.

I met him in the corridor. I think I had followed him to the rest rooms and waited outside. When he walked out, I think I had fallen over him then...intentionally, no doubt. I had held on to the collars of his grey Armani, taking in the deep musky scent that emanated from him, more like layers of soft mist floating over a transient lake. His scent was blended in it too, manly and human...and for a moment, I had heard our heartbeats drumming together...beating together with promises of life.

'Careful, madamji,' his hands had slowly disengaged my body. My hands grasped him, refusing to let go. 'You...OKAY?' he had then asked, his voice drifting and then disappearing into the chaotic din of my own heart.

'What would you want me to be?' I had heard myself say. Shocked and stunned at my own brazenness, my hands were shamelessly tapping his chest. I think he was amused. He was not surprised, for women falling over men intentionally no longer remains a shocking prospect.

'Anything that you would want to be, madamji.' Now there was humour in the tone, naughty and teasing.

'Trying to hit on me, are you?' my finger pointed to him. I had prodded him on.

'Would you want me to?' he had played along.

'Depends on if you want me to want,' I had replied, my voice now slurring and my senses nearly blurring.

'In that case, I would say, very much, madamji. I would like it very much indeed. Whatever it is that we are seeming to want, I would like to want it very much indeed,' he had said putting an end to the dual word play and leaving me for a moment, with a loss of an equable repartee.

Words drifted out from my mouth, that was already steaming out vapours of the vodka and tequila that I had vigorously consumed...words undesigned and impromptu.

'I would want you to want to kiss me,' I had said, standing straight, hands loose by my side, swaying back and forth and looking straight into his eyes.

His hands had then taken hold of my shoulders. His fingers biting into my flesh, he had pulled me closer. Instances such as these are momentary and rather impacting...more like collisions; planes and cars suddenly ramming into another object approaching from the opposite direction. Ditto that. There was no time to think, and no time for reactions...only the repercussions are felt, stunning aftermaths that linger on...stick on rather, stinging and ravenous. His lips were on mine, soft and beseeching. I think my hands had moved up, feeling his skin, tender and warm. I drowned there instantly, voices around me disappeared in a haze.

Sanju broke Sanjeevani's engagement with Nabin Shah, a rich relative of the ruling royal clan, and with it she broke many expectations of many people that mattered to Sanjeevani.

My father had kept quiet. I saw the little I did of him thereon, sitting by himself, in silent contemplation, his head vigorously bobbing. He did not get angry with me, at least not in words, nor did he speak to me then...nor does he much now. Two years have now passed and the silence remains between the two of us. It is a still, calm, quietness that keeps mounting with unsaid words – his dissatisfaction over my choices for myself. As for my mother, she killed me the day her beloved son died. I no longer exist for her.

Her priorities, her obligations along with her love and care, if she is still capable of feeling at all, are now reserved for Dada's daughter. As for me, she has buried me along with the painful memories of Dada and the mountain of her other unmet desires. I am for her a pile of useless garbage and having me around would only fill her with an unpleasant odour.

As for Nabin, he walked away gracefully, considering the fact that I had let him down and even hampered his own social status in some way. He did not make it a big issue. Our engagement had lasted a little more than six months and I cannot say I did not like him. He is a good man—quiet, calm and maintains a very balanced approach to life. Perhaps it was this very last trait of him that did not go down well with my own nomadic soul. I have to admit that my heart is fickle as is my mind. We could not have ever been happy together. He was too complacent for me and I was too wild. And of course, he never did create a furore in my heart...that sizzling ache that keeps one alert and alive each day.

There had to be sighs of relief from many quarters at our broken engagement as it brought the most eligible bachelor back onto the prospective matrimonial list of many a mother seeking a match for her daughter. As for myself, I began to be shunned and subtly excluded from the society of the rich and the proper, who had but very recently begun to accept me into their glittering crowd. Not that I missed this society after Nabin for I was ever a pariah amongst them...this intruder...this girl from the remotes of the jungles of Kailali, who had suddenly appeared and harnessed herself to an object of many a desires. When I walked with Nabin, people welcomed me, hugged me but I knew that I was being watched at all times; assessed with stern, critical, disapproving and judgemental eyes pinning me down and many a time making me want to run for shelter.

'Hi Sanjeevani! Look at you...you look so beautiful in this dress. But darling, do something with your hair...it's a mess!

'Aaah! I know what you are wearing. That's a Chanel dress, isn't it, deariee? What a waste! You should have worn it for Kartika's party, I believe the whole of Kathmandu is invited?'

'That's a nice bag you are carrying, Sanjeevani. Todds, right? This must definitely be Nabin's choice...I tell you, he is one hell of a perfect man...sure knows how to win a woman.'

In a word, with Nabin, wherever I went, whoever I met seemed to talk only of designers, brands, jewellery, clothes, shoes, bags, perfumes, sunglasses and always the latest fashion. Not that I did not try and blend in...for the choice was always mine. I had chosen to brave it all, smile complacently and play along to the innuendoes that were lashed out at me every now and then. I think after a while I had started amusing myself with my own assessment of each person I met in Nabin's circle. These were women bored to sullenness and hysteria. They were lost in their own vanity, and ones who had never seen the other side of life. For these are people who drink filtered water and have never defecated in the open fields. How can they ever feel my pulse?

My life back home in Kailali stood in contrast to what I saw around me. We were still living in the dark ages out there. Our place was an hour's flight away from Kathmandu, but the difference was of a lifetime. And for this very difference was my own brother killed. My brother, who had never set his eye on designer wear, who was content with his faded Chinese jeans bought in the Dhangadi market, whose dreams never went beyond the boundaries of his own fields in Ganeshpur. Yet, my brother was killed, or rather brutally murdered, to set a trend, to begin a revolution that would narrow the gap between the haves and the have nots.

Who is to blame for this gap? Who is to shoulder the responsibility of widening this gap? Who? The rulers and the leaders? Yet they seem busy with their own little squabbles of retaining power and authority here in the capital. Kailali and its likes are forgotten as stepchildren and left to fend for themselves, whereas Kathmandu is pampered as the favourite child. Surely, there has to be a discord, there has to be an animosity between the favourite and the neglected. And that is exactly what Dr Baburam Bhattarai and Prachanda are talking about in the jungles with their warring cadres. The cadres are going village to village promoting the same sentiment.

I do not say I support communism...I don't...I cannot...but somewhere inside me, I can see the fair side of it all. I admit there are more privileged people than my own family as there are under privileged, but definitely the ones lacking are many more.

'Why is it that bad things happen to good people?' Razat had once asked me when I had asked him why only the remote areas were affected by the Maoist insurgency while the Capital and its people not only remained unaffected but also in a state of denial of the sufferings of the people under Maoist atrocities. 'Why do these remain unaffected and why do the likes of my family have to suffer at the hands of the Maoists? Not that there are no affluent families here in Kathmandu. Now look at yourself, Razat...compare your lifestyle with my own parents. What do they have in comparison to your wealth here, Razat? Your land here in Kathmandu is enough to buy nearly all my father's lands in Kailali. Why then must the Maoists attack the likes of my poor father who barely have the means to survive hand to mouth?'

'Why is it that only the poor bear the brunt of the havocs of nature? Why is it, Sanju, that only the poor are affected drastically by floods, earthquakes, landslides, droughts...why?' he had asked, with the same smile on his face. My Krishna smile...the very smile that even after two years of dating, still managed to fill me with the same warmth...a warmth that more than anything else, made me feel snug and secure.

'Once you know the answer to that, Sanju, all your other questions will subsequently be answered. The problem with you,

Sanju, is that you think too much...so much that you unconsciously make a mountain out of a molehill,' he had concluded, gentle mirth in his laughter.

'You think that? Razat, I cannot believe you just said that,' I had retorted back in self-defence. 'Mountain out of a molehill, my fucking ass! Razat, you live in your perfect world here. You are the same as everyone around you. What is happening in the country doesn't affect you as long as the share bazaar does well, remittance comes and the land value here in Kathmandu goes up. Making bucks is all that you care about, Razat Aggarwal. Finally I can see Jijumua's words hold true about you...you are merchants who care only about profits...nothing else...bloody Marwari.'

Razat laughed, he always did...an affectionate laugh, an undermining laugh. Yet I knew it was a caring laugh and a laugh that was for me alone.

'You are insensitive to the pains of the afflicted in the remotes of the country, Razat...you will always remain insensitive. What is happening out there is just another piece of news for you, isn't it? What do you care about the families displaced, sons and brothers killed, houses burnt...what do you care? For you have enough here...and enough elsewhere. All you care about is making money and more money.'

Then his arms had wrapped around me. Instinctively, my head had rested on his chest, his heartbeat soothing my pent-up fury, my resentment with the world around me.

'It is not all about money, Sanju. You know that I have enough to eat, a decent place to live in and perhaps even more than what I require. Yet I wake up each day and go out there and fight a battle for more. But the drive to achieve, the high of a challenge is what keeps me going.'

More than the words, it has always been his voice, the feel of his living flesh against mine, and his hot, lingering breath over mine that has helped in calming my agitation, neutralising the venom that is in me. A rancid acid it is...that I am filled up from within, that is sizzling from within, and slowly scorching my restless soul.

'What am I angry with?' I have asked myself often times, but the reason for my own vendetta against the world around me has always escaped me and I remain shifty, disconcerted, disappointed and extremely unfulfilled at all times. It is only with Razat that the constant fever in my brain seems to subside. With him, I want to believe that I am at peace and sheltered. I want to believe that Razat understands me whereas the fact is that no one does...not even myself. I have remained a piercing mystery to my own self. My conduct based upon my decisions, has always faced contradictions from my own conscience, not exactly my conscience but from within myself...I rebel and contradict my own self.

I try focussing on my priorities.

Razat.

My parents.

My job.

My volunteering with Rashtriya Prajatantra Party.

Saving the monarchy.

Helping to improve the country.

Writing my novel.

Who am I fooling? I don't care a shit about any of these. My parents, I love, I know I do...but that's about it. They are not my priority.

Razat...I have him but for how long? Is there really a future for the two of us?

My job...I work to sustain myself everyday. That's about it. There is no drive, no challenge steering me on.

My volunteering with the Rashtriya Prajatantra Party is mainly to fill the vacant times that are so obviously empty, bare and even suffocating.

Helping to improve the country and to save the monarchy...now that's where I am fooling myself totally. Do I give a donkey's ass to what is happening to this country and the monarchy...the king, the crown, the palace, the generations of the Shah dynasty that my father feels is the foundation of our own identity?

Having said it all, I think it is my writing that is saving me from disappearing into the thicket of this hypocritical sham that everyone else around me has taken for the truth. I see them walk around in denial of their actual selves believing more in the roles, and the masks that each one has dawned over themselves. Are they not taunted by their lamenting soul? Do they not despair for what they have become? Do they not fight their jeering phantoms? Indeed, the world around me is a chaotic stage and I the apathetic narrator.

Sanat

It has been so many months since Sanat stopped counting the torturous days and nights that have come in between her own home and herself. Now she merely looks forward to the days...only to wonder whether the day will be bright, whether the sun will shine or instead, will it rain. And if it rains, will it in silence, soft and beseeching, or will it come down in forceful showers, roaring and thundering.

Sanat now wakes up to watch the sun slowly emerge from the crimson horizon, gradually alter shades in shifting hues; soft, mellow, bright and then flaring, it seizes the entire sky and as it does, it spreads a glaring brightness that in turn ensnares everything that comes its way, absolving the beauty of it all. The skies disappear, the hills and the fields wane out, the entire ambience seems to take a backseat as people begin to walk, talk, taking the reins of the rest of the day. It is only in the evening that Sanat peeps out of her shadows to see the setting sun sending a tranquil sweep all around. Giant shadows begin to fall. Hill after hill begins to darken; there is a sense of serenity in this retirement of the sun; it holds out promises to Sanat. Promises of a better dawn.

Sanat soon begins to adjust and blend in with the domesticity of her husband's domain. She has taught herself not to run but to walk slowly, not shout but speak softly, not laugh but smile quietly, not wander off alone but to take a suitable chaperone, not to think of her home left behind but instead, force her mind into this new life that is gradually beginning to seem familiar.

Her days are spent doing nothing, as there are servants to do all her necessary chores. She does not even have to dress herself; there are maids assigned to her. They wash her, dress her, decorate her with gold and silver, paint her face and do up her hair each day in a different fashion. Sanat is led from room to room, surrounded by maids, voices, laughter and singing. Rooms are filled with artistic furniture, lounging chairs, tables made of marble, glittering mirrors and walls filled with portraits and gigantic elephant tusks, gilded in gold and silver. Sanat stares at these with incredulous awe and marvels at the mysteries of the world beyond which these articles have been brought... a world that is alive with wisdom and progress, a world that with every passing day, is leaving them behind, making a headway, alone in its own listless tangent towards the procurement of more and more of these luxuries. And slowly, Sanat begins to get absorbed into her new life.

She has encountered her husband on few occasions. He is tall, well-built and stately. Not only does he inspire respect and subservience but Sanat cannot help feeling a sense of terror when with him. He has not spoken much to her; all the instructions are given to his Nani Sahebs, Tara or Chanda, the maid of his dead wife in Kathmandu, who he has brought along as his new mistress.

Sanat cannot help bonding better with Chanda than with Tara.

'There are chariots drawn by four and even eight horses. The durbars are made of shining marble, and the gardens have fountains that flow all day long. You will see, Rani Saheb, for yourself, women glittering in jewels, men suave and polished with English boots and smoking pipes. It is a different world altogether, Rani Saheb...'

Chanda speaks in a sing-song manner, leaving Sanat in a state of amazement, her wondering gaze falling over the hills that spread on peak after peak to a distant land of mysteries.

'Rani Saheb, there is much for you to learn. This place is just a retreat for Raja Saheb. One day he shall return to Kathmandu, proud and victorious...' With a dream in her eye, Chanda continues to unfold Sanat's imagination.

'Victorious of what, Chanda?' Sanat asks, naïve and ignorant. To this, Chanda laughs... a sweet, soft symphony that floats across the room. Chanda, with her face heavily painted, is not beautiful, but undoubtedly, she is a charmer. Her hands with painted nails, flay in the air; her little head decorated with stars and moons, thrown back, she begins to reminisce about the old days of sheer merry making.

'Your husband is in exile, Rani Saheb... the Teen Sarkar in the capital doesn't want him to needle with the politics there.' Chanda is bent over Sanat, her dexterous fingers, moving effortlessly over Sanat's forehead, shaping her thick brows and in its stead, drawing a straight line with the black soot of the night lamp.

'Is he in trouble? But for what?' Instantly there is concern in Sanat for the husband she does not know.

'He will be if he returns... until his allies working from Calcutta, Benares, Dehradun manage to oust the Teen Sarkar and help Raja Tribhuvan to gain control of governance.'

'You know so much, Chanda.' There is awe in little Sanat's voice, and apprehension too. 'I will not know what to talk to him. Neither can I talk of Teen Sarkars nor am I able to discuss matters of the house. I know nothing for Tara won't let me involve myself anywhere, neither in the kitchen, nor in the stores. Honestly, how do I spend my days doing nothing?'

Chanda's arms go around Sanat to give a warm hug. Chanda positions her face next to Sanat's. Peering into the mirror, she consoles Sanat. 'With time, you will know how to conduct yourself with your husband. Now you say, you have only idle hours on your hands but a day will come, my dear Rani Saheb, when you will have no time for yourself. Believe me.'

Sanat has finally begun to menstruate and is out of her thirteen day isolation, where she had been locked up in a dark room, as she was considered tainted and impure for those particular days. Now she has been bathed, cleansed and made ready for the first night with her husband.

Women and girls crowd her room; joking and bantering is in full sway. Chanda is dressed as a man and she dances around with a huge carrot tied to her waist. It falls on her crotch symbolising a man's penis. As the other women sing and clap and even beat on the madal, Chanda thrusts her flanks, swinging the carrot on the squealing women's faces. There is a moment when she rides another woman, who is prostrate on the ground. The carrot in her hand is pushed into the crotch of the other woman.

Peals of laughter and cheerful banter continue until Tara comes in. Stern and sober, she is clearly not in the mood to join the raillery. 'Raja Saheb is ready.' Sanat has begun to understand this contemptuous tone of Tara's. She has held command and importance for too long on Raja Saheb's domain; and now the legal wife is soon to make her influence, slowly but surely.

'Enough of your silly bantering! Get Rani Saheb ready for the night.' This too is said with the same officious contempt.

They swarm over Sanat. The excited women are giggling, joking, pinching and teasing. Sanat is nervous and frightened, yet eager to know what is in store. After her bath this morning in the stream, she had shut herself alone in her room, taken off her clothes and felt her naked body with her hands that were cold and trembling. She imagined his hands, warm and gentle, stroking her body, her neck, her breasts that were soft and supple and moving down her flat stomach, resting there perhaps for a while and then moving down. She sighed; a strange sensation – sweet and exciting – making her inner thighs go hot in a queer desire.

He sits by the bed, reclined on a lounging chair, smoking his hookah. The curtains on his four poster bed sway with the gentle breeze that filters in through an open window.

'Sit down,' he says finding her standing, mute and motionless by his chair. She begins to squat on the floor before him. 'Not there, come sit by my side.' The tone is the same that he would use with any of the servants in the house, careless and overbearing.

Loud thuds begin to resound in her wildly beating chest as Sanat places herself by her husband's feet. He watches her; a scrutinising look that moves down her entire form. 'You are too thin.' It is a casual complaint. Placing his pipe on the floor, he sits up and takes her hands, which were visibly shivering now with fear and mortification for not being fleshy enough for her husband's liking.

'You have nice hands, long and delicate fingers, very ladylike.' It is a relief for Sanat that he actually likes something about her. 'Let down your hair,' he orders and watches her as she untangles her braided hair, allowing thick, black ruffles to fall over her face and shoulders.

He picks up his pipe and begins to smoke again, his eyes glued on to her trembling frame. Sanat has not looked up once to see her husband but she can feel his roving eyes move down her body. She can feel his hot, desirous look scan her inch by inch.

'Take off your clothes and wait for me on the bed.' Yet another indifferent order.

Sanat walks towards the bed and slowly begins to unfasten her blouse. He notices her hesitation. He walks up to the night lamp and brings the wick down so that there is now a still darkness in the room. Sanat fumbles with her clothes and finally stands naked and fearfully trembling.

She cannot see him in the darkness but can smell his odour, hot and pungent. His hands begin to roam all over body and his mouth is close...very close. She can almost feel the coarseness of his moustache on her face.

There is a stirring in Sanat, hot and consuming, and she is suddenly filled with a desire she has never known. A fire burns between her legs. She can feel his hands push her thighs apart. Before she can gasp for air, he is on top of her and pushing into her – a piercing pain. It begins to hurt Sanat more each time he bangs into her, careless and reckless and with a frenzy that drives out all the feelings of passion that she had started out with. Now there is only pain, searing pain. She tightens herself with each banging. Hands clenched, eyes closed, lips forced together so that she doesn't let out a scream, Sanat hopes and prays for the nightmarish ordeal to end.

Sanjeevani

The wrought iron gate is missing; only the hinges remain, rusted and ready to fall. I walk in and look around. The tall brick fence around the house is now a ruin. There are gaping holes as bricks have been stolen from here and there. In many places, the entire wall is uprooted. They did not even spare the trees around here. The age-old seesams that bordered the fence are all gone along with the mango trees that stood in a cluster by the house. They had been cut and taken away by the villagers for fuel and construction.

'Bastards...Bastards!' I want to scream out. There is anger in me. I am filled with hatred but all I can do is look around, helpless. Towards my left used to be the kitchen garden – a patch of land separated from the fields by a fence made of sturdy tree trunks, laid parallel, one over another. Here I sat on many afternoons, my feet dangling, chewing languidly on pods of green peas and staring listlessly at the neat patches of spring onions, coriander, tomatoes, spinach, brinjals, cabbages, chillies, all sprawled in a merry assortment. I waited for the cattle to return from the jungles. And when they did, the tinkling of the bells tied to their necks would alert me much before they crossed the river. That's when I would begin to run towards the river and ask Dangwa, the keeper of our herds, to help me onto the first buffalo. The ride back each evening would be accompanied by the sun setting behind the river, the tinkling of the bells, the calling of the calves for their mothers, the click of their hooves as they charged into their sheds for the night. I would help Dangwa, quietly enchanted while watching him place huge logs of wood, one over the other, making a parallel railing to keep the cattle in for the night in the shed. The males were kept in one with the calves and the females in the other. In the mornings, Laata would come with two buckets and brought in the calves to the female shed. Here, he milked the cows and I used to watch, squatting on the ground, my hands perched under my chin, with the same enthusiasm each morning.

I stand in front of the house, my heart drumming and my mind in a furore. The house, my house, our house stands in front of me, remainder sad of a brutal molestation and a chilling abandonment. Patches of moist, cold and dismal, are spread across the façade. Weed and moss peep out precariously from the cracks that have emerged in the thick rounded walls. It is now left to decay. All these years, it has stood deserted and alone, braving all the vagaries of nature and humans alike.

I do not enter the house but walk around it first... looking and assessing and even more, reminiscising. Each part of the house bears a memory. The portico in front of the house, was the place where my father and uncle met the men of the village. Their discussions, sometimes lasting hours, even stretching on until late at night. The fire would then be lit up here for them and they all sat around it, nodding, discussing, and sometimes even shouting their opinions. I would sit with them and watch the yellow embers from the fire... rising in giant flames and slowly disappearing into the night.

'Birendra Sarkar shows promises of a benevolent king... he will surely make the Shah dynasty proud.' That's my Thulubua, blind follower of the monarchy. Praises of the monarchy just flow out of him, effortless and ceaseless.

'Yet, I do feel that the Birendra Sarkar lacks the firm resolute mind that Mahendra Sarkar had...something tells me that King Birendra is not as assertive and openly critical to opposing parties as was his father.'

That's my father speaking and though his words then made little sense to me, I believed in each word that was spoken by him. For me then my father was my be all and end all. He knew everything, he could do anything and indeed my father was always right.

I walk to the back of the house where the stoned courtyard separates the Bhancha ghar from the main house. This used to be the women's zone. Here all the women of the house spent their days knitting, assorting vegetables, cutting vegetables, drying chillies on cots lying in the sun, filling jars of mango and chilli pickles, picking lice from our heads, reading the Hindi novels...every chore of the women was done in this area. And along with them, I remember spending many an idle afternoon here, lying in the shade of the mango tree...doing nothing but whisking the hovering flies away from myself as I listened to the women, gossiping in hushed tones so as not to make their words be heard by my grandmother who lay on the next cot, enjoying her afternoon siesta.

I would squeal sometimes. 'Jijumua, Jijumua, you know what Mamu was telling Thulumua this afternoon?' I would whisper mischievously into my grandmother's ears, when we sat by the hearth after dinner, warming ourselves. I would get reproaching looks from my mother and aunts, but there never was any fear in me. I did what I wanted, I said what I wanted at any given time.

'No...I don't know what they say of me. You tell me,' Jijumua would stop blowing on her hookah and pick me up onto her lap. 'Mamu told Thulumua that times have changed and that we all must change with the times...there is no sense in walking down all the way to the well on the far ends of the fields to fetch water for your daily puja when water can be had right here from the hand pump.'

'Oh! She said that, did she?' my grandmother would say not looking at my mother.

I glide around like a restless ghost. This ruin has many memories...memories of my past, the past that was me. I am everywhere...by the river, splashing water on the buffaloes that are there half immersed to ward off the heat, running along the fields, in the barn, hiding behind the thresher and watching the labouring cow give birth to a new calf. In the kharihans where the harvest is stacked in piles, I can see myself climb up and jump from one pile to another...I can see myself coaxing Dangwa to take the strongest bulls out and attach them to the bullock cart and take off with the half-naked children of the village into the nearby jungles.

What did I do to spend my days? Nothing.

I stared, to be honest. I love to stare at things...trees, clouds, birds nesting on branches of trees, faces, sunsets, the rustle of leaves...everything around me seems enchanted...and I wonder why I remain immune to the tranquil that is all around me.

What am I doing here?

A passing thought provokes my saddened senses and yet again I am filled with that yearning...the desire to belong...to cling on.

I miss Razat. It has been months now, since I last saw and even spoke with him. Did we quarrel?

I guess not. I guess I began to slowly withdraw myself from him. I'm now left with stinging questions that keep rising within me much like a nauseating acidic bile.

I cringe. I sigh. Is this agony real? I ask myself.

Did I run away?

Should I fight back?

Will I ever...ever get Razat for myself?

Is Razat all I want in this life?

What kind of a pathetic loser am I not to know what I want in life?

Razat had made it very clear from the beginning of our relationship that I could never be a part of his family. I was his other part, he said ... a significant part, and his wife his other part ... the essential part but the two parts of his life could not and must never come together, he had said.

I complied to all of Razat's terms and conditions. Not only, that I have to admit when it comes to Razat I become like this little pet dog ... wagging its tail and bouncing all around him to keep him entertained and in return, maybe get a bite of a goodie. The goodie, in my case, is his company. I am addicted to Razat's company.

With him, I feel secure. With him, time passes effortlessly, and with him, I can genuinely laugh and more than anything else, I think it is the sense of contentment which is so fulfilling. I seem to want nothing else. I am at peace, ease and truly happy. It is when I am not with Razat that the world begins to look ugly, scary, and utterly depressing.

Each time Sangeeta came to Kathmandu with his children during their holidays, I conveniently slipped away. I led my own life. I would be alone, despondent yet hopeful; knowing that once she would go back to Hong Kong, my life which had taken a sudden pause, would resume with the same exuberance as before. I would be back in Razat's sturdy arms, I would feel his naked skin again, and find myself sailing along with Razat's firm convictions.

Yes! That's what it is all about, I guess. I think Sanju clings on to Razat's confidence in himself.

Perhaps I want to be a part of his undaunting spirit. There is always a spark in Razat's eyes. A glint that speaks volumes of his enthusiasm for life. He lives each day with a passion as though every day were a battlefield where he must go out armoured with his ceaseless spirits and fight. Razat savours his life and I am sure he loves living his life. I am convinced that being with him, sharing brief moments with him, his triumphs and defeats, his worries, his concerns, makes me satisfied.

I admit I live a false life; Razat's pains are his, not mine; Razat's success is his, not mine; Razat's life is his, not mine. After all, Razat is a separate individual and now I know that Razat was never mine.

To sum it all, Razat was never mine. He always belonged to his family. I have never fitted in. He never placed me with the little jumbles that he has sorted out and made into a perfect picture of his family. I am the one who looks from the outside into this completed jigsaw and sighs for my own emptiness.

This dawned on me late...two years late. After having steered my life to a totally different direction from where it was headed, after having slurried my name and become a social shame for my parents, I realise now that Razat and I have no future together.

It hurts still, when I say it. I cannot imagine going back to Kathmandu and not seeing Razat again. All these months that I have stayed away from Razat...I have longed for him every moment. There is a pain inside me...a sour, bitter pain that just does not give me rest. I am lonely, I am shattered and not a moment goes by when I do not think of him.

I left Razat and along with him my job with the *Kashthamandap Weekly*. I ran away from Kathmandu after that fateful night.

Can I ever forget that night? We were together. Only I am an accomplice to Razat's drinking...did I not get him into it to begin with. It is almost unethical in his Marwari society to indulge in alcohol and smoking. It is not only considered indecent and improper but also shunned as an unhealthy and unreligious vice. Which undoubtedly it is...but there are so many other things in life with the same effect which we conveniently adopt. Say, for instance, ambition, greed for money and material things, backbiting, devious intentions...my list could go on.

Razat and I had countless discussions on this topic. And I guess I did manage to instill some of my indecorous vices into him. He does take a few puffs from my cigarettes now and then and occasionally does switch from his Virgin Marys to a strong Bloody Mary.

The night Razat was abducted by the Maoists, I admit I was relishing this impropriety of mine. I was totally wasted, having downed five or six vodkas and coerced Razat into matching the intake of his Bloody Marys with mine. We talked nonsense and we laughed a lot and he kept saying, 'Who am I, Sanju? Who am I?' and I laughed each time he said this with an innocence on his face that was nearly childlike. It was always amusing to see Razat get drunk with his first Bloody Mary. He would behave like a child then, innocent, curious and even demanding; very different from the Razat Aggarwal that the world recognised him as – the business tycoon, the king of the Nepalese stock markets, suave, tenacious, determined and successful.

Before he dropped me back to my shack that night, he had taken hold of my hands, looked straight into my eyes and said 'What have you made me...Sanju?'

I was then too drunk to comprehend and even answer that question...but God knows I have gone over these words again and again in my mind, trying to answer it. The rational answer to it, the one that makes sense keeps throbbing at my temples as though it were a terrible headache.

I have ruined Razat as he has me. We have both wrecked one another and our relationship is a lost case with no directions. Just like myself.

I had disentangled my hands from his grip and taken hold of his head and forced it down; placing my lips, that are always craving for his, on his forehead. I had kissed him all over his face...tasting his skin, his warm flesh, feeling along the breath of life that emanated out of each pore of him.

Razat dropped me to my place that night and never got back to his. I began to sense something was wrong when he did not respond as he always did to my SMS on his mobile. Each time Razat left me for the night, I would text him, as I did that night too. I wrote: 'Razat' taking for granted that soon a 'yes, dear', would appear on the screen of my mobile phone. This had been a routine affair. We had done this religiously every night since we started seeing each other. His 'yes dear' was like a last prayer of the day for me before I closed my eyes. That night these words did not appear at all. I had started calling him but he did not answer and soon, the line on his end went dead on me.

I knew something had gone terribly wrong.

He was in the headlines the next morning. News channels, radio stations and my entire editorial team at the *Kashthamandap Weekly* spoke of nothing but the abduction of Razat Aggarwal for ransom by the Maoists.

I suffered alone. While the rest of my colleagues went frantic in collecting the latest news of him, I sat stunned at my desk, staring at the harsh words on my computer – 'Businessman kidnapped for ransom'.

I knew Razat was a difficult man, stubborn and unrelenting in many ways, but I knew that he was a sensible man too. Besides, he is a Marwari, and Marwaris know best how to conveniently slip out of a dicey situation. 'It is in your genes...' I had often joked about it with Razat. 'You Marwaris know well which side your bread is buttered and will lick the side which is. You can twist and turn a situation to your advantage and liking...I don't mean it as an offence, Razat, but you guys can really deal with difficult situations.'

He had laughed then, with confidence and pride in his laugh. 'That's the racist Samanti Maharani speaking again,' he had said amidst peals of laughter.

I cringed at the thought of his vanity and pride in himself being hurt, this very minute. I imagined the blows, the kicks, the spits, the abuses that he was probably getting from the Maoist cadres. And I knew that Razat was suffering all this while not as much from the physical abuse that he was probably receiving but from the thought that the entire country would know of his miserable predicament.

My suffering was mine alone.

The next day Sangeeta arrived and I waited alongwith a crowd of journalists at the airport. As soon as the Thai Airways from Bangkok landed, I could feel the vibrant energy all around me—cameras getting fixed, dictaphones getting ready, and journalists even pushing and shoving to get closer to the reception aisle.

She walked out. Her head held high, her hair tied up in a bun, her eyes shaded with Chanel sun glasses, a Fendi bag slung carelessly on her shoulder and holding on to her two children on both sides.

Cameras began to flash, people began to shove and get closer to her as they began to scream their questions aloud. I froze as I saw Prateek, our photographer rush to the frontline with the other cameramen.

Sangeeta walked towards us, the hollering journalist crowd. I watched her in awe, still frozen to my spot. She had a flawless complexion and her features were bold and clearly defined...indeed, she was beautiful. She seemed to have a proud air about her...not really proud I decided, but an air of contentment. After all, she had Razat; what more could she want? Ignoring all the jumbled queries that were being thrown at her, I watched her speak.

'My husband, Razat Aggarwal, has been kidnapped for ransom. We have received an alert asking for ten million for his release. I am ready to release the ransom amount hoping that it would be issued for a humane and just purpose. I pray to God that my husband is safe and request his kidnappers to release him at the earliest.'

Suddenly, all around me was a dark eerie gloom that seemed to foretell horrific days ahead for me. I had nothing. Razat was taken away to a place where I could not reach him, or share his fears. I could not even be a part of the negotiations that were going on for his release. I suddenly felt left out, abandoned and extremely helpless.

I feared for his life and even thought of his predicament in captivity, but strangely what troubled me most were my own pains. My selfish reasons that I was left out, and not there for him during this calamity. Nor could I help during the negotiations for his release; nor later, when he returned after a week.

I was all of a sudden shut out. Completely denied access to Razat. In normal circumstances when Sangeeta came to Kathmandu, she stayed for a fortnight or a month at the most. But this time she stayed on for three months. There was no knowing whether she was here for good.

I could not meet Razat, and for three months I could not speak with him as he refused to take my calls.

I will never know what troubles me more; the fact that I could not be with Razat or the fact that I was deserted by Razat.

For some time, I consoled and comforted myself saying that he was the talk of the town lately, his kidnapping still fresh with the media and even the locals. So perhaps he was avoiding me only to keep a low profile. But then he could have texted me, emailed me. If Razat wanted, we could actually continue the way we were prior to his kidnapping. After all, he had resumed his daily life as before. He was going to work, attending seminars and business lunches. He was even on television sometimes debating on political issues and the effect on the business community that further highlighted its negative impact on the national revenue.

It took some time for me to admit that Razat was deliberately keeping himself away from me.

Imagine my plight. I was angry, I was hurt. I was shaken and I was terrified. I did not know what to do with myself.

My mother then started her matchmaking again.

'No good family will accept you here in Kathmandu, Sanjeevani,' she said to me in the kitchen that night. I rarely visit my parents, unless it is for some family function or when I am summoned by them. They seem to enhance reasons for my self-pity.

I had gone over that evening to be with my family as they mourned King Birendra's death. Although it was not announced officially, there were rumours that it could have been his own son, the crown prince who had killed nine members of his family, including himself, the previous night.

I knew this was an unexpected blow on my father's hopes and that the king's death would affect him as would a tragedy of his own. My father had placed all his hopes upon the king. It was an innocent child-like wish. It was as though the king would wave his wand one day, and all the Maobadis would disappear, and our home would be returned to us and with it, our pride and our social status.

Today, my father was not falling off to sleep in front of the television set as he habitually did – his dishevelled grey hair, always in need of a cut, half falling on his heaving chest, his mouth slightly open, saliva sliding down from the corner of his open mouth and the sound of his snoring louder than the sound of the TV. Today, he was alert, sitting cross-legged on the couch, his torso inclined towards the television, he was flicking channels in a near child-like excitement.

'Dhana...Dhana...Indeed, the kalyug has come upon us,' he was calling out to my mother who was in the kitchen.

From where I stood, I could see the television clearly. There was utter chaos and even the news anchor was crying. She had tears in her eyes which she wiped just before the live clipping of the general public gathered outside the gates of the Naraynahiti Palace was shown.

People came together to mourn their king. Men with shaven heads, women, and children, were all weeping and placing flowers. Not one person out there was not crying. How vain, how forgiving the Nepalese people are, I had thought, watching people crying, wailing and muttering prayers for the dead members of the royal family. 'These are the same people who chanted 'Pampha Devi *hai, hai*! Birendra *chor*, desh *chor*!' during the 1990 Democratic movement. Now they all weep. More than that I was amazed at my own feelings when last night at around 11 p.m., we were all summoned to the editorial room and told the news.

'King Birendra is no more...' Suddenly I wished the world would come to an end. There is so much evil, pain and suffering, what was the point of going on? More than that, I felt orphaned. It was a weird feeling of being left alone for I barely knew the man. But there was a strange gloom hovering about me as though I had indeed lost someone very near and very dear. My own wounds seemed to be magnified with the cruel death of our king; and when I mourn now along with the nation, I also weep for my own shattered soul... 'Nepti, come here my little sis. Feel me growing, Nepti...my dearest sister...mero banu. Yes my Nepti...feel it harder...'

'Death is the only sanctuary...death is the only reprieve, I can hear my inner phantoms scream back at me. I want to drown in the chaos that is there on my father's television screen.

'Who could have done this, but the Maobadis. They must have a hand in this. 'Perhaps it was done in collaboration with India...' My father was mumbling in shock.

I did not tell him then that I had spoken to a lieutenant of the palace guards who was on duty at the palace last night. He had unofficially leaked out that it was the Crown Prince Dipendra who had shot eight members of the royal family before shooting a bullet through his own head.

This news had already become fodder for gossip in the past twenty-four hours, blending in with many other possibilities.

My head was throbbing with terrible pain. I had not had any sleep since the night before last. Suddenly, I did not see the point of any discussions. What had to happen had happened and what has to happen would naturally happen.

What was the point of calling up people, getting together, airing your opinions as though all that would make any difference.

I felt a strong urge to turn around and run back to my rented room, shut the door, draw the curtains and close my eyes to the world of news, gossip, conversations, suggestions, commands...oh, I was so tired.

'Call your mother, will you? What is she doing in the kitchen when the country has collapsed? We have no king...tell her to come out and watch this immediately.'

While walking towards the kitchen, it struck me that he had not asked me once how I was. It had been over a month since I had seen him last. I knew he was excited as was the rest of the country but he could have at least said something personal to me. 'How is your work going?' 'Or even how are you?'

My parents had moved lodgings three times last year. 'Not for long should our whereabouts be known.' My father's fear of being followed by the Maoists even in Kathmandu. 'We keep changing our lodging and they will never trace us.'

'But Bua, they are not after you,' I would try and make him understand.

'Yes! Why do you think they killed my son? Indeed, they are after me.' He would shout in anger.

'They did that to prove a point to the community. Dada was like the symbol of oppression. And what happened that night was a way to claim to the rest that families like ours are nothing. They are humans just as everyone else and can get hurt and even killed,'

I had said, explaining the reason more to my own self than to my father.

But my father is adamant in believing that the Maoists have a personal vendetta against him. Perhaps they do, but what he fails to realise is, that in Kathmandu he is just a little fly hovering around, useless and worthless. No one cares in this bustling city about where he lives and who he is.

This house completely depressed me. It had three bedrooms, cold and damp, and no sunlight and no privacy as the house was surrounded on all four sides by other similar houses nearly joined to one another.

Jijumua was now living with my parents after my Thulubua's death along with Thulumua, my dead uncle's, eldest wife. I have two aunts. The eldest is Thulumua. She is the Jaat ko buhari, the socially accepted one but never accepted by her own husband. The youngest is Aunty.

Coming back to my parent's apartment and my marriage proposal, I went to the kitchen to call my mother. There were vegetable peels all around. My mother refused to throw them in the bin as she cut them. She waited for the entire meal to be ready before she began to clean the kitchen. At times, the floor would be mucky, wet and slippery. There was no dining table; we sat on pidkas on the floor to eat. Often, this reminded me of all the wooden, bulky wooden furniture that my family had left behind. At one time we had our own factory. Bua used to cut down trees at his will. We had hired two Muslim carpenters from a neighbouring Indian town, and we made our own furniture. It was nothing fancy but we had everything. This was when my father was in the timber business. My Uncle was the forest minister then I guess that was why we felt we had the right to cut down any number of trees at our will and even trade at our will. The details escape me, for I was only five or six years old then. Every thing seemed right then.

My mother had finished cooking our meal and was just putting some rice in the cooker for Jijumua. Jijumua never ate food cooked by anyone but her bahuns. Now there were no more bahuns, and even if there were, we could not afford to keep one, just to cook her meals. So my mother cooked the vegetables for her and washed and placed the rice in the electric cooker that was placed in the far corner of the kitchen. Jijimua would come and plug it in and eat food in her secluded corner. She complained many times when she remembered her old days, when an entire team of bahuns would cook her food in a separate kitchen where there was no meat, garlic or onions.

'Now I have to make do with whatever there is. They cut my vegetables with the same knife that they use to cut the meat in this house. I am left with no choice but to ignore it all. At this age what can I do but say Hare Ram and turn a deaf ear and a blind eye to all the tainted new ways and customs,' she would say.

'There...Sanju is here. Kanchi Buhari, tell her to cook my tarkari...I am sick of the same taste every day, a different hand cooking would perhaps alter the taste,' Jijumua said, sitting in her corner, waiting for her rice to get cooked.

'Darshan, Jijumua,' 'I said mechanically. 'Ma, give me that. I will cook the mismaas for Jijumua. You go to Bua. He is calling you.'

'I have to talk to you first Sanju. Even your Bua. All of us need to talk to you. He didn't mention it already to you, did he? You must have said "No".'

What she was saying went over my worn out, sleep-deficit head. 'What, Ma? Bua has not said anything. He only wants you to watch the news, the cremation ceremony of maharajdhiraj is soon going to be on air...'

'That's there, Sanju, but...' I could see that she was excited now. She had some command to give yet again. The urge to run became stronger. 'A proposal has come for you, Sanju.'

I did not want to run any more...that would take time – to turn around, go out of the kitchen, back into the living room, to the main door and then out to the little porch and then the gate. It was not possible to run; my mother would catch up. Instead, I wished the ground below me would open instantly and swallow me up.

'He does not live here. He has been in America, working there for the past fifteen years. He has made enough for himself there...and now wants a wife who is smart, can get a job, and take care of his two children from his dead wife.'

'Ma...stop it,' I had said. 'You know I do not wish to get married yet.'

This infuriated her. 'She banged the ladle with which she was mixing Jijumua's vegetable curry, banged on the plate next to the sink, washed her hands and stood staring at me...her eyes fiery and her body trembling with agitation.

'You would jump and marry this very minute if that Marwari wanted to...wouldn't you, Sanjeevani?' I could even see the veins tightening on her skin. Her face was only inches away from mine now. 'But you won't marry a good, decent man, of our own caste...who is ready to accept you after knowing all your indecencies.'

I knew that she knew that I no longer was a virgin. That I had purged my religion and bedded a married Marwari man.

'Ma...please, it is my life,' I had begun to say. Just then I felt a smarting sting on my left cheek. She had slapped me and had turned around, her face buried in the pallu of her sari. She had started to cry. Then she turned around.

She was pale. It was as if all her blood had been sucked out. 'Your life, Sanju...is indebted to us. I carried you in my womb for nine months and nourished you, I gave birth to you, we brought you up, fed you, clothed you, educated you and you call it your life. Tell me one thing you have done for yourself that has not given you bad name and along with it dragged our name into a pit of shame. Your old, sonless father has lost everything, Sanju; he has nothing left but he holds onto his family pride. Keep that up for him, will you? Marry this man. Sanju, lead a respectable life, help us hold our heads in dignity in the society.'

Saying this she had rushed out of the kitchen and my heart went out to her. I was miserable. I had never seen my mother cry. She was a strong woman and never revealed her emotions publicly, not even to us, her children and family.

I stayed back, stunned and grieving for my mother's pride. It was Jijumua who spoke then...

'Sanju...' she said, walking towards me, 'your mother is right in her own way...but it is your life, Sanju.'

I remember hugging her then, burying my face into her drooping shoulders, and letting my misery flow. 'I am bad. Bad...evil, that's what I am,' I wept.

'Quiet, my child. It is not you but the times that are bad, circumstances that are bad. And times change. Sanju your parents will soon learn to accept that...I did. With time, I saw people change, places change, customs change...and myself adapting to all these changes. I rebelled, I fought hard...but fate is something no one can change.'

Sanat

'This time it is a girl for sure.' Tara is assessing Sanat's eight-month pregnant stomach. 'You can tell whether it will be a boy or a girl just by looking at the rise of the belly. Small and round with a slight peak at the naval is surely a boy but this time Rani Saheb, your bulge is huge. The weight is uniformly distributed. This indicates that it's a girl for sure.'

Tara is giving a massage to Prabhat. She is warming her hands with the heat of the brazier and then mechanically placing them on the one-year-old boy's chest. The room reeks of camphor and hot oil, with which Sanat's first born is being massaged.

'I so wish your words would come true, Tara! I really want a daughter this time.' There is longing in Sanat's eyes as her hands begin to caress her protruding stomach. She is clicking her tongue to the bitter taste of the lemon that she is diligently sucking on. 'All the symptoms are so different this time. I don't feel as sick as I used to when I was carrying Prabhat. But with this one, I get weird cravings...'

'Tell me about it, Rani Saheb! Your cravings could drive one up the wall. I had to send Laata all the way to Khaptad to get you the sweet you wanted. And then one day, in the middle of the night, you wake me up wanting chukani. Now how is one to get chukani in the middle of the night when there is no farsi available? Yet, I brought it for you. And this time have I not seen you sneak out to the fields and come back with your mouth sending tell-tale signs of you having eaten mud again?' Tara continues her rambling as she takes a handful of hot oil in her palm and begins to pat it on the infant boy's soft head.

Tara's initial hostile stance towards Sanat has altered to a warm affectionate patronage. The hostility was only because of Tara's own feeling of insecurity. Now, Sanat looks upon Tara as a mentor and guide. In the last few years, Tara, too, has started taking a liking to this girl who she knows will keep alive the honourable reputation of her own beloved, Raja Saheb. Tara is sensible to see that Sanat is sharp, shrewd, rational and most of all, enduring – a trait that will take her far in life. Tara has seen Sanat crouch in pain, forcing her legs to walk straight. She has also seen her blow away the tears that well up in her eyes, tears of despondency and tears of sheer helplessness. Nor has Tara missed the lost glint that comes into Sanat's eyes from time to time; a glint of sadness, a glint of her hopes dashed and the very glint that she so stoically replaces by steering her mind to other inanities of life.

'She is an intelligent girl and I am sure she will learn soon enough. Besides, she is not the same as Chanda and I. She is your wife, someone who will walk by your side in the fine society of Calcutta and Kathmandu. And most importantly, she is the mother of your heir and will bring up your son and other children. It is imperative for her to be educated.' Tara puts a new thought across to Raja Saheb. He lies with his face buried in her lap and she tenderly picks out the strands of grey hair that have not only begun to flood his scalp but totally take over.

Tehsildar Harka is called for and he brings along with him Fatteh Baje who has educated himself in Benaras and now moves from estate to estate, family to family, educating young boys and girls in the attempt to make them well-groomed and well-informed adults who will outshine all others around them, making the latter subservient to their knowledge and command.

Tehsildar Harka is here to hand over Raja Saheb's share from the revenue of the lands that he holds in control as Talukdar. Although the Tehsil of Kanda does have a government appointed official, it is Raja Saheb who dictates the laws of administration and jurisdiction in this area. This is partly because he is the Talukdar and mainly because there is nobody else to refute his feudalism. Therefore, the Raja Saheb's family has ruled this area for generations as supreme lords – supervising the administration, monopolising the land revenue and even holding their own court of jurisdiction for crimes and pardons. Besides, Kanda is yet another distant land, one that is of barely any consequence for rulers in Kathmandu. The decisions made for such remote areas by the central government is neither communicated nor ever known to such disregarded corners of Nepal.

'Kanda is not forgotten, Harka,' the Raja Saheb announces to his guests, as the two begin to nod in consent while chewing on beaten rice that has been offered to them along with a bowl of curd. 'We may as well not exist for the Teen Sarkar in the capital. We are too far away for them to bother about us. The little means that the Teen Sarkar has for development that you so strongly speak of, Harka, is utilised either in developing new durbars in Kathmandu or on improving lifestyles of the members of the Teen Sarkars.'

An orderly has come in with the Raja Saheb's hookah. He wipes the table, places the hookah on it, and adjusts its gold plated pipe into the waiting mouth of the Raja Saheb, who instantly begins to blow out ringlets of tobacco smoke. The orderly squats at the feet of the Raja Saheb, waiting to refill the cup of the hookah with fresh tobacco when the need arises. Until then he shall massage the feet of the Raja, languorously spread on the low seated French couch.

'It is true, hajoor, but they say that the Teen Sarkar is soon to fall,' says Fatteh Baje, his mouth full of beaten rice. He speaks his turn, knowing well that the Raja Saheb is a supporter of the underground Congresss movement, initiated by the banished and rebelling defacto of Hiranya Shamsher, Rudra Shamsher and Mahabir Shamsher, under the guidance of whom the Nepalese Congress is steadily growing in spirits in Calcutta.

But Raja Saheb is smarter than Fatteh Baje. He speaks without revealing his hostile intentions to the Teen Sarkar. 'Remember Devi Prasad Sapkota, Fatteh Baje?' Raja Saheb blows out rings of smoke that blend and disappear into the vastness of his grand baithak. Behind him hangs a life-size portrait of his late wife. Richly dressed and decorated with precious jewels, she stands leaning on an armoire, her delicate fingers sparkling with the largest diamonds that neither Harka nor Fatteh Baje have seen for real.

But both of them are fully aware that this luxury and grandeur that Raja Saheb lives amidst is all due to his late wife.

Being a Rana's daughter, she had brought along a big dowry most of which was said to be stored in Calcutta. The remaining was in the form of pieces of land in Kathmandu.

'In 1903, Sapkota had started his weekly paper, calling it "Gorkhali",' the Raja Saheb is informing the two as their furtive glances shift to the big, thick walls of this mansion. It is said that the Raja Saheb has stored bricks of gold and silver in between the bricks.

'If I am right, it was printed and distributed from Benaras. Remember how this paper made big news for nearly four years? And then what happens? Chandra Shamsher the then prime minister, shuts it down with the help of the British in India.' The Raja Saheb has a deep frown upon his forehead. In his state of distress, he begins to twirl the tip of his moustache as he continues in his own lost tangent. 'And can we forget Krishna Prasad Koirala and Krishna Bir

Kami? Both ended up dying in imprisonment for starting an anti-Rana propaganda in Kathmandu. Nothing will change in Nepal, Fatteh Baje, until the British in neighbouring India are first removed. The Ranas are self-imposed dictators here, just as the British are in India. As long as the two keep supporting one another, hardly any change can be hoped in both countries. Take for instance, the Charkha movement in 1930. What happened then?'

The two silent recipients of Raja Saheb's political reflections do not bother to respond and continue chewing on their beaten rice, slurping in between the thick curd that gets stuck onto their fingers in their attempt at scooping it out from the bowl.

'Tulasi Meher is serving a life imprisonment sentence for it today,' Raja Saheb answers his own query. 'Had it not been for the Rana's help, I tell you, it would have been impossible for the British to curb the Swadeshi movement. You see, until they stop this act of scratching each others' backs, the Ranas and the British, this will continue. The king will remain where he is, peerless and insignificant and the junta will be herded on as ignorant cattle, and the Ranas will continue to flourish in power and wealth. What can one do, but resign to the fact that we are all but slaves of one big destiny?'

The disappointment is clear as is the resolve; this strong urge to rectify. Raja Saheb takes a deep breath, a sigh of helpless surrender as it were, and kicks the orderly, nudging him to continue the massage.

'Hajoor, this time it is big,' Fatteh Baje has shifted closer now to the Raja Saheb. 'People all around the country are slowly but surely waking up to the oppression of the Ranas. They want a change now and this sentiment is fast becoming a general slogan. Praises of King Tribhuvan and the Shah dynasty are being sung all over the country. Ballads are going around the villages criticising the Rana oligarchy and bards are openly singing the "naivedya" song of Dharni Dhar Sharma. And hajoor, I have found out from a viable

source that a Praja Panchayat has been formed and that it will now
work to end the oppressive Rana rule.'

If the Raja Saheb has any hopes from this revelation he is adept
at hiding it. 'It will fail as did the Prachanda Gorkha movement.'
And presuming that Fatteh Baje has never heard of this movement,
the Raja Saheb begins to explain.

'Umesh Bikram Shah, a relative of the king started this formation.
His aspirations were great as were his motives noble. Yet, a coup
détat, ha, ha, ha!' Throwing his head back, he begins to laugh, as
though he could clearly see the folly of it all. 'The plot was to murder
forty important Ranas on Diwali day amidst the gambling that goes
on when the entire clan assembles in one place. But of course as
fate would have it, their plans were leaked and he was arrested
along with his allies, Khanda Man and Khadga Man Singh...how
they were tortured! Khanda Man's sufferings were the worst – he
was tied down with a heavy iron chain that went round his ankles,
wrist and neck. Imagine his suffering!'

He is lost in his own reflections that seem to pain him, too. For
a shadow of regret has come upon his face. 'The rest were exiled
from Kathmandu,' he finally concludes.

'What do we care, Hajoor?' Fatteh Baje sighs, as though
fathoming the silent reflections of the Raja Saheb. 'We live in our
own world here. What do we care about who leads the government
there in Kathmandu? Powers may shuffle there, prime ministers
keep getting new titles, native and foreign, but in no way does that
affect our lives here...neither for good nor for worse. We continue
living here in the remotes. Our lives remain unaltered, irrespective
of any variations in the Capital.'

When Sanat is called in, political discussions have waned away
and have been replaced by discussions on livestock and harvest. She
is introduced to her tutor. 'You can take along Dane. He is nearly
twelve years now and illiterate as a cow.'

Raja Saheb instructs Sanat to take his bastard child to the school room.

That night, her son is brought to her, moist and sticky with his last oil massage of the day, wrapped in a bundle with a khasto. She unfastens her blouse and helps the child place his tiny mouth on her nipple. As Prabhat begins to suck, his tiny fingers clasped around her thumb, Sanat wonders about the exciting prospects of being educated. Finally, she thinks, smiling with content as her son continues to suckle, his eyes lined with kohl, fixed on her,

'Words that resembled twisted and turned figures will finally begin to make sense now. All the books lined up in Raja Saheb's drawing room with pictures of places and people will now no longer seem inane and futile. Soon, I will master the alphabet and will be able to read. Sitting here in Kanda, I can access the stupefying mystery that is this world.'

Sanjeevani

I am convinced that I am mad, for normal people do not feel like me. They are not continually restless and surely they would not want to continue to want a person like Razat. I have tried living my life without Razat, but then without him there is no laughter, there is no sunshine. Without him, eating is a burden, talking is a compulsion and sleep – that dear, dear sleep – is a distant stranger. I feel like a dead piece of meat walking around aimlessly. I might as well be a ghost...living yet not living.

As I drove back that night from my parents' place to my own, Kathmandu began to scare me. There was so much sadness in the air. I could feel myself suffocate. The sleeping capital, Kathmandu – the land of promise seemed more like an ugly trap that was filled with greed and ambition that brought along with it so much of despair. Everything around me seemed to disclose ugliness. The buildings, the bridges, the roads and even the lights filtering out of the windows behind which people lived. My hatred seemed to reach out to them too. Swarms of people have inhabited this city with expectations of a better job, better income, better lifestyle and even a better social status. But somehow, in this rat race, each one seems to have given away their mental peace. 'All this for what?' I had asked myself trying to peer through windows that reflected bright lights from within.

I drove on, crossed the Thapathali Bridge, the rotting smell of the sacred Bagmati rushing through my nostrils, mocking me with its putrid odour. This is what we have become – a farce. Nine out of ten houses in this valley worship this river, hold it sacred and yet let it rot away. The houses that stood like tall clusters of giant concrete exaggerations seemed to look down on me. It seemed very strangling and suffocating.

Suddenly, I was seized by this longing to return...return to the sheer innocence of the remote, to the laughter of naked children splashing in the stream. I started imagining the joy of seeing buffaloes half-immersed in the cool waters of dear Kanda; returning to the dust of the muddy tracks that blew with the warm summer evenings; cows returning to the call of the calves as they trod back from the nearby jungles to their sheds for the night; return to the chorus of the crickets at dusk, to lay myself down on a *khatiya* under the shade of the mango tree and slowly close my eyes to the shimmer of twinkling stars in the vastness of the sky above.

'Your eyes have pieces of the sky in them, Sanju,' Razat had once said to me, his face inches away from mine. 'The stars, the moon...you have the entire galaxy swimming in there.' What Razat did not know then was that the shimmer in my eyes were mere reflections from his. The light and laughter in his eyes reflected in mine. Without him there is just darkness...sad and hurting darkness

It was then that I decided to return home; home to the scent of the lemons; to the calls of the jackals at night broken only by the sound of the crickets in the fields, and the sweet smell of the *raat ki rani*, mingled with the warm breeze that hung in the air. The sound of the hoopoe digging its beak in the bark of the mango tree, the drifting voices of Kanchi ordering the tharu servants to arrange the cots in the courtyard for the night....

My home, my village – Ganeshpur. Where there was still some innocence left in the ignorant minds of my villagers; where this very ignorance had not yet managed to tamper with the laws of nature. I desperately wanted to return home where the trees were still green, where the fields still stretched out to long distances, where the waters still sparkled in the rivers and where children still covered themselves with leaves and branches on hearing the sound of an aeroplane in the sky, screaming 'Cheel gari...cheel gari!', thinking it to be a monstrous eagle that would seize them in its giant claws and fly away to lands unknown, just as the chickens were taken away by the intruding eagles that they saw.

The next day, I gave my resignation at the *Kashthamandap Weekly*, called Samanata Shah, the president of Naari, an NGO that works against domestic violence. I had once interviewed her and knew that they had branches of Naari in western Nepal. As luck would have it, they had recently opened a shelter for women and children in Dhangadi and were looking for a person to hold the post of the project coordinator and supervisor for the two shelters. It was the perfect job for me. I would have all the privacy and time to work on my novel.

In a week's time I was out of Kathmandu and in Dhangadi. Staring out of the window of the night bus to Dhangadi, as it made its exit out of the valley, I began to feel a sense of exhilaration. The feeling that keeps me conscious of my being alive and the very sense that never manages to stay...leaving me fumbling, aimless and directionless, and completely lost within my jeering phantoms.

Having crossed Narayanghat we entered the Bhaluwang jungles around midnight. The bus stopped. I could hear murmurs, and then one after another, the occupants were made to alight. It was a security check. I walked along with the others for nearly a mile, staring at the endless trail of buses, trucks and even small cars waiting in line to be given the green signal by the armed police. There were women walking along with me, old grandmothers and new mothers with their babies tied to their backs. Some of them were struggling along with their toddlers, who were wailing and screaming for being disturbed from their sleep. After an hour we got back to our bus but an hour later, the bus stopped and voices, this time louder, yelled in from the windows.

'It's the Maobadis,' the woman sitting next to me whispered, her mouth concealed by her shawl.

'But why?' I asked, as we stood in line on the side of the highway while a group of loud, commanding figures began to inspect us. They were peering into our faces, emptying out our handbags and even screening our identity cards.

'On the lookout for journos, security men on leave and even district and local level politicians,' the woman replied, her voice muffled. 'Look...look,' she had pointed out to the far end of our line where a man was beginning to get kicked. 'But I am only going home to my wife and old parents,' was the last we heard of him as we saw him being tied, blindfolded and pushed into the thickets of the jungle on the other side of the road.

Nobody spoke during the rest of the journey. I doubt if anyone slept. All must have been imagining the worst for the abducted man. As for me, I sat stunned, staring into the stark darkness that swept by. So much hatred, so much violence, so much disruption, so much disparity, so much discrepancies... for what? At the end of the day, do we not all, irrespective of caste, class, creed or colour, close our eyes to the same eternal darkness?

When the bus entered Dhangadi in the late hours of the next morning, the sun was bright and very hot. I looked around, shading my eyes with the palm of my hand. I was assessing the differences that had come over my hometown. The most significant of all changes was the air of fear, suspicion and wariness that hung uncomfortably. Once upon a time, these people were carefree and always smiling and ready for a chat with any stranger. Now, as I trudged along with my bag into the main road in search of a rickshaw, I noticed people clearly avoiding strangers with furtive glances.

'*Hasanpur jaina ba. Katra lebo?*' I asked the rickshaw puller.

'Ten rupees,' he answered, not looking at me, but pretending to fix the bell on the handle of his rickshaw.

'Okay, take me there,' I said without bothering to bargain for the fare.

I had rented an apartment through Samaanta who had in turn asked one of her staff from the shelter to get me a place in a decent and safe neighbourhood. 'The owners live on the first floor and are letting out the ground floor, Sanjeevani. I think this would be perfect for you,' Samaanta had said when we had decided on the place. I had merely nodded then and did not bother to say that I hardly cared for my safety. It was peace of mind that I wanted more than anything. The lack of it made me wish each day that I do not live to see the next.

While travelling on the rickshaw I felt nostalgic on seeing the familiar structures. Structurally, Dhangadi had not changed in years. The same main road runs straight with shops on either side. Moti Mahal, Merina Stores, Ahmad Tailors, the old ones that were there since I was a toddler, stand where they were; only the boards have become bigger and brighter. As for the people, they remain the same, too – complacent and with little hope of the future.

My lodging was a simple three-bedroom apartment with a small kitchen. What I loved most about it was the little verandah with its painted cement railing. A small flight of stairs went down from the verandah to the pathway that led to the gate. Beyond the gate were stretches of fields that were then followed by a jungle.

I stood there on the verandah, staring out into the vast openness, while my heart ached for Razat. Everything around me seemed beautiful – the fields, the jungles beyond that, the chirping of the birds, yet inside me, this gloom prevailed.

'Razat,' I let his name escape and blow away with the gentle breeze that swept past me. 'My Krishna...my shyaam.'

I felt choked. When this feeling of suffocation comes over me from time to time, all I can do is just look around, helpless and disoriented, knowing that there is no reprieve.

'I must go back home the first thing tomorrow, before I join work,' I had heard myself say before opening the netted swinging door of my new lodging.

And here I am in Ganeshpur now, my village, forty kilometres away from the bustling town of Dhangadi, but a world apart. There are so many memories linked with this place. Some are inert and buried, and some fresh and alive. They flitter around me, faces, places, instances, happy moments and sad; all surge towards me as though in want of belonging. And with these memories comes along the thought of the night that brought on a doom over my family. A curse, I call it, intended for others but sadly falling on my brother.

Back in Kathmandu, people are starting to forget the reason for Dada's murder. It has come down to 'Sanjay's death'. Very conveniently, people talk as though it was a normal death. No, it was not. My brother was killed! Brutally assaulted, beaten and mauled . . . and that is why he died. Not only the reason for his death, but also the man – Sanjay Bahadur Singh – are slowly being erased from public memory. It is as if he never was. The world around us has moved on; his vacancy filled in by this one and that. His wife has moved on, and his daughter shall never know him. His friends have other friends. It is only me who walks around with this empty gash and does not know how to fill it.

I am standing in the courtyard of my house, the place where my brother was killed. He was dragged out from the *bhanchaghar*, where he had just sat down to eat his dinner. They had stormed in with guns, violent glares staring out from the masks that covered their faces. They had pushed him, sworn at him, kicked him, hit him with lathis, guns and even bare hands. They had even spat at

him. He had walked out, grim, silent yet hopeful and had even tried
to reason out with them.

'*Basera kura garun na...*' he had said. But they had all come with
an intention – motives that had reaches beyond the torturing of my
brother. They had come to set an example, to start a new trend, to
put an end to the old one. Insult the feudalists – the samantabadi –
beat them to pulp, drain out all your grievances against feudalism
all on this one man – Sanjay Bahadur Singh.

'Samanti...' I can hear myself say aloud. I walk to the little
altar made of bricks and cement at the corner of the courtyard.
My Jijumua's peepal used to be here. Each morning she placed her
'chokho jal' onto this peepal before raising her hands to the rising
sun. The peepal is not there. Instead, wild grass stretches out like
ugly claws. 'Samanti...Samantibaaad,' I can hear myself repeating
the words as though they were a mantra.

I am laughing now, fighting samanti. My ass, samanti! My editor,
back in Kathmandu is a samanti. He used to dictate terms and
conditions as though we were his slaves. All the columnists who force
their minds on their readers are samantis; Prachanda is a samanti
forcing his Maoist ideology upon the entire country with his violence;
Girija is a samanti – dictating terms and conditions over his party
along with the entire nation; all the political leaders – Sher Bahadur
Deuba, Madhav Kumar Nepal, Lokendra Bhadur Chand – everyone
of these is a samanti for luring and fooling the general public, and
promising them a better country. All the people back in Kathmandu,
living peacefully are samantis for remaining in denial. And they killed
my brother, calling him a samanti? My brother?

The irony of it all makes me laugh. And I do. Loud and clear,
my voice echoes in the empty courtyard.

He was a good man, my brother. He had a good heart and
he led his life, separate from the rest of the world. For that was
my Dada, aloof and alienated, always drowned in his own silent

thoughts. If you ask me, he was killed that night not for who he was but for whose son he was.

Do I blame my father for Dada's death? Not anymore, I think. I do try and make sense of his murder but I fail...I really do.

It is getting dark now and looking at my watch I know it will be difficult for me to catch the last bus to Dhangadi town. The curfew rules around this area are rather strong now. I will have to walk back ten to fifteen kilometres to get to the highway and God knows whether I would be lucky in getting a bus there. I will probably have to stay back in the village for the night

I begin to walk out of our compound and walk towards the village. I don't take the road, clearly to avoid the red, blatant posters of the Maoists. I go through the fields. It would also help me reach Badki's house quicker.

I stop at the far end of our fields at the well. It is still there. I peep into it but because of the lack of light, I see nothing below. The mango grove by the well is still there. As a child I remember covering my head as I passed this way. For there was this ghost – Jamjutwa they called him – who is supposed to have lived here in one of the trees. I never really believed in the gossip at first, and even if I did, I did not want others to know; for I was always a proud girl and wanted everyone to believe that I was brave.

I clearly remember gathering all my friends from the village and scheming a plan.

My cousins Ladhe and Kallu were there, too. Shital and Anil and my two best friends, Dongli and Ramkuari accompanied us. We made the perfect secret seven team, just like in the books I used to read in school. We even had our secret hideout and I had made it compulsory to cover our heads with a cape when we attended our meetings...the idea had come after reading about a certain cult in some comic.

'Maiya...na karo...' Kallu had said, his eyes flashing bright through his dark face. 'Jamjutwa does not like people trespassing into his domain after sunset. Remember Ganga, Malkunji's grandson? He went to steal some mangoes at night and the Jamjutwa got him.'

'How? What did Jamjutwa do to Ganga?' We had shouted out loud. We were all excited and nervous at the same time.

'Ganga never spoke after he was found the next morning on the road that led back to the village. But then, everyone said the Jamjutwa had gotten into Ganga.' Kallu's eyes were bright with an expression of being the one who knew. His voice had a hint of pride. In his excitement he had stood up and walked around with a stick in his hand. His loin cloth clearly demarcated his black, sun-burnt buttocks into two charred halves.

'Then what happened, Kallu? Come to the point!' I had said, fiddling with the dying embers of the fire. We were all assembled in the Kharihan. This is where my father's harvest was stacked initially after being brought from the fields. A watchman guarded the harvest at nights and left early in the morning. It was then that we all got together by the place where he had lit a fire. By the time we reached, the fire would be dying. We used to place corn in the warm ashes, watching them pop up and then eating and planning our day's adventures.

'Maiya,' Kallu said, swinging the stick in his hand for reasons that only he knew. Perhaps he felt that the stick was giving more weight to the feeling of self-importance that had suddenly swept over him. It was as though he were striking something. 'His body burned and became hotter and hotter by the minute. The *guruwa* was called. He sat down by the Ganga. The sacrificial chicken was brought and slaughtered right there.'

'Why? Why did they kill the chicken?' I had inquired.

'To awaken the Jamjutwa inside Ganga, Maiya,' Kallu had said in a matter of fact tone that also hinted clearly of how foolish the rest of us were for not knowing something as simple as that. 'Then the blood dripping from the headless chicken was poured over Ganga's head. The *guruwa* recited mantras and sprinkled rice all around the room. I was there, I saw,' Kallu was thumping his chest proudly with his hand. 'Ganga opened his eyes. The black of his eyes began to tremble and then as the *guruwa* began to jitter and bounce in his seat, the black part disappeared.'

Thre was a loud 'NO' from all us children. 'What happened then, Kallu? Go on. Why do you keep stopping?' I had snatched the stick from Kallu's hand and hit him gently with it, intending to prod him on.

He squatted then, the little bulge between his legs poking out of his loin cloth. This made Ramkuari, Dongli and myself laugh; I remember going into squeals of laughter with our hands covering our faces. Ladhe, the eldest of the lot, understood first, and chided his younger brother promptly.

'Sit properly in front of Maiya sa'b.'

'Go on, Kallu, tell us quickly what happened?' I had said settling back to shuffling the corn in the ash pit.

'Then Ganga's body began trembling. He started throwing his legs in the air and his hands fluttered aimlessly around. Everyone said it was Jamjutwa inside that made Ganga do such things. Then it stopped as the *guruwa* went around sprinkling water and hitting Ganga's body with a long, thick bundle of elephant grass.'

'It stopped?' I had asked, nearly in despair for the thrill of the entire tale was coming to an end now.

'Yes, Maiya,' Kallu said. 'It stopped. Ganga was still like a log. The *guruwa* looked at all of us and whispered that the Jamjutwa had left the body.'

'And then?' With baited breath, I had interrupted again, knowing that now the climax was to be revealed. 'Ganga never woke up after that. Everyone cried and the *guruwa* said that Jamjutwa takes away the spirit and soul along with him when he leaves the body of anyone.'

There was silence for a long time. No one spoke. I knew that each was wondering whether to undertake such a risky task along with me that night. But I was adamant. I stood up.

'That could have been anything. It is not proven. They teach me in school that such practices are called black magic and are complete nonsense. We can prove it. Be brave. Ganga was alone. We are seven of us. Perhaps we could capture the Jamjutwa.'

My word was law. I knew that if all of them wanted to stay on in my playgroup, eat the food cooked in my house and wear my discarded clothes, they had to give in and come along with me that night.

Seven of us sneaked out of our houses after dinner that night. I had carried along a sack with me to put the Jamjutwa in, in case we did manage to catch it.

It was a full moon that night. So, we had no problem locating our way to the mangrove. But there were clouds, dark and heavy, beginning to gather in the sky. Lightning struck somewhere in the distance and we knew we had to rush before the rain came pouring down. I remember the loud thuds in my chest as we got closer. I had deliberately kept Shital and Anil in front to lead and Kallu and Ladhe at the back. In between them, I walked, flanked on either side by Dongli and Ramkuari.

When we got there, Kallu began hopping from one tree to another, throwing stones, so that the noise would wake the Jamjutwa. Behind him, all of us walked with the sack in our hands. The mouth of the sack was opened wide so that the Jamjutwa would fall into it easily.

'Hurrah...hurrah...' Kallu kept repeating his call to the Jamjutwa, continuing to jump up and even hit the highest branches. Then something jumped down and with it all of us screamed. It was a cat! A black cat, with red glaring eyes.

'It could be him...the Jamjutwa in the cat,' Ramkuari was nearly draped around me with fear, and I did not seem to mind it for I too felt a bit secure with her body close to mine.

'Shut up!' I said and looked ahead to see whether Kallu had made any progress.

Suddenly, we heard loud thunder and lightning very close by. Frightened, we huddled together in a circle. It started raining immediately. Though it was dark and the rain was torrential, I think we all distinctly saw something jump out of one of the mango trees and leap into the nearby fields.

The next morning I was down with fever. My friends disappeared for days fearing Jijumua's wrath. Despite running a high temperature, I kept insisting on having seen the Jamjutwa. My mother and Jijumua were hovering around me, placing wet towels all over my body, bringing in the camphor burning on coals and feeding me hot chicken soup all at the same time.

'Kanchi Buhari, close the windows, the cold will get to her all the more,' my grandmother was complaining.

'Her body is too hot. And Dr Dixit in Kathmandu has told me to get the body temperature down first, in case of high fever like this,' my mother was insisting.

'The chicken broth will do her good. Drink it, *chora...gyanu.* Drink it...' my Thulumua was pleading.

And in the midst of this chaos no one heard and even if they did, did not bother to take heed, to my sincere assertions.

'I saw Jamjutwa! I saw it jump down from the tree and leap away. I saw Jamjutwa!'

Although it was soon forgotten by the others, this incident left a lasting impression on me. And now, while passing the same mango grove, I can feel the same eerie chill go down me. I quicken my pace.

I have nearly reached the village now. A cluster of twenty or so houses are standing parallel against the river that ran below the edge of the land. 'Fifty years from now, these houses will have to move, as the Shivganga will cut into the land...' I remember Dada telling me and myself wondering why these houses were built so precariously close. They should have begun to move out immediately. Probably they never wondered about where they would move.

A stray dog barked somewhere and then there were voices. I had felt the air of hostility upon arriving here earlier. Faces stared at me with a hateful awe. Stray dogs had barked at me while naked children ran alongside; they were giggling, laughing and some even were even pulling my clothes. The adults and the youth of Ganeshpur stared from their courtyards, eyes curious but blatantly aggressive.

I was the outsider now. I was the educated one, the one better off and I was the enemy. My home had become a cold, unreceptive foreign land. I knew that there would not be many who recognised me from the old days but I had not expected the few who did, to turn away as though I was a diseased dog to be kept at bay. I think I can understand this fear in their eyes; it is of ignorance, poverty and most of all, it is the fear of the armed rebels that lurk in every face.

Cots are being laid out in the courtyards, lanterns are lit. I can see piles of hay are being readied to sleep on. I knew our old kamaiya, Dangwa was still living in the village. Last I heard of him was ten years ago; he had paid off his bond to my father and even saved some money to buy a piece of land in the village. I remember feeling bad then, that Dangwa wouldn't work for us anymore. I had grown a bit attached to his family, his wife Badki, his sons, Mangru, Ladhe and Kallu and his daughter Dongli. I was certain he would give me a bed for the night.

At the first house, I stop. Faces stare back at me.

'Which is Dangwa's house?' I ask in Tharu. For an instance I get no response. Then a little child speaks, 'Dangwa kaka is dead. But his wife lives there,' she prattles, her hand stretched to the direction of Dangwa's house, not very far from where I stand. 'Dhanyabad,' I say, smiling at the child and walking towards the direction given to me.

I see Badki in her courtyard. She is there with a girl of about fifteen or sixteen. Although the girl is dressed in a modern adaptation of the old lehenga, a printed wrap around and a blouse, Badki is the same as before. I recognise her instantly. Though she has grown older, she looks the same. She does not recognise me at first and stares back. 'Badki,' I say, walking towards her. 'It's me, tohar Maiya.' And then, she springs up as though waking up from a dream and begins to charge towards me.

'Maiya *ree, hamar* Maiya!' She nearly screams in excitement.

'Many years! Come, come, sit down.' She forces me down on a woven stool. Water is given to me by the other girl as we sit in the courtyard. There is a bullock cart, unharnessed and stacked in one corner and besides it is an empty pigsty. Across this is the water stand. Two tree trunks supporting another laid horizontal on the top upon which are the clay pots with water in them. I do not bother that it was not filtered and realise how thirsty I was once I begin to gulp the water down my parched throat.

'*Eee ka hui gail,* Maiya? What has happened, Maiya? Everything has changed. Nothing is the same as before. What a fool I am to start complaining as soon as you have arrived. I should ask you how you are. How are Raja and Rani Sahib? Where are they? And what brings you here at this hour?'

All her queries spilled out in one go. Her coarse, aged hands are feeling me all over. Caressing my knees, my shins and sometimes even grasping hold of my hands, she continues talking. There is a weary look in Badki's eyes – the same look that I see in Jijumua's eyes. Perhaps it comes with old age. It is like a longing but a longing for what? An end?

I take hold of Badki's coarse shrivelled-up hands into my own and press them. I too want an end, I want to tell her. Even I am weary of dragging on one day to the next, hopelessly and aimlessly. Instead, I hear myself say, 'Can I stay here for the night, Badki? I don't think I can get a bus back now. I will leave the first thing in the morning.'

'Maiya,' Badki smiles, her teeth are nearly all gone and the few that remain are decaying. 'I'm so glad to meet you after such a long time. You stay for how many ever days you want, Maiya. It is too late now but tomorrow morning I will kill a rooster for you and make hot, spicy curry with some mango pickle...just the way you liked.'

She was grinning now. The girl standing behind her, is a bit alarmed after knowing who I am and which family I belong to.

'This is Batasha, my daughter-in-law, Kallu's wife. You remember Kallu, Maiya? How you used to sneak him out of the house to play with you. And how I used to grumble about it because he had to help his father in the fields.'

Badki looks behind at the girl and pushes her forward towards me as she speaks. I can see Batasha is shy and more than that, alarmed. 'Go in,' Badki tells Batasha. 'Get some food ready for Maiya. And don't worry. Maiya will eat anything. Some rice and pickle will do for her, no Maiya?' she has let go of Batasha and is staring at me again with the same toothless grin.

'Yes Badki, anything will do for me,' I say while pressing her hands again. 'Where are your sons?'

'Mangru is in Dhangadi with his wife and children. He has three of them – two daughters and a son. He makes a good earning there, driving a rickshaw.' Here she stops. A haze has come over her face. A sad, apprehensive look.

'What of the other two?' I ask.

'Kallu and Ladhe, both have joined the comrade party, Maiya.' Now she is pressing my hands. 'Not that they wanted to, but they were forced.'

'When did this happen?' I ask.

'Soon, after Sanjay Raja's death. After that wretched night, nothing remained the same around here. Before that they were living in the jungles but after that they boldly moved into the village, bag and baggage. They sleep in this one's house one night and someone else's the next. They eat our food at their will. What can we do, Maiya? We give in with fear. Tomorrow you will see, Maiya, there won't be any boys left here. Only old men, who can barely drag themselves to the fields, would remain. The rest have been taken by the Maobadi's or have fled to Dhangadi or India. But I guess it is for the best. At least they are occupied somewhere. It was either that or the harassment from the security forces that come in to the village from time to time. Say "Mother fucker, where are your friends?" They say it as though each one of us has to know where they are. Sometimes they create a ruckus, beat and threaten and go back. But sometimes they drag the boys along saying they are informers of the comrade party. Kallu was beaten black and blue before he joined the comrade party, Maiya.'

Badki stands with both her hands on her hips and staring out into the far distance, beyond the bend of the river and beyond the jungles after that. Then she begins to explain. She is contemplating as she talks.

'They broke his hand. He had bruises all over his face and back. I kept him at home and applied besar all over his body instead of sending him to the Dhangadi Hospital. There again they would have asked him countless questions like "Who hurt you like this and why?" And if he did not answer properly they would have beaten him more and perhaps even put him in jail. It took him nearly three months to recover, Maiya. But when he did, he resolved to join the comrade party. "Take me to the Maodbadis," he said. "Since I have been beaten cruelly for being one of them, I am now determined to be one of them." I let him go, Maiya. What could I have done?'

'Oh!' I say, for that's all I can think of.

'Kallu has been sent elsewhere, somewhere in the east, I hear. But Ladhe is with the regiment here. He comes over sometimes with his lot and I feed them. What can I do, Maiya? I am a mother and hope my sons will be safe wherever they are.'

'Yes Badki, I understand,' I say. And to steer the conversation elsewhere, I ask, 'Does Ladhe have children?'

'Yes, Maiya...yes! He has two sons. They are sleeping inside. Come see them.'

She pulls me up and we walk into the house. Batasha is squatting by the hearth. She is digging out some leftover rice from the pot and putting it in a plate for me. I recognise the melamine plate with blue flowers on the rim. It belonged to my family. I look around. There are many other familiar articles here from my house. The rug on which the two children are now sleeping is one, the two tin trunks with my brother's and my name painted on them once belonged to us, too.

Following my speculative eyes, Badki begins to explain. 'Everyone took, Maiya. They said it was up for grabs. Tractors and bullock carts were taken to the kothar. People even came from neighbouring villages to grab whatever they could. We took what we got. It was me who brought all this in. I went there last, only to see what they had done and picked up whatever was left.'

Pictures of Gods from Jijumua's puja room were hung on the walls and beside them was my mother's mirror.

'Shall we eat?' I say and sit down besides Batasha. She gets up and goes out with an empty glass to get some more water for me. I can feel her fear. It is clear she does not like the fact that I am shacking up with them. I am the enemy of her husband's employer. Besides, I belong to a family that was shamefully thrown out of the village. I am a threat to her.

After eating, I am given a bedsheet, old and worn-out but clean. Although it is cooler outside, I tell Badki I will sleep inside with the children. She quickly unfolds a woven mat on the cot by the children. 'If you want I can arrange some hay underneath the mat,' she says, looking nervous.

'I'll be fine this way, Badki. Don't worry,' I say, covering myself with the sheet that is given to me. She leaves to sleep in the courtyard but Batasha is in the same room with me. I can see her crouched by her children. Her eyes are shut and she wants me to believe that she is asleep. Clearly, she does not want to talk to me.

I stare at the thatched ceiling. There are gaps here and there. I wonder how Badki will patch these gaps before the rains arrive. I remember, as a child, convoys of bullock carts going into the jungles and returning days after with stuff to cover up the roofs for the monsoons ahead. When the men returned, it would be celebration time. Chickens were killed and cooked; there was singing and dancing at nights; and during the day, all the men got together to help each other in fixing the roofs.

'Perhaps Kallu will do something about it. He must be considered an influential man around here, now that he has joined the Maobadis,' I think to myself staring at the roof. A lizard crawls in from one of the gaps and I look away. One of the children begins to cry and Batasha, with her eyes shut, unbuttons her blouse and shoves a brown nipple into his mouth. I can hear a chorus of crickets in the fields, the silent flow of the river close by and every now and then, a dog barks somewhere.

I am woken with loud talking outside the door. Badki's voice is the loudest. I look around my surroundings, Batasha is not in her bed but her two children are sitting up, quiet and staring at the open door. A faint light is streaming in shafts from outside and with the crow of the rooster on the roof, I know it is dawn.

I walk out, stretching my limbs. My back feels a bit stiff from sleeping on a cot with no mattress. But that is not my concern right now. I am convinced, with the noise outside in the courtyard, the Maoist forces are here for me.

Outside, the air is still. I see them first as a cluster. As I move into the courtyard, faces emerge, young and fierce.

They are around twelve in number – mostly children around the ages of fourteen, fifteen and sixteen. There is a man who is sitting on the bullock cart stacked on the side of the courtyard. He is fiddling with his 12 bore gun. Looking around I realise that each one seems to be holding one.

I can feel fire around my temples. I can feel the blood rush to my brains. 'Murderers!' I want to scream out to them, 'You killed my brother, you destroyed my home! You uprooted my family!' But the impulse fades even as I open my mouth.

My heartbeat is drumming fast and loud now. In want of something to do, I start scanning faces. Each face is staring at me, hostile and alert. A girl not yet sixteen, dressed in the same camouflage uniform walks forward towards me. Half her face is covered with a red scarf. A naked gun hangs carelessly around her shoulders. Her eyes glare as would a provoked wild animal.

'What is your name?' she asks in Nepali.

'Sanjeevani Singh,' I reply, my voice slightly shaking as I wonder to myself, 'Why?' I had heard stories of the PLA and local Maoist squads like this one going into villages and interrogating villagers, and even torturing and killing ones they were convinced were informers to security forces or having faint affiliations to the Congress party and the reactionary parties like the Rashtriya Prajantra Party and the UML. Even the elected members of the village district committees were not spared. Sometimes their families were harassed, too. I had heard of journalists being tortured and killed, just because of their inclinations towards a particular political party.

I was a clear enemy; daughter of the zamindar whose family had monopolised and controlled all jurisdictions of this area – social, judicial and financial – for years.

'Any affiliations with Prashant Bahadur Singh and his family?' she asks knowing well enough that I do. The reason they are here is evidence they know I am affiliated with the family.

'I am his daughter,' I say, not looking at her but peering into the cluster of faces that have begun to scatter around in the courtyard.

'What brings you here?' she asks, her anger for my like apparent in her query.

'Love for my homeland, I guess,' I say, shrugging my shoulders and now looking at the girl's face. There is conviction in her anger, a strong determination and sincerity for a cause that has made her leave her home and join a band of killers that feel that giving up their own lives is nothing compared to what they shall leave behind – a new Nepal, fair and right.

She must have walked for miles in the heat, rain and cold. She must have braved herself for the bullet that could one day be the end of her. I wonder how one can cling on to a conviction? My mind has always played games, shifting allegiance from one thought to another. One minute I am resolute on one decision but then soon enough, I begin to falter. I see my conviction and my dedication disappear into a haze of uncertainty; everything seems fabricated...even myself.

'Remembering one's home on a vacation is easy, my dear.' She spits on the ground and her accent clearly tells that she is from the eastern hills. She has her arm on my shoulder now and is walking me to the verandah of Badki's house. 'What good will anyone gain of your visit? You nor your home.' Her mouth is near my ear and she is whispering into it – a taunting murmur.

I shrug her hand away from my shoulder and look at her straight in the eye. 'One does not need to gain anything by wanting to come back to one's home. Besides, it was your people who forced us out of our homes. Your people killed my brother. Your people have made my old parents into refugees in their own country. Your people have made my house into a...'

While I say all this, I do not notice that my hands are tugging at her arms as I pull her to end of the courtyard from where my house is visible, doleful and in shambles. 'That's what you have done to my home...my family,' I say.

My eyes are brimming with tears of vulnerability and resignation alike. I can feel the trickles slip down my cheek but I don't care.

'You leave today.' It is clearly an order. I can feel her prying eyes on me. She wants to know more, more of me and more of my mind. 'And...' she says suddenly, her voice transforming into a trance. A severe sense of dedication can be felt in her voice. 'This is a people's war. A war between the feudalists that have sucked on the nation's wealth, and the common masses who have been made slaves and kept in utter poverty and ignorance. Your brother was killed along with many others and will be forgotten about soon enough. But it is our cause that shall live on forever. You say your brother was innocent but so am I. Yet, I willingly give my life for my country.'

Her words do seem to make sense, but I do not want to resign. 'How many innocent lives are you going to take?' Words fly out, adamant and hostile.

'As many that come in our way to our goal of a new Nepal.' She is beginning to enjoy herself, I think, debating with me.

'Is that fair? You all want yourselves to be heard by killing and torturing people?'

'All is fair in love and war, my dear. And this is war. Without arms no one hears...I can make you listen. Not only that my dear city girl, I can even make you dance...such is the power of the gun. Now you pack your bags and leave Ganeshpur immediately. And no word to our Saru Dais back in Dhangadi, Okay? Or else...' She makes a throat slashing gesture with her finger against her own neck. 'We will have our eyes on you, Sanjeevani Singh.'

It is here that I see him. He is standing by the pigsty assessing the entire episode. His eyes speak to me first. He has aggressive eyes. But somehow, I know that they are gentle as is the smile prominent below the thick bushy moustache that he sports – a perfect blend of a subtle smirk and a shy bearing.

He seems older than most of the cadets here who are clearly not more than eighteen. Perhaps, he's in his late twenties.

He does not carry a rifle across his shoulders as do most of his colleagues but under his shirt, around the waist, I can see a bulge and I know that's where the pistol is.

I can feel his eyes scanning me. It is a feeling of being undressed in public and the smirk on his face is adamantly persistent. I hate him instantly but it is strange how my hatred is reflected in his eyes. Silently potent, it blatantly stares back at me.

I am overwhelmed at my own feelings, for in me I can feel a passion grow; a soft sentiment rushing in fast to become a steadfast feeling that begins to gnaw at my chest. I do not know whether I hate him for being who he is – a rebel, or inclined towards him as I too am a rebel.

Sanat

Sanat watches her sons walk out of the Dashain Ghar behind their father. Their foreheads are smeared with red and yellow vermillion paste and around their necks hang the garlands weaved of the sacred jamara. Prabhat holds his four-year-old head high, almost arrogant but clearly deferential to his father's standing. Prashant, now nearly three, holds on to the index finger of his father's free hand and looks up at him with an innocent awe. Throngs of people stand outside Raja Sahab's Dashain Ghar, where since the past eight days, intensive rituals have been taking place behind the shades of black curtains by an assemblage of family priests. On this day of *Nawami*, the family sword of the Singh clan is brought out. The naked blade glistening in the brilliance of the October sun gets reflected onto the Raja Sahebs's raised hand that holds it proudly and firmly.

The sword is passed on to the eldest Chautaria. He decides who would have the privilege of being the first sacrifice. Then, the slaughtering begins. The sword begins to fall unheeded on waiting necks of lines and lines of *raangas*. One after another, the insensible beasts begin falling, their heads decapitated, eyes gaping wide, as the beheaded body lives a moment longer, writhing and jostling its feet in its last desperate moments. The bloodied sword is passed on from one relative of the Raja Saheb to another. The kith and kin having finished with the sacrifices, the villagers move in. The

Thapas come first. They have been brought along from Baajhyang and Bajura by the ancestors of the Raja Saheb with an intention to have chetris around him. Behind them, the damais and the kaamis and the baadis follow. Each one gets a turn to bring out the animal in him, rough and brutal on this day of the Mahanavratri.

Celebrations follow, with drinking, gambling and lots of merry-making. For days the village of Kanda and the surrounding villages relish the abundance of meat from the sacrifice. Inside the Durbar, mutton is cooked, fried, curried and roasted in every meal. Women and children run around the courtyards rejoicing in the festive mood. The Raja Saheb lounges in his balcony, content and pleased with himself. He smokes his hookah, blowing out rings of smoke in between flickering smiles that come upon his stately face for no reason apparent to others around him. But the Raja Saheb has reasons to gloat.

B.P. Koirala has sent out a press release from Patna stating that an inevitable political change in Nepal is now evident following the independence of India. He has taken an initiative to form the Nepali National Congress party and the party is determined to launch a movement in Nepal to replace the Rana regime with a constitutional monarchy. The party in its Calcutta session has even received complimentary messages from noted Indian leaders such as Acharya Kriplani, Vijay Lakshmi Pandit, Jayaprakash Narayan, Ram Manohar Lohiya and Acharya Narendra Dev.

The Raja Saheb has recently returned from Calcutta, attending as a member of the Prajatantrik Party led by Subarna Shamsher, a joint session that his party had with the National Congress led by B.P. Koirala in Calcutta's Tiger Hall. There, the two parties agreed to resolve their differences and merge as one Nepali Congress, with a policy statement of fundamental rights, democratic system of government, economic welfare and immediate intensification of the struggle against the Ranas.

Soon there will be consequential action taken by the Congress Party. So thinks the Raja Saheb secretly to himself; he is very excited and hopeful about it.

Sanat glides around her festive household, giving orders in the kitchen that has moved out into the courtyard and expanded into additional mud baked ovens. Massive brass cauldrons steam out spicy aromas; trays after trays are spread out with sel, feeni, khurma and other sweets. Trunks of these delicacies are packed and sent off to married sisters. After five years of arrange, Sanat has become proficient in dispensing her duties. Standing in the courtyard, she hands out sacks of rice to the poor of the village. She also gives old clothes and coins of silver to a few as she hollers out her own orders.

Tired at night she watches her sons fall off to sleep. 'Muajiu...tell me a story...the one with kauguji...'

Her maids come in with a silver pan and jug. Sanat washes her hands and face and sits by her mirror. The glow of the night lamps burning bright in various corners of the room fall on her reflection in the mirror. Sanat smiles but in a strange way; she does not feel the smile. Instinctively, her hands move up to her face, fingers making sure whether it was indeed a smile or mere suggestions from somewhere inside her. Of late there is this piercing vacuum that Sanat has begun to feel. Deep inside her is an emptiness that she is unable to define and thus she walks around, mechanically dispensing her duties as wife, mother and mistress.

Laata, the deaf and dumb boy, sleeps on the floor by the door. He is a playmate for her sons and it is they who insisted that Laata sleep there. Sanat watches him while he sleeps, a look of charming innocence writ over his face. His head rests on his hands, and the little ringlets of his curly hair fall on the creamy white skin of his face.

It was Sanat who had brought this boy in from the cattleshed where he helped in herding the cattle, gathering fodder and even cleaning the sheds. She had found him, crouching and hugging himself to ward off the winter chill by the cattle shed, where she had gone to check on a cow in labour. His face then was dirty with days of unwashed mud and dust. His mouth was open, perhaps to facilitate breathing, as his nostrils were jammed with thick snot.

Out of pity, Sanat had brought the little boy in. She gave him a rug and instructed him to sleep in the corridors outside her door. This is where he had been sleeping on the night that the Raja Saheb had found him. Raja Saheb had nudged him with his leather boots. The boy had not moved. Having walked for hours, taking the cattle to graze to the luscious pastures of Khaptad, the ordeals of the day had pushed him into the comforts of a soothing sleep. Raja Saheb had watched and wondered at the beauty of his innocent charm. He had looked over his shoulders; there was no one in the corridor at that time of the night and so he had bent down. Kneeling on one knee, he had let his hands roam over the creamy white skin of the boy. A surging thrill had moved his groin instantly and the Raja Saheb sprung up on his feet, shocked and shaken by a completely strange sensation.

For days, he had stared at the boy. He used to ask for him to be sent down to fill his hookah, massage his feet and even pluck out the grey hair from his scalp. And when the fire in his groins refused to subside, enflaming his carnal passions obliterating his sense of right and wrong, the Raja Saheb grabbed the creamy white hand of Laata and forced it upon his hot pulsating penis.

When Sanat entered her husband's room with a glass full of hot milk, without which her husband did not go to bed, she found him standing by his bed, his pants down, and Laata's face buried in his groin.

This had left Sanat shocked but more than that, irrevocably disgusted. Standing there at the doorway, watching her husband's face contort from passionate frenzy to a frenzied alarm at being caught,

Sanat had clearly felt her own sensuous passions—that existed still somewhere in her, waiting as though for miraculous revival—die an instant death.

Forlorn and frigid, Sanat now walks around watching other women. Smiling to their own secrets, they put flowers on their hair, scent their breasts and hum along a beautiful song. She wonders why, completely failing to understand their sentiment.

A maid knocks at her door and asks for Laata. 'Raja Saheb wants his feet massaged,' she says with a furtive glance, that told Sanat that she, too, knew.

'Tell him Laata is very tired and already asleep. Ask him to have someone else massage his feet tonight.'

Sanat sees the maid's face darken with fearful apprehension of the Raja Saheb's wrath.

'Rani Saheb ...' the maid pleads, her eyes pathetically imploring.

'Take him ...' Sanat rests her own heavy head onto her pillow, and with her hands cups her eyes that suddenly feel heavy with tears.

The next morning, the sun shines again, the hens cackle in the pen, the horses neigh in the stables, clicking and stamping their hooves on the cobbled pathways below. The bars of the cow shed are opened and cattle stream out. They are steered towards the Khaptad hills for the day and with it, the din of the morning chores begins. Maids walk up and down the house, plates and utensils clatter, Tara hustles up and down giving her first orders of the day and children run around, screaming, laughing and crying. Chanda runs behind them, her hair let loose, a hint of laughter in her voice as she begins to round up all the children of the Raja Saheb, both legitimate and illegitimate, for the morning milk after which they will be led to the school room and be deposited in the firm hands of Fatteh Baje.

Sanat has stopped going to the school room for a very long time. She can read and write and feels this qualification is sufficient for her to get by. Besides, what more can she learn and what use would it have, anyway. There are other more important issues to be taken care of by her as wife, mother and mistress; they demand most of her time. Now she drops in once in a while to the school room only to peep at her own children who have begun to learn the basics.

'*Kapuri Ka, Kharayo kha,*' Fatteh Baje is saying with a stick in his hand that is pointing out to alphabets on a chart that is hung on the wall. The six children repeat in a sing-song manner after him – '*Kapoooreee Kaaa...Kharaaaayoooo Khaaa.*'

In between this rhythmic recitation, her younger son, Prashant, raises his tiny hand in the air, waving it to draw attention from his teacher. 'Yes Kancha Raja, what is it now? You want to go urinate yet again?'

Prashant nods his head up and down as an answer. 'Go and come back fast,' Fatteh Baje says sternly, showing him the stick in his hand, reminding the little boy of consequences if he does not come back on time.

Sanat quickly conceals herself, stifling a giggle and watches her son. Clasping his hands behind his back, his head lowered in a manner of concentration, he walks out of the school room. Once out, he begins to walk slowly, joining the heel of the front foot with the toes of the foot behind; then, the foot behind would come in front, its heel sticking close to the toes of the one behind. Prashant drags himself slowly to the toilet. Having reached there, he urinates. His eyes are dreamy and sleepy; he walks back taking the same, slow and monotonous steps. Sanat creeps up from behind, surprising him with a squeal. Prashant, happy to see his mother, snuggles against her, his little hands lovingly embracing his mother and his tiny head buried in her bosom.

'Muajiu, I am sleepy, can I not skip classes today?' He yawns, his tiny mouth opening wide while his black shimmering eyes fix on his mother in a desperate plea.

'*Mero sano raja*, if you do not go back to the school room then the Kauguji will come, creeping from behind, pounce on you and then take you away to far off distant lands...'

She is carrying Prashant now. She begins to walk to the school room. Prashant, with his hands circled around his mother's neck, innocently enquires, 'Which distant land will the Kauguji take me to, Muajiu?'

'To the lands where naughty boys are taken.'

'What is it like there?'

'It is dark and cold and one has to carry stones, heavy stones, from one end to the other and then come back the same way carrying a bigger and a heavier stone.' Sanat has just made up a story of her own to scare her boy from neglecting his studies. Prashant, however, is thinking on a different tangent.

'I'd rather do that, Muajiu – carry stones than sit in that classroom that smells of Fatteh Baje's fart of rotten onions and garlic all the time,' Prashant snuggles his podgy face against the softness of his mother's as she carries him along, insisting that he go back to class.

'You will be a big boy some day, Prashant. Just like your Buajiu, you will travel to places, meet many people, wear a tie and suit and be a business man. And that will make your Maujiu proud. Now, do you want to make me proud?' Sanat asks Prashant, a tender smile on her face and to which he begins to nod his head up and down again.

'Yes, Muajiu. Yes, I will make you proud. I will be a big man one day.'

It is on her way back to the house from the school room that Sanat meets Tara. White and bloodless in the face, Tara grabs hold of Sanat. Her eyes still and lost in a haze, she whispers, 'Raja Saheb has had a stroke.'

Instantly, Sanat disengages herself from Tara's desperate grip and begins to run. Her mind empty, her heart furiously beating, she runs blindly to the courtyard, where her husband is lying, his eyes wide open but the glint is gone; his mouth is open too, in his last attempt to gasp air. Sanat bends over, her head on his chest. Not a sound comes from within. He is stiff as a log. She takes his hands, ice cold and stiff in her own, and begins to rub them, hoping that with the heat of her palms, she could revive him. Surely his blood would begin to flow again and he would blink his eyes and ask in the same haughty tone, what he was doing lying on the ground in the courtyard.

But the harder Sanat rubbed her husband's lifeless hands, the more she realised that her husband was now dead. Not even twenty-years-old, she was now a widow with two little sons to care for.

And then Sanat looks up at the gaping faces around her, some of which are staring dumfounded; some are beginning to cry and some are shouting out instructions. But to her, none of these faces seem to have a name. All of these seem a jumble of contorted faces peering out through a thick haze. With her heart drumming inside her, bewildered, lost and helpless, Sanat hears her own voice coming from somewhere totally alien to her.

'Have the Dittha alert the entire family and bring down his bed. Shade him with an umbrella until the other men of the family get here and get the boys down here from the school room.'

Sanjeevani

It is raining outside. Raindrops race down the windowsill, tip-tapping happily. It has been pouring for the past few weeks. Not that it bothers me in any way; on the contrary, I have enjoyed every bit of it. I also know this same monsoon is wreaking havoc somewhere or the other. I wonder how Badki is coping with the rains and whether she has managed to have her roof fixed? And what of the armed rebels? How are they managing in the jungles with the crawling leeches, earthworms and snakes? I think the monsoon must have put a pause to their extortions from the local farmers. Perhaps not. Perhaps the rains have driven more of them into the villages, forcing them upon the helpless villagers. Ganeshpur is now totally isolated from the rest of the world and completely in the hands of the Maoist cadres. The two rivers encircling it must be furiously over-flooded and since there are no bridges, the little villages of Ramshikharjhala have learnt to survive the monsoons, alienated from the rest of the world. Irrespective, the rain shall fall...soft and beseeching, hard and devouring. For me the rain is like a balm, a soothing, comforting balm that seems to lull my senses into sweet sedation.

The room around me is engulfed in darkness. Last night's storm has probably blown out a transformer somewhere. Last night was bad. I could not write; the fan was not working and sleep did not come easy. I spent the entire night sitting by this very window, staring out into the thickness of the night, alone with the murmurings of the mosquitoes by my ears and the torturous mumbling that seem to come from somewhere inside me...jeering at my incapacities.

Voices jabbing at me in the dark...the voices are familiar, and yet they make me cringe... 'Nepti...Nepti! Come to your Hemant Da...Sanju, my dear Sanju...my crafty angel... Razat...my Krishna...my Shyaam.' Voices blending, voices parting....They make me shiver. I woke up with a start to the sound of the telephone ringing in the sitting room. The ring had rescued me from the nightmare. I suddenly realised that I had tears in my eyes and my body was drenched with sweat. My mother had called. Although she had much to say regarding my coming to Dhangadi, my being selfish, irresponsible and the list that never ended, I do think that she also feels that my staying in Dhangadi would keep me away from Razat. And, therefore, this could turn out to be a boon in disguise for me and her as well. So, when she calls, her words are not all that harsh as they can be.

'Sanju,' she had said this afternoon sounding overly tender and affectionate, 'since you are there already, your Bua thinks that you should get in touch with...the chief district officer there. He has also asked me to give you Tika Kar saab's number. Remember him? His youngest brother is married to Sanu. He is at the Teghari Barrack now. Who knows when you might need assistance? Babu, times are not good. But of course, you know that already. You are big enough now not to be told what is right and what is wrong.'

'You want to protect me Mamu? Then protect me from myself...from these voices that come from within, from my jeering phantoms...save me Mamu' I wanted to say all this. I wanted to fall down on my knees, hold the receiver to my chest and weep and weep. Instead, I mumbled the usual – 'Don't worry, Mamu, I'll be fine.' I had obediently and mechanically jotted down the numbers she had for me. She also informed me that Aunty was coming down to Dhangadi. 'She is taking the night bus and should be there tomorrow morning. You don't need to bother about picking her from the bus stop, but I think she will stay with you and not at our place.'

We had ended on a good note. I had placed the receiver back and hardened myself to face the sham that was all around me.

Aunty staying here is no problem for me. There is enough space in this apartment. Besides the two rooms that I use as my bedroom and writing room, there is another one; but it has no furniture. I could ask my landlord to lend me some mattresses if he can or else go into town and get a cheap cot and a mattress. Something inside tells me that going for the latter option would be better for there is no knowing how many more people my mother is going to send down here to spy on me.

Sunk in my thoughts, standing by the window and watching the rain fall in its forceful urgency, I do not notice the lights that come on. The fan begins to swirl, in slow rotations initially, and then gathers momentum.

My thoughts revert to Razat. Am I mad? Perhaps there is a chemical imbalance in me. Or am I simply in love? Do all people in love feel this way – hurt, tormented and lonely all the time? I miss Razat but when do I not? He has become this constant pain, somewhere inside me, that just won't subside. During the day I don't feel that mind-numbing ache that much as my mind is occupied with work at the shelter; but when I get back here, to the apartment, thoughts of him follow me around from room to room.

Working on my novel seems to ease the pain a bit, but then, the pain keeps returning from time to time, a forceful reminder of my utter weakness. It is strange...I have not seen the man in the past six months. Haven't heard from him either. But his face is clear in my memory...his naughty smile, those endearing eyes, that comforting voice and the little flashes of the priceless moments spent with him; the memories cruelly mock me.

'Did you know your teeth are magnetic, Razat?' I had once told him, fighting my instinct to feel those immaculately glistening set of teeth. When he smiled, revealing his perfectly placed teeth, his face suddenly lit up. Illumined I should say, for to me then, Razat seemed the perfect image of a perfect God – beautiful, serene and so very enticing.

'I know, my darling Sanju. My astrologer says that I must take care of my teeth, for the secret of my success lies in my teeth... without these I am nothing,' he had said, grinning back and flashing those pearly whites at me.

I walk back to my writing desk where my laptop is waiting. I stare at the words on the screen...

'Sanat peeps out...out of her shadows; the setting sun bids adieu to the day by sweeping the sky with a tranquil shade of purple and orange. Giant shadows fall, hill after hill beginning to darken. There is a sense of serenity in this retirement of the sun; it holds promises for Sanat...promises of a better dawn.'

'What a life!' I say aloud as I think of my grandmother now, confined to a tiny, dark and damp room. Her old age has become more of an imprisonment. Does she still hope? But for what...annihilation?

My fingers begin to flow over the keyboard. Instinctively, words appear as though they were always meant to be. I stop and read. Am I creating this story or is it my factual past trying to assert itself for a want of recognition?

The phone rings. It is Sarala Didi, the warden at the shelter. A child has fainted. I give quick instructions.

'Call for a rickshaw and take her immediately to the hospital. Take Hari with you and ask for Dr Pathak and tell him you are from the Naari Bishram Kendra. I will join you there.'

I rush to the hospital. I ride a bicycle here in Dhangadi, the easiest and the most economical way to commute. People still stare at me with curiosity. But I refuse to care. I am soon at the Seti Zonal hospital. Hari, the shelter peon, meets me at the reception.

'Sanjeevani Didi,' he says, muttering and half eating his words in his state of excitement. 'Aastha has gone into a coma.'

'Where is she?' I ask, ignoring him, for I know the child is not all that critical as Hari has portrayed. Hari is used to exaggerations. He is a dreamer like myself and can imagine anything under the sun while sitting on his wooden chair outside my office door. Hari's dramatic imagination would have assumed that she is in a coma and would wake up after another fifteen years, just like it is shown in the Hindi soaps. The shelter thrives on Hindi soaps. From the peon, to the two ayahs and all the twenty-three children along with the eight women—victims of physical abuse staying away from their husbands—are hooked onto the saas-bahu cult. Sometimes I think if nothing else, all these children will easily make a good career in the theatre business. Even the youngest ones deliver the soap dialogues with proficient ease and brilliance. I am amazed at how easily each one has picked up Hindi without any guidance. I wonder why mothers have to complain about television and its addictive hold on their children...at least they get to learn something or the other from it.

Dr Pathak is attending to Aastha in the emergency ward. The repulsive stench from the toilets nearby is mingled with the strong smell of Dettol. There are around eight beds in this room, and all are occupied. On the floor, upon mats, other patients. Astha is on a bed and is being given an intravenous saline solution. She had been suffering from a severe case of diarrhoea for the past few days. Since the medical budget is barely sufficient for purchasing the necessary first aid requirements, I supervise minor health problems at the shelter myself.

I had sent an email to Samaanta complaining about this matter last month. The complaint was the immediate consequence of one of the children being admitted to the hospital for nearly two weeks with a severe case of jaundice. 'It is the best we can manage from here, Sanjeevani. You know the Kailali shelter is functioning on the leftover budget from the Bardiya and the Kathmandu shelters. But I am trying to rope in extra funding just for your shelter there. Hopefully, in my trip to France this October, I'll manage to get a donor specifically for Kailali. Till then, babes...'she had laughed and said, '...manage with whatever you have.'

I did manage somehow. I brought the entire Seti Zonal hospital down, screaming my lungs out at the reception, asking for a bed without any fee. This also brought to my attention how adjusting and easily giving in the Nepalese people have become. One has to be firm and rigid with one's decision no matter how inane ones need is; and that's when people begin to give in. I guess they don't like hassles or is it that the Nepalese mind is too lazy to deal with hassles. Well whatever their reasons, my hollering and demanding immediate attention had brought Dr Pathak, a senior doctor, out of his cabin. He had eventually given in to my demand for a free bed and medical attention for my ward.

'Sanju...Ma'am,' Aastha smiles weakly at me, and stretches out her hand. I sit on the bed.

'She will be fine,' Dr Pathak says. 'You don't look too well yourself...Sanjeevani.'

'It's the sleepless night, doctor saab,' I reply.

'Yes, it's the same with everyone. No electricity at night and it is just too hot and humid inside the room. How is one to get any sleep? I wait for nights when it does not rain and make a bed for myself on the terrace. It is best to sleep there. There's always a pleasant breeze the entire night and there is no fear of the lights going off at any random time.'

Although Dr Pathak has completely missed my reason for lack of sleep, I do not bother to correct him. 'Yes, indeed,' I say. Remembering my childhood days back here in Dhangadi when our entire gang – Dada, his friends, a few cousins, my mother and father and even the servants – used to take cots and mattresses to the terrace each evening. My father slept on a cot while the rest of us were comfortable on the mats laid on the floor.

There used to be a lot of chatting and singing every evening. We talked a lot those days and most of it was nonsense. We laughed a lot too, but those were good times, easy times... when the mind did not think too much and easily adapted itself to anything and any situation.

'I have prescribed Metrodinazole, four times a day. The child will need Cetamol till her fever subsides and will need to be on the saline for the next twenty-four hours. After that, let us see whether we can give her some light meals, soups maybe...'

Dr Pathak is now standing across the bed. His eyes are always probing into mine. But strangely, I do not take this as an encroachment. Perhaps he is lonely and in constant search for someone who appeals to his mind and soul.

'Thank you, doctor saab,' I say, looking away from him and staring at another corner of the room. Across the room, on a bed, is a woman. She has her head covered with a cloth. There are patches of dark bruises all over face, neck and arms. I can see stains of blood on her crumpled bedsheet. She is lying with her hand on her stomach, watching us with a dead look in her eyes.

'Anything for you, Sanjeevani.' Dr Pathak has a smile on his face, and he is quick to notice my object of curiosity. 'She is from Malakheti. They brought her in last night. She had lost a lot of blood along with her eighteen-week-old foetus. She will be fine,' he said. 'Care for a cup of tea?'

'Yes, I think I won't mind one,' I say, and stand up. 'Aastha is sleeping now.'

'Sarala Didi, you and Hari take turns to sit by her side and call me at the office if anything comes up. I will be going there now and later in the evening. I shall send Malati or Dhimni to substitute,' I tell the hostel warden as I walk away, taking a quick, last glance at Aastha.

'But what happened to her?' I ask Dr Pathak on our way out. The stench of urine coming from the toilets is unbearable now, and I am speaking with my nose and mouth covered with my hand.

'Oh, the same old story,' Dr Pathak replies, opening the glass door at the end of the corridor for me to pass. We are in the reception now and it is packed with people ailing with this and that. 'A pregnant woman getting beaten up and losing a child is a regular story here.'

'And you people don't complain to the authorities? Outrageous!' I am angry now.

'Who has time, Sanjeevani? Most days, we don't even get enough time to attend to all our patients, for there are just five of us doctors attending to more than a hundred patients a day here. You have only seen the emergency ward. At the general ward, everyday twenty to twenty-five people are admitted, and all of them are insurgency victims. Victims from both sides of the warring factions – the security forces and the PLA. Some come with broken limbs, some with amputations and some with internal hemorrhages. We doctors merely do our jobs and don't think about which side has inflicted the harm. We don't have time for hassles. Social service, madam, for us doctors is not a privilege we can afford.'

We are out in the lawn now. Across this is the in-patients department building made not many years ago, but beginning to look shabby and old due to lack of maintenance. Under the banyan tree by the gateway is where we are headed, to the small tea stall run by a woman and her two children.

'But then, someone should inform NGOs like mine. We are here to help. I am going to file a police case. You, for one, better cooperate,' I say to Dr Pathak, my finger pointing at him.

'Anything for you, Sanjeevani, but you will have to get the woman to speak first.' He is smiling again. We sit on the bench by the tea stall and Dr Pathak asks for two cups of tea, which is instantly brought to us.

I sip my tea and watch the road outside the gate... rickshaws and cycles and people walking up and down. There is a chemist shop, Deepu's Medical Store, right opposite the gate. I remember this one well as we used to get all our medical supplies from this store at one time.

There are a few people at the store, waiting at the counter. Then I see him. He turns around towards the road for a brief moment and I catch his eye. Even from that distance, I can clearly see that inquiring look, the kind that asks too many questions but does not accept many answers. I am certain he is the same man, the one who had come with the cadres that morning to Badki's house looking for me. He is wearing a pair of jeans and a blue shirt. Over his head is a peak cap. I know he has seen me and even recognised me. Instantly he turns around and nudges the man by his side.

I place my cup on the bench. 'I'll be right back,' I mumble to Dr Pathak as I begin to run across the lawn towards the gate and towards him.

He is beginning to move away from Deepu's Medical Store. I see him shove a huge package of medical supplies into a small rucksack, zip it up and fling it across his shoulders as he walks.

I reach them as another man joins them from the adjoining chemist store. He too is carrying a rucksack probably filled with medical supplies.

'Dai... Dai,' I call out nearly panting from the running. They are briskly walking away now, clearly ignoring my calls. 'Dai!' I call out again. I am right behind them and can even stretch out my hand and touch them if I want to, but I don't.

He turns around while the other two don't stop. 'You are from Ganeshpur, aren't you?' I say loudly through my heavy breathing.

He does not reply but waits for me to first catch my breath. He is looking at me now, assessing me as it were with an amused glint in his eye. 'How is Badki?' I ask, having nothing else to say in order to keep him occupied. I am filled with an urgent need to keep him there, in front of me, tangible and real.

'She is fine . . .' he replies and I catch a subtle smile playing around his lips. His lips quiver for a second and I hold back my hands that nearly reach out to feel that smile.

'You know my name . . . Sanjeevani . . . what are you called?' Not for a moment do I think of the fact that this man is an armed rebel and is probably carrying a pistol under his shirt; that if his identity is revealed, he can be instantly shot down by the armed police force members of which are standing and chatting in their make-shift booths by the hospital gate.

All I know is that I am overwhelmed and completely seized by my warring phantoms. His proximity seems to challenge me in a strange way, drawing me closer to him. I do not want to let go of him.

'Chandra . . . my name is Chandra.' He is actually talking back to me! I feel thrilled! It is as if each atom that makes me has suddenly come alive. I remain ecstatic in my own awakening.

'Chandra,' I hear myself say his name aloud with ease as though I have been saying it every day. 'Take my telephone number. Call me some time, whenever you can, whenever you come into town.'

I quickly take out a pen from my bag and scribble my name and number into my little diary, tear the page out and hand it over to him. He takes it and does not ask why. Perhaps he understands, perhaps he feels the same longing, the same yearning to reach out as I do for him.

I watch him put the paper away in his pocket and then he looks up at me. There is a lot said, sometimes with silence . . . I can feel my hands rise and move towards him and then move all over his face. 'So different,' I hear myself say from somewhere inside of me... 'this is not Razat... Razat lives in a box, a conventional box and this man is a wandering soul... look he's even wearing a cheap faded cap with Mickey Mouse printed on it... and he walks the town in his chappals.' A sudden challenge comes over me... a challenge to conquer and be conquered. 'Is this lust?' I ask myself again. Feeling his skin and wanting to negate the repulsion that bounces back from the negated depths of my conscience.

The world around us has come to a standstill. I can feel his hand now, gently clasp mine and remove it from his face. But then I do not let go off his hand, and for the longest time, he does not make an effort to release his hand from my desperate grasp. We stand in silence, hand in hand as the world around us begins to resume its activities. A car passes by, a rickshaw driver tinkles the bells on the rickshaw, a crow is cawing somewhere, rustles of feet all around, people begin to talk. Then he lets go, turns around and leaves. I stand fixed to the ground watching his back, sturdy and firm, walk away from me.

I return to my seat by the tea stall. I breathe again. The world around me returns to normal. The stall owner is still hollering her menu out to passersby, her two boys are still running around attending to customers spread all over the lawn, Dr Pathak is still sipping his tea but I can feel an enormous change in me... it is as if a heavy weight has been lifted from my chest, it is as if I have suddenly come upon an opening in the dark, this opening leading me towards light, towards what I really want. Have always wanted.

'Someone from my village,' I explain without being asked. Have I become one of them? Am I an enemy of the state now? The thrills of these silent queries bubbling inside begin to excite me further.

I quickly finish my tea and walk back with Dr Pathak to the hospital. Sarala Didi is asleep on a stool by Aastha's bed. There is another woman sitting by her sick son and feeding him some boiled rice and dal out of the tiffin carrier; a man is standing and fixing the drip that is attached to an old lady who is mumbling in her sleep. There is a child sucking his mother's breast while the mother is sprawled unconscious on the bed.

I walk to the woman on the bed at the farthest corner of the room. Both her hands tightly held together, rest on her stomach while she stares at the ceiling fan. I am standing at the foot of the bed and watching her; she does not move. Even her eyelids don't flutter. I cough – a strangled effort to draw her attention. Getting no response from her, I walk to the side of the bed, bend over and turn her face around towards myself.

'Bahini...' I begin to say, 'I work in an NGO. It is called Naari and we work against physical and mental abuse of women. My name is Sanjeevani. I am its regional coordinator and run the shelter for victims of physical abuse.'

I receive an empty look in response. Thinking that perhaps she has not understood me, I begin to explain with revised and simpler words.

'Look,' I say, sitting on the edge of her bed and forcefully taking hold of her hands. They are cold and still trembling. 'Your husband beat you. That is wrong. It is a criminal offence and he can even go to jail for this. You must not allow that ever by anyone, not only your husband. A hand raised to beat once, can even kill you the next time.'

Before I could say more, she begins to cry. The cries then turn into loud heart-wrenching wails that draw everybody's attention. Two nurses run in, alarmed.

'*Maryo, mero bachha maryo*...he killed my baby.' This is followed by curses. 'He will die like a diseased dog, his flesh will rot and decay as he watches it rot. He will burn in hell...and be reborn as a dog and will be kicked at and spat at by all.'

'That is assumption,' I say, patting her hand. 'He may kill you first and who knows what happens after death. You have to make him pay for this before your own eyes. Bahini, there are ways to do things. You have to file a complaint against him with the police. The doctors here will certify to your statement regarding your physical condition.'

Raising my voice to calm her down does seem to help and she stares back, silent and in deep contemplation. 'We have a shelter here. There are other women living there. Just like you, they too have taken a stand against physical abuse. They will stay there until they manage an independent income for themselves. Once you are discharged from here I can take you to the Bishram Kendra. What is your name?'

'Sharmila...Sharmila Bhandari,' she whispers back, still holding my hands and staring at me with a hope in her eyes that suddenly begins to gnaw at me, setting off an uneasy panic. I disentangle myself from her clutch. I take out my diary from my handbag and begin to note down the contact details and necessary information of her husband.

I leave the hospital and cycle to the district police station just down the road. Sometimes it helps to have friends in places like these. I like to believe that I have friends here but the truth is they associate with me only because I shock them. I guess my unconventional ways and mannerisms are what they find refreshing. They probably laugh at me behind my back, giving me names and even pairing me with this one and that in their drunken stupor. But when they are with me, I keep them enthralled and totally captivated in my mysterious charms.

I had met this bunch of policemen a few weeks after arriving here. I was returning to my apartment from the shelter that night after having dinner there. I had not set up my own kitchen then; not that I can boast of a fully functional kitchen even now. I don't cook. I can't cook. So I just have this electric kettle in which I boil water to make coffee and a pan that works as a toaster and a means to cook eggs too. I normally skip lunch or eat something with the children at the shelter and take back leftovers for my dinner...so, I hardly feel the need to use utensils.

Coming back to the first encounter with my drinking buddies from the police station...that night I was cycling back and got stopped by this bunch of policemen, swaying with the intoxication of authority and cheap tharra alcohol. All four of them were in uniform and were swaying their batons in the air, in front of my face. They forced me to get off my bike.

At first, I had felt something like fear. I even thought that I was going to get raped and thrown into the gutters of the Mohana river and that would be the end of my distasteful life. But then, assessing them, while showing them my citizenship ID card given to me by Naari mentioning my designation, I concluded that they were just a bunch of bums, bored out of their lives and in need of some entertainment during their night patrol.

'Where are you going at this hour?' asked one of them as the other three stared at my face, trying their best to look and sound authoritative.

'As you can see, I work at this shelter and am returning home for the night,' I had replied, shoving my hands into the pockets of my track pants, and shrugging my shoulders at the same time.

'It's not safe for a girl to walk around alone at this hour,' I had heard one of them say as faces bore down on me, grinning by now.

'Ya, so many dangers around...one does not know who the enemy is any more – the police or the Maobadis,' I had said, bending my torso a little forward.

'Why do you say that? Our job is to serve and to protect. We are here for the general public's safety. We protect you from harm.'

'Ya, ya,' I had said, while taking back my identifications and putting them back into my bag. 'I could be taken in by you all now and the world would not know where I went! So much for your protection!'

'Don't say that, bahini, we are not all that bad as portrayed to be,' said one of them. He seemed to be the commanding one of the lot. Hardly more than twenty-four, hope and aspiration from life were blatantly visible upon his countenance.

'Stop calling me bahini,' I had said, taking hold of the handles of my bike. 'My name is Sanjeevani, did you not read that in my ID card?'

'Okay, Sanjeevani, go straight home. You should not wander around unnecessarily at night. If you want, we could escort you back. Where do you live?' I had read his name by now – Gopal Adhikari and he was an assistant sub-inspector.

'Assai saab,' I had said, now beginning to enjoy myself, 'I am capable of taking myself home safely but since you seem to be in dire need of female company, I shall not deprive you of that. Let's all go to my place and share a few drinks together.'

They readily came along. I had smuggled them in quietly so as not to alarm my landlord on the floor above. Sitting on the floor of my sitting room, the five of us finished an entire bottle of Russian vodka by the break of dawn.

That night, we truly bonded, realising that deep within each one of us was the same fear, the same frustrations and the same hopes and aspirations. Each one of us wanted peace.

I see Gore Rokaya standing by the long verandah of the Jilla Prahari Karyalaya (Ji. Pr. Ka.). He does not notice me walking up to him, as he stands there, staring aimlessly. 'Gore dai,' I wave my hand in front of his face and he seems to awaken from his trance. 'Ke ho? See a beautiful face there, do you, you daydreamer?' I tease him and ask him the whereabouts of his assistant sub-inspector.

He gives a sheepish laugh and tells me to sit and wait on one of the wooden benches laid in long lines across the length of the verandah. He walks off, humming to himself, in search of Gopal Ahikari. Soon enough, Gopal arrives flanked on either side by the other two. I tell them the reason for my visit and we walk back to the hospital.

Here, Sharmila files her complaint and a medical report is given to Gopal by Dr Pathak.

By the end of it, I am not only feeling tired but also sweaty and dirty from all the walking and cycling around. 'I desperately need a shower,' I say to myself, while simultaneously feeling a strange sweet sensation of accomplishment somewhere inside me. My encounter with Chandra has also left this tingling sensation in my body that seems to have stimulated all my senses. I suddenly feel alive...tired but alive.

'We will call the husband over. Will let you know,' Gopal says to me as we walk out of the hospital.

'*Dherai dherai, dhanyabad*, Gopal sir.' Waving one hand to him, I unlock my bicycle as we part ways at the gate.

It is nearly four in the evening now, but the glare of the summer sun is still at its peak. I look up at the sky to see whether there are any chances of a drizzle, but the sky is distinctively blue with not a smear of the grey clouds I wish to see. There is a slight warm breeze – not in any way a consolation. Cycling to the shelter, I am drenched with my own perspiration.

At the shelter there is not much to do. Children have just returned from the day school. They will now change, have some bread and jam with tea, play for a while and then sit down in the common room for their homework, which I normally supervise while working on my novel.

Today, I feel tired. Or is it just that I want to rush back to my apartment, to be alone with my thoughts? My thoughts of Chandra, of Razat...and of what the hell I want in life.

'Dhimni, why don't you go down to the hospital and wait on Aastha. Send Sarala Didi and Hari back so that Hari can replace you after dinner and stay there for the night. I don't feel too well. So, I think Sarala Didi will have to supervise the children's homework today.' The seventeen-year-old-girl, Dhimni, came as a victim of domestic abuse a few months back and I decided to employ her at the shelter. The thought of her forty-year-old, smelly husband and the nights of forceful, drunken rapes, would not allow me to send her back to her family. There are times when she comes and whispers, 'Sanju Didi, do you think I should go back?' I turn around and glare at her. I guess that was enough to remind her of the torturous nights that she has left behind.

Back at my place, I take a quick, cold shower, pouring mug after mug of water from the bucket over my head. It does little to cool the heat of my body. I raise the entire bucket and pour the water in one go over myself. I stand wet and naked, staring at myself in the mirror, watching little drops of water slip down the skin of my face.

Am I lonely? Am I happy in my loneliness? Is this what I want – estrangement from family and friends? Am I content with my work? Is this all that I am capable of or is it that I seek no more? Even as I ask myself I know I am not content. My job does not satisfy me. I want to do something different, something that really touches my innermost being... something like going back to my village, feeling its earth and becoming a part of it.

Questions hound me as I begin to towel myself dry. They flitter around me, poking me, nudging me as I walk out into the verandah. I sit down on the wooden chair given by my landlord and look out into stretches of open land that merge with the jungle at the far end. There are a few one-storeyed houses in between. The owners of the vacant land must be living elsewhere, probably in Kathmandu, waiting for the opportune time to come back, and build a house to let it out on rent in the future. A soft breeze is blowing and the heat has considerably lessened. I feel a tug at my stomach from inside and realise I have not eaten anything the entire day. In my rush to leave, I forgot to bring back food for the night from the shelter.

I walk into the kitchen to see if I have anything there. I find packets of Wai Wai noodles inside a polythene bag along with some long-forgotten biscuits. I cook the Wai Wai and carry it back, steaming in a bowl, to my chair in the verandah.

On my way there, the phone rings. I want to ignore it. The urge to cling on to my isolation is overtaken by the possibility of the call being from the shelter or from the hospital. I answer it.

'Hello? Hello? Hellooo?'

I am about to hang up, dismissing it as a silly crank call when he speaks from the other end.

'Sanjeevani...' My name sounds different when he says it. Not different but perfect...just the way it should be said...stressing on 'jeevani'...soft but demanding.

'Yes, yes...this is Sanjeevani,' I quickly say, expecting him to hangup any moment. 'Is it Chandra?' I ask with the same urgency.

'Yes, Sanjeevani, I did not go back to Ramshikharjhala with my comrades. I stayed back so that I could see you today. If it's possible, where shall we meet?'

I tell him to come to my apartment after it gets dark while realising what a severe gamble he is taking with me. I could be an informant and have him arrested.

I sit on the verandah, watching the sun set behind the fields. My heart is chaotically beating. Am I over Razat? If not, then why is it that I yearn for Chandra...this stranger, this enemy of the state, this man who believes in a change, a belief that killed my brother and shattered my family?

'Sanjeevani...Sanjeevani,' I hear my landlord's wife holler out to me from her window above the verandah. 'They have attacked the jail. I just got a call from Mangalaa, who lives near the prison compound...and she says she heard a loud blast.'

Even before she ended her sentence, we begin to hear blasts, one after the other, piercing the silence of the night. I stand up and walk towards the gate. Frightened neighbours are beginning to assemble outside their houses.

'The army along with the armed police is out there...fighting the Maobadis. There is no reason to fear,' someone says in the dark, a tremor in his voice betraying his own fear.

'Let us stay indoors and switch off all the lights,' says someone else. People begin to rush back in panic.

Inside, sitting in the darkness, listening to the gunshots coming from the direction of the jail, I can almost see Chandra shooting one of them; his eyes masked with the same indifferent look. I can picture him – daring, persistent and adamant.

Chandra comes to me just before dawn, when the gunshots have died down, the streets are quiet and the people, now comforted by the silence outside, have fallen into deep slumber. He arrives wearing the same peak cap. Sitting on the verandah, my heart is racing like never before. Seeing him walk up to the house, I quickly sneak him in.

I feel no emotion now and I know the lust for him is purely animalistic. There is no need for an exchange of words as we communicate with our instincts. He undresses me first. His quick hands move over my body in a blind instinctive caress. I watch his helpless desire as he begins to take off his clothes one after another. His fingers unbutton his shirt; his arms, with their taut muscles, moving down to unzip his pants. His sturdy hips are revealed. Instinctively, my hands grasp his determined flanks. He bends forward, takes hold of my hands and pushes me gently onto the bed.

I do not let go of his eyes. They stare back at me with the same naked passion. He works like an animal, brooding, patient and withdrawn. As I watch him, silently pleading, his hands begin to roam all over my naked flesh and stop with a sudden jerk at my navel.

I hold his face, my lips trembling; I begin to taste his skin, my tongue desperate in its queer longing to penetrate the deepest core of him. I can taste him now... the trickles of his hot salty sweat, seeping into my flesh. I am in a frenzy now, a desperate, urgent frenzy. I want him so much...I begin to moan holding the back of his head. His face is buried into my stomach. I can feel his hot tongue swivel in my navel.

A quiver of exquisite pleasure passes through me; he draws me into his arms and looks into my imploring eyes. His quivering lips search for mine; hot, smouldering and instinctively demanding kisses are showered on me. Insensitive of time, we probe deeper and deeper with an insatiable want. I cling on to him desperately in awe and almost in terror as I begin to feel his stirring. He enters me, demanding and challenging, and defiantly insistent.

'Razat...my Shyaam,' I weep in my soul before I begin to cry as Chandra releases me from myself.

Sanat

A new era has begun. King Tribhuvan has returned from New Delhi. With the aid of the Indian Embassy in Kathmandu, he had fled from here and received political asylum in New Delhi. He left behind the Nepali National Congress, which has launched an armed struggle in the country. The nation's simmering discontent with the Rana regime has burst out into a blatant revolution. In the east, the Kiratis break out; Rudra Shamsher the Bada Hakim of Palpa has revolted with a troop of his own, alongwith a large number of C-class Ranas who have also started speaking up for the restoration of the king's sovereignty.

The volunteers of the Nepali Congress, armed with weapons obtained from Burma, have stormed into Birgunj and occupied the Indian border town. Biratnagar and Amlekhgunj have become victims to the conflict between the Congress Mukti Sena and the government deployed troops.

Finally, the Indian government intervenes, without the cooperation of whom the Ranas cannot sustain themselves. This has forced Mohan Shamsher, the prime minister, to announce an election in order to form a Constituent Assembly that will draw up a Constitution for the country.

The interim Constitution of Nepal has been drafted and adopted. The king approves this act because it recognises the supremacy of the institution of monarchy in the dealings of the state. As for the Nepali Congress, they seem to be content in having ended the Rana regime and having slashed the powers of the Rana prime minister.

King Tribhuvan has constituted a new cabinet and made Matrika Prasad Koirala the prime minister. The sovereign role of the prime minister is reduced to communicating all administration related decisions of the cabinet to the king. The new prime minister withdraws restrictions on sale, transfers, mortgages, gifts and subdivision of Birta lands that carry traditional importance for the monarchy. The other political parties begin to feel they could come to power by winning the King's personal favours. Thus a vacuum begins to be created in the political scenario of Nepal. The political parties begin bickering amongst themselves, giving the king the authority to assume more power in terms of tradition, culture and even politics.

But these turbulent moments in the political scenario are the least of Sanat's concerns. She has more important issues to attend to. She refuses to let her sons be doomed to the confines of the Kanda hills and is determined to educate them and make them finer men than their own father. Sanat moves to the tarai. Tara refuses to move.

'I have taken care of this home for Raja Saheb. It is a part of me now and I cannot bear the thought of separating myself from it. Raja Saheb has gone, and I don't know how long I will be able to continue. But Rani Saheb, take my son, Dane. Make him a gentleman. Educate him and make him worthy of his father's blood,' Tara had said, staring into the distant fields, with a firm determination in her eyes.

Sanat travels along with Chanda, past the towering hills that have secluded Kanda from the rest of the progressing world. For weeks her entourage moves, crossing one hill after another, camping at night and moving on the next morning. Porters carry trunks, heavy with clothes, ration and even gold and silver. Armed security, maids and orderlies, family priests, friends and relatives trudge along with their wives, husbands, children, and livestock from their abandoned homes along with their meagre belongings. And thus Sanat moves into a foreign land, ready to start a new settlement of her own. Her entourage is alive with the melodious songs of the maids, the playing of the madal by the errand boys and the cheerful laughter of the children. Sweeps of mist cover the convoy like a dark veil, but the procession moves on. Children doze off, the singing of the maids slowly stops echoing from the valley below, but Sanat remains alert.

They arrive in Ramshikharjhala in the thick of the night. It is in the morning, when Sanat walks out of her tent, that she instantly falls in love with the dawn of the tarai. In the east, the sky is lighting up with a scarlet blush. Before long, the sun rises to throw its sanguine glow upon the immense stretches of fields. Sanant had never seen such vastness of land, and is instantly absorbed by the grandeur of it all.

Serious discussions take place with her manager, the Kothari. The location of the house to be constructed is the prime focus. 'I want it away from the village...a little distance always helps in easing tensions that arise from close proximity.' Instantly, the Kothari begins gathering the natives – black, nearly naked and alert with curiosity.

Maharaja Bir Shamsher had let out this arable land for sale and lease to the highest bidders with the sole intention of populating these four jillas of Kailali, Kanchanpur, Banke and Bardia. All these were lands returned to Nepal from the Sugaulie treaty, as a reward for its aid in the Awadh war. Sanat has now bought a total of two thousand bighas paying a total sum of seven thousand gold coins.

The Mahajan is called for, and from him Sanat buys her first three bonded labourers, each for a sum of one hundred gold coins.

A mud baked house is made for Sanat that soon begins to expand. A kitchen house is added across the courtyard, a granary house beside it, a cattleshed made across that and a kitchen garden separated from the fields springs up soon enough. Sanat has made three tiny houses for her three Kamaiyas and names it the Teen Gharua that with time begins sprouting up more tiny mud huts, one after the other as Sanat begins requiring more help in the fields, and acquiring more bonded labour.

With time, Sanat's establishment prospers and grows in population as more and more of her household begin to migrate from Kanda and establish themselves around her; to some she sells her own land and for the others, she helps procure land from other landowners. Before long, Sanat is established as a prominent zamindar of the Ramshikharjhala Gaon Panchayat.

The boys are growing up and although still under the tutelage of Fatteh Baje, Sanat is not really convinced of the quality of their education. She worries while watching them spend their time running around the fields, chasing Kamalarhi girls, pulling up their lehangas and peeping between their legs to satisfy their pubescent curiosity.

More than Prashant it is her eldest offspring Prabhat for whom Sanat worries. During the day, he rides his horse, proud and rather overbearing. He has begun to enjoy intimidating the ignorant villagers for no particular reason.

'It is because he has nothing better to do, Rani Saheb,' Chanda says to Sanat, tying the latter's hair in a Grecian bandeaux and decorating it with jasmine flowers.

'Who says he has nothing to do? He has lands to take care of, attend to the production, the sales and even the handling of the revenues. But no . . . he will ride his horse as a Sahibzaada and while away his hours chasing Tharunis who run from him as though he were a devil. And why won't they, when he pinches them, bites them and even pulls at their lehengas.'

Chanda laughs. 'He is big boy now, he is curious, Rani Saheb...all boys are.' Chanda gazes out into the softly shifting wheat in the fields and sighs. 'Our days are gone Rani Saheb...we have lived enough. Now it is our children's turn to live and enjoy.'

'I agree, Chanda. But life is not all fun and enjoyment. There are responsibilities, too. My sons will be married one day, have children of their own and it is now that I must prepare them for the challenges of life that they are bound to meet with sooner or later.'

Sanat has walked up to her writing desk and is now beginning to look at papers in rolls, thin sheets of lokta, written in ink and stamped with fingerprints.

'Their father wanted his boys to help the monarchy. We Thakuris are the founding base of the monarchy, he said. And the monarchy for us is a protective shield without which we cannot survive.' Still not looking up, Sanat continues voicing her concerns.

'I have decided to send the boys to Calcutta for their further education.'

'Muajiu, I will not leave you and go anywhere.' Prashant, with a prominent frown on his forehead, is kicking his heels and creating a ruckus.

Sanat pulls her little boy from where he stands, forlorn and agitated, and places him lovingly on her lap. Caressing his brooding little head with her hands, she consoles him, 'And how will my kancha raja become a suited, booted man with a tie if he does not go to school?'

'I can do that by staying right here with you, Muajiu...please don't send me away from you. I promise to study with Fatteh Baje and not miss any of my lessons,' he pleads, his big innocent eyes brimming with tears again.

'Fatteh Baje can teach you only about the little that he knows. And what you don't know my kancha raja is that to be a big man, one has to be far more knowledgeable than Fatteh Baje. Otherwise, wouldn't he have been a gentleman, big and famous by now?'

The day they leave, Sanat spends an extra hour in her puja room. She stares at the little idols of gods spread out in front, nearly drowned with her offerings of flowers, fruits and sweets. Folding her hands in reverence, she comforts her aching heart and prays to her Gods to strengthen her will and resoluteness. She is shattered at the thought of separation from her children... the only people who gave a meaning to her life.

Sanat watches her sons depart. A line of bullock carts can be seen trailing in the distance. She waves her handkerchief till the dust raised from the departing convoy settles. All around is a mournful silence. A cuckoo flies from somewhere and silently settles on a branch of the Ashoka trees that she has planted to border her house. For the longest time, Sanat stares at the lonely bird, and feels a familiar emptiness rise and engulf her with a sense of gloomy barrenness.

Sanjeevani

The attack on the prison was the talk of the town for days after Chandra left that night. The Maobadis had succeeded in destroying the jail, killing a few security personnel and taking off with all their imprisoned comrades. However, for me, nothing seemed to matter. Chandra had left in me a sweet sensation, a comforting sedation, that began to slowly subdue the conflicting voices from within me...the ridicules, the derisions, the mocking and even the luring of my deeper phantoms. Strange enough, I can feel the constant ache and longing for Razat begin to ease.

I do not say that I have stopped loving Razat. I wish I could, but he lingers on in me, jeering at my weakness. God knows I want him out of my system. What wouldn't I give to wake up without his name whispering from under my skin and to close my eyes at night without repeating to myself, 'I have to get over Razat...everything is going to be fine.' For hours together, I chant my mantra for peace; my eyes squeezed shut, I force myself to believe that I will someday stop longing for him. Now there is Chandra.

'If it is destined, we shall meet again, Sanjeevani,' he had said sitting on the edge of my bed, his hands lying listless on his lap. There was so much to say, so much to ask and so much to complain about...but strangely, all of it remained cooped in a jumble of unsaid words in the pit of my stomach. I felt a pinch of pain, a pain that was both bitter and sweet.

Who is Chandra? A Maobadi? An enemy of the state? A class enemy?

I am filled with venom that begins to spread through my body and sting my conscience. Yet, I fucked him...yet, I allowed my hands to dig into his skin seeking for a reprieve. *Why, Sanjeevani?* Perhaps, it is the hatred that I feel for his kind, for everyone around me, and even for myself. I want it out! I want to feel this hatred for real and perhaps even vanquish it, for good.

With Chandra, I felt myself come to terms with this hatred and for once, I felt my phantoms come alive.

Chandra had left when it was still dark. The neighbourhood dogs had run after him, barking and then returning to their corners. Tired after the chase, they stood with their tongues out, panting and staring at me standing in my verandah. It was as though they knew my secret.

The next morning Aunty had arrived, her rickshaw spilling over with her tin trunk, bedding and bags. Bottles of pickles, ghee, oils, sel roti and other knick-knacks wrapped in plastic packets were the other accompaniments. She had hustled into my apartment and very soon taken over its maintenance as her mission in life. I did not mind her intrusion as long as she gave me my space, which remains, now after three months, almost a wishful thinking.

I can hear her in the kitchen as she cooks, screaming out to the landlord who is basking in the sun in his kitchen garden asking for some mula. 'Gharbetijiu, eklai, eklai... If you would spare some mula, I'd make some achar and send it up for your family too.'

Aunty has barely changed. She remains the same jovial fun-loving person I remember as a child. Life has not worn her spirits away. My Thulubua married her to feel the vibrancy of her youth and perhaps even to understand her love for life. She is his third wife, the prettiest and definitely the liveliest of the lot. She is always brimming with life even in her worst times. I remember her always smiling and ever hopeful.

'Sanju, should I bring your lunch out to the beranda?' I can hear her voice, pleasant and loud and still full of laughter. How can she be so forgiving, and so optimistic with life, I think to myself. Switching off my computer, I walk towards the kitchen, which is alive with the sounds and smells of delicious food cooking.

'Babu, take the jug of water and go out to the beranda. I will bring your food there,' she says indulgently. 'Aunty, you cooked so many varieties again. You know, since you've come here, I must have put on five to six kilos already.' I complain lightly, holding onto her shoulders and peeping into the little bowls that are holding the little portions of various dishes.

Outside in the verandah, she stands by me ready with a fan in her hand to whisk away the hovering flies while I eat. 'Aunty,' I breathe in, beginning to get restless with her, 'I refuse to eat alone. Get your food and let's eat together.'

'I can eat any time,' she begins to say but I interrupt her, placing the food back in my plate. 'Aunty, there is no fun eating alone. Go in and get your food now or else I too shall eat later whenever you are ready to eat.'

She smiles as she goes in to get her plate of food and I begin to mix the rice on my plate, with some dal and fried vegetables. A soft breeze is blowing outside, cool and comforting. 'Autumn is the best time in tarai, neither too cold nor too hot,' I think quietly to myself.

Aunty comes back with her plate and sits on the stairs going down to the porch from the veranda. We do not speak for a while as we pretend to concentrate on our food. I know Aunty is worried. It has been nearly three months now that she first came here to try and get her land back from the grasp of the Maoists so that she can sell it and return to her life back in Kathmandu.

I had tried my best and even got a buyer for her although it was not that easy. I managed to convince this man, who worked in Bombay as a security guard and had his entire family living there with him to invest some of his earnings into my aunt's land. 'This crisis will not last forever. You can see good days coming now that the useless Girija government has gone. His majesty King Gyanendra seems to have something up his sleeve and will make sure that this Deuba government produces results'.

Words had flown out of my mouth, not making any sense to my own self as I desperately hoped that this potential buyer I had met would be convinced. He was sitting on the same staircase where my aunt sat now in the verandah. 'But what of the rebels? Will they allow land seized by them to be sold to another?' he had asked scratching his head in deep contemplation.

'Why not?' I was persistent. 'The second round of peace talks is going on between the government and the rebels in Bardiya as we speak. I am certain this will result in something fruitful. Besides, peace talks mean resting time for both the warring parties. This is the best time to buy and sell land, harka daju.'

I was ashamed of my persistence. I knew well enough that the peace talks had barely stopped the Maoists from functioning. They had taken this period for mass mobilisations – holding open conferences and airing their idealism and philosophies to the masses, and it was common knowledge that their extortions and tortures had not receded either. Yet I went on convincing him that nothing would go wrong. 'We do not even have to go to the village to do this. Aunty has the lalpurja with her here and it can be done here at the jilla malpot in Dhangadi'

We had gone to the District Land Revenue Department the next day, having convinced old harka and having fixed the price to the liking of both my Aunty and him. The place was brimming with flies and people alike. The stench of urine from the nearby toilets and cigarette smoke mixed with the pungent smell of perspiration hanging stubbornly in the air. There were people sprawled languorously in bunches of twos and threes all over the front lawn. The long veranda was packed with people, some coughing and spitting right where they stood, some scratching their heads, some even their crotches, some shuffling papers, some looking excited in their discussions and some stood by, resting against pillars in silent contemplation.

I had prepared the necessary papers the day before, so we walked straight to the registration counter. This was a big hall-like room, with desks specifying various designations of different class officers placed all over the room. Behind the desks were aluminium racks stacked with files. A fire in here and all the documents of land ownership would be gone. Why don't they start using computers, I thought, smiling artificially at the man behind the registration desk.

This man, a second class officer, screened the papers. He was chewing on paan, and even as I stood with Aunty by my side, he had spat on the floor, splashing the wall by his side. Wiping his mouth with one hand, he had placed Aunty's papers on his table and stared, a keen, speculative stare at us. Then he had pushed the papers back.

'Nothing can be done to this land,' he had said leaning back in his chair and holding both his hands together in front of his face.

'Subba saab, don't say that, we know, you can handle this,' I had said bending over his table. 'If there are extra expenditures to be met, we are ready to cover that also.' I had nearly whispered, hoping that his refusal to register my aunt's application papers was only an informal way to ask for some bribe.

He had glared back at me through his glasses that were nearly falling off his nose and growled back. 'Your papers are not complete.'

'But Subba saab...' I had begun to say that we had made these papers through a lawyer and all the neccessary documents – my aunt's citizenship, the transfer of the land in her name from her dead husband's name, the lalpurja of the land – were in there. But he interrupted me with a wave of his hand and called the next person waiting in line.

I had feared this even before coming here, but had wanted to give it a try and had known all along that it would be difficult to sell land that belonged to my family. The subba knew that once the news got to the controlling Maoist cadres back in Ganeshpur, he would be targetted by them.

We had walked back in silence and taken a rickshaw home. Aunty did not speak for a long time. It was not in Aunty's nature to keep silent for very long. But now, she was staring ahead, lost in her own thoughts.

Later that evening, after dinner I had brought up the topic again. 'Aunty...I think, we should wait a few months. Things will not always be the same. These are terrorists, killing people, kidnapping, extorting money, confiscating lands...it's so bloody insane, and if our government is going to watch and do jackshit about it, the international community is not going to keep shut for a long time. America has taken a firm stance and labelled them as terrorists. Since the 9/11 attack, India too is showing their support; I believe they are giving weapons and helicopters to the security forces to fight the Maoists. And China has clearly disowned them.'

My words seem to give Aunty little hope. She had other problems, financial mostly, since she had divorced her husband and moved away from the family.

The base of the Singh family pride had then shook for the first time. Although the tremors were light and did very little damage, the initial days after that night when Aunty decided not to return home, having quietly slipped out in her tattered blouse and a stained petticoat around her waist, shocked the entire family. There were phone calls to relatives, my father must have visited all the emergency departments of all the hospitals in Kathmandu and had come back home, his head bobbing up and down as though it were attached to a spring.

Indeed it was a shocking affair. Thulubua thrashing Aunty black and blue was nothing extraordinary. He had once beaten her throughout the night. Thinking her dead, at the break of dawn, he asked my father to dump her lifeless body somewhere. My father had driven round the entire town, with his brother's wife unconscious at the back of the car, wondering how to get his brother out of that situation. She had stirred in the back seat, and moaned, and that had saved my father from becoming an accomplice in a murder.

Aunty always came back. Sometimes she took temporary asylum with relatives, her brother mostly, but she returned, smiling as though the battering had never taken place. I remember as a child, sitting outside Aunty's room and hearing her stifled cries alongwith loud curses from Thulubua. I would wonder why no one did anything. Others, the elders, would pass the bolted door and sometimes even press their ears to the door when there was silence, but move away as soon as they heard Aunty's painful cries. I guess her cries from inside was a reassurance in a way, telling the rest of the family that he had not killed her yet.

There was a time when my mother had woken up my father in the middle of the night. 'He has gone too far this time. He will kill her tonight. You must intervene.' My father had just turned over and put the pillow over his head and tried to go back to sleep. My Aunty's agonizing calls for help were heart-wrenching and with each bang and thud that came from inside that room, I flinched. I stared at the ceiling trying to think of other things, good thoughts and drifted off to sleep dreaming that Aunty had died and gone to heaven and she was smiling, her pretty face shining the most amongst the stars. She seemed so happy there, twinkling in her state of peace.

At times, Aunty managed to run away during her thrashing sessions. She would hide in the fields and Thulubua would roar like a mad bull and sway his big frame, smelling of alcohol and invade our rooms. He would kick things around, throw things around, stutter and mutter nonsensical words and leave the house. My father followed him around, entire nights as his brother went into the village, screaming shouting, destroying anything that came in his way. I have this hazy memory of my uncle swaying in the dark with a huge mashal that flared its bright light in the night, going into the fields in search of his wife and, not finding her there, setting the entire field of rice on fire.

The aftermath is clear and distinct in my mind. My father standing on the terrace, his head bobbing up and down and screaming orders to the servants, the servants running out with buckets of water, the dogs barking around Jijumua, Jijumua standing in the middle of the courtyard quiet, looking concerned and very angry, and my mother rushing with blankets and a paraffin lamp on her way to sneak the other two wives of my uncle out of the house, just in case he returned to direct all his anger on these two.

A bullock cart had been made ready at Teen Gharua. That night the elder two wives of my uncle were smuggled out of the village. I had stood by mother, clinging on to her waist and crying. 'Ma . . . why does Thulubua become an animal at nights?' I had asked my mother as we slowly walked back home through the fields.

'It is because all men are animals. It is up to us women to domesticate them and turn them into sensible and considerate human beings. With your Thulubua it is a no-win cause. He is an animal and no one can do anything about it, not even his three wives.' This was said with so much contempt and dislike that for me, then an infant, it was clear that my mother did not like my uncle very much. Later on with age and wisdom I understood why. My father, her husband, was completely dominated by his elder brother. I had heard my parents quarrel.

'Raja, your children are grown up, it is time we separated from your brother. He is selling off all the common land and spending it on his drinking, womanising, and his so-called politics which seems to be getting him nowhere anyway,' I had heard her say.

'Not again, Dhana,' my father had replied, 'You know, I cannot ask for that, unless Muajiu or Dai himself suggests it. Besides, he is my elder brother, my sibling, my blood and flesh and it is to him that I owe my upbringing. I am what I am for him.'

'Oh! Stop saddling yourself with his benevolence. He did what he had to do. He has given you nothing that is not yours. If he educated you it was with the money that belonged to you too. If he bought you clothes, that too was with your share of the money. He got you married with your share of the money. And in return he has taken enough from you. Have you not quit your government job and come down here to take care of the farms at his behest, while he stays in Kathmandu pretending to be a big politician there and squanders all your hard-earned money from here? You have to start thinking of your own increasing expenditures now; your son will soon go to college, your daughter needs to be married off some day. We have to start getting her silver and gold ready. Not that you don't have that already, but I bet you will not claim that from your mother and brother and we will end up buying the required gold and silver for our children's wedding from our income.'

'We will discuss this sometime later. Now is not a good time.' My father always ended my mother's bickering like this.

But that night in Kathmandu, Aunty never returned and a few days later, my grandmother got a telephone call from Aunty's brother saying she was going to be living separately from her husband from that day and he hoped that the family would understand and support her decision.

'If she wants to leave, what can we do? We understand that she had suffered a lot but one does not leave ones husband for that.

What a shame! Deplorable shame!' My Jijumua had assembled her
entire family around her and most of us were there in Kathmandu
as Thulubua was then the Home Minister and had also made a
huge house for himself that could accommodate us all. Besides, it
was the beginning of precarious times back home. The grassroot
were just awakening to the knowledge of a democracy that defied
autocracy and the dominance of families such as mine. Feeling safer
in Thulubua's police guarded house, my family had chosen to stay
away from the insulting slogans and parades of a new Nepal all
around our village that were getting bolder by the day.

'To be a woman is not easy. Have we all not had our own share
of troubles? Life is all about troubles, yet you do not run away from
life because there are troubles. You face it, after all, endurance is
the other name for a woman. Which woman leaves her home and
husband and walks away? What will society have to say for this
scandalous behaviour? What answer am I to give my own gods...my
son is not dead yet and his wife wants to live the life of a widow?
What blasphemy are you showing me lord?'

While the rest chose to keep quiet, I had looked at my brother
who was sitting in his corner trying not to laugh. I had thrown a
naughty smile back at him. He had turned his face away, knowing
I always got him into trouble. I had shifted restlessly; I wanted to
run out onto the terrace where my kite waited to compete with the
neighbour's son. I tried to catch Dada's attention so that he would
come along, but as always, he had chosen to be the good boy, the
obedient successor of the Singh family traditions. As I slipped away,
I heard my father saying, 'Muajiu, Kanchi Bhauju has decided to
stay away for a reason. But we cannot let the world know that she
has left us for good. Probably she will come back, for it is not easy
for a woman to live outside by herself. People are sure to talk, but
we must make certain that she is welcome whenever she wants to
return.'

Aunty remained a part of our family, joining us during festivals and on religious occasions; she even fasted on Teej, dressed in red and proudly displaying her tilahari and pote but she never returned to her husband's bed and continued to live on her own. And people did talk, the world gave her ugly names. People kept wondering what she did for an income. Yet all these years Aunty has smiled her way through, never letting a hint of her disappointments from life appear on her pretty face.

I watched her now. Aunty was suddenly looking old and resigned and looking at her, something in me died.

'Aunty, wait till Dashain. Every one is in a festive mood then. We will go down to the village and talk directly to the janasarkar there. I know a boy who is with the commandoes there, we can ask him for some help. Everything will be fine, Aunty. Look at Bua; he is having the same problem, he cannot sell his land and he's got his wife, Dada's wife, Dada's daughter to fend for at this old age. What can he do, nothing but wait and hope.'

'Then you do something for your old father and dead brother's family. Get married to a rich man and take care of your family.'

It was clear that it was her anger with her own helplessness that was the reason behind her outburst, but her words managed to pinch my conscience.

My concern for my aging parents, living in exile in Kathmandu with no source of income was beginning to haunt me. It was guilt, I guess, guilt of abandoning them when they have no one else to lean on; yet I cannot see myself fitting into their dreams...I never have.

I left the kitchen without saying a word and the next morning Aunty had returned to her bubbly façade again.

'Aunty...I think we should make a trip to Ganeshpur once.'

Suddenly everything seems light, weightless around me. A cuckoo flies and nestles in the shifting branches of my landlords jack fruit tree. I see Aunty sitting on the stairs, her food half-eaten on her plate, staring at the tree with the same delight as it is bringing to me. The sky is blue, speckless and the fields stand out bold, brazen, proudly displaying the harvest piled here and there. The thought of my village, my home, my own fields, brings a smile on my face, and I can see Aunty smiling at my smile. Then we laugh together, for the sheer joy of life.

Before we can change our plans, the two of us are on a bus to Ganeshpur. The bus is packed, brimming with people nearly hanging out the window and through the open door. There are as many sitting inside as on the roof of the bus. And I am one of them. I could not bear the smell of sweat and fart, noise of babies crying, women jabbering and lecherous looks of men. Here, it is better, with fresh air and the open skies to look upon.

The bus stops every ten minutes dropping off and reloading new passengers at each village that crops up on the way. At the Khutiya river the bus refuses to move. The engine goes kaput in the middle of the slow-flowing current. There is a slight commotion. Men around me begin to jump down and push the bus forward. All passengers are made to get off the bus and we cross the river, women holding up their sarees, men with pants folded up to the thighs, children giggling and parents running behind to bring back their playing children some.

Finally the bus begins to roll with a stuttering sound, leaving behind the men pushing it. We board the bus again and move ahead. Chaumala comes and goes, then Mussooria, and then starts the dense thicket, once a dense jungle with long dune like curves for a road. Finally we are in Pahalmanpur. Here we get off. Pahalmanpur is on its way to slowly but gradually and eventually becoming a little town. There are electric poles on the sides of the road and in the fields are sprouting up tiny-one and two-bedroom brick houses with TV antennnas proudly displayed on the roofs. At the crossroad where the bus has left us there seems to be a total makeover since Dada's days, when he came here in his fit of depression and got himself drunk.

Dada had taken to drinking in his last years. But his drinking sprees were different than Thulubua's, where as Thulubua's drinking created a spontaneous terror all around him, Dada's made everyone to worry about him alone. Why was he drinking? Was he fine? Has he eaten? What is pushing him to this destruction of body and mind? He drank to drown his frustrations from life. I had dragged him many times from the bhattis in Pahalmanpur as he swayed, his body lunging forward and back as though his feet had suddenly developed palsy and were unable to hold the weight of his body.

Dada smiled when he was drunk; a sheepish smile as though he were vaguely conscious of his uselessness. Even in the most drunken state Dada never became violent. He laughed always as though he were mocking life itself. He had strange ways, my brother, and all of us failed to understand him.

Aunty and I now run behind a bullock cart that is going down the pitched road and into the rough track that slips into the jungles. It is headed towards my village. I ask for a ride and jump onto the moving cart, giving my Aunt my hand to climb up.

The man behind the bullocks does not care that we have forced ourselves on him. He is a bit shy, though, and speaks without looking at us.

Aunty asks him in his language about the situation of the terrorists in the village. 'They are there always...bossing around and bullying. Local boys join them only to feel the power that comes with being associated with the red commandoes. They don't care and even know what they are doing, but little-little boys are ready to take up arms, leave their homes and go into the jungle, only to feel brave and come back home and feel great.'

'Why have you not joined them,' Aunty asks.

'Who will feed my family if I go into the jungles? Besides, it is dangerous being a red commando. Any day you might get killed. They say now if the peace talks fail between the sarkar and the Maoists, the army will finish these terrorists.'

He might as well have been speaking to himself for his words were soft and barely audible and not once does he look back. 'It is difficult as it is,' he continues talking as he whips the lash in hand gently on one of the bullocks, tugging at the same time at the reins, steering the animal towards the right, where we are headed. 'The Maobadis come in one day. Force themselves on us, eat our food and take away our rations sometimes, pointing their guns at us and the next day, the police come in and beat us up calling us traitors and even asking, who came? How many came and what did they look like? Where did they go? What did they say? We are squashed in between and honestly if you ask me now we don't care who wins this war but only hope for the war to end. What do we have to lose and gain anyway? We only want go on with our lives and earn a comfortable two meals a day.'

'Yes... you are right. We all want this war to end now,' Aunty is saying to him. She is now sitting right behind him at the front as the weight of us both at the back was pushing the cart down.

We have crossed the Shivganga that has come flowing down all the way, sidetracking my village. And I can begin to feel my heart beat in excitement. I am getting closer to meeting Chandra. And as we pass the scarecrows standing in the middle of the fields, I smile back.

I feel the same excitement that I felt as a child returning home for holidays after nine months in boarding school. It is now six months since I was here last, alone, despondent and feeling totally alienated from my homeland and its people. But today, I feel different. There is a thrill of meeting Chandra and this thrill brings back in a strange way my attachment to my village.

I stand up on the cart, holding onto its sides, and look ahead. The entire flat land of Ganeshpur, encircled with two tributaries of the Shivganga on two sides, sprawled in a happy assortment of clusters of huts, fields, groves of trees and in the distant end, the curve of the foothills beginning to grow.

'This is my home...' I say to myself. 'This is where I belong.'

Dogs are running by the cart, barking: I see a flock of parrots take off from a cluster of seesam trees on the side of the road, children half-naked begin to jump on to the cart and the owner of the cart for the first time turns around and whips his lash, threatening the children. The angry glare in his eyes seems nice to me, the laughter of the children seems nice to me, the wind blowing the dust from the road and powdering our faces nearly white seems nice to me and even the faces peering from different courtyards as we pass seem nice to me. I can feel myself blend in this time.

We get off at Badki's house and I thank the man for giving us a ride. Although I wish to pay, I know that it will hurt his pride. Instead, Aunty passes the little tiffin with puris and vegetables to him. He takes it happily and we walk into Badki's courtyard.

Badki has red chillies spread out on a cot to dry and is sitting by her verandah, grinding something with a pestle. Her two grandchildren are sitting by her, naked waist upwards, with snot trailing down their noses and nearly slipping into their mouths. Flies buzz around them. Badki's head is bent down, her hands moving rhythmically as one thrusts the pestle into the mortar and the other removes and refills its contents. Her eyes are fixed with total concentration on her occupation. She does not notice us walking towards her.

'Badki...' She looks up hearing her name called out.

'Nepalni Hajoor...' She has recognised Aunty and, leaving her pestle tilted inside the mortar she comes running to us. Aunty got the title Nepalni Hajoor as she belonged to Kathmandu. Thulubua's eldest wife was addressed by the Tharu staff and the others of the village as Badki Hajoor or Thuli Rani saheb by the paharis, and the second wife as the Manjhli Hajoor but since the Kanchi Hajoor title was already taken by my mother, when Aunty moved into the family, people called her Nepalni Hajoor, from distant land of Nepal. Later it came to my understanding that for these people in the far west, Nepal was Kathmandu, where life was, where all the glories and whence came the lovely stories.

I remember, as a child Aunty seemed a fantasy to us all. The way she dressed, the way she laughed, her laughter ringing as would a sweet symphony echoing in the air till much after, were all different than ours we all thought. She was a constant object of curiosity: she was so full of life and laughter. But it was her accent that clearly demarcated her from the rest of us; we spoke Nepali in the Madhesi accent, our diction slightly different than hers. She would laugh and make jokes of our ways at first and we all felt stupid and ignorant in front of her, for she was the one who came from Nepal, the land of fairy tales.

Later as we sit in the evening on the cots layed out for the two of us, I ask Badki about the whereabouts of the controlling Maobadis of the area.

'They do not stay in one place more than a night, Maiya.' Badki tells me, stirring the fish broth which she has insisted she must make for us, her guests. Aunty is sprawled on her cot, a thin sheet covering her body but both her feet sticking out from the two sides of the sheet. She is tired from the day's travel.

Badki is cooking the broth in her special aluminium pot, which is testing on a small iron tripod with wood burning slowly underneath. She wipes her eyes that are streaming with tears due to the sting of the smoke. 'Last I heard of them was through Bhalmansa. He had met them one night while returning from his daughter's place in Janakpur. They were camped in the jungles of Madhakunti.'

I am rubbing some mosquito repellent ointment onto my arms; although it will soon be winter, the last of the mosquitoes are still around.

'Aunty, you rub some, too' I pass the tube of Odomos to Aunty who takes it reluctantly. 'Oh! I have spent many summers here, in the village, out in the fields, by the river, in the jungles everywhere without any mosquito repellent and my body has done just fine.'

But she rubs the ointment on her arms and neck anyway. 'Aunty these are different mosquitoes than the ones in those days. These have evolved, they are mosquitoes of a new Nepal, these go slow but the sting is more piercing and the itch will remain longer and perhaps even leave a mark on your skin.'

I laugh to my own silly connotation and then remember that Badki was telling me of the whereabouts of the PLA in the area. 'Yes, Badki, go on...' I say, picking up the glass filled with Badki's homemade fermented rice alcohol and taking a sip.

'Not too bitter not too sweet, no Maiya? My jaanr is the best in Ganeshpur,' Badki chuckles and grins. 'They gave jaanr that night to Bhalmansa. He was treated with respect as a visitor because of Kallu. And Bhalmansa says they danced and sang the entire night.'

I could imagine Chandra standing aloof from the singing and dancing crowd, perhaps sitting alone on the edge of the fields and thinking. His deep thoughtful eyes, probing into the darkness of the night as his mind reaped thoughts of where his life was headed. Perhaps he even thought of me.

'Is there a way that I can go meet them Badki? Maybe you could send a word to Kallu and perhaps he could arrange for a meeting with their area commander?'

'Let me see, Maiya...' Now Badki's eyes have become curious. 'I will talk to some old men in the village tomorrow and find out if anyone knows where they are and I will send my someone to fetch Kallu for you, Maiya.'

When Kallu comes the next day, I am sitting by the ponds on our property. They are dry, with not a drop of water in them. They are now big gashes on the land. Deep craters that hold nothing but caking mud. I have been here the entire afternoon, walking around and thinking and the more I think, the more I know that this where I belong and this where I want to be the most. For this is my home, these fields, the crumbling house, the ponds... and here is where I decide that, come what may, I will make this place alive again.

I will renovate the house, I will fill up the ponds, they will have fish in them once more; the kitchen garden will bloom once again; the stables will be full with cows; and this time I will start a poultry. Dhangadi town is bustling with people, all refugees who have come from the hills and the neighbouring villages and there has to be a bigger market for eggs and chicken there. I shall cultivate vegetables and sell them in the Dhangadi market. I could involve the entire village and make it a community project...

I was dreaming again... but this time my dream seems real. I do not hear Kallu come up to me. 'Maiya...' The sound of my name jerks me out of my thoughts.

He is a smiling Kallu, wearing jeans and t-shirt and a peak cap, he looks different this time. As his name suggests, Kallu is dark and has become darker, I think, walking to him and embracing him. Kallu steps back with a shy smile on his face and looks down at his feet and begins to scuff the earth.

'Oh Kallu, you look so different.' My hands gripping his elbows, I begin to jump with sheer joy. 'You have become a man, a thinner but handsome man.' I move back and assess him from head to toe. Kallu is wearing shoes. As children, I was the only one with shoes amongst my playmates and Kallu with the other children ran around bare foot regardless of weather or terrain.

'But you are just the same Maiya,' he says, smiling and still shy. 'Only more beautiful.'

'Oh Kallu, you really have not changed! Let's walk back to the village together. We have so much to talk about, so much to exchange.'

I convince Kallu to take me to his squad leader. Kallu had initially hesitated. 'Maiya, he is not like us. He can be rude and very aggressive and you may not like it.'

'I don't care, Kallu, for I have been insulted enough already. I now lie grovelling in the dirtiest mud, there is nothing now to feel lower than this. If I have to go anywhere from here, it is surely upwards and higher.' I smiled and patted his hands in reassurance.

I am offered a chair this time and a steaming glass of tea is brought to me. I sip my tea as others around stare at me in silence, coughing and shuffling their feet in the earth.

I am a marvel to them, a puzzling phenomenon of acute curiosity. Each one stares at me as though studying an extraterrestrial being.

I tell them Aunty's problem. 'She is alone, with no other source of income. She could start some occupation if she were allowed to sell her lands here in Gairakhera.'

I seem to be begging but that does not make me falter. 'I don't care I have no fear, I have no shame,' I silently tell myself as my eyes wander around in search of Chandra. And then I find him. He is resting against a sturdy tree right in front of me. He is in his warring gear, the camouflaged uniform of the Maoists, and is sharpening the blade of his khukuri against a stone slab at his feet. At once I am filled with hatred again. I can feel it rise from within me as a giant surge, pinching, tugging, pulling, making me susceptible to my own self. It is as if I can feel, understand each molecule that makes me. It is in him too, I know... this hatred, this loathing. I can see it in his eyes, in the stiff muscles of his arms, the curve of his back. I am convinced that we are connected, attracted and bonded by this very hatred and yet, strange as is everything around me, I feel secure, safe in the midst of the enemy.

Although we have not acknowledged each other yet, watching him I feel safe in the midst of this jungle and the gun-toting Maoist cadres walking around me. I could be shot or even hacked to pieces and no one would know.

'Your Aunt's lands cannot be returned as all the lands confiscated by the Peoples Liberation Army have been seized for a just cause. They will be worked upon as a community by all, the produce of which shall be shared equally by all.'

This man speaking to me is firm in his mind. He looks it, stern and non-condescending. 'But since you have made such an effort and come down all this way, your request, if submitted in writing to the Jana Adalat, could be considered.'

I could hardly believe my ears, but he has just said, could be considered. This was certainly a frist.

'Dhanyabad, comrade, and lal salaam,' I said, standing up from my rickety chair and walking towards him so that I could shake hands with him. But I am stopped. Immediately surrounded by boys and girls, looking at me with threatening eyes and pointing their guns menacingly at me.

'I was only going to shake hands with him.' I explain and at the far end, I hear Chandra laugh. He walks closer and tells his gunmen to disperse.

'It is a policy of war that no outsider can be totally trusted,' he begins to explain. His words fall on me as soft showers after a long dry summer. 'Come let's walk,' he says.

We pass the cooking area. I can see little boys peeling and cutting vegetables around a makeshift oven. 'Stay for dinner and I will drop you back at dawn tomorrow,' he says not looking at me but straight ahead.

We sit by a little stream and watch the soft waters swiftly gurgle by. He is throwing pebbles into the water and I touch his arm. He places his hands on mine and for the longest time we sit staring at the water flow, an incessant stretch of tranquil and calm.

By dinner time, everyone in this platoon knows me by name and has even understood that I am an intimate of their platoon commander, and although they are still sceptical regarding my spending the night at their camp, they seem to have developed a tolerance for me.

'It is eleven years now since the panchayat system was ended and constitutional monarchical multi-party parliamentary system established. During this period, state control has shuffled hands between a tripartite government, a single-party government of the Nepali Congress, as minority government of the UML, a Nepali Congress and Sadhbhavana coalition. The trend seems endless, Sanjeevani. But instead of making progress the country seems to have gone further downhill. The gap between the rich and the poor and towns and villages has become increasingly wider.'

His head was inclined and his face touching mine from one side; on his other cheek I could feel the warmth from the burning fire around which we sit.

'Our war is not with the people, Sanjeevani, but against a system that has failed and refuses to resign. It is also an awakening call to all Nepalese people to realise the mistakes that have been made and to make amendments now.'

'You are certain that your leaders who make big promises to you will not let you down once they have accomplished their own design?' I ask.

'This people's war may be led by a few, may be initiated by others but I have joined in with a sincere belief of my own. I have left my family behind, my old parents who can barely walk to the water source to fend for themselves. I know I have endangered their lives by leaving them alone, where they can be tortured by the security forces as I scour jungle after jungle. Yet, Sanjeevani, the calling is from deep within. I could have chosen to stay back like the others or run away to Kathmandu or even India, but would my conscience then be free? At least now I feel satisfied that even if I die, I will die for a cause that held sincere promises to me.'

His smile is divine and his words begin to drill into me. I fight back, I can feel the resilience, the need to shrug off his optimism, his patriotism for his cause, as useless and baseless but it is there, staring back at me. Indignantly. Instinctively my hands reach out to touch him, to feel his skin again and he is there; a real, tangible inspiration.

'And must you terrorise, torture, kidnap and kill non-communists?' I whisper knowing the others watch us with a fusion of emotions.

'Class struggle led by revolutionary communists is not aimed at eliminating non-communists as you say, Sanjeevani, but instead the aim is to be rid of feudalism and bureaucratic capitalism. Now that you are here in the remotes, does it not strike you, the disparity, the unfairness of it all. A man tills his land, sweating in the heat of the sun and gets barely enough to eat at the end of the day and a man drives to office in a Mercedes Benz, sits in a revolving chair in his air conditioned office and has much more than he needs?'

'That is something no one can answer, Chandra. No one, not even God himself. Even in America, that is the biggest democracy in the world, there is a disparity between the rich and the poor. Capture of power through an armed class struggle...don't you think, Chandra, that this is just a far-fetched dream?'

There is a desperate urge for me to get my point through, to get him to fathom my reasoning as clearly as I do his. But I falter and fail.

He is smiling now and it is a benign smile, one that a father would have for his five-year-old child trying to understand his father's motives.

'Each revolution is a dream before it is made, Sanjeevani. Think of the French revolution, the Chinese revolution or even the

Bolshevik revolution. Were they not all tall claims and just dreams before they were actually realised? I am firm in my conviction, for I believe in the science of Marxism-Leninism-Maoism and the one thing I remain convinced about is that a class-divided society cannot last forever and, some day or the other, a fair and an equal, class-less society has to emerge for humanity to sustain on this planet.'

There is sincere belief in each word that he has spoken and there is a strong urge in me to make him falter as do I, to make him shake.

'You Maoists are under a fake belief that you are on the right track only because the preceding governments have failed to deliver. That normally is the case in juvenile democracies, we learn from our mistakes. But this failure of the past governments, you Maoist have taken personally, and made yourself seem all the more self-righteous and vociferous. What you have forgotten are the basics of Mao's directions, which clearly implied that the revolutionary leadership should wait patiently until the people are ready for action. Until then they should mobilise their forces in educating the masses, instilling them with notions of right and wrong and give them to understand the notion and finally accept the revolution as their own. This, Chandra, as far as I know, was Mao's famous, mass line...and without heeding this sentiment, I clearly see your people's war degenerating into a war without the people.'

I can see he is shaken but not in the way that I would want him to be. My words have excited him to defend his cause with an added ardour.

'You have it wrong, Sanjeevani,' he says, leaning towards me, and I gloat over the twinkle in his eyes and the vigour in his voice, owing all that to myself. 'Mao's theory clearly states that the process of a protracted people's war is also a process of training the masses to run a society in a different manner, to ideologically and politically transform the masses and society prior to capturing nationwide power and the building of a new socialist society. There, you are right. But what you don't understand maybe because you do not know that we have also taken up the classic Chinese three magic weapons – Party, Army and the United Front. Whereas the Party stimulates the masses with its ideologies, the Army engages itself against the opposing enemies and the United Front maintains a diplomatic stance with a view to creating the requirement for the cause. Now you see, Sanjeevani, how we function? We have not given up Mao's theory but we have imbibed some of our own and from others too in the course of this war.'

Here he stops advocating his cause, and bends down to place a few more logs into the fire. I watch him, half-interested, half-amused and strangely stimulated.

'I will quote Comrade Mao as he said we had nothing at first. We had millet so we ate millet. We got some rifles so we began to use them and we began to capture but then we did not know what to hit and what not to hit. It shows clearly that the Chinese revolutionist were learning as they moved along. So are we.'

I cannot pull back the sigh that escapes me. 'But Chandra,' I say, 'How can you feel good about yourself after having killed, after maiming another human being, torturing your own species? All this bloodshed, this cruelty does not go down well with me.'

'Are we left with a choice, Sanjeevani?' Now his eyes are flaring. I can see that his conviction, that led him in the first instance to end another life, is beginning to take him over. His face tightens and I can clearly see the muscles on his neck, the veins become darker and blood in them flow in great speed to his furious brain. But then as quickly as it came, his defence begins to soften.

'Comrade Mao also clearly stated that cleansing of a society is necessary. Destruction is necessary before construction. Unlike what people think about war, that it is dirty and destructive. What people like you need to understand, Sanjeevani, is that war in itself is a great process of construction. And you see, once this war is ended, it will definitely have a sweeping cleansing effect.' He stops to take a breath and a long silence follows. We stare at the flames from the fire rise in waves, heaving up and down. 'I have killed, Sanjeevani, I have sliced throats, hacked limbs.' He is staring, a vacant void now created on his face. There is a thin layer that has come over his eyes, a shield as it were for veiling his feelings. 'But I tell myself that it is cleansing. If I have killed I will create some day. I want to create life, Sanjeevani, life that breathes and lives and laughs and sings.'

Chandra begins to laugh, a soft laughter. 'That is my dream, my fantasy.'

Time has lapsed beyond our understanding and we are left alone by the dying fire. The rest have retired for the night. I can see shadows of the night guards on duty move in the thickets. There is an owl perched on the tree right in front of us and it watches us tilting its head to each side as though perplexed by our teaming.

I laugh along with Chandra but actually I laugh at myself, 'Even I don't understand what is happening,' I want to say to the curious owl. This man is a hard core revolutionist and people of his mindframe have killed my brother and displaced my family and would, given the first chance, hack my father to pieces. And yet I am sitting in the midst of this jungle where I was brought blindfolded, reasoning out philosophies of twisted idealism. But what strikes me more is my yearning for him. This deeper call from within that wants to grab him, tear off his clothes and blend his naked skin with mine. Bone to bone, skin to skin, breath by breath I want us to merge, the hatred inside both of us to merge and become one. I stop reasoning to myself, for my senses seem to be shadowed by this overwhelming desire, the desperate urge to flee from my own self into the firm conviction that is Chandra.

'Oh I have been going on talking for too long, you must be tired?' I like the concern for myself in his words. I smile. 'Not really.'

'My tent is over there behind the trees. If you want, you could share it for the night.' He says sheepishly, beginning to stand up in his state of edginess.

I grab hold of his hands and place my lips on them. He moves closer and I bury my face into his stomach and he holds me still there, his hands gently caressing the back of my head. 'Chandra...' I look up and his fingers begin to travel all over my face as though in search of something. He finds my lips and he wets his fingers in my mouth and then he is down, kneeling on the floor and holding my face right in front of his own, he whispers 'Sanjeevani... I want you. Since I met you first, I seem to be challenging myself. Daring myself to take yet another step forward towards you...tell me Sanjeevani... what is this between us?' I can feel his breath, hot and consuming over my face, my neck and slipping down in a stream of moist sweat down between my breasts.

'Everything is going to be fine... I need to get over Razat... Razat for me does not exist...everything is going to be fine...'

There is an urgent need to flee, to run and keep running until the voices in me fade. Instead, I lift my face, shut my eyes and bind my lips to Chandra's quivering ones...indeed, this is a moment of complete harmony, if not bliss of two contradictory minds.

Sanat

Prabhat is in love...or so he thinks. His eyes, surreptitiously and with much longing, in follow Badki walk in with the other Kamlaharis. She is different – her walk, talk, even the way she carries the water pot on her head, the manner in which she squats on the ground, her slender fingers plastering the floors of the house with cow dung, her slender back, exposed and bent over in the courtyard as she sweeps, the jerk of her head and neck as she sits in the granary sifting grains of rice...everything about Badki is different. That's what Prabhat thinks, ensnared with a longing that is nearly devotional.

That afternoon, while Dangwa is off herding the cows in the nearby Badka Banua jungles, Prabhat sneaks into his house. Badki sits by the fire, her eyes red from the smoke from the hearth that has clogged the room like a thick, blinding curtain. Bent over the fire, Badki blows into it, her hands rubbing her eyes that are stinging from the smoke. She has a white wrap-around that flows from her waist to her knees and another white cloth that has been tied around her chest. Her thick black hair has been tied into a knot at the back of her head with a slender stick pierced through it to hold it in place.

Prabhat creeps in from behind and grabs hold of Badki, making her scream aloud in a startled alarm. She is small and tiny but voluptuous. Prabhat grabs hold of her full, rounded hips, drags her onto the cot by the corner of the room and pushes her onto the bundle of hay piled on it. Having recognised who he is now, Badki has stopped screaming but stares in speechless panic.

Clumsy in his juvenile attempt at lovemaking, Prabhat fumbles while grabbing, pinching, biting, and licking Badki's bare skin. As he continues, squeezing her ball-like breasts with shaking hands, trembling with a strange frenzy on exploring a completely new terrain, Badki, plastered between the cot and this obsessed young boy, begins to feel her own sexual passions being ignited.

She grabs hold of his hand and pushes it inside her skirt, guiding him to her fiery organ; with the other hand she helps him discover his own potent manliness.

That evening, Prabhat returns home in a drunken stupor, loud and echoing in the silence of the night.

Sanat stands with a wicker lamp in her hand, watching Laata and the Kothari drag his drunken body, limp and staggering, across the courtyard in their attempt to get him inside the house.

'I am in looooove...' he sings, his eyes droopy with intoxication and his voice slurring with the same effect.

Chanda is out of her room too. Startled and shaken, she stands by Sanat's side, watching her from the corner of her eye. She knows well that Sanat will not take this unruly behavior very well.

They drag Prabhat on to the verandah while he continues crooning, 'I am loooooove.' As he passes his mother, standing stiff and still, staring ahead with a pensive but determined look, Prabhat flings his drunken self on his mother. His mouth reeking with rancid smell of fermented rice, he hugs her as she stands still; not an expression betrays her unease.

'Muajiu, get me married. I want a bride and I want a white stallion to ride on and a garland around my neck and then, I shall go to Badki's house and bring her here as my wife. *Jhwaikuti,*

jhwaikuti jhwaikuti jhwaikuti jhwai.' His hands begin to beat in the air as though he were playing the madal. 'Give the paaji jaantha of her husband some land. Muajiu, give him some land, some cattle and I shall drink with him like a man and take away his wife. I am in looooove . . .'

Sanat has requested the palace secretary for a Darshan Bhet with his Majesty King Mahendra for her sons. Before their vacations are over and prior to their visit to the capital city, Sanat sends her Kothari to Baitadi and asks for the hand of her brother's wife's, brother's daughter in hand for marriage with her eldest son, Prabhat. The offer instantly agreed upon, the girl, still in her pre-pubescent age, is sent with considerable fanfare and a little convoy to her new home.

'I would rather have an ignorant girl from my own caste for a daughter-in-law than a black tharuni and wife of my cattle herder,' Chanda heard Sanat. Although Chanda had felt the need to remind Sanat that times had changed and that Prabhat was of a different generation and would probably want a wife to match his own caliber in the sense of education and grooming, she had kept shut, noticing the firm and resolute look on Sanat's face.

Durga was a small, thin and ordinary-looking woman, crouched and coiled into a bundle of distress and complete disarray. On the day of the wedding, the couple sat for tedious hours in front of the sacred fire with the family priests chanting holy verses and uniting Prabhat and Durga as man and wife. The same night, with not so much as even a flickering glance at his new bride, Prabhat wanders off towards the Teen Gharua.

Sitting on a wicker stool in Badki's courtyard, he gulps pots after pots of jaanr that Badki has made in celebration of her master's wedding. She has little caskets of mud installed all around her courtyard and in these she pours in mustard oil. Placing little cotton wickers in each, Badki lights her entire courtyard up. Taking two of these shimmering candles in her hands she begins to dance for her master as he sits drowning his reckless mind into pots and pots of jaanr.

'What good will it do your ugly shrivelled up face? This powder, this kajal, tika and laali? Throw it out! You don't need it!' Prabhat kicks his wife's silver vanity case as she sits with it open by her dresser, the cosmetics inside it clearly on display.

Durga is shaken by this rude and offensive behaviour. She looks at her husband, surprised and hurt at the same time, her tiny eyes instantly flooding with tears of gloom.

One night Prabhat enters their room, where Durga is spread out, unconscious in deep sleep. He begins to feel her body all over. Durga wakes up, alert and intimidated, and coils herself into a bundle of self-protection. He begins to enjoy this intimidation. He climbs on the bed and begins to poke her with his fingers, on her face, her neck, her breasts, her knees, her hands and in retaliation, the terrified girl hits him back, a gentle tap on his encroaching fingers.

'You hit me!' Prabhat roars. 'You have the audacity to strike at me! You good for nothing, ugly creature!' And then, smack! He sends her tiny form flying across the bed. Terrified, she begins to cry. Durga's helpless, vulnerable figure suddenly begins to excite Prabhat with a strange obsession and he stand over her, his tall legs spread apart above her, more like a towering bridge. Petrified, Durga covers her face with her hands and begins to sob.

'You know, you wretch, you have ruined my life. And I will make yours as miserable as you have made mine,' he says between her sobs as he forces her up and pushes her back on the bed. Lifting the ends of her sari, he pulls her feet apart. Frenzied with alcohol, he begins to force himself into her.

Prabhat begins to drink every evening. After dinner, he has his chair brought out on the verandah and sits with a cigar in his mouth. His eyes distant and aloof, he gulps glass after glass of whiskey and when that is not available, he makes do with the home brewed local jaanr brought in from Badki's house.

Sanat has understood that there is something amiss in the relationship between her son and his wife. She has been noticing Durga scuttling about as would a terrified mouse, her face covered with the ends of her sari, refusing to let go of her.

'Go to your husband now Durga, you have massaged my feet enough for today,' she tells her daughter-in-law – shy, timid and exceedingly obliging, bent over her feet, massaging them with her tender hands.

'Muajiu, can I not sleep with you instead?' Durga whispers, her face still covered with the ends of her sari the edges of which, she is beginning to bite in her state of nervousness.

'But why would you want to do that, my dear girl? Your place is with your husband and not with me. It is enough that you follow me around the entire day as though you were my shadow. But it is imperative that you go back to your husband at night. Or else my dear girl, he will bring in another woman.' Sanat tries to be jocular.

'I wish he would, Muajiu...bring in another wife.' This is said simply and very clearly although in a hushed tone and it jolts Sanat's reclining body. Putting down the hookah that once belonged to her husband and that she is now addicted to, she asks, 'Why in the name of God would you want your husband to bring another wife? Do you not like him, Durga? Is it because he drinks alcohol? But that my dear girl every man does. I guess it makes them feel more manly when they are intoxicated and wasted...'

'It is not that, Muajiu.' Durga is still bent over Sanat's legs; her hands still moving in a rhythmic manner, pressing and massaging. 'Raja does not like me. He does not find me pretty enough and I think he is right. I am not worthy enough for him.'

The same night, Sanat hears clear and loud noises coming from Prabhat's room. They begin with small rustles as though things were being thrown around, then turn into loud dashes of huge articles being smashed, tables and chairs being thrown, murmurs coming in from there begin to get louder and clearer...

'You whore! You slut! Spread open your legs!' Bang! It is as though a table is smashed and then another bang, followed by a loud painful cry from Durga. The bangs become louder and so do Durga's painful cries. Sanat cannot take it any more. She walks to Prabhat's door, adamant on putting an end to this cruel and heartless behaviour of her son that was becoming more of a nightly trend. She bangs on his door but the din of the chaos inside drowns the sound of her knockings. She goes up to the terrace where Prashant is sleeping out in the open with his step brothers. His cot is covered by a sagging mosquito net. He is awake listening to the noise coming from downstairs but pretends to sleep and squeezes his eyelids tight, sensing his mother standing by his side.

Sanat shakes him. 'Go down this minute and break open the door if you must, but I want Durga out of there right now.'

It is an order, a firm and a forceful command. Not that Prashant would not heed any of his mother's wishes; after all, he had always been a docile and compliant boy craving his mother's attention.

Prashant walks down, clearly disturbed at this predicament. There was his mother on one side and his brother on the other; offending any of the two was not to Prashant's liking. So, he stands brooding outside his brother's room. The screams and abuses along with the sounds of physical violence pervade clearly through the door. He slowly moves his body away from the door, making sure to keep distance and then charges into the door with all his force. The door falls open. Prashant charges back to the terrace. Covering himself with a sheet, he clenches his eyes shut, his heart wildly beating against his chest; he waits for the worst to occur.

When the boys get ready to leave for Kathmandu to meet the King, Sanat offers her special prayers and asks the family priests to determine the best day and hour for them to leave so as to avoid any obstacles on the way.

On the day fixed for their departure, Sanat garlands her sons with dubo and flowers, feeds them a spoonsful of curd and makes them bite into a piece of banana each.

'Remember,' she says, 'king Mahendra is a friend of your father. Someone whom your dead father backed in his dire days and with good cause and reason. After all, we are his subjects. He is a king now, having succeeded his father. Then he was only the Crown Prince but what is more important is your allegiance to the institution of monarchy, without which we Thakuris have no semblance of our own.'

In Kathmandu, the boys met the king who was duly impressed with the sons of his old acquaintance and who now stood before him pledging their honest allegiance. He could use them in the west. After all, he needed young blood. He needed young men who could be trusted to handle his political affairs. What better candidates than the offsprings of a ruling clan with a standing of their own in their region? 'For the forthcoming elections, I want you to stand as a candidate Prabhat, from Bajura the king said, smiling benevolently at Prabhat.

That winter, Sanat receives a letter from Prashant with an enclosed photograph of a girl, standing with books in her hands, in a long corridor of his college. The letter says:

My respects to you, Muajiu.

I am writing this letter hopeful that it reaches you in good health. I am well and am preparing for the final year examinations of the bachelors degree. You will be proud to know that I am prepared well and am determined to come up with good results.

I have received the draft of 1000 rupees that you had sent via post. Thank you very much for it and you will be pleased to know that

I have put it in good use, having paid off my room rent and my tuition fees for the month. I have also brought a pair of jeans and a new shirt.

Muajiu, do forgive me if you can for my insolence, but I have to admit that I have given my heart to this young lady who is two years junior to me in college. We have exchanged handkerchiefs and with it our hearts too. I feel that after my graduation and with your respectful blessings, the two of us should get married. I repeat, only if it is acceptable to you will I suggest this to her, or else I shall let this flame die out slowly but surely in my own heart.

I'm sure you must be wondering about her family and background. Anju is of our own caste belonging to the Chautaria family of Chisapani. Muajiu would probably know her family more than myself. I must state that she is educated and also pretty as you must have already seen in the photograph.

Do forgive me if my insolence has offended you, Muajiu, and do be assured that your son will not take any decision without your consent.

I end my letter here, my dear Muajiu, with all my love and respects. Hoping for an answer from your side soon.
Your obedient and loving son,

Prashant.

Sanat folds the letter and places the photograph on her table. She stares at it for a while, silently contemplating and then says aloud to herself, 'May have been just as well. She is pretty and seems to be a confident girl. Perhaps she will rub off some of her own confidence onto Prashant as well. He so needs to be convinced of his capabilities. She's his choice and comes from a respectable family. Why not? At least he won't thrash a wife of his own choice.'

Sanjeevani

Dhangadi is alive and elated. The streets are being swept, gutters cleaned, hedges trimmed, plants being planted on either sides of the roads, houses repainted from the outside, and people have even made new clothes for the occasion. Aunty had gone last week to the Indian border and brought for herself a new green sari. She coerced me to wear a yellow chiffon with light pink flowers on it. 'It's more your colour, Sanju,' she had said passing me the sari. I could see she was excited as is the rest of the town. Along with the many others, she too is hopeful that the king's visit will bring about a change, and in a miraculous way, put a balm on their sufferings. More than anything else, I think it is an assurance that all these people in the remotes are seeking...an assurance that they are not alone in this ordeal. The king's visit to Western Nepal has suddenly awoken this remote area into an ecstatic furore.

People are walking around with hope in their eyes. Thousands have swarmed into Dhangadi from all over the far western region. Dadeldhura, Baitadi, Mahendranagar and more from little villages that the king does not even know exist.

This is the second time the king of Nepal has visited Dhangadi since the early eighties. Then it was King Birendra who had flown down with Queen Aishwarya, and I remember, a wild boar had been flown in by a helicopter from my village to the Tegi, the local government bodies. I had watched the queen, sit in her dark glasses, her head held at a tilted angle, her delicate hands fanning her pretty face. King Birendra sat beside her, in an army uniform, smiling and gently nodding his head at people nearly crawling up the dais to greet him. They had seemed like larger than life figures to me, fabulous but fictitious. Sitting on the grand stand with an entire army garrison around them, they were indeed illusory . . . more like a far-fetched dream that makes one smile but cannot be touched or reached.

I kept staring at the people coming to greet the royal couple, hasty, shifty and more than anything – hopeful. From where I sat, they seemed like a long trail of ants to me, hobbling and shoving forward. Time and again, I had looked up at the king, wanting to read how he saw this endless trail of people. Whether he even noticed their excitement, and their curiosity.

I knew Kallu was amongst the crowd and had stood in the queue five times only to repeatedly look at the king. 'Maiya, it was unbelievable. He shines like the almighty and his smile is so divine,' he had said later, delighted at his good fortune. He seemed to be in a trance for the rest of the day.

Nearly two decades later, I stand in the same queue to receive another king, and Kallu is in some jungle, trudging along with a heavy weight on his back and fighting the army that the king has mobilised, to kill him and his like. I am restless and the April heat is hot and dry. Regardless, around me, where I stand with the prominent women of Western Nepal, journalists, women representing local NGOs and development bodies, the air buzzes with excitement. I can see women peering into their little hand mirrors to check whether their make-up is intact, settling their hair, and the folds of their saris. Some are even mumbling to themselves . . . probably rehearsing their words prepared for the king. I totally fail to share the same eager, thrill with the rest around me as I see my father sitting with the reception committee created for this occasion. He is excited and probably nervous too. But I am certain that deep within it all is a sense of pride, his lost pride soaring up again. He smiles as he shifts to one side and lends his ear to the chairman of the reception committee. The two of them then throw back their heads and laugh. There is a hint of the glory of the old days in him again, a suggestion of the same vanity...the feeling of being important, the pride of being one of the king's men.

It is not that I do not believe in the monarchy...that I do; how can I not? I am my father's daughter. I was born to believe in the king, loyalty to the king and the Crown. A Nepal without a king, I can see shattering and falling to pieces.

This is where Chandra and myself can never agree. 'Monarchy is the holding factor. Without it this country will break into countless ethnic pieces, Chandra. Newars, Tamangs, Bahuns, Chetris, Tharus, Paharis, Madhesis, Janjaatis; the king holds us all together as one Nepal and one people. He is the symbol of unity, Chandra. Can't you get that?'

'Monarchy is nothing but a symbol of autocracy for one class, the ruling class,' he had said, with sincerity and belief in his own words. 'As for holding the country together, that can be done without a king. Love for the country has to be promoted. With that a sense of patriotism and pride for one's nation will come along, and with that will come the sense of being one nation and one people. There is no need to sing praises of the king and base the entire national anthem on that.'

We argued more than we talked, never reaching any agreement. However, sometimes, while talking to Chandra, I get a feeling that I too am a bit inclined towards the Left. I am not as radical as Chandra, but I think I believe in a democracy with a social face, not an autocratic communist regime that Chandra and his lot are striving for. Yet, he talks about certain things, principles, and objectives of his Leftist theory that make sense to me.

Do I try to alter his views and his political opinions? I guess not. Come to think of it, I have learnt to love Chandra for who he is. I love him for his mind, and his dedication and diligence. Yet there is always an urge in me to agitate him, to rekindle his spirits rather, and when that is done, I rest and watch him – his eyes shining, his facial muscles taut, his deep voice defending his cause. Sometimes I marvel at his selflessness.

'Chandra, do you realise you may die, get killed?' I had said to him, standing naked, and wrapped around him from the back as he stood staring into the ceaseless flow of the Kandra. He was leaving that day for Mangalsen although I had not known that then. He had sent a word earlier, through Kallu, saying he would be leaving Kailali for some time and had expressed his wish to see me. Since a state of Emergency had been declared two months earlier, Chandra had been taking extra precautions while meeting me or contacting me. He was now a direct and an open enemy of the State. Since then three major attacks had been conducted by the Maoists, two in the west and one in the east, with strong counteractions from the Nepalese Army aided by the Armed Police Force and the Police Force. Besides the recent one in December in Bhakundebesi where they had attacked the Area Police Office, the previous two in the west aimed to gain control over the Telecom Security Camps in Ratmate and Kapurkot. These were serious failures for the Maoists with large casualties on their side. A chilly fear had swept through me, fear for Chandra's life, and I had rushed to Ganeshpur from Dhangadi the evening before.

We had camped alone, by the Kandra. It was early February and although the days were beginning to get warmer, the mornings and nights in the tarai were still chilly. We had lit a fire after dinner comprising rice, dal and some mutton curry that Kallu had brought down from the village. Kallu left after helping Chandra pitch a small two-man tent just above the river, where the beach ended and the thickets of the Badka Banua forest began.

Chandra had not spoken much the entire evening, but had stared at me, his eyes fixed tenaciously on me as I sat eating and talking with Kallu. I could make out that he was overtly quiet since I had arrived. He had appeared from behind the trees. He just walked up to me, took me into his arms, hugged me tight and kissed me all over my face. Later, watching him fiddle around with his food, looking uninterested, I was certain that Chandra was going for a major operation, yet again.

After Kallu left, I had straddled myself over Chandra's lap as he sat on a log by the fire. His hands had instantly clasped my waist in an embrace and he had buried his face into my chest.

For the longest time none of us spoke. He stayed there, his face buried between my breasts, his hands on my back, his fingers pressed into the depths of my skin. I had let him be, for I remained overwhelmed at my own drumming heart. His head in my clasp, I let my fingers carelessly caress his head.

I then spoke, my voice drifting out of my mouth and blending with the furore of the raging Kandra nearby. 'I don't know what I am doing here with you, Chandra. I have never stopped to think about the reasons. We are class enemies. My blood churns when I walk in the village and see terror imposed by your lot. Yet, I rush to you for solace... solace from my own warring phantoms?'

He had looked up then, his face aligned right below mine. 'Sanjeevani, my Sanjeevani booti, you are indeed my only healing ointment. With you all my bruises are healed, my soul is refreshed and my spirits rise to a stronger will.' He was smiling, his mouth open and his teeth revealed, perfectly placed giving an enhancing appeal to his smile. 'We feel the same pain, Sanjee... which is why we are together. There is a silent understanding between the two of us that reaches out to mine for you and yours for me.'

I could see the hatred in his eyes as clear as the loud beating of my heart 'There is so much poverty in this country, Sanjee. And the select privileged few continue to live in denial. They even hoard their excesses in foreign lands, while the rest of the country continues to suffer. I had a younger brother, Sanjee. He was small and very weak and his heart was weaker. I could do nothing to save him. I walked around Kathmandu, staring at lavish bungalows, fancy hotels, cars, people, shops... and the hordes of accessories available for the rich and only the rich. It disgusted me... provoked me. I had no money for a heart transplant operation, and so I let my little brother die. I left him staring at me in his helpless state from his hospital bed, and I ran. Since then, I have just been running. In a way, it is a slight reprieve having given myself to this war that will finally drill an opening for the poor and the needy.'

Chandra had cried then and watching him release his own pent-up devils, I wept too. I cried for Razat, I cried for Dada, I cried for my parents... I cried for a bewildered country, and I cried for myself...

The next morning, Chandra woke up when it was still dark. I had fumbled for him in the dark of the tent. Finding his side of the bed empty, I had walked out of the tent and found him standing naked, his back to the tent and me, and staring into the river.

Quietly, I had crept up to him and wrapped my naked self around him. My fingers clamped to his chest, I had whispered into his ear, 'Chandra, do you realise you may get killed?'

His hands had covered my trembling fingers on his bare chest. They were cold too and we stood there, skin to skin, shivering in the cold, and perhaps, in anticipation of the unknown.

Chandra turned around, took hold of my face in his hands and peering into my eyes, had said, 'And I will kill too, Sanjeevani. Taking someone else's life, putting an end to a train of continual breath... Am I scared, Sanjeevani? Am I hesitant, Sanjeevani? I think not and I wonder whether I am still a human. I must kill or get killed for my principles. But you will live on Sanjeevani, and you will get to see the new Nepal. My dream will be realised through your eyes, my dearest.'

Tears slipped down my cheeks, but I had not cared; the cold biting into my naked flesh seemed not to bother me anymore. It was as if the world had shrivelled and with it, I had too. We were nothing, our pains nothing, our sorrows were nothing; the only thing I saw was Chandra and his selflessness, his dedication and conviction to a cause for which he was ready to give his life. For what? For the likes of me and the rest... who did not know him, leave alone care when he died. His body would be collected by the army, perhaps. Perhaps, it would lie there in some field, headless and unclaimed, left to rot but who would care? No one. And he was ready to give his life for us, for our following generations? I wanted to laugh, throw back my head and laugh.

Trumpets are blaring, and with them a medley of drums. Finally King Gyanendra has arrived. I watch him walk up, his head aligned at an arrogant angle, and a smile – a haughty smile. He waves his hand and at times even reaches out to people behind the ropes as his security walk besides him, tense and pushing back the hysterical crowd.

'Daring,' someone says next to me. 'Very daring of him to come down at such a time and mingle with a massive crowd like this. Anything could happen... can happen. Who knows there could be Maobadi with a bomb or a gun in there with the jostling crowd.'

'Daring my ass! Ask me what daring is all about. People dare to wake up not knowing whether they will get to feed their children that day. People dare to walk days and weeks with their sick ones on their backs looking for a health post. Pregnant women working in the fields go into labour and deliver a baby right there as do women with cancer who pick up their fallen uterus and shove it right back in along with the pieces of grass, leaves and twigs stuck to their fallen organ and continue cutting the harvest. People turn off their lamps each night and close their eyes, knowing that an insurgent could walk in any time, kick him, beat him and even kill him for no real reason; and people go out to war, not knowing whether they will be alive to see the sun rise the next morning. That, dearie, is daring. Walking into a crowd, with security buzzing around you is hardly daring,' I wanted to retort, but forced myself not to.

Suddenly watching the king meant nothing to me; the monarchy meant nothing to me; the cheering populace around meant nothing to me; my father's pride, as he stood smiling with a bulky garland in his hands, his head bobbing up and down with his excitement, meant nothing to me. We had suddenly shrunk, the thousands of cheering people, the grand stand, the blaring music...everything shrunk to a tiny, insignificant size, and over it, seemed to loom large, my Chandra's courage, my Chandra's convictions and my Chandra's dream for a new Nepal.

'Poverty does not have to mean indignity, Sanjeevani.' I can hear his voice clear and loud in my ear through the blaring din of the medley of music being played from the corner of this open field that once was used as the landing place for the first planes and helicopters that came in the seventies from Kathmandu.

I look around. People are shoving, pushing, grabbing and nearly crawling at the feet of a man who holds the entire nation in his grasp. What do they want from him? What can he give them? Yet I can see lines after lines of faces, hopeful and wishful. Is this indignity – begging for hope, asking for basic essentials?

There is a glint in the king's eyes. A glint of vanity perhaps, the cheering crowd must have given his kingly pride, I think while looking at the stretch of people, assembled to put forth their grievances to their king again in hope. Water, food, shelter, roads, electricity, medical supplies, education, protection, the list could go on...

'Sudoor Paschim Anchal has always been treated like a step child by all governments. We have proudly given to the nation, Kumar Indrajit Singh, Lokendra Bahdur Chand, Sher Bahadur Deuba – three prime ministers; yet, we are left behind and neglected as the last priority.' I remember Bua complaining to me about the Deuba government in one of his states of depression. Actually he was talking aloud to himself. He does that more often now...just goes on speaking aloud his trail of thought, irrespective of any acknowledgement.

Being here in Kailali, the hub of far western Nepal, I can see his words make sense now. There is so much more poverty compared to the east. No roads, no bridges, no electricity, no drinking water, food shortage, and our neighbouring countries are all hoarding money for nuclear weapons. Talk of disparities! It never ends. Perhaps I should tell Chandra about this the next time I meet him... only for the sake of an argument – why only ravage a country asking for equality? Let's go global. Why let America, European countries or any other country be better off than Nepal? Let's ask to be equal with all.

'That is not impossible, Sanjeevani,' I can nearly hear Chandra's slow but impactful words. 'It will take time, but with sincere dedication and severe diligence, we too can place our country in the global economic rat race. It might pinch you, but it is a fact that we lag behind by nearly a century from the rest of the world. All thanks to your Rana regime, that wanted it to be secluded from the rest of the world. Kept the inhabitants ignorant and docile so that they could continue their autocratic dictation. And so we were kept segregated in the dark as the rest of the world moved ahead. It will take time, Sanjeevani, but we will definitely catch up.'

The king is walking up to where I stand. Women around me become tense in their excitement. The ones behind me begin to push forward and I am flung onto the parapet that separates the red carpeted aisle from the rest of us.

I feel his hands on mine as he helps me stand up. 'Are you okay?' he asks, smiling. The smirk in his smile gives his face a constant image of absolute arrogance. 'Thank you, Your Majesty,' I mumble as I hand him the little bouquet – insignificant, measly and nearly withering.

He takes it and nods his head at a tilted angle as I catch a glint in his eyes – a glint that shows his unabashed confidence. He knows all these people, including me, are here for him; we believe in him, we hope from him and therefore we are his subjects. And so, he walks along, confident, content and a happy king.

'The quintessence of our Nepal's identity is the strong bond between the king and the people, nurtured by mutual affection and confidence. Nepal has been able to maintain her independent identity and self-respect throughout her history only because of the people's unwavering trust in the institution of monarchy and the monarchy's unqualified dedication to the people...

'It is but natural to have differences of opinion and competition in a multi-party democracy. However, the converging point of all these different opinions must be patriotism. A monarchy ever devoted towards the country and the people and a people with an innate love for their land, is the glorious past of Nepal's history, its present and its future.' Slow, clear and in a monotonous manner, the words are spelt out by the king. Other than his imperial voice that resounds in the near still air, there is dead silence all around. We listen, hopeful, yet...

'Is this what the people want to hear?' I ask myself. Allegiance to the monarchy and the bond between the people and the monarchy – are all these people assembled here to be reminded only of that? Or is it that they have traversed great distances, bearing upon themselves the traumas of nature and the terror of the rebelling Maoists to get some assurance...from their king? They've come here to get real tangible assurance, and not words of patriotic philosophy. They want to receive actual aid and assistance.'

My head begins to spin. The sun is directly overhead, and there is not a trace of a breeze. The jostling crowd around me is only making it stiflingly hotter by the minute. In the podium, we have chairs to sit comfortably. But a little ahead, where the masses stand, there is nothing – men, women, the aged and children are either standing or sitting on the naked grass with no shade over their heads.

I reach for my bottle of mineral water, take a sip and decide to leave without seeing the performance of my shelter's children. There was no innocence left in these children. Poverty had deprived them off their basics – family, love and security, and snatched their purity. Sometimes, I detected hatred in them – a strong hatred for life. And today, these 'have-nots' were to dance and sing for a man who has everything. I feel a rebellious force emerge from inside that urges me to leave and leave now. I crane my head to look at my father, busy with his introductions to the king, and know that he will not miss my absence. He had rushed down, a fortnight back, ignoring the threats to his own life here in Kailali only to be a part of the reception committee for the king's visit to an area that once was his homeland.

I push my way through the hysterical crowd and manage to get out through the back exit. Aimlessly, I walk by the hospital and into the main bazaar. The streets are vacant. Shops have their shutters down, rickshaws are stacked neatly by the side of the roads. The stillness is overwhelming.

'Shri Panch Maharajdhiraj ko jai, Shri Panch Bada Maharani ko Jai' Bold laudations for the royal couple painted in red and white are hung everywhere on walls, on shutters and all over the streets. And through these I walk alone, listless and purposeless.

I clearly do not see any hope for the monarchy to sustain in Nepal. Irrespective of my father's confidence that the monarchy is essential and will get its footing back in the political scenario, I feel that there are going to be great changes made soon; or else this war, this killing and culling of people will never end.

Indeed, the king has received a grand reception in Western Nepal. Thousands have thronged to see him, meet him but little does he know that many have been forced and lured down to Dhangadi to attend the function. Tractors and trucks had been sent down to the villages coercing people to attend, convincing them that their grievances would be laid before the king. Many were even bribed. The ones who came on their own came only out of sheer curiosity, and many more for a day of recreation.

Little does the king know that, here in the remotes, left to fend for and protect themselves, these people have stopped caring. There are other issues prominent in their minds apart from the patriotic bond with the monarchy that the king speaks off; issues of hunger, health and now safety.

Not only the king but his Capital, the entire populace of Kathmandu remain unaffected by the ongoings here. People are starving, getting killed, kidnapped and tortured both by the security forces and the armed rebels; yet, life goes on in Kathmandu as though it were a different land altogether. The king will fly back and be safe and snug in his Narayanhiti Palace and the populace of Kailali and its likes will continue their struggle... waking up each day to the chill of the unknown.

I was shocked, and completely scandalised upon my visit to Kathmandu a month back. The complacent attitude of the people there made me want to feel sorry for their ignorance. It was not that the media was not propagating the happenings from all around the country but, here too, I felt that the news supplied to the people was biased. Biased because the media was not relating events but taking sides. News channels and all the local papers, big and small, were all inclined to various political parties. Besides, King Gyanendra had started his reign on a wrong footing with the media. The arrest of *Kantipur's* editor-in-chief, Yubraj Ghimre along with Binod Raj Gyawali and Kailash Sirohiya, the newspaper's director and managing director respectively, for publishing an opinion piece of Dr Babu Ram Bhattarai. The article clearly accused the United States of America and India in having a hand behind the royal massacre. This had created a spark of antagonism and mistrust in the media for the monarchy and now they seemed to be having a ball in degrading and demoralising each act of King Gyanendra. And the political parties were yet again at their power struggles. Some intellectuals, the likes of Deepak Thapa, Aditya Man Shreshta, Kanak and Kunda Dixit were seeming to get the picture of devastation right but even their articles seemed to be more of attempts to enhance their own intellectual vanity, as each one debated endlessly about the validity of the state of emergency declared by the king.

The Amnesty International was in an uproar of its own, debating that the suspension of the sub-clauses a, b and c of Clause 2 of Article 12, Clause 1 of Article 13 and Articles 15, 16, 17, 22 and 23 of the Constitution is a downright violation of Nepal's obligation to the Human Rights Treaty with the commission.

The expatriate community was the one completely bluffed, I thought, or was it that they were never able to grasp the truth that is Nepal.

'The king is a monster, a bloody dictator!' was their general dictum as they went about their chores feeling they knew this country and its inhabitants better than the Nepalese themselves.

The armed conflict between the Nepalese Army and the Armed rebels in the remotes had become to the people in Kathmandu a tripartite conflict between the political parties versus the Maobadis versus the monarchy; and each was slandering the other and nearly disregarding the killings going on in the war zones of the remotes.

As for the people of Kathmandu, little remained for them but to switch off their television sets after the news and go back to their daily lives and to go on pretending that Kailali, Bardia, Rukmu and Rolpa were a million years away from them. Stifling with the effects of war were but mere portraits on the television screen, lifeless and feeling-less.

As for the prime minister, he was trembling in his own instability. The prospects of his prime ministerial tenure seemed bleaker and bleaker to him as the war between the security forces and the armed rebels ceased to come to a conclusive halt.

Throughout my week-long stay in Kathmandu, the city had seemed to me a theatrical stage where all actors remained busy with their own histrionics and in the backdrop, a war continues to rage. People are getting killed every single day, and in between, the narrator comes in to say that Prime Minister Sher Bahadur Deuba has announced a price on the heads of Maoist leaders caught dead or alive. The pamphlet in the hand says '5 million for the top leaders and 2.5 for the top commanders.'

'Come with a head of a Maoist in a bag and go back with the same bag filled with the prize cash,' says another minister, baring all his teeth in a grin that had filled me with a contempt for myself, for my having to be a Nepali just like him.

I felt stifled wherever I went – the denials, the assumptions, the valuations of the war was all that people talked about, yet none was ever a part.

I met Razat then. I went over to his office in Tripureshwar; a tall, four-storyed building – cold, concrete and plain ugly from the outside; but inside, it was bustling with people and the money that came in whoppers as remittances from all over the world.

'These bloody Maoists should be all sent away to other countries. They create a ruckus here for there is no job for them, no income for them. Once they are earning, once they have cash in their hands they will begin to look at life from a different perspective. They too will begin to enjoy life. And the remittance that they send back home will also help the country more than their guns and violence will ever do,' Razat had said to me once, while randomly browsing news channels on his television set. 'Instead of wasting money on weapons and fighting the Maoists, the government should start setting up vocational training institutes all over the country. They should begin to send skilled labourers abroad. Remittances will be better and the standard of living will begin to go up. Secondly, the third generation from now, there will be no need to send labourers out. Nepal will have earned enough to be self-sufficient. That's one hell of an idea no, Sanju? Perhaps I should invest in training the labour going out of the country. Who knows, my son, one day, might just end up sending doctors and engineers out of the country.'

I had laughed with him. 'You! Why don't you ever mention your daughter. It is always "my son will take over this and my son will do that". Why not your daughter? She could turn out more efficient than your son. Ever thought of it that way?' I had punched him lightly in his belly and then begun to tickle him all over.

'Hear…hear the feminist speak!' Razat had guffawed, his head falling back on the sofa.

Standing at the reception and asking for Razat, I did not feel awkward, nor did I feel hesitant. I wanted to see him, so I was there. Plain and simple. Walking around the bustling din of the Asan market, the thought of him had just sprung up somewhere and I had walked into his office.

I was called in immediately to his conference room where perhaps he had just finished attending an important meeting. I walked in to the familiar scent of Razat, the same smile…my Krishna smile, pure and gentle. For an instant, it was as if time had never come in between. But time with Razat was always calculated and ever so little. He had stood up and walked to the door to usher me in and we had even embraced, a polite hug.

I could see he was shifty but strangely, I was not. My heart did not thump wildly against my chest yet the familiar longing for him, and the moments spent with him seemed to shift inside of me, wanting to assert their existence. His hair over his forehead had slumped down due to the pressure of the cap that he had just taken off. And then I remembered that it was a Thursday and on Thursdays, Razat dressed informally in jeans and a casual shirt. On other days of the week, he wore formal suits and expected his entire staff, which mostly consisted of pretty girls, to follow the same dress code as himself. Razat always liked perfection. He liked perfect things, perfect décor, perfect decorum, and he just loved his perfect life. During Dipawali, Razat distributed chocolates, packed in smart and neat packets, flown all the way from Hong Kong to all his business associates. 'Nepalese sweets make it look cheap. Besides, everyone exchanges the same sweets from Aangan. Razat Aggrawal is different; he does things in a different way,' he would say, pompously swinging his hands in the air. It all began to rush in like a swift wind, gushing and howling for acceptance, each memory of Razat as he sat in front of me, nervous yet smiling.

'Did you ever love me, Razat?' I had asked, looking straight into his eyes. He did not flinch, his lashes did not flutter and his facial muscles did not contract.

'Yes,' he had said, staring back at me, earnest and firm.

'Why did you shut me away after your abduction? Why did you never bother to contact me all these months?'

He leant back then on his swivel chair, his fingers on the table, gently tapping the dark glass. But he did not look away. Our eyes were caught together, forcing each one's way but being pushed back with the resistance of the other.

'You know, Sanju, while I was in captivity, I thought of no one as much as you. Not of Sangeeta, not of the children...it was only you that kept pinching my heart. It was as though I was accepting my sins, my wrong-doings. What future did we have together, Sanju? What had I given you other than a bad name and reputation? How long could we go on living a life that could never be ... I had to let you go. I had to stop being selfish.' Razat had said, eyes still caught with mine, his fingers still tapping the table.

'I thought as much,' I had said. 'But Razat, that was not what I wanted. I wanted you; you did what others wanted. You left me for others, Razat. For others felt that it was wrong. I never did. All I cared for was you. The little time spent with you was happiness for me. I never did nor do I now bother about what others have to say or judge of my actions. I don't live for others, I live for myself. Tell me Razat, what is happiness? Do we ever really get it?'

He did not answer for the longest time but kept staring at me and in his staring was the same reminiscence, the same longing.

'In truth, happiness is an illusion, Sanju, a figment of our imagination, of our personal perception of what and how things should be around and for us ... I guess.'

'And we go on living with this illusion, Razat? This illusion of happiness and what not we do to achieve it? Don't you think that illusions are necessary, imperative rather, to survive. That we need to tell each other beautiful though illusory stories of love, of glory, of patriotism?'

He was nodding, slowly in agreement to my train of thoughts.

'Without these stories, the reality of us would be so drab, so boring and not worth living for.'

Then he leaned forward towards the table, leaving the back of his chair with an impression of his back dug onto the sinking black leather and exclaimed in a near whisper, 'You haven't changed a bit, Sanju. You are still the old dreamy self, living in another world.'

'Ya Razat,' I had said, smiling now. 'You live in a tangible world, with real people but I have always preferred my seclusion, away from this humdrum. For me, other things matter; for me, emotions are tangible; for me laughter is tangible. A sigh escaped is beautiful, the rush of the wind against my skin holds more meaning to me than this commercial life of yours. It's a wonder we stuck to each other for as long as we did. We are poles apart, Razat, our thinking, our wanting... we never clicked yet we loved, we craved one another, did we not, Razat?'

He did not answer. 'How is the novel coming up, Sanju?' he had asked instead.

'Very well, Razat. The more I write, the more I feel that I was born only to do this – to write, to be this silent god. Secluded from the rest of the world. Condemned to witness and suffer, but also blessed with fleeting moments of sudden clarity before the wonder and beauty of the world fades again – revealing colourless barren landscapes; the world at its worst. I feel, Razat, that from my pedestal, I observe and assess this tangible world, marvel at it even but strangely never feel a part of it.'

Now he was really laughing. For Razat,. my writing had always seemed a futile vocation, an indulgence to keep myself busy. What he never understood was that my writing helped me escape from a world where I was always a misfit.

Someone brought tea. A young girl, smartly dressed and very eager, it seemed, to impress her boss. Razat was always a proud man. He took pride in everything he did – his work, his style of working, his staff, his décor... everything that he did had to make him proud. Even this girl he must have assessed, I had thought, drilled his philosophy, of dedicated hard work that only leads to success, into her. Must have commented on her dressing style until he made her into what she was now, a necessity like his Vaio laptop. She left setting the tea cups on the table, ever-willing to please her boss.

'Enough of me,' I had said, smiling at my thoughts of him. 'You tell me how is money-making going on. Loads of it must be rolling in, now more than ever. This war has become a boon to you money transfer guys. More people leaving the country meaning more money going into your pockets, right? And then, I believe you have started buying land like peanuts all over the valley. On my way in, I could not help noticing the model of your new venture. You are a smart man indeed, Razat.'

'Oh that! That is my dream, Sanju. I want to make the first tallest building in Nepal, a one-stop market and around it I aim to create the finest financial hub. Come, let me show it to you.'

We then walked out to the reception area where the model of his latest venture stood tall and proud. 'Twenty-five storeys in all, my dear,' he smiled again, his eyes genuinely delighted. 'The first three storeys will accommodate upto three hundred cars for parking, the next ten floors will have the commercial space for select brand outlets and the ten floors above these will have commercial spaces for financial institutions. Above these the last two floors will be extremely elite and premium penthouses. I am redefining commercial spaces now. Sanju, this will be the first, plush business ambience that will be both exclusive and efficient and it will indeed reshape and revolutionise the existing financial structure of Nepal. This is also the best time to procure land, Sanju, this is the worst economic crisis that the country is facing... There is only one way now and that is upwards. Once the country settles down, value of land will go further up; until then I will make homes for all the destitute people that have thronged into the city. They need homes after all, roofs over their heads and someone has to make it for them, why not me?'

Chandra had then flashed before my eyes, roofless and shelter-less... maybe even without food, rummaging the forests, with a rucksack on his back, a .303 in his hands and a dream in his eyes.

Will the two ever meet? I had asked myself in silence.

'Will the two ever meet?' I ask myself yet again walking in the drab and near silent street of the Dhangadi market. I think of Badki sitting in her courtyard, her white hair falling over her wrinkled face, her toothless grin, her retiring eyes stretch into the distant horizon, watching the sun rise, the sun set and then rise again. Did she ever have dreams, hopes and aspirations for a better life? No, I think. For she never knew that a better life existed... that somewhere there are cars with leather upholstery, that there are hotels with fancy marble floors and glittering chandeliers hanging from the high ceilings, that a flight attendant comes with a smile and a glass of sparkling champagne on an aeroplane that seems to squeeze the planet in size. For Badki has seen only the bare earth, the dust that rises with the breeze and the yellow shifting of the sun into a red glow when the sun sets and to this Badki closes her eyes.

Sanat

King Mahendra succeeded his father, on the Shah throne. His succession was followed immediately by the dismantling of the political structure set up by his late father, which he thought was a juvenile democracy that required many alterations. This was how the Panchayat system was promulgated on 16 December 1962, the constitution of which declared Nepal to be an 'independent, indivisible and sovereign monarchial Hindu state'. This Panchayat constitution conceived of a multi-tier political set-up led by the king himself, in whom the sovereignty of Nepal was rooted. All the powers – the Executive, Legislature and Judiciary – were eventually answerable to the king himself. The Panchayat system put the village and Town Panchayats at the lowest rung of this system, displaying this as proof of the decentralisation of power. Above these come the District Panchayats and over these, the Anchal Panchayats. The Rashtriya Panchayat is situated at the pinnacle.

Members in the Rashtriya Panchayat are elected from the immediate lower levels of the Panchayat hierarchy. Members were also elected from professional organsiations, some of whom were university graduates and members of faculties. Sixteen members of the total lot were directly nominated by the king himself. The Rahstriya Panchayat advised the king. It also includes the Raj

Sabha, the Supreme Court whose judges were also appointed by the king.

In 1967, the adjective, 'partyless democracy' was added to the Preamble to the Constitution which firmly states that 'no political party or any other organisation, union or association motivated by party politics shall be formed or caused to be formed or run.' Simply put, political parties are banned.

Now an Environment and Forest Minister, Prabhat lives in Kathmandu. He has put on weight, wears a daura surwal and drives a Mercedes Benz to Singh Durbar and is contentedly in love with his life as he is with Sushma – a young, pretty and extremely vivacious trainee nurse at the Bir Hospital. He sends her flowers every morning and his car waits at the parking lot of the hospital. Sushma jumps in and is driven to Baluwatar, the place where Prabhat has made a house on his father's old property.

They drink Johnny Walker, smoke Cuban Havanas and sing together. Prabhat watches her, enamoured by her love for life. She has a pretty smile and she laughs, throwing back her head...her lively laughter ringing out in the air as a melodious symphony and seeming to enchant Prabhat all the more, as he sits licking the tips of his moustache and then twirling the tips with his fingers, the whiskey running through his veins, shrouding his senses in an enthralling captivation.

'This is the kind of wife, I need. Witty, smart, intelligent, pretty and someone I can show around to my friends and colleagues and even take along with myself when invited to the Palace dinners. Not someone dull and ignorant as Durga; she would not know how to raise her glass of champagne when the queen felicitates her husband.'

He sends for his brother, Prashant, who is taking care of the farms back home in Kailali. Taking his brother with him to Gujeshwari, Prabhat makes Sushma his wife.

Prashant had wanted to start his career in the land revenue department where he had been accepted as a land administrator but someone was required at the farm as their mother was now getting old and the family had increased in number. 'You don't need a career as a government official, Prashant. The measly income would not even buy you your cigarettes; it's for the mediocre people, this civil service. You have our lands to take care of. The powers I hold as a minister will help me take care of the rest.'

So, Prabhat had returned to Kailali, taking back his flustered and much disappointed wife, Anju, whose dreams of having a small apartment in Bhakatapur, where she would live alone with her husband, away from the dictates of her mother-in-law, had been shattered. A dream where he went to work each morning and she too would take up a job as a teacher in one of the neighbouring schools. The two of them would return in the evenings, tired but content and then spend the evening at Ratna Park or to the cinemas with friends and colleagues.

Anju returned with Prashant, but complaining and cribbing. 'Why must you always listen to your brother? It is alright for him to leave his wife and children in the village, make a big career for himself and live in Kathmandu as a prince, and you have to go back to toil in the farms and take all the responsibility of Muajiu, and his wife and his kids. Preposterous! Another Lakshman in the making. I tell you, you are like his pet dog. He says sit, you sit; he says wag your tail, you do the same,' she had complained, her brows knit together into a frown, and her thin lips quivering.

'Does it matter where we live, my dearest Anju, or what we do for a living as long as we are together wherever we are? How we spend our time together is more significant. If the village, dust, mud, flies and mosquitoes are fated for us, so shall it be, but it is left to us to make that life beautiful with our love.'

Prashant had embraced his wife and kissed her and they had returned to the village where in due time, Anju had adapted to the hardship of village life. If that was not enough, she had surprised her husband and mother-in-law by taking the reins of farming into her hands. She woke up at dawn during sowing-time, walked with a lantern in her hand to Teen Gharua waking up the bonded labourers. With them she went to the fields, managing the sowing of seeds, watching her workers, sunk knee-deep in wet marshes during the monsoon. Soon, Anju began enjoying the soft drizzles that kept going on for the entire day. The leeches and water snakes stopped bothering her as did the cockroaches and the mosquitoes. Lizards, crawling over her bedside and flies hovering all over her during hot summer afternoons, a stray whiff of a breeze were all deeply exhilarating for Anju and became an inevitable part of her life. She established her position as a manager in the fields as well of the house.

It is when the children return on vacation from the boarding school that Sanat feels comforted the most and even content with her accomplishments. The house is alive with children laughing, talking and even quarrelling. Extra help is brought in from the Teen Gharua. Even children from the village begin to come in during those days, some quietly staring at the toys and books that are sent down from Kathmandu by Prabhat, and some join in as playmates.

The two boys, Hemant and Sanjay, sleep for most of the morning, waking up at noon and then loiter around in their pyjamas listening to cricket commentaries on the radio or playing cricket themselves. Hemlata, the eldest of the lot, is a quiet girl. She follows her mother and is submissive and docile. She is happy to help with the chores of the house and spends the entire vacation hovering around her grandmother; fetching water for her puja from the well, cleaning her idols in the prayer room, having her hookah filled with fresh coal, reading out verses from the Bhagvad Gita; she is indeed the pride of the entire family. As for the youngest, Sanjeevani, she is a brat. She is never in one place. Spending her day foraging the nearby jungles, splashing in the rivers, hiding in the thickets of the slowly ripening wheat in the fields. She prances about the entire day and doesn't care for anyone in the world, not even herself. She is never afraid, neither of the wild, nor of the dark and not even of the reprimands from her elders.

It is only at nights that the eight-year-old Sanjeevani, exhausted with fatigue from her day of gallivanting, snuggles with her aging grandmother. Staring into the fire around which the entire family sits after dinner, she insists on being told yet another story. Sanat gives in to her granddaughter's request and begins with '*Ekaa desh ma, euta thiye raja ani unki thin euti rani...*'

Her eyes widen and her little black pupils glisten with awe and wonder as she begins to fantasise about the fictitious characters, feeling their joys, their pains as though they were real indeed. By the time the tale comes to an end and Sanat concludes it with...

> '*Sunne lai sun ko maala*
> *Bhanne lai phool ko Maala...*
> *Yo katha baikuntha jaalaa.*'

Sanjeevani is fast asleep. A smile on her face, content and clearly pleased.

She is the first to wake up and creeps out in the dark. The stars are slowly fading; the cocks begin to crow one after another hailing a new dawn. From the village the sounds of the dhikki chiau begins to softly merge with the chirping of the birds nestled for the night in the sal, seesam, asok and the mango trees. Sanjeevani tiptoes towards the shed. She knows it is time for Laata to milk the cows.

She finds him leading the young calves to their mothers and as the calves rush and attach themselves to the teats of the hanging breasts of their mothers and Laata begins to milk the cows, his hands moving up and down the voluptuous teats, spraying forth thick, white rushes of milk that stream into the bucket placed right under the cow. Sanjeevani watches, enthralled. Communicating with Laata with gestures of her hands, she waits for him to finish milking. Then she helps him carry the buckets into the *bhancha ghar*, where Kanchi has started a fire. The milk is poured into huge pitchers and made to simmer on the fire after adding cinnamon, cloves, cardamom, cashew nuts and pistachios to make it more appetising.

Sanjeevani squats by the hearth, warming her hands by the heat of the fire and watches Laata flirt with Kanchi, his hands gesturing his love for her and Kanchi frowning to his speechless banter, showing him her raised palm, meaning to say that she would slap him if he did not stop. Laata laughs a muted laugh, but his face lights up in sheer delight and his old body shakes with his silent laughter.

Durga comes back, washed and cleaned after taking a bath in the river, her hair wet and tied in an untidy bun over her head, and takes some milk for Sanat in a silver glass perched on a silver tray. Sanjeevani follows her.

Inside Sanat's room, the morning bustle is in full swing. The maids are doing up the bed. Sanat sits on the floor mattress, she has just washed up in the silver pan that is brought to her every morning. She is waiting by the brazier for her glass of milk. She looks radiant from the glow of the fresh hot coal burning bright.

'Brahma Bishnu Sadashiv...' she chants her religious prayers as Sanjeevani cuddles in with Hemlata who is sitting by the brazier wrapped in a blanket.

'Bhictoria went into labour last night, but all the kittens came out dead,' Durga is informing Sanat about the pregnant cat. Instantly, Sanjeevani is tense and alert. She nudges Hemlata, 'Please Hemlata Dijju...please help me make the stretchers.'

The two of them go the courtyard where gentle shafts of the rising sun have begun to fall. Hemlata cuts stems from the bamboo thicket there, and begins to tie them up with jute ropes. Her stretcher ready, Sanjeevani places the dead kittens on it. Carrying this stretcher she begins her march to the fields, followed by Hemlata who is smiling and giving in to her younger cousin's fancy.

In the field, Laata digs up a small pit just enough to bury the three kittens and Sanjeevani buries them there, placing a flower on top of each of the dead kittens. On her way back, she is wrestling and punching Laata. As he bends over, his hands clasping his stomach in a gesture of mock pain, Sanjeevani hears her mother call her to come and drink her morning glass of milk. She twists her mouth in a gesture of dislike and takes off with Laata into the fields, thick with wheat that has begun to sprout. They hide there. A serious look of concern on Sanjeevani's face is accompanied by Laata's play-along look of grimace. Soon, the entire household is screaming and shouting, looking for Sanjeevani.

Hemant spots Sanjeevani crouched in Laata's lap, her face buried in his chest, as he stands by the hand-pump brushing his teeth. 'Nepti...' he calls out to her slyly, flinging open the blanket wrapped around him. 'Come, hide in here, no one will see you.'

Sanjeevani looks up at Laata's face, wanting to know whether it is a good idea to leave her hiding place. Laata smiles back. With a nod of his graying head, he prods her to go to her new hideout. She runs out and charges into the open blanket that quickly folds around her. As Sanjeevani hugs Hemant, her heart beating wild with excitement, she whispers in between her pants, 'Hemant da, have they seen me?' She feels his hands go around her, inside the blanket and push her tiny frame closer to his body.

The next day is Maghi Sangranti. The entire family is up before dawn. The bullock carts are ready. Rice, dal, vegetables, flour for the puris, oil to cook, masalas to be added... are packed in trunks and baskets and loaded on to the waiting carts.

Anju has made sure that the children are kept warm with jackets, woolen caps and mufflers. All the children are made to sit together in one cart with the women and the men following in the last cart. They will go to the hot spring at Seeta Kunda for the annual sacred bath.

Slowly, the convoy moves in the dark, the buffaloes dragging the heavy carts downhill on the embankments of the Shivganga. Across it is the jungle of Madhakunti where the dead of the villagers are buried.

'The Jamjutwa lives in there,' Sanjay whispers into his sister's ears. Instantly, her eyes widen with curiosity and apprehension as she looks up at her brother's face.

'Where?' she whispers back, shifting closer to him to feeling safe. 'There...do you see those trees? He could be lurking behind any of them,' he says, pointing with his outstretched hand. 'And do you see cots lying upturned on those mounds of mud? That is where the dead are buried...'

Sanjay is enjoying himself, scaring his sister and using all his powers of self-control to stop himself from laughing. 'Do you see pots and pans there?'

'Yes, I do,' Sanjeevani whispers back, straining her neck to the direction her brother is pointing to.

'Those were all full with food, and offerings to the dead. The Jamjutwa comes and eats on their behalf. But now since the pots and pans are all empty, he must be hungry...'

'Nooooo! Now?' Sanjay cannot hold back his pent-up laughter and turns his head sideways and lets out a muffled giggle.

'Now the Jamjutwa is on the prowl, looking for food. He likes chicken. If he doesn't get that, he goes for little children,' he continues scaring his sister.

'Really?' Sanjeevani asks, nearly choked with fright.

'Really!' Sanjay repeats. 'Just think, Sanju, if he finds you today, what should happen?'

Sanjeevani begins to cry, attracting attention from her mother who begins to scold Sanjay for frightening his little sister. 'Spoilt brat of the first order!' he mumbles and begins to stare at the dark figures of the trees looming large over their heads, their branches sprawled out into the skies like claws desperate for a clasp.

'*Seeta maiya darshan deo,*' Sanat chants. Whenever Sanat chanted, Sanjeevani felt that the water seemed to surge up in a wave at the Seeta Kunda

'Once more, Jijumua,' she pleads.

They have all bathed and are now waiting for the food to be ready. It is the same time in Magh that the Tharus are in a festive mood; so not many servants come along. Besides, it is also the time for the annual circulation, when the bonded labourers leave and new ones join in.

As Durga and Anju help with the rolling of the dough and frying the puris in the hot oil, Prashant is sitting on the river bank, discussing his labour problem. Some of his old workers have left. They have either paid their debts and freed themselves or have paid their loans through some other zamindar and moved to a different village.

Although Prashant knows well that soon, groups of families will begin to come in seeking for placement, he still worries as there is so much of pending work and it is such a hassle to let go of the workers that one is used to having around. Searching and negotiating with a new family over and over again was nothing less than a nightmare.

'I give my *kamaiyas* thirty quintal dhaan. What more could they wish for? *Paaji saalas!* Just want a change of place, that's about it. No zamindar is going to give more than me, yet they leave. Ignorant fools!' he is complaining to the Kothari, who has come along for the sacred visit to the holy site.

'Hoina, Kancha Raja, their attitude has changed. These Tharus are beginning to get spoilt. They want more and more now and if you give in to each of their whims and fancies, you will be left with very little for yourself. You give them a house, a kitchen garden, quintals of dhan and yet they want more. Insolent bastards!' The Kothari is voicing his own concern as he gestures with his free hand to a Dangua to bring the umbrella to shade his master. Prashant, he has noticed, is squinting his eyes, battling the glare of the sun that is bright and right above their heads.

Sanjeevani

It is like a trail of ants trampled upon and disrupted. People run around, scattered and aimless and helpless in a frantic panic. But I cannot move; I stand transfixed watching alarmed faces pass me by; faces contorted in fear, faces anxious for a refuge, and then I see the jeep pull up. And from it jumps out the former crown prince Dipendra, wearing a combat uniform and a machine-gun hung upon his shoulder. He carries a naked khukuri in his hand. 'Mamu, run!' I scream to my mother.

I see her grab hold of my father's coat and begin to run. 'Mamu, run!' I scream again, loud and desperate, fear squeezing my heart and constricting my throat. I see my old parents – my mother frantic and pulling my father, as she runs and my father's grey head bobbing up and down – mingle with the fleeing crowd.

It is a relief to see them get away, and then I think of myself. I am still where I was and the man with the khukuri is approaching me at a deadly speed. Around me, there are others who have not been able to escape and we are surrounded by scary-looking men also dressed in military uniforms.

Quiet, submissive and anxious, we are made to follow them to this long dining table that is spread out in the open and made to sit around it. At the head of this table sits Dipendra with his naked khukuri. Behind him stand his security, stern and laden with loaded guns.

Mercilessly, he begins to slash throats then, this man Dipendra... and I watch him. His eyes are cold and frigid. He moves from chair to chair, adding to the carnage one after the other. As he nears us, our terrified hearts beat wildly.

I am the last in line as I sit on the first chair to the left of the head of the table; he has begun his bloody butchery from his right. I look at faces drained of colour and scared of impending death. Faces that begin to get familiar. I see Thulubua there somewhere, twirling the tips of his moustache and then wetting them with his tongue. Besides him sits Hemant da. He wears the same smile, the very smile that gets my stomach churning, making me so nauseous that I loathe my own existence. I can see the rhythmic motion of his right hand under the table and I quickly look away. My fleeing eyes fall on Dada. He is chewing on something; he smiles carelessly from across the table and winks at me; his old manner of telling me that we share a secret. Hemlata Dijju is there too. She looks hassled with her own troubles and seems hardly affected by the impending threat to her life. I can see her wipe the snot trailing down her son's nose with one hand and with the other, she gestures to her eldest son to sit quietly on his chair. Then there is Jijumua with her rudraksha beads, calm and collected. I can see her lips move in silence to the words of her prayers. Aunty is fixing her hair; then she catches my eye and smiles. Her pretty face lights up and with her hand she beckons me to come and take the empty seat by her side, I am about to leave my seat and walk up to the empty chair when I see it taken by Subba saab from the land revenue department. He clears his throat, spitting out a long trail of phlegm onto the ground as he sits and begins to go over my Aunty's land papers. He is shaking his head as though disagreeing with something. Kallu is nudging him from the other side trying to draw Subba's attention towards Badki. She is scratching her head with one hand and using the long nailed finger of her other hand to pick on something from her decaying teeth.

As I assess faces both familiar and strange, this man continues walking with his khukuri, his mouth now painted red with all the blood that he has been sucking. Bodies lie headless, fallen off chairs, sprawled lifeless on the ground and some even slumped on the table. There is blood everywhere; there is fear, anxiety, and chaos but strangely no sound. I can see lips move, bodies writhing and wrenching but it is as though my ears are blocked. I can feel the cries of fear, agony and pain, but no matter how hard I strain my ears to hear the sounds, I cannot. Silence looms large as I watch this man, cruel and devilish, walk up to one person after another and dismember the head from its body, bend down and slurp the flow of blood that oozes out of the open neck.

Inside me, I can feel fear. Hard and biting, it nags at my chest from the inside. Then he approaches me, his khukuri leaking with blood. I look up at his face – his eyes are blazing, his mouth splattered red. He is smiling at me now...a wicked, evil smile. He whispers into my ears, 'Sanjeevani...' I hear my name called out. 'Sanjeevani, my healing ointment...' Instantly, my head turns to look at the source of the voice and as I look on the blood-smeared face of Dipendra, the face begins to change. Slowly, the fiery eyes metamorphose into the compassionate look of Chandra's. He stands with the khukuri rested on the back of my neck; his lips stained with blood, whispering into my ears, 'Sanjeevani...Sanjeeevani. My Sanjeevani, my love, my life...'

I shudder and open my eyes. I am drenched in my own sweat – the aftermath of my preposterous dream, no doubt. I throw off the heavy cotton quilt from over me and walk to the electric heater that is burning red in the corner of the room. I switch it off and place myself on a chair next to it, stretch my legs on the floor, rest my head on the slanting backrest of the chair and stare at the expanse of the ceiling above.

'But Bua that is what I want. I really want,' I had said to him, pleading as though my life depended on his verdict there on.

'No Sanjeevani, get that silly notion out of your head. Quicker the better for your own self,' he had said, shoving in handfuls of his food into his big mouth and swallowing it instantly.

'But...Bua, what is the harm in trying anyway? Others are using your lands, feeding off them. I don't understand why I cannot do that?' I sit in front of my father with the rice pot in my hand, serving him an extra helping.

'What is the point, Sanjeevani? Say I let you go ahead with this crazy idea of yours...do you think the Maobadis are going to let you in, give you back my lands so that you can continue our family's trend, the dislike for which had your brother killed?'

I had watched his fingers, dexterously sweep in the food from his plate into his palm and from it disappear into his mouth. 'Put some tama for me, will you...' he says, straightening his back, wanting to put an end to our conversation.

I am adamant. 'What if I can fix things for you? I have been going down to Ganeshpur quite often, you know that Bua. People there have become used to seeing me around there. I have friends there now. I am no longer an enemy for them. I think they look up to me as this educated person who seems to mingle with them and who can even bring about a few changes to improve their lives,' I had insisted, pouring some tama curry into the pile of fresh rice heaped on his plate. 'Here, try some sidhra ko achar. Badki had sent some for me last week,' I add and begin to continue my insisting when my mother, who is slowly and quietly nibbling her own food, sitting beside my father, speaks up.

'That's exactly how Sanjay thought. He wanted to go on living in Ganeshpur, the only Pahari among all Tharus, and look what they did to him. He wanted the same as you. He felt the same as you. He wanted changes in Ganeshpur and even talked about improvisation in his farming techniques. "Ten years down the lane, Ganeshpur will be self-sufficient," he would say. "I will make it into a model village," and look what it has become now – a breeding ground for terrorists. Serves them right! These ignorant villagers! Let them rot, Sanjeevani, let them get ground in between the Maosits and the security forces. If my son, my Sanjay, had been alive today, he would have led the villagers, protected them, spoken for them...serves them right.'

My mother had not looked up but continued mixing the food on her plate. There was a tear silently trickling down her cheek.

'Mamu...don't you see? Dada had a dream for his village and his home, and it is left to us now to realise and achieve that dream for him. We cannot let his home and fields turn into grazing grounds.'

My father had then intervened. 'You want to till lands, you think you can stand the heat of madhes in mid June out in the open fields, the wet monsoons with the rivers flooded and you stranded in Ganeshpur for months...what if you fall sick? It is easier said than done, Sanju. They have made it clear...you till your land and eat what you sow. Are you ready to do that? Bend down with the tharunis and plant seeds in the fields, cut the harvest with them...do you think, Sanjeevani, that you can really be one of them?'

He had said all this stammering with excitement. His anger for me was explicit in the roar of his voice.

'It is my knowledge and education that sets me apart from the rest of the villagers, Bua. And that is what I want them to accept. I want them to accept my differences from them as an added asset to the village. I do not want to stand out of the lot but be one of them and lead them on. I may not be the same as them, Bua, but I am ready to join them with my own skills and knowledge of which they have little. After all, both are required. Skilled and unskilled labour. I can be a good manager. As for being one of them, Bua...when was I not? If Ganeshpur is Atwari's home, Bhalmansa's home, Sita Ram Chowdhary's home, Badki's home, it is mine too. It belongs to me as much as it does to them and with a bit of compromise and cooperation from both sides, we could make a lot of difference in Ganeshpur. Is this not what Dada wanted?'

'Nonsense...utter nonsense! You make them understand that, Sanjeevani...not me! They were the ones who packed us off saying we are different from them,' my father had said and walked out, his head trembling with agitation.

I can now feel the heat from my body leaving me. The chill of the winter night slowly begin to sweep in. I am still staring at the ceiling. I want to go back to bed, cover myself with the thick quilt and close my eyes to this ceiling, to this room, to the world and even to myself. But sleep is far gone.

I am restless. I begin to walk the expanse of the room, peeping from time to time at my laptop kept on the table by the window.

My mind is shifting, racing rather, from one thought to another. After the king left Dhangadi, leaving behind his flowery speeches that were instantly forgotten by the masses as was by him, my father had soon followed suit. He left immediately after I had applied for a loan with the Krishi Bikas Bank, here in Dhangadi. I needed some financial backup to begin my venture. I would do it in three phases, I thought. First will be the research period where I will go down to Ganeshpur and survey the land, soil, climate and temperature. Having done that I will then decide upon the best value-added crops that will reap the maximum returns. In the second phase, I will do an awareness programme in the village with the locals. We will discuss the potential of my new farming scheme. And finally, when I have convinced the villagers, we will commence the execution of the plan.

It was not as easy as I had thought it to be. Firstly, my request for a loan was denied on the basis of my father's pending loans with the bank. I could not forward any viable security against the loan either. I had nothing of my own. Some fields in my name in Ganeshpur are there but I could not mortgage that as they were in the custody of the insurgents.

So I did the research myself, making Hari, from the shelter, my assistant and my entire staff. We frequently visited Ganeshpur, talked to the locals sitting out in the courtyards on their knitted cots, and sometimes walked the fields with a few of the farmers, discussing strategies. A year since I had my discussion with my father I have realised that Ganeshpur Gaon Bikas Samiti has a little over hundred bighas of land, 50% of which belongs to my father. As a collective farm, we could grow varieties of value-added crops like tomatoes, chillies and even mushrooms. The farmers around here, I have learnt, rely mainly on wheat and rice and if the crops fail, they fall in debt. I want to change all that. Teach the farmers that money, and fast money, can be made from selling vegetables and we could easily send our vegetables to Kathmandu by the night bus to be sold every morning.

Faint light is filtering through the edges of the windows. I look at my watch. It is twenty minutes to six. Soon the neighbourhood will be alive – cocks crowing; cycle bells tinkling; Asha from the next house will begin to scream and shout at her eight-year-old son, forcing him to complete his homework; Neeraj, her husband will bang the door and leave the house for his morning jog peeping at my neighbour's window, to see whether his college-going daughter is also watching him as she brushes her hair; she herself would be getting ready for her campus classes. Round the bend of the street he will joined by, Syam Uncle, Mahesh Uncle and Paras Kaka. All three of them would have have begun jogging a short while ago but would have started panting already. As they disappear into the thicket of the morning fog, my landlord's radio set will come alive with the morning bhajans. His wife will scream down the staircase from the landing, 'Sanjeevani, can you bring the packets of milk upstairs, please?' I will then walk out, open the main door and grab the four packets of milk, keep one for myself and take the rest upstairs to my landlord's kitchen. Here she will make the first cups of tea for her family and politely invite me to join them. Sometimes I stay on, watching the morning news on their TV, the remote control of which is the bone of contention between my landlord, who will want to watch the news, his wife who will want to watch the morning yoga, and the children who will want a glance at the cartoon channel before they get ready for school.

There will be loud voices, of people, vehicles, birds, things falling, picked up, placed back again...utter chaos. The world around me will begin to move ahead. As for myself, I shall force my steps, inch by inch, languorously with little delight and no enthusiasm.

For me, each day is the same. The sun rises and it sets and around its clock I see the world around move in a chaotic humdrum, never stopping to feel the beauty that is life, the fleeting moments of epiphany, moments of sudden clarity. They never stop to feel the laughter and the pain...but I do. As an outsider I watch and observe the beauty that is life, yet miserably fail to be a part of it.

Many times I have wondered whether Chandra is a part of this swift commotion that is life; or does he stand still by my side, a smile on his lips, aloof and brooding to himself, and perhaps even marvelling at the wonder that is life.

I can see Chandra building a blockade around himself; a blockade made of strong convictions. It is like a barricade for the rest of the world...within the confines of which, Chandra wants to brood alone. I can see him slowly pushing me away, out of his self-imposed confines....I understand my Chandra...he loves and that love makes him weaker, makes him want, makes him dream for the future, dreams that seem to run parallel with his goals and objectives.

'My dearest Sanjeevani...my breath of fresh air...'

This is what his first letter said after he returned from Mangalsen. For months he remained underground but his letters came when least expected and were much to my relief.

I take you in each morning with the first rays of the sun that hit my eyes, warm and pleasant. Each night I hold you tight in my heart that beats aloud only your name.

Poetic it may sound, Sanjeevani, but I have taken you along to the edges of life. It was your name that seemed to drown the thunders of the loud bombshells blasting all around me. It was your name, Sanjeevani darling, that sped with me as I ran as a mad man, firing bullets in all directions and it was your name, my love, my life that eased the angst of watching my friends fall, lifeless all around me. Your name goaded me on, picked me from where I fell, and helped me move ahead with a courage to kill for my cause.

I have killed. I have put an end to a breathing life, making it still and lifeless. I thought of nothing then, Sanjeevani, but your name but now I seem to be hounded by these ghosts, of faces, bodies mutilated both of friends and the enemy... They laugh at me sometimes, jeer at me and often, they beg... Sanjee...they beg me for life...to go on breathing, perhaps, the name of their own loved ones.

At times, I feel that I do not want to go on living each day with the voices around me, inside of me, screaming, shouting, begging. That is not all, Sanjee. Faces dying, smeared in blood but with eyes still hopeful of life continue walking by me at all hours... making me wish in desperation that I too, as others did that night, should have given my life for my cause for a new and fair Nepal in Mangalsen.

*Having said all that, Sanjee, I know these are but repercussions of
a war. My human conscience feels the sting of being a part and
perpetrator of devastation. And I am convinced that in due time I
shall attune my mind and conscience to the same. I will then not
suffer the agonies that I have created. Don't you think so?*

*I end here, my Sanjee, my beautiful dream, my love, my
life... Sanjeevani, with a prayer that when I close my eyes to the
world, I shall do so with my heart beating its last toll with your
name.... Sanjeevani.*

I did not reply as I did not know where to send my letters. But I
held each one to my heart each night before I slept. Somehow I felt
close to Chandra when I did so; it was as if his words penned with
his own hands would blend in with the heartbeats of my life...and
the distance would not matter. He too would feel the life breathing
and beating inside of me.

Chandra was involved in many major Maoist operations after
Mangalsen. Right after, he was deployed in Lamahi. Then I heard
that he was in Lisne in the first week of May where his lot attacked
the Royal Nepalese Army base camp. But it was the attack in Khara
that had made me sit stiff by my landlord's TV. I watched the news
anchor say that the Nepalese Army had succeeded over the terrorists
that had attacked the army camp in Khara and that there was a major
fatality on the side of the armed rebels. I sat horrified, drowning
in the drumming of my heart, as I saw the footage of bodies lying
on the grass in long columns, lifeless and dead.

'What if Chandra is one of them?' I had shifted in unease trying
to peer at the dead faces but in my delirium, each had seemed the
same...the same face of death – cold, still, stiff and lifeless.

For days I had gone about as a zombie, getting startled at the
faintest of sounds. I was afraid everything, even my own solitude,

which is why I began sleeping at the shelter with the children. The nights were the worst. Thoughts that hinted at the worst streamed in into my mind. What if he is not dead but captured alive or just wounded? Perhaps he is being tortured by the security forces? Getting beaten to pulp, spat at, forcibly made to eat his own feaces...scary thoughts hounded me at all times. At the shelter, children entertained me, sang for me, danced for me, and jumped about on their beds with a joy that comes only with innocence.

I did my best to keep myself busy in the months that followed. I took a bus to Ganeshpur every weekend. I spent a day or two with Badki and the villagers. I rolled up the length of my jeans and worked in the fields, planting the first buds of the next harvest with a juvenile pride. Feeling the moist earth touch my skin made me elated. When it used to drizzle, I stood with my feet sunk in wet mud up to my knees and smiled and welcomed the soft showers. Later, I walked around the fields along with the villagers treating my eyes to the now blossoming crops, and their swaying to the gentle breeze. In between, I stopped to think of Chandra...his brooding eyes, his faltering smile and his words,...'You shall live on, Sanjee, and I shall realise my dream through your eyes...' soon stopped hurting and began to comfort me instead.

The vast stretches of green swaying to the gentle breeze became Chandra to me; the interminable flow of the Shivganga, inexhaustible and perpetual, seemed like Chandra to me; the dark shadow that fell in long sweeps when the sun set seemed like Chandra to me; the cackle of hens, bleating of goats, the shouts of the naked children on the dusty roads, Badki's toothless grin, Bhalmansa's drunken shouts in the middle of the night, the crickets in the fields, the howls of the jackals from across the jungle...all these swarmed in together to link me with a life that was pure and untainted from chaos of the demanding world outside. So what if Chandra is not with me, I kept telling myself while looking at the flight of the white cranes landing gently and settling in the midst of the fields. I have all these and his memories, for I saw all this with him once. With him did I stand by the river hand in hand, watch the sun rise, the horizon behind, the shades and hues altering with its ascent...I saw this world with Chandra; with him did I breathe the air mingled with dust and smell of cow dung; with Chandra did I begin to blend with the raw exquisiteness of nature, a beauty unadorned. With him I became one with this innate, unassuming, unpretentious world, that is Ganeshpur.

'All this will change, Sanjee. The river will be gone, dried up and thick with muck and sewage. The trees will be cut down, the empty dusty roads will be pitched and crowded, the thatched cluster of houses will in few years become a tangle of unfinished ugly structures.' Chandra had once said this to me while staring ahead at the village, standing on the terrace of the ruins of my father's house.

'Why does it have to be that way, Chandra? Why can we not preserve this pristine beauty?' I had sighed, my head slowly resting on his shoulder

'It is because we crave for development and progress and for that, destruction is imperative. The old rickety house must be brought down in order to make a new flamboyant one, my dear. That is how history is made, layers and layers of modulations piled one on top of the other. So, it will be with us. We will destroy the old world in order to make a new one and that is how the world shall move...'

And thus I passed my days in a haze, listless and careless to the world around me. I did not care that King Gyanendra had declared a state of Emergency; I did not care for his visit to Kailali; I did not care that he dissolved the Parliament; it didn't matter to me when the date of the mid-term elections were announced and when this announcement was petitioned against at the Supreme Court; it did not matter to me when all the contesting parties met the prime minister and unanimously decided that the elections could not go ahead with the terrorists in action; it did not matter to me when King Gyanendra addressed the nation stating that the elections could not take place on the date specified earlier and thus Sher Bahadur Deuba would need to shoulder the blame and resign from his post as prime minister. Little did it matter to me that Lokendra Bahadur Chand was now the prime minister appointed by the king and little did that excite me as it did my father, adding on new hopes for him. The entire team of political parties came out in opposition of the king's actions, determined, rebellious and slandering, onto the roads. I did not care when a ceasefire was announced as little did I care for the press release given by the Maoist president, Pushpakamal Dahal saying, 'In order to facilitate a peace talk, the government has agreed to take back the terrorist tag, head value and red corner notice against us. Considering the decisions of the government to be a positive note, we have decided on a ceasefire and will participate in the recommended peace talks.' Nor did I care when Narayan Singh Pun was made to lead the peace talk team by the government.

I continued to roam in my own world of nightmares, of little thoughts of Razat, my village, of Chandra and completely immersed myself into writing my novel.

Weeks later, I received a letter from Chandra. Stunned and shivering, I had opened it and rushed through the words scribbled in ink in the same, neat and composite hand of my Chandra's.

'Congratulations, my dearest Sanjee, on your new prime minister.' The letter started with a hint of banter. *'I wish you all the best hoping that Mr Lokendra Bahadur Chand will indeed take Nepal to a totally new level of development and progress. Ha ha! Sanjeevani, my dearest, I am now convinced of the final victory not being too far ahead. The king is making a grave mistake. He has clearly negated*

the norms of pure and fair democracy and has blatantly joined in the war with his active power politics. We welcome him as a new player but remain convinced of bearing the victory flag.

I know you have been worried for me, wondering whether I am dead or alive, but darling, times were such that I had to remain underground, informing none of my whereabouts. My darling, in all these days and nights, weeks and months, not a moment has gone by when I have not thought of you. The angst of our separation could only be mellowed by the fact that I was with the supreme commander himself, Prachanda. Imagine Sanjee, my good fortune to be of service to such a noble mind and to learn from him and be trained by him. Indeed, I am honoured and consider myself extremely privileged.

After the Khalanga defeat, our spirit was shaken. The best of the few that had survived were selected to be trained under Prachanda himself. From dawn to dusk, I hovered around him like a thirsty fly. In the early hours of the morning, I used to bring him fresh buffalo milk and turn on his radio for news. Till the end of the day, tired and nearly delirious, I would watch over his bunker. And you would be interested to know, Sanjee, that he has a human face too. There were times when he joked about Karishma Manandhar and called her the Madhuri Dixit of Nepal. We sang songs together on some nights. I watched him, dazed and enthralled. Sanjee, it is him who leads me on. It is his words of inspiration that make my life seem insignificant to the vastness of my cause. "There is no alternative to people's war and the gun is the only tool for social transformation," he said to me, finding me alone one evening. He had sensed the harrowing questions in my mind without even having spoken them aloud. Amazing isn't it, Sanjee? "Remember always, Bikral, that you are a significant figure now in the People's Liberation Army. Without us and our sacrifices the people out there have nothing. We fight for the people, we kill for the people and we get killed for the people", he said. And then, *pointing to my gun, he said, "Remember Bikral, that political power grows out of the barrel of a gun." Oh, I have not mentioned earlier that I am now called Bikral and am promoted to the position of a battalion commander by the great Comrade Prachanda.*

Do I not seem like an excited child? I feel that walking the rugged terrains with Prachanda and listening to his promising words, have given me a fresh outlook to my cause. I am ready to leap, Sanjee, without any hesitation or regret. I am now finally ready to take the great leap into the great Prachanda path.

Along with Comrade Prachanda, I was fortunate to inspect and examine a few base areas in Rukum and Rolpa. After the military victories of the Peoples Liberation Army, the Military has confined itself to District Headquarters. Therefore, these regions are now more or less liberated. It is interesting to note, Sanjee, that elections of the local and district level of the Peoples' Government here have already been completed. Whereas the local government has been directly elected by the public, the representatives of the local peoples power have elected the district peoples' government. These governments are known as the Local United Peoples Committees and District United Peoples Committees. These remain the prime Legislative, Judicial and Executive organs in these base areas. The Peoples' Government is composed of different departments, like the construction department, land reform department, cooperative department, forest conservation department, health department, security department, education and culture department and so on. The best part is that each department is working with diligence, focused on a certain goal and a deadline, with dedication and sincerity to the final objective. I was told, Sanjee, that soon a central committee will be formed in order to organise these Local Peoples' governments' defence, consolidation, expansion and coordination of the local peoples' governments. The party has also put forward a separate programme of autonomy for the oppressed.

This policy and programme reflects a revolutionary policy to unite and struggle on a democratic basis against the nemesis policy of divide and rule.

My dearest Sanjeevani, it is our party's strong conviction that the central Peoples' Government Organising Committee will not only coordinate with the local Peoples' government but also play a vital role in the preparing the future insurgency.

I think I have gone too far with my eagerness and am certain that you may not share my enthusiasm, for I know well, my Sanjeevani has her own rigid mind, her own set of opinions and a dream that belongs only to her...Is it not?

I look forward to meeting you very soon, my dearest...

Yours and only yours...

Chandra

I had read and re-read the letter many times until I thought that I knew each word by heart and by the end of it I did...Chandra was moving away from me...taken by his principles, his motives and his movement. I now stood distant and apart, a pariah, not understanding, not sharing, not being a part of his cause.

I must have dozed off on my chair beside the heater, for when I opened my eyes, the curtains are drawn, and a flood of light hits my eye. Aunty stands in front of me with a cup of tea. Aunty has been suspecting that I have something up my sleeve and that I have not told a soul. I can clearly see the glint of a wary question in her and she hovers around me, stares at me and sometimes even incites me into heated discussions about myself hoping that in the heat of the moment I might spill out some source of information.

'What time is it Aunty?'

'A little over nine, Ba. I have come in twice already to wake you but you were sleeping with such a peaceful look on your face. And you were even smiling, something I have not seen you do for a long time now. I just did not have the heart to take you away from a dream that seemed to give you so much happiness,' She is spurring me on again. 'Here, drink this tea. I have heated and re-heated it three times now.'

I take my cup of tea and walk out to the sitting room. It has been dusted and cleaned, tables wiped and fresh flowers placed into the green plastic vases that Aunty had brought along from Gauri Phanta.

'Will you be having lunch at home today, Sanju?'

Aunty is asking me a question but I feel my throat is clamped, I cannot answer her back. I do not want to. Instead I want to stare out into the faint outline of the green foliage of the distant jungles, visible from the open windows.

'Sanju... Babu are you not well?' Now there is alarm in her voice as she stands by my side, her face contorted in a curious look and eyes peering into mine.

'I am okay, Aunty. Don't worry. It's just that I could not sleep well last night,' the words escape like a sigh.

'You worry too much, Babu. You worry for the world uselessly. Let the world go to the dogs for all we care. We have our own lives to live, Sanjeevani. Live it well and you make a difference anyway.'

I can see her pretty face already masked for the day. She pats on a cushion next to her on the couch, gesturing me to come sit by her. I don't. Standing by the window I ask, 'And do you think you have a significant impact upon this world? Do you think anyone will remember you once you are dead and gone? No, Aunty, you will be forgotten as we have forgotten Dada...'

'Sanju, my poor child, don't talk like that. We all remember Sanjay. He will remain in our hearts forever but one has to move on. We have to continue living our lives irrespective...'

'Irrespective of what, Aunty?' Suddenly my voice is loud. I can hear it thundering against my own ears; loud splatters of hatred, disgust and even desolation. 'Irrespective of whether we are happy or not, whether we are satisfied or not? Why do we go on, Aunty, alone and yearning all the time? Why do we?'

'That is what life is all about, Sanjeevani.' She is patting my head and staring along with me at the vast stretches of fields that are now yellow with...

'Is Jijumua happy? No, she is not. She is reduced to this old, crinkled up woman, with nothing remaining of her wealth and grandeur. One of her sons is dead, her grandson is dead, her silver *peek daan* has been sold away, her silver *borsi* has been sold away, her diamond and gold jewellery, if there is any left, she will never wear. What is the point, Aunty? Of anything, of life, of ambitions of undertakings and endeavours? Why do we strive? To end up with nothing... to be taken to the ghats and burned there...'

Across the open fields, the yellow cover of the ripe mustard moves in waves in tandem with the gentle breeze. I see myself, a child of nine or ten maybe, hiding under the its lush cover...

'Sanju...Sanju...Maharani...Sanjeevani...Maiya...' I hear voices of people calling me in different names, different tones. I wait, crouching further and smiling a naughty smile. I know Mamu is looking for me with a glass of milk in her hand. Ladhe and Kallu are helping her in her search and from the courtyard, Jijumua calls too, blowing out puffs from her silver-lined smoking pipe.

I can hear the calls getting nearer and shift further into the thicket of the mustard. 'Sometimes there are snakes in there, Sanju, in the fields...Ladhe caught one just yesterday...' My mother is prodding me on, hoping that in fear of the snake I will walk out of my hideout...I don't. I keep smiling and trying my best to stifle the laughter that is bubbling inside me, forcing itself out in loud peals.

'Rani sa'b, there is Maiya!' That is Kallu, and I know he has found me...

'*Moro...kale tharu...*' I am running after him now, across the field towards the kharihan but then he changes course and charges instead towards the courtyard. I blindly chase him, not understanding that it is a trap...I am caught at the hand pump. Actually, I slip and fall over the greasy remains of the dishes that are washed there before and after every meal.

'*Macha maryo...*'

I struggle, twisting and turning my little frame, hoping to get free from Bua's arms that have wrapped me in a bundle. 'Let me...go, Bua...I don't want to drink that milk!' I say puffing and panting.

But his hold is strong and so are his arms. I relent then, burying my face into the immensity of his chest and feeling the loud thuds coming from his heart and somewhere blending with mine. From the corner of my eye I see, Laata bringing his axe down on the fallen log. Besides him stands Kanchi, gesturing with her hands. He cannot hear or talk. Kanchi is telling him to speed up with the cutting of the wood. Behind them a trail of Kamlaharis walk, baskets over their heads and their rounded hips swaying in a perfect synchrony.

'Is that someone you know, Sanju? Sanju, that man is waving at you from outside the gate. Do you know him?'

Her voice comes from a distance, a different land and time altogether, it seems at first but. Then I am brought back to my surroundings. My heart is heavy again with a gloom that is stifling.

'Who? What man?' caring little, I ask anyway.

'Look, Sanju, that man with a cap, just outside our gate...' Aunty turns my head towards the front gate...and there I see him, his black peek cap with white Mickey Mouse printed all over, the brooding eyes just below.

'Chandra!' I scream. 'Chandra!' I scream again and rush outside, across the verandah, over the little pathway and to the gate.

I hold him tight. 'Chandra, I am lost...I am lost, Chandra. Help me, Chandra...'

He cups my face in his hands that are firm as are his conviction. 'My dearest Sanjee, no one helps no one.' As we sit on the verandah staring into the thick of the darkness all around 'What you are looking for is within you, not outside. Nature, places, people and even myself...we are mere mediums, my'darling, for you to reach yourself.'

He is smiling at me and I stare into his eyes – the very eyes that are ever so cautious but always curious and in them I see myself...lost. Instantly, I hear myself...is that me or is it reflections of his own inert sentiments?

Sanat

Sanat watches Sanjay stand listlessly in the middle of the fields. The wheat is ripe and stretches of yellow mixed with contrasting shades of husk brown and even gold spread in the distance. From where she stands in the courtyard, shading her eyes with the palm of her hand, Sanat can clearly make out that Sanjay is tense and worried. The wheat is ready for cutting and there are no labourers.

Unlike the old days, the Kamaiyas don't come searching for a place to work. One has to go out looking for them and then bicker with them, for their attitudes have changed as have their demands. As for Sanjay, he is facing blatant hostility from the local villagers who have in recent years woken up to the sentiment of equality. This is making them resent Sanat's family, and their years of dictatorship. It is as if these same villagers seem to want an explanation for all the years of exploitation and subordination that they were subjected to. Clearly, Sanjay faces a difficult time ahead; more so with the Maoist cadres slowly sweeping in, promoting their propaganda and even forcefully asserting the strong sentiment of a fair and an egalitarian society. 'How can they expect a man living in a leaking hut with barely any land, to be of the same standing as one who has so much?' Sanat thinks quietly to herself, still watching her grandson.

Prashant has fled. There is now a direct threat to his life. If he returns to the village, the despise and resentment for the likes of her family would be too much to bear. It was Sanat who beseeched and implored Prashant to leave the area on the day they had found Bhek Bahadur Shahi's head strung up on a pole near the highway. It was a clear indication that other zamindars could be victims to the same fate. 'Babu, I think...it is time that you left,' Sanat had said that night after the servants, the few that were left, had come trailing in a line and touched her feet, a custom that had been in practice since she could remember. This was done every evening when the lamps were lit and repeated every morning when milk was brought to her.

His head was bobbing up and down, a clear indication of Prashant's distress. He did not want to leave. This was home, these were his farms that bore years of hard work to make it what it is today. Yet, Prashant knew that he was standing at the threshold of a drastic change that was soon to rush in, and capsize their own lives. He was worried for his son, too. Prashant had enforced this burden of continuing to pursue the family vocation of farming on him.

'I think I shall sell everything and move for good to some other country,' Prashant had said, thinking at the same time that living in this country made no sense now. It had suddenly become a different land, with strange people and their hostile and rather offensive attitudes.

'No one is going to buy our lands until this Maoist crisis is over, Bua,' Sanjay had let out his concerned opinion from the other end of the room, where he sat playing with his daughter who sat on his lap, happily gurgling.

'Besides, what will you get for this land? It is nothing but a stretch of mud, barely holding any value, in comparison to our lands in Kathmandu that you and Thulubua kept selling as if they were peanuts each time he stood up for elections.' Just as soon as these words came out, he regretted it instantly. His face had gone red for his own insolence.

'Th...th...that's what you think, Sanjay? That Dai and myself
have sold off everything for nothing, do you? My dear boy, how
do you think we've been faring all these years, making ends meet,
educating the four of you, getting Hemant married, building a house
for him in Kathmandu, getting Himani married, her dowry, getting
you married? And Sanju is yet to be married. Besides, Dai being the
person he was...state minister and all...always wanted to maintain
a certain kind of lifestyle in Kathmandu. How were we to meet all
those expenses? We had to sell off land there and here, too. For the
income, as you know very well now, from these lands, is only so
much.' Loud and assertive, Prashant was clearly moved.

   Sanjay had retreated to his compliant self, quiet and distanced.
'My apologies, Bua,' he said softly. 'I should not have said that. But
as Jijumua says, you should not stay in Ganeshpur. I am here to
take care of the farming until this crisis...'

   'What makes you think you will be safe here?' Prashant had
turned around dramatically, and stared defiantly at his son.

   'I have not harmed anyone here. They don't hold a grudge
against me. It is you and Thulubua they are after. Besides, I feel if
I stay here, I can even try to bring things around. You know, blend
in with them and their sentimentality, so that they begin to slowly
shed off the resentment they hold against our family.' But as Sanjay
said this, he knew that the resentment against his family was strong.
Besides, promises of distributing the land belonging to the affluent
were being made by the Maobadis to the poor.

   Prashant had left, taking Anju with him, who had quietly wiped
her tears and blessed her son for taking on the responsibilities of
his father.

   Sanat walks back to her cot laid out under the shade of the mango
trees. 'Hare Ram!' she breathes in. Resting her walking stick by the
cot, she sits and pulls her hookah closer. The coal in the chillum is
cold; she wants it replaced and looks around for someone. There is

no one there. She can hear Shanti, Sanjay's wife, inside the house, trying to feed the baby who in turn is yelling. Kanchi must be in the kitchen preparing lunch, and Laata must be sprawled, drunk and insensate, by the pile of logs near the shed or in the shed itself, splattered in cow dung and mud. Placing the pipe on the cot, Sanat decides not to smoke.

'So much has changed...new trends, new faces. The old are either dead or slowly waning off as distant dreams, hazy in sight yet vividly clear to the mind. Tara is dead, so is her maid Phool Maya. Chanda has moved with her son to Gaindakheda. Having taken her share of the property, she now spends her days staring at the sun during the day and at the fire during nights. Inert and unreceptive, she might as well be dead. When the two of us meet, we sit in silence, refusing to go back, to reminisce the past, lives that belonged once to them and were not mere reflections of others,' recalls Sanat. 'We have lived our lives, we live no more, we walk around now, like mere shadows of our own past. The future belongs to these...to Sanjay...to Hemanta, to Hemlata and to Sanju...' she meditates.

It is at this moment Sanat remembers that Sanjeevani is here, somewhere; that is if she has not gone off wandering into the nearby jungles or is not out by the banks of the river, aimlessly staring into it, captivated by its gurgling waters. The thought of Sanjeevani brings back in Sanat the same feeling of guilt and even remorse of a certain kind.

'I should have known years ago, and harnessed that spirit...yet I did not,' Sanat can hear her own self...regretting. 'I had my selfish reasons, for did I not revel in it myself? Feel her over-powering defiance filter into me as would a warm ray of the morning sun, bright and comforting. I yielded to the many assertions of life. Sanju is different. I knew from her early years that this life, with its demanding stances, would be confining for her wandering spirit. Yet, I let her soar, never attempting to harness her.'

Sanat heaves a deep heavy sigh and begins to concentrate on the verses of the Bhagvata Purana. But she fails to concentrate. 'What is she going to do now. Marry that Marwari and shame her father, hurt him...and kill his pride...'

Prashant was still recovering from the trauma inflicted on him when Sanjeevani had broken her engagement with Nabin. He walks around looking beaten and ashamed. That night as they eat, their food laid out on the *khandethaal*, Sanat watches her two grandchildren eat and talk, debate and disagree. Yet she feels a strong bond between the two, though they are complete opposites in mind – Sanjay, the obedient son, and Sanjeevani, the rebel.

It is right then that the dogs in the courtyard begin to bark and growl. There are voices, sharp and domineering. There is a loud thud, the sound of a stick slamming onto something. A dog begins to whimper and Kanchi comes in running, white-faced and speechless. She merely gestures with a wave of her hand, indicating that the Maoists are here.

Sanat freezes and watches mute as Sanjay confidently stands up, leaving his dinner uneaten. He washes his hands and begins to walk out of the house. Sanjeevani follows her brother defiantly. She is protective but is clearly worried. Shanti clings on for comfort to her infant daughter.

Outside, the moon is shining in all its brilliance. Streaks of silver fall on the golden shafts of wheat that softly sway with the tender breeze. The green silhouettes of seesam, sal and ashok stand tall, reflecting the softrays of the scintillating moon. But in the courtyard, a dark menace prevails.

There are about forty of them. They are armed; some of them are wearing combat uniform, their faces masked with scarves covering their mouths and noses, sparing only their eyes, defiant and blazing with hatred.

Instinctively, Sanjeevani grasps hold of her brother's arms, her grip firm and reassuring. The two walk towards the mute group.

'Sanjay Singh,' one of them says.

'Yes, that is me,' Sanjay replies, polite and obliging.

Sanjeevani notices that her cousins have been brought along from the neighbouring villages – Tara's grandsons from Ratipur, and Chanda's grandsons from Gaindakheda. They stand, hands bound behind their backs, eyes flickering with the fear of the unknown. They look much like the sacrificial goats during the Dashain slaughter, thinks Sanjeevani, beginning to tighten her grasp on her brother's arm.

'Take this girl along with the other women and shut them up inside the house,' one of the masked men says. A few girls, young and severely determined to a cause, begin to walk towards Sanjeevani.

'Please let us sit down and talk, comrades.' Sanjay begins to ease the tension.

'Shut up!' one of them says, as another one shouts, 'Gone are the days of your talking, now you listen and we talk.'

'Samantibaad murdabad loktantra jindaabad!' A man from the crowd begins to shout a slogan and Sanjeevani suddenly notices that the man who shouted the slogan is her father's old kamaiya. Besides him, stands Bhalmansa, his son-in-law, Khushi Ram. With them are also Shankar Kathait and Biswas Bhatta, her brother's cricket partners. Many a time, these very people had eaten meals with her family, played cards and even helped with chores that sprung up unexpectedly. But now, they stand hostile, glaring at Sanjay with a disdainful look. Sanjeevani cannot help but think that this feeling must have been there always, but carefully camouflaged.

And then there is a chaotic hustle in the courtyard. Men grab hold of Sanjay, flinging Sanjeevani across the courtyard. 'Dada!' she calls out, concerned but confident still. As she is dragged away to the inside of the house, she sees her brother being tied with ropes. Along with him, her cousins are all pushed into the middle of the courtyard.

Sanjeevani is taken to her grandmother's room. Two girls in combatant uniforms stand guarding the door and soon Sanat, Shanti the baby and Kanchi are forced into the room.

'Babu, take what you want but leave my grandsons. Please do not harm them.' She is pleading with her hands folded. Shanti sobs quietly, embracing her daughter tightly against her wildly beating heart.

The Maoist cadres do not bother to respond and ignore the pathetic pleadings of Sanat.

There is a lot of noise coming from outside – abuses, accusations and in between shaky explanations and arguments in self-defence.

'This is not the right solution, comrade. You have put your ideas across and we understand. We are fully with you with and will give all the support we can give,' Sanjay can be heard and then there are noises of batons, sticks, and butts of guns coming down.

Sanjeevani slumps on the floor by the window, helpless and tormented. She can hear painful cries and the moans of her cousins with each sound of smashing, whipping and thrashing. Sanjeevani can see it clearly even though her eyes are clamped shut. She can see the vision of her brother helplessly taking the physical assault upon him.

This violent foray stretches into the night. The baby is asleep and Shanti is weeping. Her body is trembling with her sobs and she clings onto the frail, aging self of Sanat, who sits staring quietly, listening to the heart-wrenching cries of her grandsons.

It is near dawn that they hear Sanjay scream out, a desperate plea. 'Stop! Stop! Please stop, he is dead...' and he begins to cry. His distressed wails ringing out loud and clear and disappearing into the dismal silence of the breaking dawn.

'And you still standing?' Thud! And a bang! Then a loud painful 'Aieeaaaah!' from Sanjay.

'Dada...' Sanjeevani begins to cry. Her head buried in between her knees, her body sways back and forth. 'Dada!' she sobs, wishing she were outside with him to share with him his pains. She knew her cousins were all either dead, knocked out or had simply given in to their helpless predicament. Except for Sanjay's, not a sound comes from outside. His agonising cries seem to pierce through Sanjeevani as though she were actually receiving the assault herself.

Then there is silence and sounds of people leaving. The cadres guarding the door unlock it and come in for a brief moment with shining torches in their hands.

'Take them and leave! And don't ever think of coming back!' says one of them, stern and severe.

All the women rush out. Bodies lie scattered all over the courtyard.

'Kanchi, go down to Pahalmanpur and bring some help from the Wada Prahari Karyaly there. And make a call to Bua from a telephone line and tell him to come down immediately with some police escort.'

She rushes to her brother. Bruised and bleeding, his legs lie limp and fractured in front of him; but he is sitting up, his hands over his stomach. As Sanjeevani nears him, she sees Sanjay throw up. A long thick trail of blood spurts out and he falls back on the ground.

'Dada!' she screams, tears blinding her eyes. He takes her hand and asks for water. Shanti runs in to the kitchen and rushes back with a glass of water. 'Ashok is dead,' he says. His eyes are dull with anguish. He then smiles – a quiet, peaceful smile and with it comes a glint in his eyes, a sudden flicker of approaching relief.

'Maa . . .' he calls out for his mother. As Sanjeevani sits, stunned with dismay, she watches her brother immerse himself into the depths of an enticing sleep. She can see the expressions of pain slowly fade from his face, as do the ones of regret and remorse and, finally, a tranquil smile, still and everlasting, settles on his face.

When Prashant arrives with his wife, Sanjeevani braves herself to meet her parents. There is a sudden urge to flee. She has seen enough and cannot think of enduring her father's pathetic plight.

There is commotion all around. Police vans and ambulances and people come to comfort and console. Sanjeevani stands, aloof and apart from the mourning crowd, watching the rest – weeping, wailing, fainting and preparing the bodies for cremation.

It is when Sanjay's body is ready to be lifted and taken away to be burnt to ashes, that she feels her father's hand on hers. Large, warm and loving as it had always felt but now it lacks the strength that his grasp had always given her. Now it holds on to hers, as though in need of assurance, support and encouragement.

With one hand, he caresses his son's dead face. 'Go, my son. It is here we part.' he says, his face rigid with stoicism.

Sanjeevani can't dare to look at her father's face. She stares at her brother's dead body being lifted and taken away. Her hand firmly held on to her father's, her eyes blank and dry, she begins to fortify her shattered soul.

Sanjeevani

The emptiness in me is overwhelming. There are times when I wonder if there are others, too, who feel like a pariah in their own bodies? There is a feeling of gloominess that weighs me down at all times. It refuses to leave me. It hovers around me like a heavy burden on my mind...dark and menacing. So, I carry it along – this feeling of not belonging anywhere, not even to myself. I walk into one day from another in a numbed daze.

I look at Jijumua. Each day she grows frail and older. She puffs and pants while walking to the bathroom. There is a cotton mat laid on the floor next to her bed, neatly covered with a worn-out sheet. She will emerge from the bathroom and sit there, breathing heavily. Though she is slowly losing sight, she will insist on finger-reading the words on her copy of the Bhagvadgita each morning. She knows each word spoken by Lord Krishna to Arjun by heart now. Yet, she flips over the pages once she has completed reciting the previous one. It is as though she were actually reading out from the book.

I watch her quietly from a corner of the room. She has not noticed my presence. She fumbles with her nightgown, trying to secure the hooks around her chest. Unable to do so, she lets it be. Her silver hair is in a mess with odd streaks falling over her wrinkled face. Instinctively, her trembling hand moves up and her fingers tuck away the meddling strands behind her ears. Aunty is menstruating and therefore she has moved into my room for the next five days. Jijumua is now my responsibility.

Jijumua had come down to Dhangadi a few months ago, to evade the biting cold of the winter in Kathmandu. But the tarai winter this year had been a severe one. We did not see the sun for days; a stubborn fog lingered around the entire day causing a constant chill to seep into the flesh and bones. Yet, she refused going back to Kathmandu at the end of winter when my father had called to send her back in March.

'For me it is the same now. Whether I am living in Kathmandu or here with you in Dhangadi, I am dependant here and will be begging people in Kathmandu, too. Why am I not taken away? How much more are you going to make me suffer, oh lord?' She is mumbling to herself as she fiddles around to locate her Bhagavadgita book that was bound in red velvet.

'In Kathmandu, it will not be so hot, Jijumua. It will be easy for you there,' I say, moving towards where she sits, with a hairbrush in my hand.

'Is that you, Sanjeevani?' she asks, squinting her eyes and craning her neck forward in an attempt to figure out my presence.

'Yes, Jijumua, it is me.' I raise my voice to speak to her as she cannot hear otherwise. 'Let me brush your hair, Jijumua,' I shout out loud as I first fasten her gown.

'Sanju,' she mumbles. It is more of an admission to her own self than an address to me.

'Jijumua, I think we can go the doctor today. Dr Pathak will sit in his clinic after five. It's best to see him there as the hospital is very crowded,' I shout out loud again.

'There is no need, Sanju, to waste money on the doctor. It's only the cold. My bones and body are too frail to fight it. Let it be,

Baa. No doctor can do anything about this body now. It has been patched and mended many times. It is time for this body to be thrown away. How many days do I have left anyway? I don't think this crumbling body of mine is going to survive this winter.'

I take extra care to be gentle with her hair as I brush the scanty and thin white strands on her aged scalp. I remember how long and thick her hair used to be. At one time, it used to be neatly plaited and many times tied into a high bun. She had been pretty. Old photographs of her were proof enough. In the black and white pictures that I found, her hair was done up in trendy styles; in some, her eyebrows were shaped straight and in others, they were curving upwards. Fancy saris adorned her voluptuous frame in style; she seemed to have had a very impressive personality as she posed elegantly, sitting on a couch with her husband standing by her side.

The immensity of change in a human being is striking and as I continue brushing the balding head of my grandmother, I reason silently to myself – the rationale of being born, helpless, and incompetent; then gradually grow in size and mind and become able, skilled, knowledgeable, only to deteriorate back to the same infantile incapacities. Is all this to disappear one day? It just does not make sense to me – the human cycle, the lifecycle and the purpose of our living.

'You said that last winter when you were sick with chest infection, then last summer when you were down for days with diarrhea, too. Jijumua, you've been saying this for the past many years now. Each season to you seems the last. But we shall each go when it is time. I guess it is left to the almighty to decide when the time is right for each one of us,' I say, finishing brushing her hair and tying it up with a thick rubber band.

'He is unfair in his dealings; taking away lives hardly lived and keeping ones tied to life by the thinnest thread to go on enduring the hassles of life,' she says, the note of despondency clear in her trembling voice.

I dust her tiny table that she uses to place her Bhagvadgita when she pretends to read from it. I place the red velvet-bound book on it, place a cotton rug on her knees and help her move towards her bed. As I get the bed ready for her to sleep, I watch my grandmother sprinkle some water with a bundle of grass onto the cover of the Bhagvadgita. She then slowly turns to the first page and begins to recite the verses with the index finger of her right hand tracing each word on the page as though the words were indeed clearly visible to her.

Soon, I will have to get her meal ready. She is used to having a proper meal by 10 a.m. I will cook the dal and vegetables. When I get ready to place the rice into the cooker, she will insist on coming into the kitchen only to plug on the cooker and wait there until the green light comes on to alert that the rice is cooked. This of course she cannot see and has to be informed by me. After lunch, she will nap for a while, not on her bed but on the floor mattress. She needs to be woken up with a cup of tea at 2 p.m. and then she will need someone to talk with for some time. Normally, Aunty would sit by her and the two would talk of the good old days when there is no one else visiting Jijumua. People here come in hordes each day – relatives, relatives of relatives and even friends and neighbours of relatives. In comparison to Kathmandu, it is amazing to see how much time people here have to while away their hours on someone distant and old and yet not grudge it. For this, I am thankful. It keeps Jijumua occupied all day. To me, these are just beaming faces and people who are dressed up in bright coloured clothes; some carry polythene packets with fruits, some come with boxes of sweets and some come with long trails of shrieking and bratty children, who run around my apartment as though it were a playground, forcing me to lock my bedroom in fear that one of them might someday innocently damage or destroy my manuscript or my computer.

I have never had patience for socialising. After some time, people, company, and voices begin to scare me. It's more of a claustrophobic feeling. I am overcome with a strong urge to flee, to dissociate myself from companionship.

Jijumua is loud, nearly singing the verses of the Bhagvadgita. Having made her bed, I walk out to the drawing room. Through the open door, I can see Aunty sitting out in the verandah, picking out stones and other waste material from grains of rice spread on a plate. I walk to the telephone and call the shelter.

A lot has changed there in the past five years. I have seen women, children, and even employees coming and leaving, and then soon becoming a hazy memory, distant and apart. Although Hari, the peon, and Sarala Di and Dhimni are still employees of the Naari Bishram Kendra, many others have left and have been replaced by new ones. No one is permanent at the shelter – not the employed staff nor the asylum seekers, children and women included. As for the children, there is now a waiting list. There are so many destitute children, more so due to the war. Quite a few have run away from their homes in the hills for many reasons. Although most of them run and end up in India, willingly or even by force and malpractices, some are brought to us by locals, and some by the police and security forces.

The phone is answered by Sharmila Bhatta. She considers herself as a member of the permanent staff of the Naari Bishram Kendra. Since the first time she was rescued from the hospital by me, she has come in to the shelter often seeking refuge and left months after. 'He has changed for good now, Sanju Madam,' or even, 'Sanju Madam, *dharmo dharma*. I spoke to his sister and she feels the same. It was the effect of some bad *grahas* on him that made him behave the way he did – drinking and abusing. But now the *grahas* have passed over. Now I am certain he is a changed man for good.'

With each reason that Sharmila gave, she went back to him but returned shortly, bruised and battered again. The last time she returned was a year back, when she arrived on a rickshaw, her neck and hands completely burnt by the acid that her drunk husband had poured over her. That perhaps, had jolted Sharmila Bhatta out of her indecisiveness. She is now convinced that he is indeed a threat to her life: Having worked with battered women for nearly half a decade, I am convinced that women need rude awakenings to understand their own capacities.

Sharmila Bhatta has now started her own beauty parlour for women and men and calls it the 'Kathmandu Beauty Parlour'. Whenever she gets free time, she comes and helps out in the shelter, that has become an extended home and family for her.

'Helloooo, Nari Bishram Kendra,' Sharmila screams on the other end of the line.

'It is me, Sharmila. Sanjeevani, and for God's sakes, one can hear you alright, so do keep the volume low,' I complain.

'Sanju Madam, good that you called as I was going to call you myself. There was a trunk call from Kathmandu for you. A gentleman had called. I have written his name and number down as you had taught me to do and even said "thank you for calling, sir" before hanging up...just the way you had instructed.'

There is a buzzing sound on Sharmila's end; she is probably looking for the piece of paper where she has noted the caller's name.

A fly buzzes around my face and I flick it away with a careless wave of my hand as my eyes scan the room, languorously moving from one object to another. I can see the green vase with the red and yellow plastic flowers in it on the centre table. A layer of dust has accumulated over the flowers. 'This room needs a bit of dusting,' I tell myself, looking at the ceiling where the fan is hanging, patches of cobweb draped around it. I think I shall stay back home today and clean this place. As it is, Jijumua will need some company, with Aunty being of no use to her now. Hari, she cannot tolerate for his insolence. 'Budi mua...' he calls her with a naughty grin on his face, making her fume.

'Cheeky boy! Teach him some manners, Sanju. I am not his grandmother for him to call me Budi Mua. And I don't like him addressing you as Sanju Di. Tell him to call you Maiya Saab or something as respectable.'

I am certain that this is Jijumua's defense mechanism. She is not comfortable with the fact that a young boy, although much younger than me is living in the same house and laughs and talks to me, blatantly disregarding the protocol between servant and employer. Besides, he is a male...a species never to be trusted, thinks my grandmother, especially with an unmarried girl like myself around.

I can hear Hari singing to himself in the kitchen, loud and happy with himself for no apparent reason. Hari is loud, boisterous, and rude but I cannot help appreciate his careless attitude towards life. He has nothing. No family, no land, no home and barely any income...yet he is so content. He seems to have no grudges against his present and little hope from the future. Yet he goes on living each day with a zeal and vigour that seems a hazy illusion to me.

'Here, I have it Sanju Ma'm,' Sharmila is so loud that I have to move away the phone from my ear. 'Yes...this is it.' She is still shouting on the other end.

'Razat Aggarwal. Would you like his contact number? He has given his mobile number, Sanju Ma'm, and he said he wanted to urgently speak to you. Take down the number, Sanju Ma'am. I shall wait till you get a pen and paper.'

'That won't be necessary, Sharmila,' said I, my voice distant and alien to my own senses.

I am stunned as I put the receiver down. It has been nearly two years since I last met Razat in Kathmandu. 'Have lunch with me,' he had said when I was about to leave his conference room.

'This late? You haven't eaten? It's nearly five!' I had exclaimed, my eyes instinctively falling on the wall clock behind him.

'We have no fixed time for meals, madam! That is our last priority. We eat whenever there is time. Seriously, Sanju, join me for lunch. We could order something, some South Indian food perhaps?'

'OK,' I had said carelessly, pulling back the chair I had stood up from and seating myself again. 'I have nothing else to do anyway but to wander around town, staring at faces and places.'

Lunch was brought from Aangan. However, we did not eat in the conference room where we had been sitting. I was escorted to the fourth floor where Razat had his private cabin and taken into a room adjacent to it. It was a huge hall and against one wall was a raised platform upon which were placed mattresses neatly covered with white bed sheets – something I had grown up seeing in the shops of Dhangadi as a child. Fat merchants in white dhotis used to sit on it, bargaining prices, eating, and even napping on it.

'Wow!' I had exclaimed, for this setting was so against Razat's personality. He was a modern man, with modern tastes.

'This used to be my father's office,' he had explained, understanding my unspoken bafflement. 'He uses it sometimes, with his old colleagues and friends.'

Against the opposite wall was a wooden cabinet. 'But mostly we use this room now to store gifts that come in from business associates and other unnecessary items,' Razat had explained, drawing my attention to the opposite wall where a massive wooden cabinet stood towering down from the ceiling. In front of it was a round table with four chairs around it and it was here that we had sat down to eat. There were some hot cases containing his lunch sent from home. And perhaps, thinking that his wife had sent food only enough for him, Razat had ordered some vada pau and a masala dosa from Aangan.

The table had been set before our arrival and a peon-like man had bustled around serving the two of us with the South Indian dishes alongside the food sent from Razat's home, probably cooked and packed by his wife.

'It's good to see you again, Sanju,' Razat had mumbled, looking down at his plate and seeming to concentrate on his food.

I had not replied but only smiled in agreement.

'You know, Sanju, I have always believed in destiny. I have always been finicky about starting new ventures without having the positive aspects of it aligned with my stars and destiny. There are certain things that are meant for you, written down as your fate and no matter what you do about it, fate will take its own course. I have done well in my business, perhaps because it was fated. I consider myself lucky. And sometimes, close associates, friends, relatives and even business associates make an impact on our fate, Sanju.'

Razat had put down his fork and spoon on his plate and had started gesticulating with his free hands.

'Come to the point, Razat,' I had prodded him on, getting a feeling that I was not going to like whatever was soon going to be said.

'You see, Sanju...we are all bound by our destiny and we will go wherever it leads us. We may or may not accept its prominence in our lives but the fact remains that we do whatever is fated for us.' His hands drew an imaginary line across his forehead while saying the last sentence.

'So?' I had asked, tasting the bhindi that had come from his house and silently complimenting Sangeeta's culinary skills.

'So, Sanju, I mean to say...we met because it was predestined. And we have come all this way and met again because perhaps we were destined to meet again. And Sanju, if distances have crept between us, it is because we were destined to move away.'

The metal locket of some God around his neck, and the thick bundle of white, yellow and red thread bound around his wrist had never seemed so constricting. It was as if, his belief and his faith were the prime reasons for me being an outsider for him.

'Stop! Stop right there, Razat Aggarwal!' I had butted in.

'We moved away not because of our destiny but because you chose to and dictated your wish on me. And our first meeting was not any predestined encounter but all my doing. I saw you, I liked you and so I made an effort. And if you must know, our relationship lasted as long as it did due to my efforts. I chose to acquiesce, I chose to forget my own wishes, giving precedence to yours...'

There was a stunned silence and I could hear my voice loud, clear and forceful resounding against the huge walls of the room.

'I made myself a puppet, dancing to your tunes, Razat. You said come, I came. You said go, I left. Did I have any say? Any at all? Be honest to yourself, Razat. Did I ever have any say at all in our relationship? No. It was bloody dictated by your whims, fancies and your timings. Yet, I loved you Razat, selflessly. I gave myself to you, for I loved you for what you were and not for what I would have wanted you to be.'

Perhaps somewhere in between this outburst, I had heard Razat say, 'Sanju, stop! Let me explain.'

But something had happened inside my head and there was no stopping me now, for the words that were being released came out with a conviction that was both forceful and awakening. Finally I was admitting to myself, that I had been used by Razat...and that I had been dumped by him. That throughout all this I had not had any say.

'I was the flip side of your coin, Razat. On one you had your pretty wife, your homemaker, mother of your children, this elegant piece that you carried with yourself...for she was appreciated, and accepted by the society that meant the world to you. As for me, I was the other side...your mistress. The sexy young thing who was there to give you a sense of liberation from the the demands of a proper life. I was your alter ego, Razat. You saw in me the freedom that you have always craved for. The escape from the monotony of your constricted life.'

I could feel the wet trickles of tears slide down my cheeks. But I did not care to wipe them away. It was comforting, somehow, to feel these tears, warm and wet...a palpable acceptance of my latent grief.

I had cried shamelessly, sitting in Razat's father's very baniya style meeting room, munching on the food that his wife had sent for him but clearly releasing myself out of his clutches.

Or so, I think now. For the mere mention of his name after two years has managed to hold me in a state of trance again. I can feel my heart beats thump with a crazy sort of excitement. 'Excitement for what?' I ask myself, sitting down on the nearest chair by the phone.

Thoughts, many of them, begin to race in my mind. Many whys and as many ifs begin to dance in my mind. I know the questions are there but none of them seem to make any sense to me; my mind for an instance is a chaotic whirlpool.

'Chandra...Chandra,' I hear myself say aloud, staring into my palms. I am seized by the fear of letting myself be vulnerable again. I can sense myself split into two contradicting halves. One cautioning me against Razat, and the other luring me towards him, prompting my inert senses to admit his significance to my wandering soul.

'Don't...Don't Sanju. Don't do it,' I can hear myself say. Despite trying to control all my desires, I can feel my hands pick up the phone and punch the numbers on it. After all these years of having not called Razat, I don't know how I still manage to remember his number.

I hear his voice on the other end.

'Razat?' I say.

'Yes dear?' he replies on the other end.

I spend the rest of the day doing this and that. Having cooked Jijumua's lunch, I take it to her room and watch her eat in silence. She does say a few things to me but I fail to grasp any of it and merely smile or nod my head in response. Later in the afternoon, I sit with Aunty on the verandah.

I know Aunty has noticed the sudden alteration in me.

'You look pale, Sanju,' she says with the same glint in her eye that gives away her veiled curiosity. 'Are you not well today?'

'It is nothing really, Aunty,' I begin hiding my feelings but then words begin to get stuck in my throat. It's a feeling of being choked; I feel helpless. I crawl towards her and placing my head on her lap, I begin to cry.

For the longest time, Aunty lets me cry without questioning or enquiring. I can feel my body shake in tremors, the feeling of sheer helplessness is simply overwhelming.

'Let it flow, Chori...let it out of your system. It has been pent up there for too long,' says Aunty, caressing my head.

Then I tell her about all that happened in the past five years of my life. Aunty is quiet but is warm and receptive.

'I cannot say...I do not love Chandra. If it had not been for him, I don't know what I would have done, Aunty. I was so damn lonely and frustrated with myself. Then, Chandra came along. He was this thin thread that connected me with life, with feelings and made me feel alive again. But you know what, Aunty? I made Chandra a refuge from my aches for Razat....'

At this point I look up. Aunty is gazing at the endless stretches of fields ahead. I have never seen Aunty look so firm and stoic. It says so much.

'Aunty, tell me what to do?' I begin to nudge her for she is lost in her own thoughts. 'I am tired, Aunty...tired of making decisions.

There are times when I think I should listen to Mamu and marry some old widower, but tell me, how will I breathe? How will I live? I might as well be dead then, no? But then all the choices that I have made for myself have not really worked out well for anybody, have they? Not for me, and not for my family. What the hell is it that I want, Aunty? Tell me...I am so lost.'

My head rests on her lap and tears flow uncontrollably. Then I feel her hand on my head again. Fingers begin to massage my head, strokes that are gentle and assuring.

'Sanju, it is your body, your mind and your life. Your choices, wrong or right, are yours alone. You are right in not listening to others. But Chori, we live in a society where there are certain ways and norms created by these very people. And to be a part of this society, one does need to adhere to these norms and ways. That's how it is, Sanju. Or else, we might as well begin to live like animals – raw, barbaric and dissipated. You did not marry Nabin for your own reasons and instead, you gave yourself totally to Razat. He used you and then threw you out of his life. Then you met Chandra. You think you love Chandra and would want him as a lifelong companion, but now when Razat calls you, and seems to want you back in his life, you begin to crumble for you don't know who you want...Chandra or Razat?'

Her fingers are still stroking my head. 'It has always been Razat, Aunty. Now I am convinced; he never left...he was always there. And no matter how much I forced him out wanting to place Chandra there, it never happened. Or is it now that I am feeling so? I am scared, Aunty...scared of myself, my choices. I don't know what to do.'

'Then, you go, meet him, hear him out. Why is he here? What does he want? And take it from there. He could be in Dhangadi for any reason. Perhaps he is here for some business of his and just wants to say hello to you for old time's sake. Now you freshen up and get ready to meet him. You don't want to be seen by him after years looking disheveled and white as a ghost, do you? You are a strong person, Sanju. Show him your tougher side.'

Later in the evening, I take Jijumua on a rickshaw to the market and tell Hari to follow us on foot

'Make sure you stop to buy some vegetables and papaya; try and get some curd, too, if you can... and meet me at Dr Pathak's. I have some work to attend to... And you will need to bring Jijumua back home,' I shout out loud to him as our rickshaw passes him at the gate where he stands.

Passing the open field of the old airport, we take the connecting lane to the main market road. We pass the Wada Prahari Karyala, a one-and-a-half storey building, that was speckless white but for the border of grey that ran down from the windows. I spot Gore Dai. He has now been promoted from a sipahi to a hawaldar and has been shifted here from the Ji Pra Ka. He is now a prominent figure in the Hasanpur ward. Standing outside the gate on the street, he seems to be having a light conversation with a mad man. He probably wants to shoo off the mad man.

'*Prazatantra ho Gore Dai*, everyone's democracy. You can't have problems with the public wanting to stand on the road that belongs to them.' I wave to him and he waves back smiling but I have caught the attention of the mad man and he begins to run alongside my rickshaw. His clothes are dirty and in tatters.

'Maiya... give something, anything...'

I tell the boy pulling the rickshaw to stop for a moment as I reach out for my bag and begin to look for my wallet. The mad man rests on the side of the rickshaw; noticing that I am going to give him some money, he begins to sing praises.

'You will do well in life, Maiya. Raja Gyanendra is a good man. You see, he will end the Maobadis, cut off Prachanda's head...' he sings along in his delirium.

'Is he bothering you, Sanjeevani?' Gore Dai is beginning to cross the road, swinging his baton and walking towards the gate of the land revenue department where my rikshaw had been pulled up. 'Not really, Gore Dai...he is a harmless creature. It is the people with sane and sound minds that one needs to fear.'

Gore Rokaya laughs and before putting his baton back into its sheath that hangs to a side of his waist, he thrusts it menacingly at the face of the mad man. '*Bhag bahula*...or you will get beaten up!' he threatens the mad man in a mocking way. As I hand the mad man a ten rupee note, he snatches and begins to jump in the air.

'See you around hawaldar saab. Have to take Jijumua to the doctor,' I wave to Gore as the rickshaw begins to move forward. I turn my head to look at the back and see the mad man prancing around Gore Dai in circles and shouting, 'Raja Gyanendra ko jai...now I will go to Hong Kong...then to Singapore.'

'He has no need to beg for money,' the boy pulling the rickshaw begins to tell us, assuming that we do not know the history of the mad man. I do not bother to stress that I know. 'The mother fucker has a family – three sons and has a big house and many bighas of land. He is a goddamn millionaire but chooses to run around begging in tatters,' explains the boy as he rings the bell on the rickshaw handle alerting a pedestrian crossing the road.

'Life is all about the mind, bhai. It is the mind that has the final say to life. Sane or insane is for us to speculate but I guess the body attunes itself to the decisions of the mind.'

I might as well be speaking to myself! Besides, I knew I was talking nonsense although this encounter had got me thinking of the thin demarcating line that stands between sanity and insanity. Have I not nearly crossed this demarcation many a time? And I have fought hard from taking that last step that would take me into another world...a world where nothing mattered. The boy does not bother to reply. Instead, he pulls up the rickshaw in front of Dr Pathak's clinic.

New shops have sprung up in the course of my living here. The Tin Tin restaurant besides the clinic has recently opened and has already become a favourite with the locals. It is a huge hall with simple tables and chairs with some pictures of Rara Lake and even the flowery pastures of Khaptad hung on the walls. Towards one end of the dining hall is glass partition and behind it is the bar, where I have got myself sloshed to the bones with Gore Dai and his lot, many a nights.

Looking at the Tin Tin restaurant now, I am already thinking of getting Jijumua here after the visit to the doctor. 'It would be interesting for her to sip a cup of tea here, away from the house,' I think to myself as I escort her, dressed in a beige silk sari and walking slowly, bent over her walking stick.

'I have prescribed some vitamins and a cough syrup. She seems to be fine but that wheezing needs to be controlled, Sanjeevani. Try keeping her away from the fan as much as you can and make sure she inhales some steam at least twice a day. Apart from that, nothing to worry. Her chest is clear.' Dr Pathak smiles at me, making sure he touches my hand as he hands me the prescription for Jijumua.

Dr Pathak is a married man now. He brought a wife from Doti last year. She is an educated girl and is now doing her masters in social science. She writes for the local paper, her daily columns strongly advocating the deficiencies of the West. He shows her off to all he can from time to time but I guess his old, fond feelings for me will always remain.

'Come over some time to the house, Sanjeevani. It has been a long time since you and Anupama sat down and discussed the potentials of Kailali. Ha ha! You women can really make a grain of rice seem like a sack full!' he guffaws. I notice how the past five years and a marriage have made him look healthier, content and even slightly vain.

'That's where you are wrong, Dr Pathak,' I retort back gently, as I help Jijumua out of her chair and hand over her walking stick to her. 'Your vision of Kailali is one-dimensional but we've got a multi-dimensional vision of our jilla. So much can be done here. Once the insurgency is over, you will see how this place is going to boom. We've got the best of everything here, Dr Pathak – hills and flat lands, sprawling fields, rivers and jungles, villages and villages. What more could an urban mind want for a refreshing retreat? I insist again that we should all do something to promote eco tourism in this area. Villages need to become self-sufficient in a way that will preserve the natural beauty of the place. Progress and development does not necessarily have to be narrow patched-up roads and clusters of ugly, tiny brick houses. Kailali is beautiful and we must all get together to preserve its beauty and make the most of it.'

'And how do you expect to do that, Sanjeevani?' Dr Pathak finds me amusing. My unconventional way with life is probably what attracts him to me.

'As I said...eco tourism. We have the Godavari hills, only thirty kilometres from Dhangadi. We have Ghora Ghori lake right there. We have Doti, Dadeldhura, Achcham... nearby neighbours. We have Khutiya, Shivganga, Kandra, Mohana, beautiful rivers... All we have to do is promote these places as tourist destinations. Recreate trekking routes that our grandfathers used to go to the hills from the tarai, promote model villages to be shown to the tourists... Rafting in the Kandra, Godavari...there is so much potential in Kailali itself, Dr Pathak...only people like you and me have to begin racking our brains and raising voices. Not that we do not have our boys and girls from Kailali in the tourism board... Hikmat Singh for instance...we make a team...'

From the door that is open and a green curtain that separates the street outside from his cabin, I wave my hand to him and conclude. 'When we meet next, Dr Pathak, we seriously must discuss this option... and take it forward...'

Outside, a cold wind receives us. Jijumua wraps her shawl tightly against her crumbling form. The sky above is heavy with bundles of grey clouds ready to shower down. The street is clearing up. I can see people quickening their paces to their respective destinations, many beginning to call for rickshaws. I change my plans of taking Jijumua to the Tin Tin restaurant and instead ask Hari who is waiting outside the green curtains for us to hail a cab and take Jijumua home right away before it begins to pour.

'Sanju...it is going to rain, you don't have an umbrella...how will you get back home?' there is concern in Jijumua's voice...'I'll be fine Jijumua...you tell Hari to make a hot cup of tea for you. I shall be back to cook your dinner...' I wave my hand to her and begin to walk towards the Saathi Hotel.

It is just round the bend, I know for this new extravagant hotel has recently opened up right opposite Sharmila's Kathmandu beauty parlor. And I know that she has managed to get a good business from the visiting guests of the hotel so much that she has partitioned her space into two halves now, so that she can cater also to men who come more as guests of the hotel too. Thinking of Sharmila, I decide to have myself refreshed before going in to meet with Razat.

So I walk into the Kathmandu Beauty Parlor taking off my shoes at the doorstep. Inside, Sharmila has done a good job with the décor. The floor is a chequer board of black and white marbles and the ceiling is fitted with full size mirrors so that when one sits on the red vinyl, swiveling chairs and rests ones head back, one can get a good look of ones own body being pampered by Sharmila and her to assistants who are again victims of domestic abuse brought from the shelter.

'What a surprise Sanju Ma'am...you never waste money on parlors you said once.'

She is clearly elated that I have come to receive her efficiency.

'I just wanted to see...how good you are at this...' I find myself saying sheepishly.

'You see... Sanju Ma'am... I shall transform you from this drab and boring look that you seem to walk around with, making your self look years elder to what you really are.' She says. Pushing me down on one of the swiveling red chairs.

'Whatever you have to do...do it quickly, Sharmila... I got to meet some one at six at the Saathi Hotel.' I mumble peering into my reflection in the mirror spread out wall to wall in front of me.

'OHH!' Sharmila has a naughty grin on her face and a curious twinkle in her eye. 'Why Sanju Ma'am...it's the same gentleman from Kathmandu who called this morning. Isn't it? He must be special for you to make an effort...'

Her tiny face, naughty and impish, is stuck to mine from the side. She flicks her pointer finger at me in the mirror and then begins to trace my eyebrows. 'It's jungle out here Sanju Ma'am...you've got thick bushy brows that can be well shaped...uhh! As for the hair...we have little time so we will just do a quick shampoo and then blow dry it straight...you see what a difference that will bring to your face.'

After she finishes, I look at myself...transformed. A different person seems to stare back. Straight hair falling down my shoulders and neatly curved eyebrows. Sharmila has even managed to outline my eyelids with a pencil and splatter a little rouge over the curves of my cheeks.

'There you go Sanju Ma'am...you could be an actress if you wanted to. You are so pretty but hell-bent on looking plain and boring. See what a little touch up can do. We are women, Sanju Ma'am. Only men are born beautiful...the female species, be it animals or humans, we need to make an effort to be at par with our males. Look at the peacock, the female would definitely have to adorn herself to look as beautiful as the male. So is the case with us women...why do you think beauty parlors flourish all over the world?'

I smile quietly, for she did make some sense. 'See you later, Sharmila. And thanks… I will come back again,' I say, walking out.

She opens the door for me and whispers as I walk out, 'Say, hellooo, from my side, Sanju Ma'am… I am convinced now that he is someone special.'

I cross the road and enter the gate of Saathi Hotel. It has recently opened up and is the first of its kind in Dhangadi. As I walk across the parking lot, I cannot help but applaud the courage of the promotors of this hotel. It is a gamble indeed to have invested in a luxury hotel here in the remotes. But I guess times will change and being optimistic will reap its benefits then. A few cars are parked, most of them with blue number plates belonging to Bagmati Anchal. There are few private number plates and I wonder which one of them belongs to Razat, or whether he has flown in to Dhangadi as now there are flights coming in every day of Budha air from Kathmandu.

The reception is a small room with parquet flooring and maroon couches made to fit wall to wall. Towards one corner of the room is a little counter with its wall displaying timings of major cities in the world. Behind the counter sits a young man in his twenties, talking on the phone. 'Tharu,' I think to myself after hearing his accent, as he attends to hotel guest a calling from one of the rooms.

I let him finish his talking and wait by the counter. My listless gaze then falls on the white board behind the receptionist. It has room numbers and names of their occupants scribbled with a marker on it.

As I wait, my eyes begin to slowly scroll down the list and there I find Room No. 217… Mr. Razat Aggrawal. Simultaneously, the receptionist puts the receiver down and begins to attend to me. 'Yes?' he says, giving me an enquiring look.

'I am here to meet Mr. Razat Aggrawal,' I say pointing to his name on the board.

'Name please?' he asks.

'Sanjeevani Singh,' I tell him.

'Wait a minute,' the receptionist says in the same accent as before, convincing me of his caste. Bua should see how people have changed; how the tharus have moved beyond the fields and entered better and more promising professions. I ponder over this thought while the young man calls Razat's room to ask him whether he would like to meet me.

Having gotten an approval from his guest, the young man says, 'Go up to the first floor, last room to the left,' and he returns to answering the phone on the counter which begins to ring again.

I walk up the stairs. Feeling nothing...thinking nothing. Room 217. I ring the door bell. And he stands there – my Krishna, my Shyaam...my Razat. The same smile, the same twinkle in the eye and with the same soothing, calm voice, he ushers me in.

Sanat

King Birendra is dead, along with ten other members of the royal family. Gyanendra, the second son of the late king Mahendra, is now the King. After having wept, shaved off their heads and mourned for King Birendra, the very same people are now out on the roads screaming slogans against his brother King Gyanendra. They want the end of monarchy; put an end to the two-hundred year-old institution that has been the firm base of all cultures, traditions and even the sole identity of this nation, Nepal. Sanat fails to understand why. Why the same offending and torturing Maoists who were the enemy, suddenly seem to become the only hope for a drowning country? Sanat now lives in a small, drab, and dreary rented apartment in Kathmandu. She longs for the open vastness of her own village. Here, when she looks out of the window, she sees the congested concrete jungle spread like an ugly scar over a beautiful face, gaping back at her. Disgusted, she never leaves the apartment. Besides, the thick smoke and noise of the chaotic traffic outside unnerves her. So, she confines herself to the small, dark and dingy rooms that barely receive any sunlight, and limits her mind to the thoughts of her Gods, praying to them for a quick death.

Soon after Sanjay's death, Sanat had found herself taking another blow of fate, cruel and painful. Prabhat died of a heart attack. He went out for his daily morning walk and never came back. Watching the dead body of her son, Sanat was shocked and furious at her own resilience. 'How much more can I endure?' she asks herself, frustrated and resigned. Prashant has withdrawn into a shell; he no longer remains the man he was – clear, calm and always hopeful for the best. He now spends his days brooding in front of the television; his graying scalp, nodding up and down to the beats of his heart, perhaps. Anju walks around like a ghost trapped in someone else's body. She passes the days in just conducting the daily chores; at night, her head rests against her pillow; perhaps she lets out silent tears for a life she has lived in utter futility. Her son is dead, her daughter is a rebel and a disgrace to the entire family, and her husband has withdrawn into a selfish gloom of his own.

Sanjeevani will not let go of Razat Aggarwal. And Razat Aggarwal will not give Sanjeevani's feeling a respectable status as he is already happily married with children. 'What will Sanjeevani do?' is another thought that worries Sanat while chanting from her Bhagvad Puran. Then she thinks, 'What good did it do to any of us...myself, Durga, Anju...with our marriages? We had children, too, but does that make us any happier than Sanjeevani now? At least she is free, and not burdened like the rest of us with bondages that with time, become so tight that they begin to hurt so much.'

Sanjeevani has gone back to Kailali to reclaim the family land that was seized by the Maoists. In her own small way, she has taken back some land and started a sort of community farming there. She is even renovating the old house and is determined to continue living there. Is Prashant pleased or even proud of his daughter's achievements? Sanat thinks not. He will never forgive Sanjeevani for her insolence that forced him to completely blow away his already shattered pride. He is hurt and he is resentful.

News of Sanjeevani keeps coming every other day from Kailali. Rumours have it that she has fixed strong ties with a certain Maobadi and spends days and nights in the jungles around the village, doing what is left for the rest of the family to assume and presume.

'Is that not what Sanjay wanted to do? Join hands with the Maobadi? Compromise on his life and agree to them so that he could continue earning from his land. That is exactly what Sanjeevani is doing now – trying to become one of them so that she can realise her dead brother's aspirations,' Sanat consoles the morose and extremely offended family.

As she says this, Sanat knows well that Sanjeevani has her own reasons for returning to the house where her brother was killed. She silently applauds the courage and resilience of her granddaughter while the rest of the family discards her as a wayward wanton and a disgrace to the family's name and honour.

As for Sanjeevani, she knows what others say about her. She also admits, to herself, the wrongs she as done to her parents and family; yet, she refuses to allow herself into a society that would confine her own ceaseless spirits. She is always on the lookout for an opening or a loophole that will allow her to release this suffocation of living up to the standards of others. She is Sanjeevani, and will not become anyone else.

'Who is not a misfit, Sanjeevani? Everyone is. Each of us is living this sham of being someone we are not. We develop various masks, Sanju. As I have. To shield my unease, I perform various roles like that of a father, husband, citizen, a businessman and even a lover. All this in the hope that people will not notice this emptiness in me, this loneliness. After all, Sanju, no matter how large we make our social network, we remain alone at the end of the day. When we close our eyes to sleep, it is done with a sense of relief that comes from finally returning to the actual self, the self that is indeed a loner.' Razat had explained to Sanjeevani in their initial days of getting to know each other.

'So true, my Shyam…so true,' Sanjeevani had said, resting her head on his large shoulders and beginning to play with the gold locket hung on his neck. It had an idol of some God that he believed would ward off ill omens from his daily dealings. 'You know Radha?' Sanjeevani had then asked carelessly, her fingers still entwined around the locket.

'Who Radha? The girl who sits at my reception?' he had asked, taking a sip of his Bloody Mary.

'No, you fool, not that Radha! Krishna's Radha,' Sanjeevani had said, laughing and sitting back cross-legged over the sofa. Her head now rested on the back of the couch, her eyes had distanced off.

'She has forgotten I am in the room again,' Razat had thought, watching her gaze, ponderous yet overtly aloof. But then, her hand had risen and taken hold of his. She had then lifted his hand to her own face and rested it against her own cheek.

'Did you know Razat, that Radha is worshipped as a God and even given an equal standing to that of Lord Krishna? Why?'

'Why?' Razat had bent over. His eyes twinkled and a mischievous smile hovered around his lips . . . the smile that Sanjeevani had named the 'Krishna smile'.

'Because my dear Razat, her love was selfless and so selflessly was she devoted to Krishna that her love became a medium of worship. Did you know she was married to another man and yet, she continued her ardor for her lover, Krishna? Exceeding bounds of all social norms, she gave herself, the immortal part to him. I guess that's why, instead of being called a whore and a wanton, she was raised to the pedestals of the immortals themselves,' Sanjeevani had said hinting perhaps to a certain kind of affiliation of her own sentiments for Razat with that of Radha's for Krishna.

'And did you know, my dear Sanju . . .' Razat had played along, his fingers beginning to gently caress the side of Sanjeevani neck, '. . . that Krishna, although he had over a hundred wives and as many mistresses, managed to appear and love each one of them at the same time and with the same ardor? Amazing, no?' he was grinning, the same naughty impish grin.

'That was only possible, my dear...' Sanjeevani had turned and aligned her face in direct view of Razat's humorous one and said, '...because the longing in each of those women, was selfless. Each of them wished for Krishna not thinking of the others in his life. Each of them wanted her Krishna, selflessly....as I do you.'

Gently feeling the soft curves of Razat's lips with her fingers, Sanjeevani had said, 'My longing for you is selfless. I do not expect anything from you. No commitments, no promises of a future together...it's just that I am content with your smile, your hands on mine, warmly placed, your laughter.... Moments like these with you make me happy, lighten up this darkness that is so intense and menacingly overpowering all the time. I guess I am happy just loving you...mero Shyam...my Krishna.' And then she had kissed him, long and hard and very passionate.

Stopping to gasp for air, Sanjeevani had then said, 'If only your wife would understand just as Rukmini did. She tolerated Satyabhama and the hundred other wives and mistresses of Krishna and only loved him, for her own love.'

Sanjeevani is thinking of this very incident as she climbs up the staircase of the Saathi Hotel in Dhangadi. Razat has stayed away from her; that was his way of making up for her tarnished social image. He cannot marry her, so he decides not to continue with their relationship that will only end up harming Sanjeevani. Sanjeevani too has lived in Dhangadi for the past five, away from Razat, making a life of her own and wanting to believe that this was what she actually wanted.

'Come in,' he says, standing at the door. Sanjeevani walks in looking proud, distant and indifferent. Razat closes the door and walks towards Sanjeevani who is standing in the middle of the room assessing her surroundings. It is a small sitting room with the same maroon upholstery on the sofas that she had seen at the reception. There is a table in the centre with a flower vase on it

Right in front is another door which is open and clearly revealing the master bed inside the room. The entire room is carpeted from wall to wall with maroon carpeting. Against the wall, next to the door leading to the bedroom, is a Luis Vuitton suitcase and a handbag of the same brand.

'Shall we sit down, Sanju?' Razat asks, plonking himself on a single-seater couch. Not for a moment is there a feeling of estrangement. It is as if the years in between had never come. The façade of careless indifference with which Sanjeevani had entered the room, instantly collapsed. Yet again, she sees herself, gloating in the raptures of selfless love for Razat. Though disregarded, stifled and even pushed back, it had still managed to stay alive and now it surfaces, dominant and overpowering.

'I think I need some water first,' says Sanjeevani, walking to the mini bar in the suite. Taking a bottle of mineral water out of the little fridge, she manages a quick look at the label on it. API Packaged Drinking Water, it says. Scrolling down she reads that the water is from Darchula and is packed in Dhangadi itself.

'Wow!' she says, drinking straight from the bottle and placing it down on the centre table. Sitting on the couch behind it, she seems happy. 'We make our own mineral water here in Dhangadi now...a leap for us. Backward people, ain't it, Razat?'

He smiles. It is a painful smile, one with remorse and regret. His eyes have already pleaded for redemption. Watching him through the rim of the bottle, Sanjeevani knows that she has already forgiven him.

'Sanju,' he begins to say but she stops him. Instantly she is kneeling on the floor before him. Her head rests on his lap.

'Don't say it, Razat. Don't say anything. Whatever it is, I don't think I can take it. Let time stand still, just like this. The feel of you, so close, so good.' She shuts her eyes. Tears roll down the corner of her closed lids, down her cheek and onto Razat's trousers, filtering in and seeping into his skin, warm, soft and beseeching.

'Razat...' Sanjeevani whispers, '...I'd rather have you in bits and pieces for brief, scattered moments than not have you at all. You are me, Razat, as I am you. Separate sides of one coin. We may never meet but we are one and the same.'

He bends over and pulls her up. They sit face to face; one staring at the other's tear-stained face. Before they know it, they kiss...slow and soft at first, then forceful and demanding...demanding for a sanctuary of reprieve and respite.

Sanjeevani

My entrails are churning. I can feel the acidic bile rise like a
tumultuous wave. It starts in my stomach, creeps its way to
the throat and then into my mouth. I raise myself from the cot I
am lying on and charge to the nearest bush to let it out; a long trail
of my lunch jet-sprays out in a pounded pulp. Tears stream down
my cheeks as I hold on to my billowing stomach and continue
retching out; but nothing remains there to be taken out now. So,
I remain squatted in front of Badki's neatly trimmed flowerbed,
mouth open, saliva dropping, panting but beginning to feel my
intestines gradually relax.

This is the third time that I have vomited today. But I feel my
situation has improved in the past few weeks. I am pregnant. It is
my fifth month and I am now a relegate...forsaken and caste away
as an unbearable shame for my family. I cry every night. I cry with
dry eyes. I can feel my body mourn for my father's shame, my
mother's shattered dreams and for all the jibes and stains on my
character that my parents are forced to hear. I am hurt. Staring at
the weeded ceiling of Badki's hut each night, I curse myself for
damaging my parents' reputation and leaving them old and helpless.
They don't have anyone to guard themselves against the taunts and
derisions of a society that is an integral part of themselves. But

with this life, breathing and growing in me, I can at least feel the
sense of being alive and aware...this is what satisfies me. I console
myself with this thought. My hands instinctively rest on the slight
bulge of my stomach.

There is a clay pot lying under the cot. From it, I pour some
water into a glass, rinse my mouth, and spit out the water. I pour
the remnants of the glass on the flowerbed to wash away the stains
of my vomit. From under the shade of the sagon tree under which
my cot is lying, I gaze up to assess the position of the glaring sun. It
has moved beyond Badki's courtyard and is slowly moving towards
the Shivganga. In a few hours, the softly flowing waters will begin
to reflect the crimson hue of the retiring sun.

It is time for my daily rounds in the fields. I collect my peek
cap from under the cot and fix it on my head. I walk to the
verandah where my umbrella stands against Badki's dhikki chiau.
Her grandchildren are lying on the floor there. They are both naked,
and insensate to the hovering flies that repeatedly rest themselves on
their naked bodies. Setu, my mongrel dog, sprawled at the doorway,
tweaks up his ears and lazily flaps his tail.

'Come along, Setu. Enough of napping,' I cajole him out of his
languorous siesta. As I walk out of Badki's courtyard and into the
dusty lane with Setu frolicking at my heels, I am joined by Bhalmansa,
who is also trudging towards the direction I am headed to.

'Going to the fields for the meeting?' I ask him. I remember
Bhalmansa from my childhood days, a close associate of my father,
as he was then the head of the village; the title 'Bhalmansa' given
to him then stays as his primary source of identification till today.
Sometimes I wonder whether he ever had a name. Even if he does,
he never uses it.

Nowadays, Bhalmansa is spinning thread to weave a new fishing
net. He carries the roll as he walks in silent contemplation. Spinning
thread is another image that associates itself almost tangibly with

Bhalmansa. Bhalmansa is learning to move on in life after facing a huge tragedy. His house was washed away by the sweeps of the raging Tengna River during this year's monsoons. He survived and was found hanging on a branch of a tree. However, he lost his entire family – wife and children – along with all his material collections earned over fifty years of hardships. It is a wonder that he still smiles and passes each day filling vacant gaps and slowly rebuilding his life yet again.

At my father's fields that spread out in one endless stretch, I meet the rest of the villagers. It is snack time. Men, women and even children, who have joined in from the government-run school that stands parallel to one side of my father's fields, are seen sitting across ledges of field partitions; wiping sweat off their brows, necks and arms. Some men and women are pouring water from clay pots to wash their faces. Some are beginning to eat, helping themselves with heaps of rice along with red chilly paste.

I can see that Badki is busy with the women. She is loud and rather imposing. She is reprimanding a group of young boys who stand in front of her with cheeky smiles on their faces. My eyes quickly span the neatly ploughed fields and search for Kallu while Setu begins to jump and lick the people he has recognised. Towards one end of the field, the water pump is roaring and releasing a forceful gush of water from the mouth of the tube well. The water is speeding down the narrow canals dug on the edges of the fields. From here, it is directed into each partition when irrigation for a particular field is required. I spot Kallu by the tube well. After having taken off his shirt, he is sprinkling water onto his naked torso.

'Maiya, you need not have come,' he begins to say, deep concern blatant upon his face. 'There are so many of us here and you have done enough. You must rest however much you can.' He begins to put on his shirt even though his body is still wet.

'I am only pregnant, Kallu; not sick nor an invalid, and if other women can bend down and work in the fields for hours, I can at least drop in once in a while for inspection. Besides, you were the one who wanted to have a meeting before the tomato seeds were planted.'

Across the tube well is the shaded nursery, where little saplings of the hybrid tomato seeds that we brought from Paliya, are beginning to sprout. Kallu has taken full charge of the nursery and proudly walks us to the source of his pride.

'Raising a healthy nursery is an essential aspect of good farming, Bhalmansa Kaka.' Kallu is boasting his new techniques to the elderly. 'So is soil preparation for tomatoes. Maiya has found out through her research that deep cultivation of land up to three feet is necessary.'

'I know... I know. I have heard this before, Kallu. You keep repeating the new method of farming as though you were born with the knowledge. Mother fucker!' Bhalmansa is piqued as intended by Kallu's boasting. 'If it were not for Maiya coming here and insisting with your lal salaam comrades to get back Raja Sahib's land, all this would not have happened.'

His gaze, fond and affectionate with a tinge of appreciation, falls on me. 'No one shall forget, Maiya Sab. No one in this village must forget your contributions to bring us here, united in working for one cause.'

'I did it for myself, Bhalmansa. I came here for my selfish reasons.' I am staring at the wreckage of my house that I have slowly begun to repair and reconstruct.

'Whatever you say, Maiya,' Kallu chipped in, 'the fact remains that you fought with the area commander to use this land as common ground for community farming, to grow vegetables that can be sold in the bigger markets of Kathmandu. It was not easy, Maiya, for you to come down here, week after week. You were blind-folded and made to walk for hours in the jungle and then sit explaining your plans to controlling comrades and even to the YCl cadres. "What if your scheme does not work?" they asked you and you bravely said, "Then cut off my head and hang it over a scarecrow in one of the same fields." I was so proud of you then, for I knew you were going to bring about enormous change.'

Kallu is so loud that he has managed to draw attention from all the others who had sat down to eat. Some of them, curious and keen, are standing near him now as he stands over a high ledge of the field. He looks like a leader giving a speech to his followers.

'Then Maiya had this enormous task of convincing all the villagers to contribute to the expenses. Remember Maiya, when we first opened an account in the Krishi Bikas Bank at Pahalmanpur? People stayed away from us at the bank. But I was proud of you when you boldly said that the account will be named under Ganeshpur village community and created a board of representatives from the village to run the account and the management.'

Being the centre of attention makes me shifty. I begin to carelessly kick at the mud near my feet and listlessly shift my peek cap. Faces turn to stare at me, still wondering at my capacities.

My cap falls from my head and is now in my hand. I look at the little white heads of Mickey Mouse printed against a black backdrop...my Chandra's cap.

'Take it Sanjee. Keep it. Besides, it suits your pretty face better. Remember me when you wear it,' Chandra had said the day after we had heard King Gyanendra on the radio.

'Taking into consideration the Clause 27 along with its Sub-clause (3) of the Constitution, and considering the imperative need of peace and security in the nation, to strengthen the democratic provisions, and to put forth in function the neglected ideologies of a democratically functioning nation, we hereby dissolve the present Cabinet of Ministers. The preceding Cabinet of Ministers shall be hereon presided by our royal person. The prime objective of the new Cabinet of Ministers shall be to bring about significant changes in the nation's security policies as well as to reinstate a multi-party democracy in the coming three years as of today.'

The world outside the periphery of the Badka Banua jungles, where Chandra and I camped, had frozen still. All forms of communication had been suddenly disconnected throughout the country. Televisions were blank and so were radio stations. His Majesty King Gyanendra had gone live exclusively on the national news channel of the television and radio.

Chandra had continued to pluck grass, acting as if he was least bothered about the royal proclamation on Radio Nepal.

Having recovered from the initial stage of being overwhelmed with a stifling feeling... a result of my mind rebelling against this near authoritarian act of the King, I asked myself, 'Why not? Perhaps he has something up his sleeve and as the King, he must feel something for the poor subjects that are being thrashed around as lifeless twigs in a windstorm. Perhaps stern authoritarian dictatorship can stabilise this chaotic stance of the country. Besides, he has clearly stressed that his conditions will apply only for the next three years. Why not?' I was silently assuring my sceptic self.

Chandra had not spoken for the longest time. After switching off the radio and placing it inside the tent, I had walked back to where he sat. He was carelessly chewing on a strand of grass. His brows were knit into a pensive arch. He was gazing into the distant thickets, his eyes still but reflective.

'Why not?' I had said aloud, perching myself on the trunk of a fallen tree behind him and lighting up a khukuri. 'I think that is what we need... an iron hand to dictate terms to us for a while. We Nepalese are nothing but a flock of sheep, willingly steered from one direction to another and in the absence of a stern herder we scatter around, lost and aimless.'

I soon realised that I was talking to myself, for Chandra seemed to be drawn into a deep reflective silence.

'What are you thinking, comrade?' I asked him teasingly. I had bent over to peer into his brooding face. Over those years, a strange camaraderie had helped strengthen the bond between Chandra and myself. He seemed to be the only person with whom I could have a decent conversation with. I enjoy the time spent with him and I know that so does he. We both seek solace for our shattered souls in each other's company.

'You really want to know, Sanjeevani...what I am thinking?' Chandra had raised his head and looked directly into my eyes. Suddenly, there is a newfound sense of antagonism between us. I knew that we were going to quarrel, yet again.

'I am thinking, Sanjeevani, that in the past five years that I have known you, I have failed to make you relate to what I believe in.'

For a split second I had imagined watching Chandra watch me watching Chandra back; clearly hostile.

'Come again? Did you just intend to say that I have to forcefully believe in what you believe in, Chandra?' There was a clear tone of disbelief in my voice.

'I did not say forcefully, Sanjeevani. What I meant to say is that I feel unsuccessful. Even if after so many years of knowing you, I have not been able to convince you about the theories that have not only defined my actions but have become an integral part of myself, then there really must be something wrong somewhere. Either I have failed as a staunch communist or you have never bothered to fathom my sincerity.'

'Or perhaps...' I had intervened, my eyes now hot with a queer resentment. '...there is something really wrong with your thinking, your principles and your hardcore communist ideology in the first place? Did that possibility never occur to you, Chandra?' There was clear spite in my tone and I saw his facial muscles tighten. The corners of his eyes had wrinkled up.

'Do you ever believe in what you say, Sanjeevani?' He was blatantly mocking me and I took it head on, defensive and offensive at the same time.

'Have you ever stopped to think, Chandra? Have you ever let your mind wander off from this straight path that you have sketched out for yourself? If you will not ever try another option, you will never know whether your option is really the right one or not. You communists are all like blind men...happy with the banal darkness that you are enveloped in, never knowing that a bright light can change hues and shades, to the effects of which the world keeps altering. Unlike you Chandra, I am open to new possibilities, I try new options. Some may work out for me, and some may not. Yet I keep myself open to new and varied experiences. I have not tied my hands and feet to one thought or ideology, Chandra, and I never will. I might as well suffocate and die than limit myself to one restraining principle.'

Breathless, I had rattled off words as they came. While I was spewing words of fire, I simultaneously noticed Chandra's face changing. The intimidating look was slowly replaced by a jovial smile. Yet, I had continued, ignoring the tug of his hand on mine. Chandra had clasped my palms and placed them between his warm and assuring ones.

'Have I ever tried to change you, Chandra? Alter your views or opinions? We may have debated but have I ever forced my principles on you? Never. Each to his own for me, Chandra. We are forced into this world. We are alone and have a mind and a brain of our own to live our own life. Do we not die alone? We don't take anything or anyone along with us, do we? Then why should we impose ourselves on one another?'

Slowly, the warmth from his palms was beginning to comfort my body and mind. I could feel my tension subside. 'No, we should not...we must not impose, Sanjeevani.' His words sounded false and clearly insincere. After a long time, recollections of my brother being abused, beaten and mauled came along in gushes along with many other incidents, some of which I had myself seen during my stay in the village. Images of heads severed and hung over a pole in the chowk of Pahalmanpur, men being tied up and herded like animals across the river and into the jungles, were swiveling in my head. Were all these not brutal and inhumane impositions?

Though Chandra was smiling and seemed to be tender and loving, for an instant, I felt that he was the identical image of my thoughts of ghastly violence to humanity. I withdrew my hand from his clasp and looked away, a part of me deriding myself for being judgmental and unreasonable. To placate myself from these derisions, I had heard my other self say, 'It's as good as him having killed my brother. Has he not killed others? Sons and brothers and other loved ones of other people?'

Instinctively, my arms had embraced myself. Suddenly, I had felt the piercing chill of being lonely, not understood and a complete misfit in the world. A sigh had escaped as I felt my body shiver in understanding. I lifted my head to look at the sky that was thick with the heavy winter fog. My eyes wanted to penetrate into the stubborn thickness of the lingering fog and search for the warm radiance of the afternoon sun...a tantalizing mirage. 'You look rather good with my cap on, Sanjee.' Chandra was trying to shake me out of this sudden gloom that had come over me. He had placed his Mickey Mouse cap on my head and was forcefully turning my head in different angles, as though he was seriously inspecting it.

The next morning he was gone. Although he did not say it and I had not asked either, I was certain that he had been called by his seniors at the headquarters to deal with the recent announcement of His Majesty, the King. Watching him pack his little rucksack and dismantling our tent, something in me had whispered, 'This calls for the final war now. This will mark an end for either one of them and hopefully there shall be peace after that. No more impositions, no more killing and culling.'

I'll be honest to myself. While waving to Chandra, as he began blending in with the foliage that he was walking into, I realised that I hardly cared about which party would bear the victory flag; the King, the alliance of the seven parties or the Maobadis.

I put on Chandra's Mickey Mouse cap and looked at the open stretches of my father's fields, neatly ploughed, well-irrigated and ready for sowing.

'Let's begin the sowing tomorrow,' I can hear someone say behind me.

'Yes, that way the Maghi rains will feed enough water to the tender saplings,' someone else has just chipped in.

'It will need constant inspection as the first few weeks are really crucial for a hybrid seed.' I can hear Kallu's 'I know the most' tone loudest in the din.

'It will need to be sprayed every ten days or so with monocrotophos that will reduce the white flies around the saplings that transmit the curling of the leaf disease.' Watching Kallu proudly show off his knowledge makes me think of our childhood days together. Then too, Kallu loved to boast about anything new that he learned. I look back at the fields. We have used five hectares of land to plant these hybrid tomatoes and if everything goes well, our first harvest should be ready for sale in March. My rough estimations for the production from each hectare was approximately thirty tons and the minimum profit from the total production would be between five to seven hundred thousand. That would amount to about Rs 15000 distributed to each household of the thirty families in the village.

'This is only the trial phase. If everything goes as planned, we can use the remaining land of my father's, still in custody with the

Maobadis,' I think to myself. 'Another forty to fifty hectares can be managed by the village in the same cooperative manner.'

Kallu is now standing beside me and noticing that the others are either busy packing up, leaving or finishing their snacks. He moves closer and looking directly at my bulging stomach, says, 'Maiya, I heard some senior commanders mentioning comrade Bikral last night.'

Kallu, along with the rest of the village has assumed that Chandra is the father of my baby. I have never bothered to accept or refute their unspoken assumptions.

Kallu continued, 'I found out that he has been in India all these months and has been negotiating terms and conditions with the Saat Dal leaders there; but now he is back in Nepal and if my source is not wrong, he is in Kathmandu. He is planning a big movement there, soon.'

I can sense Kallu's concern for me. I know he is worried about my pregnancy. He is protective and I know he wishes that Chandra would return soon to give my bulging stomach a respectable recognition for the curious society. For Kallu, I am still his delicate 'Maiya', fragile and very special.

My back hurts. It's like a burning fire at the base of my spine. Instinctively my hands begin to massage my lower back. Kallu is quick to notice my discomfiture. 'Maiya,' he rolls his black twinkling eyes at me in a rebuking manner, 'I told you to stay at home and not walk all this way to the fields. God forbid, if anything goes wrong, I shall never forgive myself. Besides, what will comrade Bikral say to us when he returns. You must take care of your body, Maiya. It is not like before. Now you are two persons.'

With a wave of his hands, Kallu signals one of the village boys cycling back home to stop. Leading me by my hand, he helps me cross the undulated ledges of the fields and although I do not need his assistance, I do not bother to refuse his over-enthusiastic help.

I ride pillion behind him as he first takes me to my father's house. It is under renovation. We enter the gateless entrance and Kallu rings the bell attached to the cycle. 'Letting the two useless buggers know that you have arrived, Maiya.' He refers to the two carpenters that I have hired on a daily-wages basis. I had not had the heart to refuse Kallu when one night, he arrived with a bullock-cart full of tall and healthy Seesam logs.

'I will have it dropped at the house,' he had said, looking very serious. Knowing well that Kallu would not take no for answer, I had silently agreed to keep the wood. I did not ask him where he brought the wood from.

I had left the ground floor as it was and started with renovations on the floor above. By the landing was a little hallway, where once the fireplace used to be. Around it were all the bedrooms that once belonged to Jijumua, Thulubua, my parents, the boys room for Dada and Hemant da and the girls room that Hemlata Dijju and myself shared. Five rooms in all. But to begin with, I was only preparing three rooms. One for the baby, one as my bedroom and the other as my work room.

The two carpenters had rushed with the jobs of making the windows and the doors. All credit goes to Kallu who has been acting as supervisor.

We saunter in through the landing and into the hallway. One of the carpenters is working on the fireplace. I have decided to have a makeshift kitchen there. A mud-baked oven would do for the time being but I am having some shelves made against the wall where I will some day keep the necessary pots and pans.

The young boy is nailing the shelves as we watch him. I look around. The boys have installed the doors to two bedrooms out of the three. The windows of all the three bedrooms had already been installed.

'Good job!' I tell the boy nailing the shelves and ask him where his partner is.

'He did not come in today,' he replies.

'And why not?' Kallu's demanding tone booms out.

'Last night he had gone to his brother-in-law's wedding. The mother fucker got so drunk and passed out in the fields, while returning home at night.' The carpenter boy is hammering nails into the wall against the fireplace. His back towards Kallu and me, he continues, 'He could not even lift his head this morning, leave alone walk down to this place and work.'

He has turned around with the hammer still in his hands. He looks at me while bending down to pick up a few more nails lying at his feet. It's a discerning look, not contemptuous but clearly alienated. 'I found him on my way here. Flat on his stomach near the ditch by the Kharihaan. I had to carry him all the way back to the village and then return to work alone. Ha ha!' he laughs to himself, probably having remembered something funny.

'Get on with your work. Remember, Maiya is paying you wages on a daily basis. The longer time you take, the more you earn and she loses out the same. You think she does not know that you are a swindler!'

Kallu is genuinely agitated, 'I told you, Maiya, to give on *thekka* basis. That way, they would have worked faster and not cheated on you. Now, with daily wages, they will come here, dilly-dally and extend their work for the longest time. The longer the better for them.'

'I still have four months to go, Kallu. Ample time to finish renovating three rooms.' I am not worried about the time frame but there are other issues on my mind like finances. Earlier, I had never bothered to think twice about money. But now, I suddenly find myself being cautious. The baby will need clothes, medicines and food. Later, I will need to begin saving for its education.

I have quit my job as Project Coordinator at Naari Bishraam Kendra and have now no source of income at all. The little money that I had saved during my tenure with the NGO has been spent in doing up this house. The little that is left will be finished by the time the work is completed. I need to construct a toilet downstairs somewhere; the old ones do not exist. The taps and commodes had been uprooted long time back and taken away by the villagers.

I have walked into the room that once belonged to my grandmother and which I have now selected for my bedroom. I have broken down an entire wall facing the fields and the village and have fitted a ceiling to wall glass window in its place. I am standing in front of it and watching the dark sweep of the evening slowly fall over the fields and slowly begin to cover the cluster of little huts of the village in a still and serene darkness.

My novel should soon be out in the market. Depending on how it is received, I will begin to get some royalty that will help me get by to a certain extent. All this I think to my brooding self, remembering at the same time, the pressure of going to meet one publisher after another in Kathmandu and receiving the same reply – 'Not enough market for fiction in Nepal at the moment.'

Then I had met Professor Upreti at Mandala Book House. Sitting on a low stool, his head covered with big black curls, he was bent over a book shelf. He was probably searching for a theme to write on for his weekly column in the *Kathmandu Post*. Professor Upreti had recognised me immediately as a student from his days of teaching English literature, years back in the Tribhuvan University. 'Sanjeevani, what a surprise!' he had said, smiling the same gentle smile that concealed an entire world in it. His eyes were the same -- aloof but curious. He had offered to take me for a cup of coffee to Delicatessen, just above the bookstore where we met.

Over coffee, we had initially reminisced the old days at the university and I reminded him of my crush on him that I had as his student. I used to stare at him, and send little love notes in the library. One day he had called and spoken to me as I sat in front of him, my eyes rolled up in sheer infatuation.

'Sanjeevani,' he had said to me, 'there are various kinds of love in this life time and the one you feel for me is more for a mentor than for a lover. You are a gifted girl, Sanjeevani, and as your teacher I feel very blessed and even satisfied, for it is rare to have such a bright and able student such as yourself.'

I had fluttered my lashes, smiled my enchantress smile, still adamant on bewitching him with my charm but clearly failed as he continued speaking in the same soft and slow manner. 'We can always be friends, Sanjeevani. You can always rely on me as a guide and mentor. This physical relationship that you so often talk about in your notes is a foolish thought that you must expel from your mind...the sooner the better.' Rebellious that I am, I had shifted in my seat. He had instantly caught my sense unease and continued. 'Consider me your soulmate, rather than your heart-mate or your bed-mate.' I had noticed that he too was uneasy and desperate for the appropriate words. I found myself feeling sorry for placing him in such a strange predicament.

'Sir,' I had said, 'Let it be. No matter what you say, my love for you will always stay. If it has to be one-sided, so be it. You don't hassle your golliwog head for it. It's my problem, I will deal with it,' I had laughed, loud, insolent and rather obstinate.

'Sanjeevani,' he had said followed with a long sigh, 'In due course, you and me will laugh about this but always remember, you are a good girl...gifted too. I am convinced that you will be known as a great writer some day. You will go very far in terms of your writing, Sanjeevani. I am sure of it. So focus on this strength of yours. Why don't you start writing something for the *Kathmandu Post*? You need to constantly channelise your energy somewhere. One cannot miss that vivacious energy in you. The problem is you do not know where to channelise it. Just walk around town and at the end of the day, write something that catches your mind, within 500 words, and submit it to me.'

And that is how I had started writing for dailies and before I knew it, had become sub-editor in the *Kashthamandap Weekly*.

'How is your creative writing going?' Professor Upreti had asked that day while sipping black coffee Delicatessen. I had told him about my novella and he had expressed desire to read it. Having done that, within a week, he had introduced me to the editor-in-chief of Nepalya Publications, who had said, 'Although it is unconventional, it does show the evolution of a woman. It could have contradictory retaliations. But the more controversial it is, the better for sales. Besides, how can I refuse or refute Professor Upreti when he says the book is promising?' He instantly agreed to publish my book.

My sense of achievement had to be pushed back for there were other more critical and more crucial announcements to be made to my family while I was still in Kathmandu. The commotion created after my announcement of being pregnant never gave me an opportunity to tell my parents that I had finished writing the novel I had worked on for over five years and had even managed to get a publisher for it.

It is completely dark outside now. Dark, still and silent. Only the crickets in the distant fields and in between, a few stray barks of the dogs could be heard.

I return to Badki's hut on Kallu's cycle. She has already prepared my dinner of rice, some boiled vegetables and spicy fish curry. 'Fish is good for baby's brain, they say, Maiya. Now you are eating for two, Maiya. So don't just taste but eat,' Badki had said, demonstrating by stuffing huge handfuls of rice into her own mouth.

Later, alone by the fire, I stare at the fierce flames that leap up from the smouldering pit. I stretch my hands out closer to the blaze, feeling the warmth seep into my flesh and then begin to sting. Spontaneously, my hands withdraw. I find myself repeating this action, moving my hands close to the heat and then remove them once the comforting warmth changes to a stinging sensation.

Badki is asleep inside with her family and so is the rest of the village. Besides the muffled clamour of some drunkards returning home from the Pahalmanpur bhatti, there is not a single sound. The stillness around me is overwhelming. It reflects the emptiness, the biting vacuum that I feel inside me. Is this hurt, or pain? What is this that I feel? I know I hurt for having hurt my family. They are ashamed of me but I am convinced that I am not ashamed.

'I am pregnant,' I had said the evening I came back home to my parents' new rental abode after my meeting with the publisher. Not ashamed but sad that my announcement would shatter my family, my voice had had been low and rather hushed.

After a shocked silence it was my mother who had spoken first, 'Why did you not drown yourself first, Sanjeevani?' And then she had cried, crouched at my father's feet, holding on to them for comfort. My father did not move nor reach out to calm or console his distraught wife. He sat still on his couch, his eyes fixed on the stillness of the air. His old, haggard eyes refused to look at me.

'Tell her to go instantly, Hemant. Take her away from our sight.' From the corner of my eyes, I had seen Hemant da, shifty but adhering to my mother's commands. He gets up from his seat and moves towards me.

'She was born to disappoint us. Did you never think of your father, Sanjeevani? We had only you to depend on. You were our only incentive to go on enduring this life. What are we to do, Raja?' My mother, in her desperation, was tugging at my father's feet.

'Nepti, come home with me. We can discuss this there. It can be taken care of.' Hemant da was standing before me, tall and pretentious. His hands stretched out towards me, as if to give me assurance.

'No,' I had stared back, hard and defiant. But inside I was trembling in my own terrible thoughts. 'No!' I had roared back. 'I have decided to keep this baby. It is mine.' I had scrambled up to my devastated parents and crouched at my father's feet.

'Bua... Ma... forgive me. I know, right now you wish, as I have always, that I had gone instead of Dada... but I didn't. I was left behind to do this... to have you bear this shame, this pain, but Ma...' I had rested my head on her slumped and grieving shoulders. 'Ma, this child is important for me to endure my life... to go on living and to tolerate myself. I don't expect any of you to ever forgive me for this but I am leaving with a hope that some day, you will understand me.'

'Go away... go away...' my mother was chanting in between her wrenching sobs. I rose to my feet, bent down and touched my father's hands that lay limp by his sides. He did not flinch as I took his hands into my trembling ones; resting my palm against his. I had peered into his despondent gaze...

'Remember, Bua, how I held on to your hands as a child? In doing so, I felt safe and secure. With you around I thought then that nothing could ever hurt me, but I guess it was only a childish belief. No one protects no one, Bua... no one lives for no one. We are born alone and we die alone as did Dada and as will all of us. And while we live, we face and fight our own phantoms, all alone...'

Conclusion

'We start to step up...a step appears.'

– Rumi

I wish I could have written my story differently. I wish it had more laughter, more songs and more sunshine. But alas! Unlike my Jijumua's tales that always seemed to end well, my story concludes in utter despair and shame. The prince does not come to rescue the princess and nor does the savior appear at the end to put right the woes of a battered nation. Instead, my climax is all hunky dory, with my Sanjeevani standing with her baby in Badki's courtyard and watching the sun go down behind the Kandra. A gentle breeze blows her ruffled hair. The sun, the mud and the roughing around in the village has taken a toll over her flawless white skin. It is now blatantly tanned. Her complexion borders on a beautiful shade of bronze and she seems to like this new colour of her skin as it gives a certain semblance to the colour of her own baby. The baby's skin colour is nutmeg brown. And right now, the gentle nutmeg skin is wrapped in a khasto, barring the tiny face from where the two shimmering eyes stare back at her. Instantly, Sanjeevani feels a desperate need to escape...escape from her jeering phantoms that have made her crouch into her own darkness. 'I have given myself in pieces,' she can hear herself whisper to her baby.

'Now I want to gather all these pieces, assemble my scattered self in one strong piece...such that none can shake nor break.' Just then the baby begins to wail. Sanjeevani lifts her baby in the air. 'You, my baby, are my compact piece. From you, I see myself emerge from the shadows of my jeering phantoms. Cry my baby, cry, let it out. Let it all out.' The baby cries, a soft muffled whimper, and she instantly springs him up in the air. 'Release it,' she whispers to the baby, a whisper that was more of a command. 'Never whimper. Cry out loud and clear, my baby.'

'My baby,' says Sanjeevani. Her voice is lifted by the wind and taken across the Kandra where the sun is nestling for the night. 'You have made me a mother. Now I shall learn to own my life and learn to appreciate it. I will value my person, my body, and myself. I realise my potential as a person and will do my best to be of use to you and my nation.

The baby smiles or so thinks Sanjeevani. Looking at the twinkle in the baby's eyes, she buries the little head into her bosom, and continues her monologue. 'Yes, my darling, I am wise but this wisdom comes with a lot of pain. Yes, I've paid the price, but look how much I have gained.

'I am wise. I am invincible. I am a woman.'

Sanat sits, reading Lord Krishna's words in the Bhagvadgita with her fingers. Outside, a nation celebrates. The decade-long fight of the Maoists has finally seen light. The centuries-old monarchy has now been abolished and a republican government will soon be set up in Nepal. In the next room, her surviving son, Prashant, sits by the television set. His graying head bobs up and down and the fingers of his hand tremble, as he fumbles with the remote switching from one channel to another. Each channel broadcasts a live telecast of the grand celebrations in the capital. Political leaders with vermillion-smeared foreheads and faces that are nearly hidden with garlands of flowers, are being hailed by the ecstatic masses.

This marks an end of an era... an elaborate epoch of kings and queens. Cultures, traditions, and lifestyles sway precariously in a state of limbo as Nepal begins writing for itself a new history. Watching it all on television, Prashant is overwhelmed with a deep sense of alienation. 'My time has ended, but I live on as a redundant phantom, insensate to the vigour of life that will continue to flow around me.'

Anju wipes the smears of tears from her eyes as she continues frying onions in oil. 'I shall cook lunch and then have enough time to wash clothes in the afternoon. There should be water in the taps today. It's Wednesday today, isn't it? Yes it is. If I don't wash clothes today I shall have to wait until Friday for the water to come in the taps. It's a nice sunny day, and the clothes will dry in no time,' she thinks silently to herself as she begins to stir the reddening pieces of onion in the simmering oil.

In one corner of the kitchen, Sushma is pumping the kerosene stove in her attempt to light it. 'Finally, we can get kerosene now,' she says. 'Two weeks of bandh is finally over. Thank God for the small mercies. The shops will finally open again. This evening we must go out to Indra Chowk and get some ration. Perhaps, we could get a glimpse of the celebrations in Tundikehel, too.'

There is denial in their stance. A denial of their suffering. Echoes of the past do come back sometimes. They are gentle as a breeze at first, but soon take over as ferocious beasts that are slow but surely devouring. But they go on dismissing these echoes. It is painful and suffocating but somewhere, there lies a faint flicker of hope. Outside too, in the minds of a celebrating nation, this very hope stands dominant. It is like waiting for Godot. A hope that the long-awaited Godot has finally arrived. The masses believe that now this drowning nation will finally be saved and sail away to a better and more prosperous day. They hope that peace shall prevail in this nation. Sons will not be killed, daughters will not be sold and that now each man shall live with his head held high and the song,

> 'Hati hoina dati rahne nepali ko baani huncha,
> Kahile na jhukne sir uthe ko swabhimani nepali huncha...
> Bishwa ko kuna kapcha ma khoja
> Nepali ko mutu ma khoja...tyaha singo Nepal huncha...'

will finally hold true, and as long as there is hope, the flag will still fly.

> 'Birds make great sky circles of their freedom. How do they learn that? They fall, and falling they are given wings.'
>
>   –Rumi

Glossary

1.	Achar	:	Pickle
2.	Ba	:	Father
3.	Bahuns	:	Priests
4.	Baithak	:	Drawing room
5.	Basera kuru garun na	:	Let us sit down and talk
6.	Bhag Bahula	:	Run, mad man
7.	Bhajans	:	Devotional songs sung to the gods
8.	Bhet	:	Meeting
9.	Bhigas	:	acre
10.	Birta land	:	Land given by the king
11.	Borsi	:	Brassiere
12.	Buajiu	:	Dear father
13.	Buhari	:	Daughter-in-law
14.	Chautaria	:	Relatives of the king
15.	Chetris	:	A caste
16.	Chokho jal	:	Sacred water
17.	Chora	:	Son
18.	Chukani	:	Sour pickle
19.	Damai	:	Tailors
20.	Dangua	:	Name of a person
21.	Darshan	:	Literally means 'sight'. Can be used in the sense of beholding of a deity (especially in image form) or revered person.

22.	Dashain ghar	:	Sacred house where the Dashain puja is done
23.	Daura surwal	:	Traditional Nepali attire
24.	Dhaan	:	Paddy
25.	Dhana	:	A name
26.	Dhara puja	:	A ritual for a newly-wed woman
27.	Dharmo dharma	:	swearing
28.	Dherai dherai, dhanyabad	:	Thank you very much
29.	Dherai	:	Many
30.	Dhikki chiau	:	an old means of beating rice
31.	Dubo	:	Grass
32.	Durbar	:	Palace
33.	Ekaa desh ma, euta thiye raja ani unki thin euti rani	:	In one country there was one king and he had one queen.
34.	Farsi	:	Pumpkin
35.	Feeni	:	Sweet bread
36.	Gharbetijiu, eklai, eklai	:	Landlord…alone…alone
37.	Gharbetiju	:	Landlord
38.	Grahas	:	Graha is a 'cosmic influencer' on the living beings. In Hindu astrology, the Nava (nine) Grahas are some of the major governing forces that could determine the behavior of the living beings.
39.	Guruwa	:	Spirtual healer
40.	Gyanu	:	Good boy
41.	Hamar	:	Ours
42.	Harka daju	:	brother
43.	Hawaldar	:	Sergeant
44.	Jaat ko buhari	:	Daughter-in-law of caste
45.	Jamara	:	Fresh shoots of barley
46.	Jamjutwa	:	The name of a ghost
47.	Janjaatis	:	Indigenous
48.	Jhwaikuti, jhwaikuti jhwaikuti jhwaikuti jhwai	:	Sound of music
49.	Ji Pra Ka	:	District police head quarters
50.	Jijumua	:	Grandmother

51.	Jila malpot	:	Distirict land revenue department
52.	Jillas	:	a district
53.	Jiunarghar	:	Dining room
54.	Kalyug	:	The age of vice
55.	Kamaiyas	:	*Kamaiya* is a traditional system of bonded labour in Nepal. The people affected by this system are also called *kamaiya* or *kamaiyas*.
56.	Kamalarhi	:	slave girl
57.	Kancha raja	:	Small king
58.	Karyalya	:	Quarters
59.	Kauguji	:	ghost
60.	Kauguji	:	Ghost
61.	Khandethaal	:	Plate with many compartments
62.	Khari hans	:	Place where the harvest is kept
63.	Kharihan	:	A place where the harvest is stacked
64.	Khasto	:	a very soft cloth that consists of three layers of the finest cotton muslin. It is usually used for baby clothing.
65.	Khatiya	:	Bed
66.	Khukuri	:	Neplese knife with a wooden handle
67.	Khurma	:	Sweet bread
68.	Lakshman	:	Lord Rama's devoted and sacrificial younger brother
69.	Lal salaam comrades	:	a salute, greeting or code word used by communists in Pakistan, India, and Nepal.
70.	Lalpurja	:	Land papers
71.	Lehengas	:	ethnic attire of women
72.	Lokta	:	Plant found in the hilly regions of nepal
73.	Macha maryo	:	Killed the fish
74.	Madal	:	A musical instrument

75.	Madhakunti	:	Place in Sanjeevani's village where the dead are buried
76.	Madhes	:	The Tarai region
77.	Madhesis	:	A name given to people living in the Tarai region of Nepal
78.	Maghi Sangranti	:	A Nepalese festival observed in the month of January on the first day of the month of Magh, bringing an end to the ill-omened month of Poush when all religious ceremonies are forbidden.
79.	Mahajan	:	great person
80.	Margh	:	Name of a month
81.	Mismaas	:	Mixed vegetables
82.	Moro...kale	:	Tharu
83.	Muajiu	:	Dear mother
84.	Mula	:	Radish
85.	Naivedya	:	Sweets offered to god
86.	Nani sahebs	:	Mistresses
87.	Nawami	:	Ninth day
88.	Newars	:	An ethnic class of people mostly found in Kathmandu
89.	Paaji jaantha	:	An abuse
90.	Paaji saalas	:	An abuse
91.	Pahari	:	People from the hills
92.	Paharis	:	A caste
93.	Peek daan	:	Spitting pan
94.	Pidkas	:	Wooden planks to sit on
95.	PLA	:	Peoples Liberation Army
96.	Pote	:	An ornament worn only by married women
97.	Prazatantra	:	Democracy
98.	Raangas	:	Buffaloes
99.	Samanti ko nash, ragat ko pukaar...Dhesh lai uddhar	:	to finish the feudalists is the call of the blood, the only way for better nation.
100.	Sanjeevani booti	:	Mythical 'herb of immortality'

101. Sano raja	:	small king
102. Sarangi	:	Musical instrument
103. Seesam	:	a type of tree
104. Seeta maiya darshan deo	:	Goddess Seeta, please show yourself
105. Sel	:	Sweets
106. Sidhra ko achar	:	Pickle made of fish
107. Silver bora	:	Bag made of silver
108. Sipahi	:	Sepoy
109. Sudoor Paschim Anchal	:	The far western region
110. Talukdar	:	The person subordinate to the tehsildar
111. Tama	:	Bamboo shoot
112. Tamangs	:	An ethnic class of people
113. Tarai	:	a belt of marshy grasslands and forests
114. Tarkari	:	Vegetables
115. Teej	:	Festival where women fast for their husbands
116. Teengharua	:	Three houses
117. Tehsil	:	Areas demarcated to collect revenue
118. Tehsildar	:	Revenue collector in the tehsils
119. Tharu	:	Tharu is the largest and oldest ethnic group of the Terai region of Nepal (southern plains along the length of Nepalese foothills). They work usually as farmers or labourers.
120. Thekka	:	Wine shop
121. Tilahari	:	an ornament
122. Tohar	:	Yours
123. UMC	:	United Marxist Communist
124. Wada Prahari	:	Ward police